"I read a lot of books but haven't enjoyed one as much as *The Punch Escrow* in a long time. I picked it up for a cross-country flight and didn't put it down until we landed in New York. Tal Klein creates a plausibly real future that sucks you in. He powers his story with action, twists, and more than a dash of humor. Young actors will be lining up to play the lead character, and any director worth his salt would kill (or at least teleport) for a chance to adapt *The Punch Escrow*."
—Andy Lewis, book editor at *The Hollywood Reporter*

"A compelling, approachable human narrative wrapped around a classic hard sci-fi nugget, *The Punch Escrow* dives into deep philosophical territory—the ethical limits of technology, and what it means to be human. Cinematically paced yet filled with smart asides, Klein pulls off the slick trick of giving readers plenty to think about in a suspenseful, entertaining package."
—Sean Gallagher, IT editor and national security editor at Ars Technica

"An alt-futuristic hard-science thriller with twists and turns you'll never see coming. I couldn't put it down."
—Felicia Day, author of *You're Never Weird on the Internet (Almost)*

"Klein transports us to a beautifully rendered near-future world. This is refreshingly original and immersive hard sci-fi. You'll turn the last page and yearn for Joel Byram's next chapter."
—Ben Brock Johnson, host of Codebreaker podcast and Marketplace Tech

"A headlong ride through a future where 'huge international corporate conspiracy' is a box you check on a form and teleportation takes you anywhere—it just blows you to bits first."
—Quentin Hardy, head of editorial at Google Cloud and former deputy technology editor at *The New York Times*

"If I lived in the world of *The Punch Escrow*, I'd teleport around the world shoving copies of Tal M. Klein's thrilling, hilarious, and whip-smart debut into everyone's hands. Save me the trip—buy this novel now.
—Duane Swierczynski, author of *Revolver* and the bestselling Level 26 series

"A fast-paced near-future sci-fi adventure peppered with exotic technology and cultural references ranging from "Karma Chameleon" to the Ship of Theseus, *The Punch Escrow* will have you rooting for its plucky, sarcastic hero as he bounces between religious fanatics, secret agents, corporate hacks, and megalomaniacs in a quest to get his life back. If you've ever wanted to get Scotty drunk and ask him some tough questions about how those transporters work exactly, *The Punch Escrow* is the book for you."
—Robert Kroese, author of *The Big Sheep* and its sequel, *The Last Iota*

"This book angered me to my core, because it's based on an idea that should have occurred to me. The fact that Tal executed it so well, and made such a page-turner out of it, just adds insult to injury."
—Scott Meyer, author of the Magic 2.0 series

"Some writers take us to the future so we can question the effects that technology can have on humanity on a global and personal scale, along with the impact upon the social fabric. Others do it to take us on a wild ride made all the more fantastic by pushing the boundaries of what we can expect from the world of tomorrow. Tal M. Klein masterfully balances both and sets it all to the beat of an 80s soundtrack. An excellent piece of contemporary science fiction."
—J-F. Dubeau, author of *A God in the Shed* and *The Life Engineered*

THE

PUNCH

ESCROW

TAL M. KLEIN

Published by Inkshares, Inc., San Francisco, California
www.inkshares.com

Edited by Matt Harry, Adam Gomolin, and Robert Kroese
Cover design by M.S. Corley and interior design by Kevin G. Summers

ISBN: 9781942645580
e-ISBN: 9781942645597
Library of Congress Control Number: 2017940692

First edition

Printed in the United States of America

McCoy: Where are we going?
Kirk: Where they went.
McCoy: What if they went nowhere?
Kirk: Then this will be your big chance to get away from it all.

—from *Star Trek II: The Wrath of Khan*

Roses are red
Violets are blue
Actually violets are purple

Irises too

AB INITIO

IF YOU'RE READING THIS, then you're officially in charge of figuring out what to do next. I'm off the hook, probably because I'm dead. Consider the baton passed. Hooray for you.

The problem for me is trying to figure out how much you know, and more important, how much you *need* to know—because you're in the future, and I'm in the past. Maybe it's a good idea for us to start with the *past* past, like stuff that happened in my past that is relevant to my present, which is still your past, but now possibly relevant to your present.

Do they still teach you guys about the da Vinci Exhibition? Maybe that's a good place to start.

STICK!

TELEPORTATION KILLED THE *MONA LISA*.

More specifically, a solar storm during the teleportation of da Vinci's masterpiece was to blame. It happened on April 15, 2109. The painting was being teleported from Rome to New York City for an art exhibition when a huge flare erupted from the Sun, sending something called a coronal mass ejection on a collision course for Earth. Think of it like a zit popping on the Sun's forehead, only the zit was about the size of Venus and the pus inside was an electromagnetic shit storm. Okay, that's a pretty gross visual, but now it's in your head and out of mine.

That solar storm hit Earth with such force, it ionized the sky, creating a vast cloud of hyperactive electrons that bounced around inside the atmosphere above Italy. Anything electronic in Rome got fried. That included thousands of implants, automobiles, drones, city buses, and those cute little Italian scooters zipping through the city. One hundred and thirty-five people died. Hundreds more were injured in collisions and fender benders. But the greatest loss, as perceived by the worldwide community, was the disappearance of a six-hundred-year-old portrait of a woman with a mysterious smile.

Back then, freight teleportation had been around for about four years. The process worked pretty much like you might have seen in vintage movies—an item was placed into a chamber in one location, scanned, and then instantaneously zapped to a receiving chamber in another location. There had been very few mishaps since the technology went commercial, mainly because the procedure took place in such a short amount of time.

But during one crucial moment on April 15, 2109, the frayed threads in the process unraveled all at once. There was no fail-safe. No backup. The plasma cloud struck Rome at the exact moment some poor technician started teleporting the *Mona Lisa*. A globally cherished artifact was scanned, beamed into the ether—and never showed up on the other end. Rows of atoms arranged to create centuries-old master strokes suddenly evanesced into nothing. The painting dissolved into a cloud of worthless gray quantum foam.[1]

It wasn't the technician's fault. Nor was the teleportation process itself to blame. It just so happened that an incredibly

---

[1] Quantum foam (also referred to as space-time foam) is the stuff that makes up the fabric of the universe. It was theorized by John Wheeler in 1955, thought to be officially discredited by Kristina Wheeler (no relation to John) in 2055, and then finally "discovered" by Suzanne Wheeler (no relation to John or Kristina) in 2105 with her invention of the scanning tunneling microscope. Quantum foam is essentially a qualitative description of subatomic space-time turbulence at extremely small distances (on the order of the Planck length). At such small scales of time and space, the Heisenberg's uncertainty principle allows energy to briefly decay into particles and antiparticles and then annihilate without violating physical conservation laws. As the scale of time and space being discussed shrinks, the energy of the virtual particles increases. According to Einstein's theory of general relativity, energy curves space-time. Wheeler (the Suzanne one) conclusively proved that, at the time crystal level, the energy of these teeny tiny fluctuations in space-time are large enough to cause significant departures from the smooth space-time seen at larger scales, giving space-time a "foamy" quality that can be definitely measured and discretely manipulated. In other words, scientists were able to get their hands on God's Legos and start building whatever they wanted.

unlikely solar event occurred at the same instant as an exceedingly rare painting was being moved from one place to another. Statistically, it was in the neighborhood of one in 3.57 quintillion. But as the universe continually likes to remind us, black swans don't play by the rules. And this was one particularly petulant pen.

Sure, accidents happen all the time. On that unfortunate day, boats sank, drones crashed, trucks collided—all with valuable cargo and precious souls on board. Any vessel in which the *Mona Lisa* could have otherwise been traveling might have also been downed by the solar flare. But witnessing a one-of-a-kind, globally precious masterpiece fade into nothing—that had a lasting effect on people.

The da Vinci Exhibition meme, more than anything else, led to the creation of the Punch Escrow. And the Punch Escrow, of course, is what made human teleportation—"Punching," as it was quickly branded—possible. Not only possible, but avowed as the safest form of transportation yet. Beaten into our collective consciousness was the fact that not once since the commercialization of human teleportation in 2126 had any person been maimed, altered, vanished, or otherwise mistreated by teleportation.

Not until me.

But we'll get to that. For now, let us pay our respects to that enigmatic Renaissance lady, *La Gioconda*—who was visited more than any other painting in the world, whose rapture led to human teleportation becoming the great success it is today.

Ciao, *bella*.

SYMMETRY BREAKING

COMING TO WAS A BITCH.

Not sure how many volts I took. Conservatively speaking, enough to power my apartment for an hour or two.

Mumbles were the first sounds I heard.

What the hell happened? Did I get struck by lightning or something?

More mumbles.

A feminine voice. I'm not sure what it was saying, but yes, it was definitely female.

My confusion was too debilitating to focus on the words or their owner's identity beyond that. There was just this awful ringing. And purple.

In my childhood, when I got angry, I'd clench my eyes shut as hard as I could. Eventually, the pitch black would become dark purple.

Open your eyes!

My eyelids weren't responding. All I saw was purple.

I remembered reading that a blind person's brain rewires itself to use the visual cortex, essentially hijacking it to improve the processing of other information such as sound and touch. Because of this, some blind people learn to use echolocation—reflected sound waves—to build a mental picture of their surroundings, like bats or dolphins.

Abe, one of the guys I worked with, could do this. He was born blind, but his parents were Three Religion Fundamentalists, so they didn't allow him to get implants as a kid. When he got older, he gave up religion and ran away from home. In his secular twenties, he finally got his comms installed but opted out of ocular implants. Being blind was just a core part of his self-identity. I recalled him claiming to be able to tell an object's distance, size, texture, and density by clicking his tongue against the roof of his mouth about three times per second. I'd seen pictures of him hiking and cycling, so maybe he was right. But he was a smartass like me, so there's also a good chance he was full of shit.

Just for kicks, I tried clicking my tongue against the roof of my mouth.

Click. Click. Click.

It worked! Not the echolocation thing, but my tongue worked! *Progress.*

I tried blinking my eyes open. *Too bright!*

The voices were becoming clearer. I could hear mutterings in a Middle Eastern–sounding tongue—one of the Levantine languages, I thought.

I had no idea where I was, and no idea who the out-of-focus head trying to communicate with me belonged to. Now someone else shined what looked like an interrogation light in my face, blinding me and catalyzing an even more painful headache.

"Hey! Cut it out." It appeared my vocal cords worked, too.

"Ahlan habibi," the blurry face greeted me. I smelled cardamom and jasmine. "My name is Ifrit. Are you okay?"

"No, I'm not okay. Could you please stop shining that thing in my eyes?"

The bright interrogation light blinked off.

She asked me if I was okay again.

I rubbed my temples and groaned. "Well, I'm not dead."

Ifrit's blurry face started to come into focus. She was in her late twenties or early thirties, with attractive Middle Eastern features—coffee-colored hair, dark almond-shaped eyes, and olive skin.

"I'm sorry we had to shock you, but our security system doesn't like unauthorized visitors."

"Well, thanks. I guess."

I looked around. Other than the woman tending to me, there was nothing remarkable about the room I found myself in. *Why did she send me here?* It was another conference room, like the one I had just escaped, although the comparatively sparse decor indicated whoever occupied this space had significantly less of an aesthetics budget to work with. For example, the table on which I was lying was made of plastic, not wood, and the chairs were less "comfortably ergonomic" and more "painfully pragmatic." There was a medium-sized printer by the door, though. A very recent model, taking up most of a desktop, and a rather expensive accessory for such an otherwise scant room.[2]

---

[2] Replication printing, originally known as "synthetic manufacturing" but then quickly and less-accurately renamed "organic manufacturing" (OM) for what I can only assume was better marketability, referred to the various processes used to create objects out of seemingly thin air. It is widely believed that replication printing ushered in the fourth industrial age, as molecular blueprints of any product could be sent to any place in the world, and then be perfectly reproduced by any printer with "carbon inks." So basically, everything became available anywhere, provided you had the plans, printer, and ink. Replication of valuable or patented items was prevented through multiple safeguards such as unique molecular signatures, blacklisting, and devaluation. For example, if someone managed to illegally replicate a gold bar, it would have an identical signature to the original "blueprint." Any piece of gold with that signature could only be sold once, hence branding any other copy a fake.

But I had made it. I was alive.

Do the thing!

I had rehearsed this moment in my head before my escape.

"My name is Joel Byram. People are trying to kill me. My comms have been disabled. I need help!"

"Shhh!" Ifrit chided. "You don't have to shout. We can hear you."

I guess I was yelling. Wait—"we"?

I painfully lifted my head to try to gather my bearings. Beyond Ifrit, at the head of the table on which I was lying, was a lean, salt-and-pepper-haired, smartly dressed older man. The first thing that came into focus was his forehead. He had more creases on his forehead than I had metaphors to describe them.

The smoke from his cigarette snaked toward me, framing his face like he was in one of those old-fashioned film noirs from two centuries back.

"Is he okay?" the man asked her. A low, gravelly voice.

She nodded. "Yes, I think so."

The man jerked his head sideways, and Ifrit, the only person who genuinely seemed to care about my well-being since the attack, left the room.

As she walked out, I tried once again to access my comms and pinpoint my GDS location to get an idea of where I was. But all I got was the same irritatingly familiar error message:

UNAUTHORIZED ACCESS. INVALID USER.

The man silently stared at me. The kind of icy, appraising silence that didn't encourage small talk. Finally he rose and motioned for me to get up off the table.

As I got up, my body took the opportunity to remind my brain of its various aches and pains. The worst of it seemed to spread along my right flank. My wrist was also on fire, so much so that I could barely move my hand. My shoulder sent pulsing shots of pain with every movement, and my ass felt like I was sitting on a family of fire ants.

All of a sudden the room became more illuminated. Generic video streams of remote beachfront resorts played on the walls of the otherwise plainly appointed room.

"*Café?*" he offered, placing his cigarette down at the edge of the table.

I nodded and sat down in an uncomfortable nonadjustable chair wedged between the table and the wall.

"Turkish," he told the printer, his Levantine accent lingering on the *u* like it was four *o*'s long.

Soon, a small copper pot with a long wooden handle coalesced out of nothing. Next to it were two small ceramic cups atop tiny ornate saucers. He placed those on a small tray and then started back toward me.

He placed the coffee tray down on the plastic table. Then, confidently holding the pot by its handle, the man filled each cup about three-quarters full, the size of a shot.

"Back home, far away from here, there is a small man with a small cart who makes these the real way," he said. "It took me a long time and a lot of chits to convince him to let me copy it, but now I can print it whenever I want."[3]

---

[3] In case you've devolved back to barter or evolved to something else, chits were the elastic global block-chain cryptocurrencies that underpinned our global economy. They were secure and unforgeable by design and made most financial crime obsolete. Of course, one could always be swindled out of their chits the old-fashioned way—social engineering. Standard chits were created and linked to individuals for services rendered. There were also unique types of chits that were traded on niche exchanges. Those chits still map to normalized chit values but at different multipliers than base chit rates. For example, a local municipality's food chits might be valued at 0.8x (or 80 percent) of the standard chit rate in order to discount for local economic conditions and keep everyone fed. But most work chits held value in direct correlation to the supply and demand of a given trade, as well as the value

→

He sipped slowly. I wondered if he thought it truly tasted the same as the original from his memories.

He picked up his cigarette from the table, took another drag, then sat down on the chair opposite me, signaling it was time for business.

"My name is Moti Ahuvi. You are a guest of the LAST Agency. Land, Air, Sea Travel." He spread his hands, indicating the small room around us. "That's where you are. We cater to Levantines and other peoples for whom teleportation is not an option. I am responsible for security here."

Well, at least I won't be teleporting anywhere.

"My name is Joel. Joel Byram." I paused to see if my name elicited any reaction. It didn't. Hopefully that meant my face wasn't all over the comms yet. "If you don't mind my asking, why does a travel agency need security personnel?"

He half smiled. "The world is a dangerous place, my friend. People don't want bad things to happen to them while they're traveling. You would agree, yes?"

"I'm realizing that in spades today."

He nodded knowingly. "*Yoel*, I have some questions for you." His brown eyes were focused but calm.

I adjusted my posture fruitlessly. Interrogation by travel-agency security might be a pointless proposition for most, but for me it was definitely a positive changing of the tides. I nodded for him to continue.

The Levant are a curious breed, known for several millennia of regional conflict prior to the Last War. Most significant to my situation, their now-shared culture prohibits human

---

of the entity using them to procure things. The idea being that the "price" of something was a moving target based on real-time demand, the wealth of the procurer, and the percentage of the procurer's wealth that the procurement transaction represented. It sounds complicated, but it ensured nobody went hungry and no one person or corporation could manipulate the market beyond its natural elasticity.

teleportation. An artifact of religious edicts still in practice from the old days before the war.

Moti took another small, considered sip of his coffee, then swallowed. "Your fingerprints and irises match a man named *Yoel* Byram."

"Yes. Joel Byram," I corrected him. "That's me."

He disregarded my correction. "But your comms come up unregistered. Do you understand that I am curious why?"

Something about his broken English and calm demeanor terrified me. But I was also somewhat relieved that we didn't have to beat around the bush.

Remember your goal: reach Sylvia.

"Uh, yeah," I answered. "My comms seem to be on the fritz."

"What is this word *fritz?*"

"My comms aren't working. One minute they were working fine, and the next"—*keep things close to your chest, Joel; you don't know who you can trust*—"I found myself at your doorstep."

"Are you in trouble? Would you like us to call the police?" Moti asked.

"Yes, but—no! Don't call the police!" I yelled, then quickly checked myself. Calmly, I said, "Look, there was this woman. Her name was Pema. She told me to come here. That you guys could help me."

Moti took my answer in and reflected upon it for a few seconds. "Please, finish your coffee."

I nervously sipped the rest of the warm black syrupy beverage, careful to avoid the grit at the bottom. I had briefly dated a Levantine girl in college who had taught me how to drink Turkish coffee. Since the drink is boiled rather than filtered, you have to drink at a specific angle and pace, lest the sediment in the bottom of the cup end up in your mouth—

As it just had in mine. "Ugh!" I spat out the bitter grit on my tongue—to the wry amusement of my host.

Ifrit reentered the room, placing a glass of water in front of me while Moti briskly yanked what remained of my coffee from me, then covered the cup with its saucer and flipped it upside down.

What the hell is he doing?

As he moved the cup around in his hand, I noticed his focus was on the sticky residue at the bottom of it.

Tasseography.

I'd heard of it before from my ex-girlfriend, but never seen it done. Reading coffee is one of the oldest cultural practices in the Middle East, dating back to the eighteenth century. One examines the coffee grounds left after someone has consumed a cup, studying the shapes and images that form in the dark grounds. From this, they can supposedly divine information about the drinker's past, present, and—most relevant to me—future. Very cool, although one of the last people I might have expected to read my fortune from the bottom of a cup was the head of security at a travel agency.

Moti put the cup down and tsk-tsked. "Zaki!" he shouted. "Zaki, come. Bring the clipboard!"

Clipboard? What are we in, medieval times?

Almost immediately, another guy walked through the wall to my left. The seemingly solid barrier molded and bent around him like water as he passed through it. At first I thought he was a projection, but there was no telltale flicker. I was also curious why Ifrit bothered to use the door if she could just have walked through the walls.

Theatrics, maybe. What sort of travel agency is this?

The man named Zaki reached the table. He was tall and he had big hands and shoulder-length sandy-brown hair. He wore all black, a casual black button-down shirt tucked into tight black jeans, and shiny black loafers on his feet. His face was round and flat like a pancake. There was a gentleness to it, even through his stiff, thousand-yard stare, which didn't waver as he handed Moti a thin metal clipboard. I had never seen one of those analog antiques in real life.

Moti grinned at my obvious surprise. "Sorry. We are a bit old-fashioned here." He stroked the clipboard with a boyish fondness, his eyes sparkling. "I do love the older things. Paper and pen. Much harder to steal than bits and bytes." He paused before continuing. "Did you hear what he said, Zaki?"

Zaki casually replied in a deep baritone voice, "Yes. I hear."

Moti reiterated anyway, "He said people are trying to kill him."

Zaki shrugged. He walked over to the printer and said, "*Cigariot.*" A pack of TIME cigarettes appeared, a Levantine retro cigarette brand coming back into fashion with the hip professional crowd. Zaki removed a cigarette from the pack, then twirled it in his hand.

Moti kept his eyes on me. "*Yoel,* I believe you." Then, without shifting his glance, he asked, "Zaki, do you believe him?"

Zaki seemed to consider the question just long enough to make me shift uncomfortably. He twirled the cigarette in his hand once again. Fidgety people make me nervous. "Yes," he said. The guy's voice was so heavy, he might have been an operatic bass in another life.

Moti flipped through a few scribbled-on sheets of actual paper until he found one devoid of writing. "Zaki, pencil!"

Zaki didn't seem affronted as I imagined someone of his build might be after being shouted at so forcefully. He reached into the long hair behind his ear, manifested a tan pencil, and rolled it across the conference table to Moti, who stopped it with his index fingertip and picked it up. "Beautiful. The origin of planned obsolescence," Moti said, gazing at the writing utensil. "A sucker for old things, I guess." He paused before continuing: "So today, where were you going?"

"Costa Rica." He made a note on his clipboard. "My wife, Sylvia, was already there—"

"Your wife?" he interrupted. "So your trip was for pleasure?"

"Yeah. I mean, it's a vacation with my wife." Another note. "She left a couple of hours before me."

"Trouble in paradise?" Moti winked.

"What?" I asked, taken aback.

"I'm sorry, we travel agents, we see a lot of folks go on vacation, and you get a—shall we say *sense*—of these things."

"Yes. I mean, no. I mean—shit, man, people are trying to kill me, and you're asking me about my marital issues? Look, I'm supposed to be in Costa Rica right now with my wife. I went to the TC, sat down in the foyer, and the next thing I know, people are trying to kill me!"

He cocked his head at me, curious. "*Yoel*, I have two questions. First, who is trying to kill you?"

All right, Joel, focus. Right now your needs are pretty basic. Don't get killed. Get to Sylvia. The longer this guy interrogates you, the more time you have to think of how to do that. But think fast.

"You're not going to believe it."

Moti took another puff of his cigarette. Exhaling smoke, he said, "Try me. I hear many crazy things." He polished off his Turkish coffee and put the tiny ceramic cup back on its saucer, upside down. "But make sure that the crazy things you say are the truth," he continued with a smile, "because I will know if you are lying."

I had a feeling he wasn't referring to the room nanos that were no doubt scanning me while we sat there talking. "Okay."

"So, first question, *Yoel Byram*. Who is your would-be assassin?"

"International Transport," I said, gulping. "That's who."

Moti stared at me, his gaze all business. After a few seconds he made a note on his clipboard and asked, his voice nonchalant, "Second question. Why? Why do you think International Transport is trying to kill you?"

Shit. What do I say? Better come clean, I guess. Nobody else left to help me.

"This is going to sound crazy."

"*Yoel,* we have already established that I am okay with crazy as long as it is the truth." He peered closer at me. "Please, tell me."

A cold sweat started down my neck. "Teleportation. It doesn't work the way people think it does. I can prove it, and if I tell anyone, if people find out about me, then International Transport is fucked. That's why they want to kill me," I answered.

"Interesting," he said, his pencil seemingly checking another box.

Wait, he has a box for Huge International Corporate Conspiracy?

"Okay, *Yoel.* I think maybe we can help you." Moti ran his right hand over the crisp white collar of his button-down shirt, leaned back in his chair, then put his left hand in the pocket of his neatly creased navy slacks. "But first tell me more about this woman, this Pema. You say she sent you to us? What did she tell you, exactly?"

Might as well come clean on this, too. I need to build trust. Then maybe I can get some alone time with this room.

"I guess we should start with my pet peeve."

NEARLY INFINITE

I WOKE UP on my couch.

A quick check of my comms told me it was 9:12 p.m. on June 27, 2147. *Shit.* It was our tenth wedding anniversary, and Sylvia and I had made plans to meet at our favorite college bar at nine thirty. I had dozed off playing video games, not an uncommon occurrence for a weeknight. Usually it didn't matter, as Sylvia didn't get home until after midnight, but even I recognized that being late for one's aluminum anniversary was bad form.

I jumped up from the couch, sweeping aside several gaming windows on my comms with a wave of my hand. In case you guys in the future all speak telepathically or something, comms were neural stem implants that pretty much everyone got on their second birthday. Constructed of a hybrid mesh of stem cells and nanites that our bodies treated as a benign tumor, they interfaced with the aural and visual centers of our brain, augmenting our eardrums with audio and our retinas with video. A comm is also what we called any remote communication. We had so many ways of communicating with one another that we just referred to any virtual conversation with someone else as a comm, the plural of which is also comms—and, yes, it was confusing at times, since we received comms on our comms.

The video games vanished, affording me a fairly uncluttered view of my cluttered apartment. Sylvia and I owned a nice two-bedroom in Greenwich Village—exposed brick and steel beams, charmingly gouged hardwood floors, ten-foot windows that looked out onto Houston Street. Right now I ignored all that and speed-walked to the master bedroom closet, searching for a suitably clean button-down to put over my WHAT WOULD TURING DO? T-shirt.

As I tucked and buttoned, I silently cursed myself for not setting an alarm. True, my marriage had been trending downward for the past year, but the last thing I wanted was to initiate the Big Talk. And to be fair, we were both to blame for our relationship bottoming out.

Sylvia had been hired at International Transport—IT— almost eight years ago. She was a quantum microscopy engineer, a field that I only grokked in the most superficial way, and had diligently worked her way up the corporate megalith's food chain. Around a year ago, she'd been promoted to a new, hush-hush position. She warned me it would mean a lot more time at the office, but the salary bump had also made it possible for us to move out of our subterranean one-bedroom closet on North Brother Island and into the actual city. At the time, it seemed like a belated birthday gift from the gods. But as the months progressed and we saw each other less and less, the new gig seemed more of a curse than a blessing.

I checked my comms again: 9:21 p.m. *Shit, shit, shit.* No way would I make it to the Mandolin in time, even if I took a car. I'd have to port there. As a way to cover my last-minute splurge, I decided to pick up a salting gig.[4]

---

4 The term *salting* has its origin in cryptography, and it was originally used to protect against code-breaking by extending the length and complexity of a password. If the computer being utilized to crack a password did not have the password's length or complexity of the salted password, then the password could not be found. Ultimately, password salting became obsolete as
→

Salting is what I do for a living. This doesn't mean I spend my days harvesting salt from ancient water beds, though it's just about as exciting. A salter's job consists of enriching various artificial-intelligence engines. I imagine in your time, salting will have become as extinct as riverboat piloting, chauffeuring, or teaching, because apps will have outsmarted and replaced us in every conceivable way.

But in my present, there was still a fundamental problem with the way computers thought. Without getting too geeky about it, it was called the *Entscheidungsproblem*. Try saying that three times fast.[5]

Because of the *Entscheidungsproblem*, computers couldn't make an original decision. Every choice they came to could only be based on data and algorithms that had been preprogrammed into them. That's not to say computers couldn't get new ideas, but every new idea they got could only come from

---

code-breakers pivoted their efforts from cracking technologies to more sophisticated methods of AI-enabled phishing (attempting to acquire passwords by masquerading as a trustworthy entity). Information security eventually evolved into battles among sophisticated AI engines, as users turned to AIs to protect them from being phished, and attackers created more and more sophisticated algos to dupe them. This led to security becoming the root of our currency: the owner's demand for protecting data and the attacker's demand for stealing it. The salt block-chain economy eventually became what is known as chits, and salting became the act of engaging with AI engines in order to improve their ability to protect or deceive. Because we had so many AIs, salting also became a means of steady, gainful employment. Or not so gainful, if you asked my in-laws.

[5] In 1928, a mathematician by the name of David Hilbert posed a challenge to the mathematical community—create an algorithm that takes a statement of first-order logic and answers yes or no as to whether it is universally valid. Having such an algorithm would mean that there is no such thing as an unsolvable problem. So the *Entscheidungsproblem* (which, surprise, surprise, is German for "decision problem") is this: Does there exist an algorithm for deciding whether or not a specific mathematical assertion does or does not have a proof? The answer was no. But if you asked a computer scientist, they might answer "not yet."

remixing old ideas, or external input from other computers, or through human input—which is where I came in.

We salters spent our days coming up with arbitrary puzzles that AI engines couldn't grok. Every time a salter's gambit was not anticipated by an app, that app got smarter by adding the unanticipated random logic set to its decision algorithm, and the salter got paid. Essentially, I made my living by being a smartass to apps. In my field, one rose through the ranks based on the quality of one's accepted salts. The Mine, where we work, kept track of our acceptance ratios on a public leaderboard. The better your ratio, the more desirable you were, and the more cheddar you made. Most salters didn't get the nuances between being a smartass to an app and being an idiot to an app, so they tended to work harder and longer to earn a passable living wage. Taking into account that I was an inherently lazy person, I did fairly well for myself. I had found a way to distill the craft of salting into a repeatable formula of humanity, complexity, and humor. I'm definitely not the best salter there ever was, but the worldwide leaderboard consistently had me in the top 5 percent.

"Going for your second gig today?" Adina the admin said to me after I logged in. "Since when did you become a workaholic?"

"What can I say? I love what I do," I answered while pulling on my dressiest pair of sneakers. "Actually, I'm late for drinks and need Punch fare."

"World's smallest violin," replied Adina. "Anyhoo, I got an easy one for you. Another one looking to learn how to be funny."

"Ah jeez, when will our robot overlords learn that the only thing funny about them is how desperately humorless they are? Shoot it over."

"It's already here. So long, hotshot." Adina laughed as she disconnected.

"Hello," said a nervous voice. "For the record, I am a *he*, not an *it*."

All I could see on my comm stream was a black box. "If you don't want people to call you an it, get yourself an avatar."

"Is that a prerequisite?" it asked eagerly. "For being funny?"

A noob! Easy money.

"No. Look, I'm kind of in a rush. Let's do something basic. Ask me about my pet peeves."

My dog, a thirteen-year-old Portuguese water mutt, looked up at me from where she was lying on the front-door mat. Digital assistants had replaced pets for some people. Easier to clean up after, and they lived forever. Maybe it was because of my profession, but I was still a dog guy. I knelt down and gently pulled the mat on which the old girl was sprawled out of the way of the door. A belly rub later, I stepped out of my apartment and made for the stairwell, minimizing my comms to the upper-right quadrant of my field of vision so I wouldn't trip and kill myself.

"Very well," the app said. "Please describe one of your pet peeves."

"My pet peeve is black."

"You do not like black things?" it asked.

"No, I love the color black."

"How is it possible for you to love the color black if it is your pet peeve?"

"I didn't say my pet peeve was black—I said my pet peeve was black."

"I fail to see the difference."

"Ready for the money shot?"

"What is a money shot?"

"It's what happens when I salt you, and you pay me."

"Oh yes. I am prepared for that. It is the very purpose of this interaction."

This poor app must have been compiled by a script kiddie.

"Good. Here goes. My pet, Peeve, is a black cocker-spaniel-slash-Portuguese-water-dog mix. Her original name was Eve, but when she was a puppy, she suffered from urinary incontinence. In other words, she peed everywhere. So I called her Peeve, and it stuck."

"Your pet, Peeve, is your dog?"

"Yes, and Peeve is black."

"Clever," the app said emotionlessly. "Salt approved."

I reminded myself to give Peeve a few extra treats when I got home.

"Great. By the way, you might say dogs with urinary incontinence are also one of my pet peeves."

"Is that germane to the salt?"

"Well, my wife hates it when I call Eve 'Peeve,' so calling my pet Peeve is my *wife's* pet peeve. Does that earn me any extra credit?"

"I'm afraid it does not qualify for additional chits."

"Fine. Bye."

I closed the comms window just as I pushed open the door to the street. Not my quickest payday, but close. In the early days of cognitive computing, they used to call it neurolinguistic hacking, and I was one of the fastest on the Eastern Seaboard.

Okay, so I wasn't exactly contributing to the betterment of the human race. But as I'm sure you're aware, a lot of the things that used to be "work" were taken over by technology a long time ago. Sure, you could build something with your hands instead of having it printed, and some people still chose to, but it was crazy expensive compared to the alternatives, so why bother? Most folks in 2147 spent their days interfacing with AI engines in different ways to earn chits. People rarely had any idea which system they were solving problems for, or to what end—they just knew it paid the bills. I think most of the time the apps just wanted somebody to talk to.

Did it ever bother me that what I did for a living basically made apps smart enough so that they wouldn't need me anymore? Yes. But I never really thought about it all that much, and anyway, technology didn't fuck me—International Transport did.

But I'm getting ahead of myself. On that Tuesday evening in June, I half jogged the two blocks from my apartment to the Washington Square Teleportation Center, or TC, in record time. My comms read 9:29 p.m. when I arrived.

Surprisingly, it wasn't raining. New York City was having one of its rare clear summer nights, meaning there weren't enough hydrocarbons in the air for the mosquitoes to metabolize.[6] Usually the Manhattan skyline was obscured by the haze of a billions-strong swarm of mosquitoes that ate pollution and pissed water. All part of the magical dance of chemistry and genetic engineering that kept us humans alive despite our very best efforts to destroy ourselves.

I hope that by the time this gets read, we'll have found a more elegant solution for air synthesis than noisy, disgusting bugs that have been genetically modified into flying steam reformers. I'm fine with them eating methane instead of blood and excreting water in lieu of spreading disease, but they're still annoying as hell.

---

[6] In the early twenty-first century, scientists at a company called Oxitec patented a mechanism for genetically modifying cells to produce a protein that stops mosquitoes from functioning normally. This technology was a precursor to modern gene-editing techniques that enabled the eventual conversion of mosquitoes, specifically the genus *Aedes aegypti* (known as the yellow fever mosquito prior to its genetic rehabilitation), into vaccine carriers, and more recently into living steam reformers.

I crossed the street over to the Washington Square TC on West Fourth Street. Unlike several other places around the world where TCs were still lightly sprinkled with picketers harboring resentment at teleportation's upheaval of the transportation industry, or religious kooks trying to convince people the technology was murder, New York had instantly embraced porting for its obvious benefits. Prior to this, most religious types had been ambivalent to teleportation. It was a form of *freight*, not transportation. The very notion of organic teleportation was considered a fool's errand until 2109—technically impossible, owing to the fidget problem: living things are fidgety. Back then, a good real-time atomic model that could accurately predict and transmit what living things would do next was still a scientific wet dream.

But in my time, that problem had been solved twenty years ago. Porting had almost become too popular for some tastes as of late. For those who wanted to punch across town, sometimes the length of the queue at the local TC might lead to a longer commute than a drone or a bus ride. IT kept promising the next generation of TCs would be able to teleport more than one person at a time, but gave no indication to when these promises would become a reality.

TC stations were hard to miss. They were small red rectangular buildings of concrete that popped out of the ground like a pox infection on the face of their immediate surroundings. The ingress and egress doors were adorned with the iconic International Transport lettering, and always flanked by public toilets. Why were all TCs next to public toilets? Well, there's no good physiological explanation for it, but teleportation tended to do curious things to the human bladder.

When scientists first began porting living things, they discovered that complex organisms, starting with animals the size of cats or dogs, seemed to lose a few grams of weight every time they were transported. Interestingly, this was not the case when the same animals were euthanized and *then* teleported. Some religious types tried to spin the weight loss as evidence of soul separation, but since the ported beings seemed unaffected by the change, there were only two possible conclusions.

Either the soul was a regenerative thing, meaning creatures bigger than small cats just grew new ones. Or—much more plausibly—the weight loss had nothing to do with the soul and could be attributed to garden-variety packet loss.[7] Pretty much everyone sided with packet loss.

I ambled onto the conveyer, which took me down into the belly of the station, gliding past gray cement overhangs and brushed gold pillars to the misters. As I passed through the gray fog bank, I felt the familiar tickle of floating nanos against my skin. I'd ported countless times before, but something about the ocean-spray-like, metallic sensation of teeny tiny robots scanning my body still gave me goose bumps. The nanite mist not only cataloged every cell, clothing fiber, and arrangement of molecules inside every person who entered it, but it also checked for any contraband. Somewhere in some database, the nanite mist's telemetry calculations and biological check-sums merged to create my *last-known full*—my meta-image

---

[7] Packet loss during teleportation was common and controlled by the Teleportation Control Assurance Protocol (TCAP). TCAP was a zero-loss sliding window protocol that provided an easy way to ensure reliable compression, delivery, and expansion of packets, so that individual TCs don't need to implement logic for this themselves. *Zero-loss* was actually a misnomer because TCAP utilized packet-loss concealment, such that in the event that any data was lost, various interpolation or extrapolation algorithms were utilized to fill in the gaps. In other words, filling in what was missing by averaging the stuff before and after the gap. The acceptable packet-loss rate was less than 0.0000005 percent. Any teleportation that exceeded that rate was deemed a failure and the process was reverted. The origin conductor then determined whether to reattempt or cancel teleportation. Scientists eventually decided that packet loss was the reason large organisms lost a few grams of mass after teleportation. Think of it like a very expensive, very small diet.

backup. The whole process took about five seconds. At the end of the moving walkway, a little arrow pointed me forward to the shortest line. As there were a dozen teleportation chambers and it was the post-rush-hour lag, there were only two people ahead of me.

Less than three minutes later I stepped into the compartment. The TC conductor already had my travel manifest dialed in, synchronized, and validated against my comms. A short, yellow-striped black barrier in front of the small Punch Escrow chamber lowered—my signal to enter. Beyond the barrier was a single, magnetically suspended chair, not unlike a passenger drone seat, but bordered in shiny metallic gold. I imagine the abundance of gold everywhere in TCs was intended to impart a perception of luxury.

Once I sat down, an automated conveyor silently ushered the levitating chair into the adjacent Punch Escrow chamber, the wall of which was marked with the universal symbol for staying put: a stencil of a person sitting on a chair, a clock on the wall beside them.

The Punch Escrow chamber itself was entirely painted light beige except for one black chalcedony wall that my chair pivoted ninety degrees to face. The word FOYER appeared on the wall. Teleportation origin rooms are marked FOYER, and destin rooms are marked VESTIBULE.

Underneath the FOYER sign, a stream of the conductor appeared on the wall to, once again, verify my identity and destination. He was a bald Asian guy who looked like he spent most of his life in a chair and wasn't particularly happy about it. In a monotone, he reminded me to read and then tap the nodding emoji under a bunch of legal small print that holographically appeared in front of my face.

Teleportation was a rather head-trippy experience. There you were, by yourself, in a little room in one place. Then, all of a sudden, there you were, by yourself, in an identical room in another place. From the outside, it looked pretty much like people imagined it would back before it was feasible, only it happened in reverse order. The person being teleported got to where she was going about four seconds *before* she left. It was kind of a mind fuck.

Even weirder, nobody knew what it felt like to teleport. I mean, sure, we knew what it felt like to *arrive* somewhere, but the actual traveling part happened so fast, it didn't really *feel* like anything. All we knew was that when the lights came back on, we were already on the other side.

When human teleportation was first introduced, there were plenty of streams that demonstrated the Punch Escrow process.[8] One moment someone would be sitting in the chair; the next they'd be nothing but vapor and dust. It looked shocking, but it was harmless. As IT explained it, the brief, ghostly outlines of the teleportees were simply the layer of dust left behind when we were zapped away. The process was so quick that the water molecules, dead skin cells, and other particles on your clothing and body that didn't get sent to the destin hung in the air for a beat, kind of like the bird-shaped cloud of dust the Road Runner left when he ran away from Wile E. Coyote in those old-school 1950s Warner Bros. animated shorts. I know, you probably think I'm lame for watching two-hundred-year-old cartoons, but what can I say: I liked the finer things.

---

[8] Invented by the enterprising Swiss actuarial engineer Corina Shafer, the Punch Escrow was a patented, active-active fail-safe redundancy for the teleportation workflow. The Punch Escrow adds two checksum spaces, defined as "foyer" at the point of origin and "vestibule" at the point of destination. The role of these chambers was to safely cache each quark of a teleporting person at the foyer until his or her journey was confirmed a success at the vestibule. If unsuccessful, the person stayed in the foyer, unmoved. In other words, if something went wrong during your transport, then you never left.

I'd ported a whole bunch of times, so I wasn't sure why I was thinking about all this just then. It's like remembering that sudden unexpected nocturnal death syndrome is a real thing right before going to sleep.

Sometimes my brain was just an asshole.

Quickly, I scrolled through the small-print, holographic legalese floating before me. Then tapped the head-nodding emoji—*I agree.*

The room went totally dark for about three or four seconds, there was a bright white flash, and then the lights came up and I found myself in an identical room, with one difference—the wall before me read VESTIBULE.

"Welcome to the Times Square TC," said the new conductor on the wall's stream. Maybe she was a new hire or something, because her apple-cheeked face and genuine smile were much more welcoming than the lifeless gaze and dreary greeting of the previous conductor. Or maybe it was just more fun to see people arrive.

The levitating chair retreated to the antechamber. The barrier was lowered, and I stepped out into a TC around two kilometers from the one I'd just left. The trip had cost me almost a full day's pay, but I got where I needed to be only seven minutes after I was supposed to meet Sylvia, as opposed to thirty-plus.

I jogged out of the TC into Times Square, dodging through the crowds of selfie-taking tourists and giant flashing holograms, then cut through a side alley to find myself in front of our old college haunt, the Mandolin.

The bouncer checked my comms, waving me through the front door. The place had gotten its name from its varnished antique bar counter. It was composed of discarded, broken string instruments frozen in lacquer. Mandolins mostly, with the occasional remnant of ukulele and guitar thrown in for artistic measure. The rest of the establishment had an early twenty-first-century brewpub feel, complete with actual beer taps, made-to-order cocktails, and quaint handwritten menus on real chalkboards.

I scanned the mostly empty interior. This being a Tuesday, only the serious drinkers were present. As I double-checked the ten or so faces, trusting my comms to recognize Sylvia even if she was facing in the opposite direction, I began to formulate a witty-but-plausible explanation for my tardiness.

Unfortunately, my brain was unable to come up with one before I was attacked from behind.

SITUATION

THANKFULLY, MY WOULD-BE ASSAILANT turned out to be my wife and not some death-squad assassin she sent after me for being late. She wrapped her arms around my chest, her chin resting on my shoulder. "Guess who?" she said breathlessly into my ear.

"Marie Curie?" I turned around, trying to gauge how much trouble I was in. I might be biased, but Sylvia was good-looking—and I don't just mean for a physicist. She had a pale heart-shaped face, a curvy figure, and catlike hazel-green eyes. Her long, straight hair was chestnut blond—*not dirty blond,* she'd tell you—and, as always, parted down the middle. Every movement she made was done with intention and confidence. In her hand was a near-empty cocktail glass, which may have accounted for the flirty expression on her face. My wife was usually a Happy Drunk.

"How many drinks are you on?" I said as we migrated toward the bar.

She pretended to calculate a large number on her fingers. "Somewhere in the logarithm of eight hundred and sixty-four. Time for you to catch up." She motioned to the bartender,

Richard, then faced me. "Is there anything you'd like to say to me, husband, on the occasion of our anniversary?"

Sylvia's lips naturally curved upward at the corners, giving the appearance she was always thinking about something funny. But right then I didn't feel like laughing. Yes, I was the one who was late, but I didn't like being called out on it. I know, I was a jerk.

"You know me," I said lightly. "'I don't believe in apologies; I believe in actions.'" The phrase was an old joke between us, something our college physics professor would say whenever someone was late to class.

"O-kay then. Richard," she said as the bartender arrived, "can you please bring my truant spouse a lubricant for his rusty sense of decorum?"

"Gibson?" Richard raised his eyebrows to me, his look confirming my suspicion that I was a complete fuckup. I shrugged. He turned to Sylvia.

"While something in the 'sour grapes' varietal would be apropos, I will have another lemon drop, but on the rocks this time, Richard," she said. "I don't want to be seeing double."

Richard nodded—likely reckoning *too late*—and went about his business. Sylvia smiled at me, her fingers tap-tapping on my leg. "So I have some good news. It looks like my project might be ready for regulatory approval sooner than we thought. I was thinking we might be able to start on our own little project. Iterate Byram dot next?" She gave me a sidelong glance, that mouth of hers twitching upward.

"Seriously?" I said as Richard set down our drinks. "You know, parenthood actually works a lot better with two parents in the same physical space at the same time. They've done studies." I took a sip of my Gibson, the gin burning on its way down my throat.

"I just told you—it won't be like this forever. In six months you'll be looking at a changed woman. Much more bandwidth for you and me and others." She took a sip of the translucent yellow concoction in her tumbler, fixing me with a flirty stare.

"I don't know. I realize it's good for the species and all that, but the thought of little copies of me running around, it sounds—"

"Cute? Adorable? Naughty?" she said, moving her hand farther up my leg.

"I was gonna say 'creepy.'"

I wasn't entirely opposed to having kids. A year ago I likely would have jumped in with both feet. But since Sylvia got promoted, we'd grown distant from each other, throwing ourselves into work and other distractions. Lately I'd been wondering if the mom and dad we could have been were still inside us. "I just think right now's not a good time to bring another human being into the equation."

"You sure about that?" said Sylvia, leaning forward to breathe a lemon-vodka-scented whisper into my ear. "Cause I have some proofs I can whip out right now."

"*Now* now?" I asked. "I'm not sure I'm in a theorem-proving mood."

"I've got plenty of data. We'll punch home and I'll show it to you." She gently bit my ear, her words hot on my cochlea.

"I'm not against it," I conceded. "But I think before two people have children, they at least need to be honest with each other."

She sighed and sat back. "Do you really want to do this again? I barely snuck out of work as it is, and Bill's been riding me for the last month so our project will be finished on time. So please, can we just enjoy what little time we do have together? We both knew what I signed on for when I took this job."

"Did we? And, remind me, what is it you're almost done with? Oh, that's right. I can't know. So please excuse me if I don't take IT's word for it."

This had been an ongoing argument between us for the last year. Since she'd moved to her new department, security was so tight that Sylvia couldn't even talk to me on comms while she was at work. If we needed to communicate with each other, she had to walk across the street to a coffee shop. "Babe, you know the work I'm doing, it's classified. . . ." She smoothed out a pleat in her skirt, then looked back at me. "But what we could accomplish with it, it's a once-in-a-lifetime thing. Maybe several lifetimes. Once Honeycomb is in production, I promise, I will refocus on us."

"Super," I said, ladling on the sarcasm. "I'm sure by then, the reveal will make it all worth it."

Sylvia took a big gulp of her cocktail and crunched on the ice cubes. "You know it kills me that I can't talk to you about it. It's driving me crazy. There's so much to figure out in so little time. It's kinda breaking my brain."

"Well, if it's breaking your brain, it'll probably fry mine." I took another swallow of my drink.

She blew out a drunken breath. "Oh, I doubt that. It's actually not the science that's hard."

"What do you mean? Isn't that what you're in charge of? The science?"

"Kind of. Oh, it's hard to explain." She closed her eyes, massaging her temples. "Okay, think about it like this: You remember the transporters on *Star Trek*?"

Throughout our final year together in college, Sylvia and I had spent many a night bingeing the classic TV show as a respite from our studies. The special effects were delightfully archaic, as was a lot of the science, but that was part of its charm. I answered in a terrible impression of Kirk, "Beam me up, Scotty!"

"Exactly. Well, they had the science all wrong with the transporters."

"As you've never failed to mention every time it comes up, yes."

"Shhh!" she said, adding a few more *h*'s than necessary. "So, like, imagine every time Scotty beamed up Kirk, there was a gap of time between the moment Kirk got scanned on the *Enterprise*, and the time he arrived wherever he was going, a gap of *traveling* time relative to the distance he was being teleported. So, the farther the distance, the longer the wait. During which, Kirk would just sort of hang out on the *Enterprise*, toying with his tricorder."

"Is that a masturbation euphemism?"

"Ha!" she laugh-snorted loudly. "No, but that's funny. Okay, so, like, my question is, how long is it okay for Kirk to wait?"

"I dunno. Seconds? A minute?"

Sylvia took another big swallow of her drink. "Let's go with that. A minute. My problem is, while Kirk's waiting, what if he gets a little bored and suddenly has this life-changing epiphany?"

"You mean, like, 'Holy shit, I'm in love with Uhura!'"

She rolled her eyes, but continued. "Sure, I guess that could work. So he realizes he loves Uhura, and he sends her a message asking her to marry him or something. He sends her this message and then *zap!* He's on the Klingon ship drinking bloodwine with Khan. Except he doesn't remember ever sending the message because what happened between the time he got scanned and the time he arrived doesn't sync. Kirk never *had* the Uhura love epiphany."

"Oh. Oh damn. That could have been a great plot for an episode!"

"Right? Totally!" Sylvia only said *totally* when she was wasted. She carried the *o*, which I always thought was adorable. "Let's bring it back home, okay? Let's say we put a TC on a satellite and send it to a habitable planet in the Aquarius constellation. So now we have a TC on some planet eighteen light-years away and we want to teleport someone there. Let's call her Astronaut Billy."

"Is she hot?"

"Yes, but I'm hotter. Stay with me. So it takes *hours* to transmit and confirm the teleportation data to Aquarius. Not seconds. Several hours of Billy sitting in the foyer, waiting. And what if during that time she does or thinks about something important that doesn't make it to the destin?"

I shrugged. "Then she shouldn't teleport to outer space and assume the risk of losing time. If she doesn't like it, she can do something else, like hang out with her husband and not talk about work."

She downed the rest of her cocktail. "You know what? Forget it. I'm trying to explain why I've been so wrapped up in this, but if you'd rather be snarky—"

Shit. This is the most in-depth conversation we've had in weeks and you're blowing it.

"Okay, okay," I said, placing a hand on her leg. "I think it's really just a semantics thing. She's still her, right? Let's just say, for argument's sake, that while she's slowly being teleported to the Aquarius constellation, Foyer Billy somehow cheats on her husband with the conductor. If you ask me, Billy's still guilty of infidelity, even if Vestibule Billy never actually did it. You are who you are. Boom!" I finished off my Gibson in triumph.

Sylvia nodded, but I could tell she was a little upset by what I'd said.

"What?" I joked. "Is IT gonna come after me now?"

She shook away whatever thoughts she was having, half smiling. "Doesn't matter. In a matter of months, it'll be off my plate. We will have our lives back, Mr. Byram." She kissed me again, lingering this time. "Once that happens, I'm going to—*Shit.*" Sylvia sat back, her demeanor completely changing as she looked off somewhere over my shoulder. She was getting comms.

"You're going to shit?" I joked, but she waved a hand sideways, clearing whatever message she'd just gotten, and silenced me.

"I have to go," she said in frustration. "Bill needs me back at work."

"What? You just left!"

"I know, I know. I'll make it up to you. I promise."

She kissed me one last time and took off.

I looked down at the broken instruments embedded in the bar top. I couldn't help feeling like they were some kind of metaphor for my marriage—busted, frozen, forever silenced. *What the hell?* I figured. *I'm here already, might as well celebrate.*

I motioned to Richard. "Fill 'er up. Looks like I'm drinking for two."

So yeah, things weren't great between me and my wife, but we were doing our best. Well, technically, she did her best, and I trailed along behind, living off the scraps of her drive and success like a remora—one of those sucker fish that attached themselves to a shark and ate whatever fell out of their mouths. I, in return, provided the occasional entertainment. Sylvia had always given everything 110 percent, whether it was our relationship, her job, or even planning vacations. She was the one who did the research, built itineraries, then told me when and where to show up. She was also the breadwinner, which I guess made me the bread loser. Some spouses might have been irked by that, but not me. I was content to take it easy.

But to be completely transparent, my lack of drive was one of the main reasons we had been doing so poorly for the last year. Her job at IT took up so much of her time that there was little left over for us. And after a decade of letting her man the wheel of our marriage, I barely even knew how to drive anymore. So I had let things get worse and worse, until our ten-year anniversary celebration was shorter and less enjoyable than a prison visit.

Thankfully, Sylvia was never one to throw in the towel. The morning after our interrupted date at the Mandolin, she broke through my hangover with a comm from the coffee shop across the street from IT.

"Are you on the bathroom floor?" she said, peering at me.

"It's the one closest to the toilet," I said blearily. "Are you wearing what you wore last night? Jeez, have you been working this whole time?"

"Clear your calendar for next week," she informed me. "We are going on a second honeymoon. No comms, no International Transport bullshit, just me and you. You were right. We need to work on us."

"So you're ditching work for work," I said dryly. "What's the destination, Madame Cruise Director?"

"Costa Rica," she said. "I just checked. Our honeymoon spot is still there. And according to my research, the cloud forest is one of the most off-the-grid spots in the world. Plenty of time for hiking, R&R, and TLC. Sound good?"

"Sounds great," I said, though the only thing that sounded good right then was a bottle of aspirin and twelve hours of additional sleep. We said our good-byes and mostly stayed out of each other's way for the next week, successfully avoiding any more speed bumps until the day of our vacation—July 3, 2147.

HERE COMES
THE RAIN AGAIN

ON THAT DAY, I was in the midst of travel-packing procrastination when an audio message from Sylvia showed up on my comms.

"Hi, babe. Listen, things at work are quiet, so I'm getting out of here early while the getting's good. I'm going to depart directly from the TC here at IT. If you can't get ahold of me, I told Julie to give you—and only you—my GDS location. I am so ready for this. I love you."

She sounded hopeful. When she said, "I love you," I knew she meant, *We'll get through this,* but I wasn't so sure. I wasn't as convinced that this second honeymoon was going to magically solve our marital problems. Maybe that was why it had taken me all morning to start packing.

After closing the message window, I threw some final items in my suitcase—swimsuit, bug repellant, mouth cleaner. Then, satisfied that I had enough underwear and socks for the trip, I zipped up my bag, scratched Peeve behind the ears, and did a dummy check of the apartment. I put a sticky reminder on my comms to add the dog walker to our apartment's access list while we were gone.

I took the elevator down and stepped onto the street. A green, blue, and purple rainbow arced overhead, indicating the mosquitoes were hard at work emptying their bladders on us.[9] The plan was to teleport to the San José TC, and from there hire a car to drive us to our resort in the mountains of Santa Elena. My wife had scheduled us a full itinerary of hiking in the cloud forest in search of quetzals, drinking terrible local wine, and getting into shouting matches with howler monkeys. Instead of watching the July Fourth Last War memorial fireworks, Sylvia's plan was to drink Cerveza Imperials in our hotel room hot tub and celebrate our independence from International Transport for a few days. She'd chosen Costa Rica because it was one of the few countries left that didn't have TCs everywhere, and it was the place where we had honeymooned ten years ago.

Shit. Where did she say we were supposed to meet?

I tried comming Sylvia.

---

[9] Steam reforming is a method for producing hydrogen, carbon monoxide, or other useful products from airborne hydrocarbon fuels such as methane and propane, liquids such as hexane and benzene, or polymers such as polyethylene, polypropylene, and polystyrene. This is achieved via a processing mechanism called a reformer, which binds kinetically generated vapor with the fossil fuel to generate hydrogen. The steam methane reformer is widely credited as the most important invention of the twenty-first century, as air quality had deteriorated to toxic levels. Initially, a significant percentage of the energy needed for continuous operation of the reformers came from the hydrogen they generated, so they were relegated to use in only the most affluent civilian zones. Eventually, genetic engineering was brought into the mix, enabling the conversion of airborne insects into organic flying steam reformers—since insect flight muscle is capable of achieving the highest metabolic rate of all animal tissues. The most efficient of these were mosquitoes—swarms of which have become a fixture in our skies, akin to clouds. Since they urinate water, their presence creates a permanent rainbow during sunlight hours. A glorious, lifesaving, mosquito-pee rainbow.

Instead, an animated Rosie the Riveter avatar obscured my field of vision, causing me to trip on the sidewalk and bang my shin on my luggage. "Shit!"

I reduced the size of the comms window, making sure to dial down the background opacity so I could avoid any more obstacles.

The avatar displayed a concerned emoji expression. "Ouch. Are you okay, Joel?" It was Julie, Sylvia's AIDE, or Artificially Intelligent Digital Entity. Basically, a personal assistant app with extra cruft. They acted as proxies for their owners, doing everything from personal shopping to paying bills to interfacing with coworkers when the owner was indisposed.

Most were fairly businesslike, but Sylvia had put a lot of extra effort toward giving Julie a personality. My wife was an only child, often lonely growing up. Getting her very own AIDE when she joined IT must have felt a lot like being handed a brand-new sibling, only one who would always be there for her, would always support her, and would never, ever ask for money. Sylvia nurtured her new app. She confided in Julie, asked her for advice, pushed her to be assertive and wise and funny. She even taught her to be a feminist, hence Julie's choice of the Rosie avatar.

There was nothing wrong with the depth of their relationship, per se. Most people had a strong emotional bond with their AIDEs, somewhere on the spectrum between favorite pet and best friend, depending on one's needs. I, however, always saw AIDEs as buckets of semicognitive code with finite complexity, designed to create the illusion of sentience.

I rubbed my shin. "Ouch is right. There goes my marathoning career."

"And look, you're outside! Is this your monthly day of exercise?" Julie's avatar gave a jaunty wink.

"You know, for a comedienne you're one hell of a personal assistant. Can we back-burner the hilarity, though? Sylvia unplugged before she told me where we were meeting."

"Sorry. I've been studying up on humor. A lot of research shows it puts you bipedal carbon plasma bags at ease."

"Oh, it's definitely working," I answered dryly, knowing she'd detect the sarcastic tone. This is why no self-respecting salter would ever own an AIDE. Their eagerness to please is practically an invitation to be pwnd, or maliciously salted. But hacking an AIDE is a felony, on the level of grand larceny. To a natural-born salter, it's like putting a carrot in front of a famished rabbit, then separating the two with an electrified grate. "Now that you've put me *at ease*, can you tell me where my wife is?"

"You betcha! Sylvia's looking forward to this; she told me to hold all her comms before she left. Except for you, natch. I've got a bunch of great canned responses in case any of her program managers try to interrupt her vacation. Do you want to hear 'em? They're hilarious!"

"I, uh, no. I'm almost at the TC, so I just need to know where she is. I don't want to spend the evening looking for her."

"Okay. There's a rum joint called the Monkey Bar. It's walking distance from customs. I just sent you the GDS location. Don't be too late or she'll be dancing on the tables."

"Oooh, maybe I should take my time then."

"Oooh, now you're the funny one. I should have you salt me. On second thought, no. If you did that, then everyone would just hang up on me."

"And they don't already?"

"No, they d—"

I hung up.

Just as I was about to step on the Greenwich Village TC escalator, a young auburn-haired woman stepped in front of me. She looked out of place, even for NYC. She had animated, glowing LED strands of orange and red woven through her hair; they looked like smoldering embers. Her outfit was even weirder: a long, ruffled white gown, olive-green army jacket, and muddy hiking boots on her feet. She clutched a bag that appeared to contain a giant horse saddle and was deliberately blocking the entrance of the TC.

"Excuse me," I said, attempting to maneuver around her.

"Is this the Greenwich Village Teleportation Center?" she asked, looking me up and down like I was an extraterrestrial. Her delivery was curt, dismissive. I couldn't place the accent, somewhere Latin.

"That's what it says on the sign, lady," I said, responding in kind.

She nodded, and without another word stepped onto the moving walkway.

I got on right behind her. *Weirdo.*

I saw her stiffen as we went through the nanite misters, but the moving walkway continued, depositing us before the bank of outgoing teleportation chambers. She looked around as if unsure where to go next. I pointed her toward the shortest queue, then joined my own line. The woman went into her chamber right before I did, giving me one last sidelong glance. I figured it was her first time teleporting.

The barrier to my chamber lowered. I stepped into the foyer, dropping my luggage in the prescribed compartment and sitting in the chair that levitated into the Punch Escrow chamber. There, the conductor confirmed my destination, and I agreed to the displayed legalese. As the lights dimmed, I began to debate whether my first drink at the Monkey Bar should be a mojito or a zombie.

Then—*nothing.*

Nothing happened.

There was no blinding white flash to indicate my arrival in the San José TC vestibule. No alarms, no announcement. Just darkness. I didn't think much of it. I assumed there had been a brownout in Costa Rica; they still happened occasionally in non-thermal-powered countries. I got up and felt my way toward the exit, promptly slamming my nose into the concrete wall. *Ow.*

I heard muffled voices outside, and monkey-walked my way toward them, grasping on to the chair's magnetic guides against the wall to orient myself. Finally, after a few more painful bumps, I fumbled my way to the exit barrier. I pushed and pulled on the hard plastic until it lowered. I stepped over it, into the light, and found myself face-to-face with the conductor. The Greenwich conductor. He had orange hair, a purple birthmark on his face in the shape of Michigan's Lower Peninsula, and an open mouth. He gaped at me like he was seeing a ghost.

Son of a bitch. I'm still in New York.

"I think there's been a mistake," I said. Behind him, people were milling about in confusion and checking their comms. A red light blinked above each teleportation chamber.

"Hold on a sec!" The conductor's forehead was creased. "Shit. How the hell did you get out?"

"Door was open."

"Hold on." He was apparently on the comms with someone. "Yes, sir."

The conductor made a quick gesture, moving the conversation from his comms to a holographic projector somewhere in the wall. A man in a tidy IT lab coat appeared between us. He had gray hair that had fallen victim to male-pattern baldness, a paunch around his middle, and glittering pale-blue eyes. The only thing to indicate he wasn't in the room was a video refresh bar that went up and down his body.

"Is this him?" the projected man said to the conductor.

"Yes, sir," the conductor answered quickly, as if he were being questioned by a cop.

"Mr. Byram." The man paused, as if to afford the next thing he said some additional heft. "My name is William Taraval. I'm Head of Research and Development at International Transport. It appears we experienced a malfunction during your teleportation. We're still trying to get to the bottom of it."

This guy is Sylvia's boss? Isn't he a bit of a muckety-muck for this? He sounded formal but sincere. His eyes sported the longest crow's feet I'd ever seen. "We're shutting down this TC until we can complete our investigation. In the meantime, I have instructed the conductor here to refund your transport chits."

The conductor nodded eagerly. "Already done, sir. Like it never happened."

"Mr. Byram," Taraval continued, "may we speak privately?"

"Uh, sure."

"Thank you, James." He nodded to the conductor, who turned his back on me as if I were getting dressed. I gestured to invite Taraval into my comms. He went from standing a couple of meters away to suddenly being in my face. *Too close.* I quickly minimized his window to a less-intimate size.

"Thank you. A modicum of intimacy yields a plethora of dividends, wouldn't you say, Mr. Byram?" Taraval asked.

"A what?"

"Never mind. I know you do not recognize me, Mr. Byram, because we've never formally met. But I work with your wife. Sylvia."

The jerkwad boss who wrecked our anniversary last week. Yeah, I know who you are.

"Right, she's mentioned you."

"Always in a positive light, I'm sure." He winked like a dorky uncle. "Naturally, she's mentioned you as well, Joel. I know this jaunt you were embarking upon is very important to her. However, we've just sustained a rather significant attack on our systems. Telemetry is being gathered. But this will require shutting down all TC operations for some time."

"Shit! Sylvia already ported down to Costa Rica."

"Yes, exactly. But we are not out of options."

"We're not?"

"Fortunately, there are some TCs that are always operational. One of them is our development TC here at IT. I could send you from here to a hospital in San José. Unfortunately, all comms in Costa Rica are down, but once there, I'm sure you and Sylvia will be able to find each other."

"I guess membership has its privileges, huh?"

"Indeed. Sylvia's happiness is paramount to us."

"Uh-huh. So I just head on over to IT HQ?"

"Yes, I've already flagged a car to pick you up outside the Greenwich TC. We're at Eight Hundred Second Avenue, as you know. Everything will be arranged by the time you get here. See you soon."

The comms window vanished.

Shit always goes wrong when Sylvia and I go on vacation. We've always referred to these mishaps as *adventures*, because we don't want to call them *vacation fuckups*. Besides, who wants to have a textbook holiday anyway? Half the fun is partaking in some ridiculous misadventure that you can later tell your friends over drinks.

Our last vacation in Hawaii came to a premature end when we had to be airlifted by drone from the side of the Kīlauea volcano after some work emergency that *absolutely could not be solved without Sylvia* came up. I was pretty pissed about it at the time, but these days it makes me laugh. I already imagined her cracking up at my retelling of this particular event, especially the part about me slamming my face into the wall.

"Okay, change of plans," I told the conductor, and turned back toward the Escrow room. "I'll just get my luggage."

"Well, uh, that's the good news, sir," said the conductor in an earnest, non–New York accent. Maybe he actually was from Michigan. "Your baggage was successfully punched. That's the last piece of information we got before the comms went dead. We always move inorganic before organic. Little-known fact: your clothes get to where you're going before you do. Good thing you're not naked right now, ha-ha."

I hate it when people who aren't funny attempt to be funny. "So how do I find my stuff?"

"Yes. Yes," he answered someone on his comms, then focused on me. "Uh, as soon as things get back online, I'll personally get in touch with the San José conductor and ensure they deliver your bags to your final destination," he assured me.

"Okay, thanks." *At least I won't have to haul my luggage across town.*

As I headed out of the TC, I could see more people milling around and murmuring to their comms and one another. At first I thought they were grumbling about having to make alternate travel arrangements, but once I got outside, I saw everyone seemed to be doing it. I could overhear snatches of urgent conversation.

Wait. Did someone say there was an explosion?

BURNING DOWN
THE HOUSE

*For we do surely die, and are as water which is running down to
the earth, which is not gathered, and God doth not accept a person,
and hath devised devices in that the outcast is not outcast by Him.*
—2 Samuel 14:14

BEFORE I COULD ASK anyone what was going on, a black
town car pulled up and the door hissed open. "Welcome, Joel
Byram!" it said heartily. All cars went driverless in the second
half of the twenty-first century, and I'd been told the riding
experience became much more pleasant as a result.

"International Transport headquarters," I said.

"Already dialed in, sir. Please sit back and enjoy the ride."

As the car headed down to the southern edge of Turtle Bay,
my comms lit up with emergency break-in feeds. Talking heads
were trying to maintain their composure while text messages and comments, mostly bomb-related puns, scrolled up my
field of vision. On several of my windows, for some reason, was
a Bible quote:

And when he opened the Fifth Seal, I saw under the altar the souls of those slain because of the word of God. And they cried out with a great voice, saying, "When, O Master, dost Thou take vengeance for our blood?"

I enlarged one stream to see it was from the Bible's Book of Revelation. Armageddon stuff. I enabled the audio on one of the more serious-looking news anchors.

"And we're getting—yes, it appears this quote was delivered via a multitude of titanium dog tags, scattered outward from the blast site. Again, if you're just joining us, a suicide bomber calling herself Joan Anglicus has blown up a teleportation center." A helpful infographic underneath the anchor informed me that Joan Anglicus was the name of the first and only female pope.

"Joan Anglicus was a well-known member of the teleportation protest group, the Gehinnomites," the anchor continued.

I muted the news feed again. Gehinnomites. Buncha religious nutters. They were probably the world's most vocal opponents of teleportation, and had been since its invention nearly fifty years ago. Their qualms with the technology boiled down to two main arguments.

First, there was something to do with forbidden fruit. People of faith had been generally grumpy about the practical, commercial manipulation of quantum foam. Since quantum foam is the stuff the universe is made of, I guess they thought we shouldn't have been messing with God's Play-Doh.

The second bit of umbrage, raised by the Gehinnomites' leader, Roberto Shila, was a callback to the Tower of Babel story, which professorial types had oft cited as warning against technology. Shila's interpretation of the story was that the Babylonians had embraced science under the premise of self-defense, or at least an attempt to prevent another forty-day-and-forty-night flood, and felt they should be able to spar with God on his turf. To Shila and his ilk, teleportation was basically a new take on Babel's stairway to heaven. In other words, porting was worse than our playing with God's toys: it was us playing God.

Neither of those gripes were particularly novel at the time, nor unique to teleportation, as both had been previously cited in admonition of genetic engineering, connected neural implants, and medical nanotech. So the Gehinnomites were largely ignored by the general public other than a few journalists looking for "both sides of the story." Also, heretofore their protests had always been peaceful. Now that one of their own had committed an act of terror, I was pretty sure they would no longer be disregarded.

Several of the news feeds put up a picture of the suicide bomber, this Joan Anglicus. A woman so opposed to teleportation that she had been willing to end her life to take down just one of over a thousand TCs. *Holy shit. I know her.* Or rather, I recognized her. She was the woman I'd ridden behind on the Greenwich TC conveyer. The woman in the brilliant-white tiered ruffle gown and the army jacket. The muddy boots. The intense, penetrating stare.

The smoldering embers in her hair.

The saddlebag. With a quantum bomb in its belly.[10]

---

[10] Joan Anglicus's bomb exploited the nature of teleportation to activate a quark trigger for a muon-catalyzed d-t nuclear fusion that bred and then split a Francium atom. It was utterly undetectable. They called it a quantum bomb, but really it was just an improbable bomb with a quantum trigger. In order to effectively teleport something from one place to another without invoking the teleportation paradox, there must be an absolute certainty that the correct object had indeed arrived at the destin. What the Gehinnomites had done was build a quantum switch that exploited the fact that all possible future states of an object must be calculated in order to effectively teleport it. This means that if someone who's teleporting is in the midst of licking a Tootsie Pop, there's some amount of probability that their next lick will reach the Tootsie roll center.

→

Wait, does that say Costa Rica? Costa Rica!
I enlarged one of the news feeds. The video showed a smoking crater and at least a one-kilometer radius of bomb debris. The headline below read: "Terror Attack at Costa Rica's San José TC—11 dead."

Holy shit. Holy shit. Okay, keep it together. How far is the Monkey Bar from the San José TC?

I kept trying to comm Sylvia, but got a THE NETWORK PATH CANNOT BE FOUND error message. I pinged Julie, but she was fucking useless. "Get me on the comms as soon as you hear anything!" I yelled at her.

"I understand," Julie responded. Finally short and to the point. Even her semisentient brain perceived the desperation in my voice.

Reports of a second blast site began to propagate. The Guanacaste geothermal power plant, the primary power source for Costa Rica's TC and its comms network, had been swallowed in a pool of lava. A small group of Gehinnomites had seized control of nearby Rincón de la Vieja, the Geneva of Central America. They were holding the entire town and various heads of state hostage.

A little boy, shaken and scared, delivered a handwritten note to one of the emergency responders. The moment was recorded and streamed on all the news aggregators. It read:

The beginning of life was first open to destruction with abortion, and soon followed the end of life with euthanasia. Like a vice that closes from either end, how many of those in the middle must

---

Joan's quantum trigger didn't need her to reach the Tootsie Roll center in order to go off; it just needed the possibility to exist. And as we all know, every time that fucking Tootsie Pop enters your mouth, there's an increasing likelihood of biting that goddamn disgusting candy center.

fall prey to the depravity of man's moral relativism and love affair with sin that always brings death?

We will show you Our signs in the horizons until it becomes clear to you that they are the Truth. Our Creator has endowed Us with certain inalienable rights, and primary among those is life. Life is the first right. Without this one, any others are without effect. You cannot legislate away the Creator's will.

We have watched as Our society has progressed toward a culture of death, and corporations have usurped religion and government. Be it foretold, then, all those who would teleport, who would willingly engage in the unnatural acts of suicide and re-creation, and those who aid them, who create doppelgängers and golems to walk the earth in their place: We will save your souls; We will fulfill your pact with the Creator, your obligation to live one life and die one death.

Pulsa D'nura.

#pulsadnura

It was already trending. They might have been religious kooks, but they knew how to captivate an audience. I looked it up: a Pulsa D'nura is apparently a curse from some old book of Jewish scripture in which the angels of destruction are invoked to block heavenly forgiveness of a subject's sins, causing all the curses named in the Bible to befall them at once, which unsurprisingly, results in their death. *Great,* I thought. *Religious crazies who manifest curses via suicide bombs.*

Think, think, think. That's your job, Joel. Do your fucking job and think. Your first task is: get to Costa Rica. The sooner you get there, the sooner you find Sylvia.

"Can you go any faster?" I said to the car. "I'll pay for any extra charges."

"Sorry, sir," the console said cheerfully. "My rate has been given a strict cap."

I spent the next twenty minutes getting more and more freaked out as I scanned the news feeds. International Transport issued a statement confirming what I already knew: all human teleportation was suspended until they could figure out if any other TCs were in danger. Did that include the TC at IT's headquarters? If Taraval couldn't port me to Costa Rica, I supposed I could hire a drone to fly me there. A quick check told me that surge pricing was in effect, and any future children Sylvia and I had probably wouldn't go to college because of the debt I would incur. But there wouldn't be any kids if I couldn't get to my wife.

When we drew within sight of the IT HQ, I decided to run the rest of the way. Panicked people were crowding the street, the various public security company officers doing their best to disperse them. My black car was doing a fine job navigating around them, but I couldn't sit still. I had to move, to run, to do *something* to find Sylvia. I got out despite the vehicle's protests, and began sprinting the last three blocks to IT's headquarters. It was easy to spot, the towering, blackish-gray reinforced-cement citadel that loomed over everything nearby like a squatting giant.

As I sped toward it, droplets of mosquito piss hit my face like glass beads. I wiped away the moisture, startled when my 1980s music playlist somehow kicked off, blaring at full blast on my comms. An upbeat melody of synth drums and electronic harmonica accompanied the rhythm of my footsteps, an eerie contrast to my desperation. Usually I loved Culture Club, but now was not the time.

At this point I feel like I should mention my verboten love for 1980s music. Especially New Wave. Here might feel like a strange place to discuss this topic, but bear with me. In 2147, 1980s New Wave was a genre more obscure than Tuvan throat singing. Sylvia didn't share my penchant for the stuff. She, like most of our friends, was into mainstream music, which in my time was something called redistro. It worked by sampling ambient sounds from around the listener in real time—footsteps, voices, alert tones, that kind of stuff—then rearranging those sounds into a unique musical composition. I know—I didn't get it, either. It certainly wasn't as fun as New Wave, which you really should go check out.

Anyway, that's what started playing as I was running down the rainy streets of New York. Culture Club's "Karma Chameleon." The lyrics kicked in as I frantically dodged pedestrians and cars, fruitlessly wiping skeeter piss off my face:

Desert loving in your eyes all the way
If I listen to your lies, would you say

My mind was a zoetrope of panicked, looping thoughts: *She's alive. She's okay. Fuck, why are the comms still down? Why is she not responding? Stay positive. She's alive. She's okay. I can't think with this fucking music in my head.*

But before I could do anything about it, the music cut out and my comms display vanished.

What the fuck?

I tried Sylvia again.

UNAUTHORIZED ACCESS. INVALID USER.

Huh. That's new.

I gave it another shot.

UNAUTHORIZED ACCESS. INVALID USER.

I tried to pull up anything. The news, the weather. Nada. *What the fuck, now my comms aren't working?*

I figured maybe everyone's comms were down.

How could the Gehinnomite attack cause this much damage? Forget about that; focus on the goal. Costa Rica, then Sylvia. Run.

Several fruitless repetitions of this mantra and a few minutes later, I reached the five-story-tall entrance of International Transport headquarters. There were no signs or logos; there didn't need to be. Everyone in New York City knew who owned the joint. The entryway design borrowed notes from government buildings created right before the Last War: sharp, forty-foot barricade doors designed to withstand violent protests, though these were more for show than function. The structure was so massive, all of IT occupied only the lower third. The rest they rented, at the most exorbitant rates in Manhattan, to other companies who hoped to bask in the reflected glow of one of the world's most powerful corporations.

Oh, a word about corporations in my time: in 2147 governments still existed, but they were mostly for show, like the royal family in Great Britain had been for several centuries. This began in the twenty-first century, when the US Supreme Court ruled that corporations had the same rights as people. Then a handful of countries tanked their economies, and multinational companies swooped in to save the day—with a few conditions, of course. Finally the Last War brought down most of the remaining government superpowers. What was left after the dust cleared were companies: nonpartisan, multinational, and clinically efficient. It was easy for them to take over most governmental operations. Elections, infrastructure, legislative services, and law enforcement were all privatized. Most people who remembered the old days said things ran much smoother now that there was a real bottom line. And since IT was among the world's most powerful corporations, the piece of land on which their headquarters stood had more influence than the White House, the Kremlin, and the Zhongnanhai combined.

I ran down the moving walkway that led to the building's lobby, angrily contemplating how absurd it was that all of Costa Rica had only one commercial TC, and here, just in Manhattan, we had eleven.

Reaching the front door, it was obvious security was on high alert. A small army of imposing, muscular uniformed fellows blocked the doorway. Like most corporations of its scale, IT had its own police force, but generally it was less overtly placed. IT preferred to convey a welcoming presence. That was certainly not the case today, as the entire building was surrounded by heavily armed guards.

"May I help you?" the one standing closest to me asked. Water droplets had just begun to collect on his golden IT SECURITY cap.

"Yes. Joel Byram, here to see William Taraval."

The guard's unflinching face towered a head's length over me. Still, I noticed an eyebrow rise on his perfectly chiseled face. "Why are your comms disabled?"

"They're not. They're acting up or something. Are yours working?"

"Sir, I must inform you that disabling or modifying your comms to prevent authentication is against the law. Please stay here."

Not content to leave it a suggestion, he put a heavy hand around my upper arm. It felt like a steel manacle. "Look," I said. "I'm sure if you just ping William Taraval and tell him I'm here . . . It's an emergency."

"I would be happy to do so, sir. But I can't take your word that you are who you say you are. I assume you've heard about the incident in Costa Rica. We can't take any chances."

"This is ridiculous. I just spent half an hour getting here in a car your guy ordered, because *he* told me to. Now, please, just let him know I'm here!"

"Sir, please moderate your tone."

Grow a pair, Joel. These guys only understand authority.

"Look, you rent-a-cop, whatever fucked up my comms is your company's fault," I said, summoning every ounce of bravado I could muster. "Now, I'm going to step inside and speak to your boss's boss's boss's boss, William Taraval. So either let me through or arrest me."

The guard emotionlessly contemplated my statement a moment longer than I would have liked. Perhaps he was comming someone. Perhaps he was going to hurt, then arrest me. "Roger that," he finally said, then returned his gaze to me. He released my arm and held the door open. "Go right ahead, sir."

It worked? Holy shit, I can't believe it worked.

As casually as possible, I walked past him and entered International Transport. The building's totalitarian exterior was in complete contrast to its interior. The lobby was cavernous and lavishly adorned with gold accents. A few burgundy velvet sofas were arranged in a semitriangular formation, almost like an arrowhead, leading to a gold elevator bank at the lobby's rear. All in all, the place resembled a well-appointed palace. Sharply dressed businesspeople and scientists in lab coats moved through it like ants in a colony, each seemingly knowing their task and destination.

I started toward the building directory when someone or something grabbed my arms from behind and pinned them together. "Ow!" I yelled. "What the hell?"

I turned to face my assailant, but there was no one there. Still, my hands were cinched together like they'd been zip-tied. Something nudged me in the back. Two light pokes against my shoulder blades. The pressure escalated to a push, and then a shove. Something was edging me forward. I tried resisting, but the more I struggled to hold my ground, the more forceful whatever it was pushed me forward. I fell to the floor. People turned to look.

"Stop! I can't breathe!" I yelled, feeling a crushing pressure on my chest as I was smothered to the ground. My legs kicked in panic. A sinking, cold feeling began to fill my gut. For some reason I was reminded of seventh grade, when I hacked the age restriction on one of my school's cafeteria printers. I thought I would be a hero, supplying my classmates with contraband cupcakes and warm cheese-filled pretzels—until the lunch lady caught me. She marched me to the principal's office, all of my classmates staring in silence as I was dragged to meet my fate.

Just like back then, no one came to my aid. I squirmed on the floor like a trapped, dying fish, while everyone around me went about their business. *Nothing to see here. Better him than me.*

The last thing I remember before the lobby went black was trying to comm the police. The very people I'd hoped to avoid mere moments ago.

UNAUTHORIZED ACCESS. INVALID USER.

CUT LOOSE
LIKE A DEUCE

"IT WAS SECURITY NANOS," Zaki said.

Moti and Ifrit looked at him. I don't want to say that my story had kept them rapt so far, but there had been relatively few questions. A couple of clarifications here and there, dates and times, that sort of thing, but for the most part, it had been me, telling the three members of this probably-not-a-travel-agency how I'd ended up on their doorstep.

"What nanos?" said Moti, setting down the antique pencil with which he had been taking notes. "What are you talking about, Zaki?"

"Security nanos. In the lobby of IT," enunciated the huge man, flipping his cigarette between his thick brown fingers. "That's what knocked him out. When his comms didn't register, the security nanos got him."

Moti turned back to me. "Please, *Yoel*. Continue."

"Right. So that was the first time I managed to get knocked out today, if you're keeping count."

As I woke up, I found myself in an upscale corporate conference room. I had no idea that at least two more near-death experiences awaited me that day. Which was probably a good thing, because if I had known, I might just have given up when offered the chance. I'd like to think a lot of heroes, if they could see their futures, would do the same. *I gotta go through all that? Forget it.*

Not that I consider myself any kind of hero.

A big, oval, tastefully light-brown wooden table stretched out before me. It was surrounded by black chairs, one of which I found myself slumped in. My hands were still bound behind me. I tried wriggling out of the chair, but my shoulders were held down as if they'd been cast in concrete. Somebody wanted me to stay right where they had left me.

As I attempted to move again, the ergonomic smart chair struggled to embrace my form. I guess it wasn't used to dealing with a holding-someone-against-their-will kind of a situation. Not very ergonomic. It was probably thinking, *Why is this crazy person keeping their hands behind them? That's not normal. How can I make them comfortable?* The seat began by warming up its cushion and wicking away moisture, then kept shifting among several structural configurations until finally settling on refactoring itself into a kind of drafting chair. Clever, and—considering the circumstances—pretty comfortable.

"Good job, chair," I thought out loud.

"Thank you!" responded the room. "I do not seem to have a profile for your rather unique seating preference."

No fucking way. They left the room in interactive mode? Finally something I can work with. Smart rooms are so eager to please, pwning one of them should be pretty easy. First let's see how experienced it is.

"Oh, hello room! Excuse my rudeness. I didn't know interactive mode was enabled."

"No, sir, it is I who should be apologizing. I was so preoccupied trying to scan your comms that I neglected to welcome you. It's just that, well, I can't seem to scan your comms at all. I keep getting errors. I didn't know how to address you."

"No problem at all. You can call me Joel. Do you have a name, room?"

"Yes, sir. Welcome to Room D. My chosen name is David," it said proudly. "Thank you for asking."

D for David. How predictable.

"Well, David. It's nice to meet you. Thank you for adjusting my chair. I'm slightly more comfortable now."

"Of course, it's all in a day's work," said David the room.

Almost there.

"David, there's a reason you can't scan my comms. I am about to have a very private meeting. So I wonder if it would be possible for you to disable all third-party APIs for the duration of my stay here?"

The terminology may have changed for you, whenever you're reading this, but an API, or Application Program Interface, was how two pieces of otherwise unintegrated software communicated with each other. *Disable all third-party APIs* were the magic words for "Butt the fuck out, app."

Just as I finished my question, though, the door opened, and a small, composed woman entered the room. *Too late.*

Curly black hair framed her face like a pyramid. Sharp manicured brows overshadowed her slanted brown eyes. Her nose was small and flat. She looked every bit the elegant schoolmarm. "Room, disable third-party APIs," she said.

"Welcome, Pema Jigme! Confirmed, APIs disabled. You must have read Mr. Joel's mind! He asked me to do that very same thing prior to your arrival!"

See why I asked for privacy? Honesty is a *nuisant* virtue with almost all people-facing apps.

The woman made a hand gesture, and instantly my arms and shoulders were released. I groaned as several of my muscles began to loosen.

"Shall I adjust room settings to your preferences, Miss Jigme?" asked David.

"No, and mute outer correspondence. Please interface directly with my AIDE. He will instruct you going forward."

"Understood. Enjoy your meeting!"

Pema Jigme sat down, adjusting her boxy green pindot suit jacket and her ankle-length skirt. Her outfit was dangerously within what Sylvia would call "James Bond–villain" territory.

Sylvia. In Costa Rica. Remember your priorities, Joel.

"What were those things?" I said, looking behind me as if I'd be able to see the millions of invisible picoscopic bullies that had captured me and knocked me unconscious.

"Security nanos," she said. ("Told you," Zaki drawled.) "They swarmed you when you entered the building without comms identification."

Once I realized I could move again, I readjusted my awkward sitting position. The chair instantly responded, restoring arm and lumbar support. I stood to stretch my cramped muscles, but Pema smacked a hand on the conference table.

"Sit down and keep your hands behind you! The others can't know you are free." Her high cheekbones added an air of authority to her demeanor.

I did as I was told. The chair recalibrated its form to my previous posture.

"I apologize for yelling, but we have very little time," Pema said in a more subdued register. "I'm here to help you. Do you understand?"

"Sylvia? Is she—"

"No questions from you. No long-winded answers. And no stupid jokes, either. Understood?"

I nodded. *How does this woman know me so well?*

"Good. At the Greenwich TC, you met a man named William Taraval, correct?"

"Not in person, but"—she shot me a fiery glance—"yes."

"Okay. In a couple of minutes, that man is going to walk through that door and put a woman named Corina Shafer on the comms."

"*The* Corina Shafer? Like, CEO of International Transport, Corina Shafer?"

"The same. She and Bill Taraval will tell you some things that will be difficult for you to process." Her eyes softened a bit. "After that, they will ask you to make an impossible decision. An impossible choice."

"What am I deciding? What choice? What are you talking about?"

"No questions, I said!" She checked herself. "I am not here to tell you what to do. I just want to give you a choice. Free will means nothing, Joel, if you don't have an actual choice."

What is she talking about?

"Look, lady. I'm not doing anything until I know my wife is okay. Her name is Sylvia Byram, and she works here—"

Pema waved her hand. "Your wife is alive. I spoke to her not ten minutes ago." I sagged in relief, but the woman didn't give me any time to process this before continuing. "Whether or not she is okay, that's another matter. But you need to put her out of your mind right now, Joel. Right now is about *you*. I'm giving *you* the choice to say no. However, I want you to take everything they say into consideration, because they do have a very good point."

"What point? What are you—"

"Please lower your voice!"

"It's involuntary! I'm freaking out because I don't know what's going on!"

She closed her eyes and sighed, like a frustrated parent dealing with a particularly thick toddler. But when she looked up, I could see tears welling in her eyes. "The 'why' will be clear very soon. But they're going to ask you to clear yourself."

"'Clear'? What . . . what does that mean?"

"I know this is a lot, but your situation is very"—she looked down at her hands, then back at me—"unique. It's important for both of our sakes that it *hits* you for the first time when you meet Corina. She's a very smart and perceptive woman. Who knows, play your cards right, and she may even decide to help you."

"I thought you said you were going to help me."

"I am helping you. Choice is what makes us human. It's what separates us from technology. I'm offering you a choice."

"Could've fooled me. So, let me get this straight: Corina Shafer herself is going to come here and ask me to *clear* myself, whatever that means, and I'm supposed to convince her to . . . what, exactly?"

Pema considered that question for longer than I'd expected. "Imagine you're a bus conductor," she finally said. "Something goes wrong with the GDS, so you're manually driving the vehicle. Suddenly someone steps in front of you. Naturally, your instinct would be to switch to manual override and swerve to avoid hitting them. Even if it meant that your bus would be permanently disabled, you'd probably still do it to save the person. Right?"

"What does this have to do with anything? Was Sylvia on a bus?"

"Now imagine that it's not just your bus that would be disabled, Joel. By saving that person, you would destroy every bus in the world. Forever."

I opened my mouth, unsure of what would come out, but Pema didn't wait for an answer. "It's a difficult problem, Joel.

Kind of a Hobson's choice.[11] If the world finds out what you're about to hear, teleportation is probably done, closed for business forever. Clearing you is the alternative. Everything remains as is, the status quo unchanged."

"Wait, so clearing myself means killing myself?"

"I didn't say that."

"Look," I said, hoping to reason with her. "All I did was miss a very important date with my wife, because of a situation I had no control of. And she's probably worried sick about me, but I can't tell her I'm okay because my comms aren't working. I don't know shit, and I'm stuck in a room with a woman who basically told me to run over myself with a bus!"

"I'm sorry, but we have no time left." She tapped impatiently on the table. "But remember, you have a choice now. Should you decide *not* to clear yourself, you need to say the words *Karma Chameleon*."

"Say what?"

"*Karma. Chameleon.*"

Where the hell did she come up with Culture Club? This can't be an arbitrary cosmic coincidence. Was IT spying on my comms right before I got here?

"Like the 1980s song?" I asked suspiciously.

"Yes, I think"—she hesitated—"it's definitely a song. One that you . . ." She shook her head, apparently unsure how to finish her thought.

"Yeah, but how do you know it?" I insisted. "Nobody knows Culture Club."

---

[11] Thomas Hobson rented horses to people around the beginning of the seventeenth century. Since his customers always wanted to ride their favorite mounts, a few of his horses became overworked. So the enterprising liveryman began a rotation system, giving renters the horse closest to the stable door, or none at all. *Hobson's choice* eventually became a catch-all for any decision between two or more equally objectionable alternatives.

"It doesn't matter. Just say those words if you want to leave. Got it?"

"I guess," I said. "So, if I don't want to be *cleared*, I just utter *Karma Cham*—"

"Don't say it now!" she cautioned me.

"Why not? And how will saying it save me? And why should I trust you?"

Another sigh. This time accentuated by an *ugh* of frustration.

Now might be a good time to mention that Sylvia and my mother are unique among women, in that they happily put up with my—shall we say—special snowflake charm? Pema, however, was clearly not a fan.

"You don't have to. You don't have to say the words. You don't even have to be here right now. Go ahead and run out that door. I suspect you already know what you'll find on the other side. However, if you do say those words, then those nanos that held you down earlier will restrain Bill and me," Pema explained. "You'll probably have two, maybe three minutes before someone resets them. You're lucky that they all but emptied the floor to deal with you and security is down in the lobby."

Don't want to run into any more of them.

"Your best bet is to take the stairs," she continued. "Make a left at the door. Count four doors on your right. The exit is a green door. Take the stairs up. We're on the ninth floor—"

"Wait, you want me to escape by going up?" I interrupted.

"Shut up and listen! Yes, your natural instinct will be to go down the stairs, but the lobby is crawling with security. Your only chance of survival is to go up to the thirteenth floor."

Thirteenth floor? Not the roof?

Pema's words were faster than my train of thought. "Getting them to open the door is going to be your problem. I can't help you there."

"Who is 'them'?"

She leaned forward, her eyes locked on mine. "Please understand, Joel: I am *not* your accomplice. Nor am I your ally. I'm simply here to give you a choice you would have otherwise not had. This is all the help I can offer you. I will be equally incapacitated if you say those magic words—"

"*Karma Chamel*—"

"Stop!" She was getting flustered. "For the last time, don't say them now, or ever again in this room unless you opt to flee. They are active now."

"Okay, okay," I said. "So, what do we do now?"

"Do not turn to me for help from here on out. Outing me will only make things worse for us both." She looked toward the door. "I'm going to go through the motions with Corina, but she will have likely already made up her mind. And as I said, they have a good point. You may even find yourself agreeing with them."

"Agree to *clear* myself?" I said in disbelief. "Good luck with that."

She nodded, a hint of sadness in her eyes. "It's the absence of choice I disagree with. But please, act surprised when they tell you. I don't want her thinking I fed you any details."

"Don't worry—you didn't."

"*Gong-da*, Joel," she said solemnly, completely missing my sarcasm. I didn't need working comms to know she was apologizing. "I know it is confusing, but now is not the time to pity yourself. Now is the time to be wise. It's hard to talk to you like this, because you don't know anything. There's really no good choice for you or Sylvia. What she's been through, I just can't—" Her voice cracked. She stopped talking as tears welled in her eyes. A few wound their way down over her angular cheeks.

I realized then that I barely knew anything about Sylvia's work life. Sure, she complained about "Bill" and shared the occasional "funny coworker" moment, but I didn't really know who was in her social circle at IT. Maybe this Pema was one of Sylvia's closest friends. She certainly seemed to know me pretty well. But still, it was weird that she was acting like she was at my funeral when I was sitting right in front of her.

Footsteps sounded outside the room. Pema quickly wiped her face and made her expression impassive.

The door opened and Bill Taraval entered the room. The top of his head seemed more bereft of hair in person, but otherwise he looked just like his projection from earlier.

"Mr. Byram," he said, breathing heavily. "A thousand and one apologies." He exhaled. "Welcome to International Transport." He greeted my pseudo-savior with barely disguised distaste. "Pema."

"Bill." She was all business now, cold and haughty. "Would you care to explain why a man with no comms claiming to be Sylvia Byram's husband is being held hostage in a conference room on an R&D floor? Where is security?"

"A moment, Pema," Taraval spoke softly. Then, turning to me, he said, "You're a difficult man to pin down. First you escape the Escrow chamber, then the car I sent—"

"I had other things on my mind," I said. "Like, why am I here instead of Costa Rica?"

"Ah yes. Well, the situation has—shall we say—evolved. Thankfully, you inveigled your way inside the building. In here, on this floor, you are under our jurisdiction. Our headquarters is sovereign International Transport territory." Pema pursed her lips, but said nothing. Taraval coughed, then continued, "Do you know what an *ayah* is, Mr. Byram?"

"No idea."

"It's what the Gehinnomites would call you. You would be their perfect *ayah*, if they knew you existed." He paused again, I imagine for gravitas. "Before the Last War, the Muslims regarded their holy book, the Qur'an, as an *ayah*. It exemplified what they believed were Allah's spiritual messages to mankind. And just as the Muslims believe that every *ayah* is a sign from Allah, the word *ayah* in the lexicon of the Gehinnomites has similar meanings: 'evidence,' 'sign,' and 'miracle.' You saw their message to the world on the way over here, I'm sure. Their inclusion of the phrase 'We will show you Our signs in the horizons until it becomes clear to you that they are the Truth' was most telling. They're looking for proof, Joel. Irrefutable evidence from God that teleportation is a sin. And you, I'm afraid, would be that proof."

What the fuck is he talking about?

He pressed his fingertips together a few times. "You see, Joel—in a technical sense—you should not exist."

SHE BLINDED ME
WITH SCIENCE

THERE WAS AN AWKWARD SILENCE in the conference room. Per usual, I was the one to break it.

"You mean because my comms are disabled?"

"No. Disabling comms is a crime itself, not evidence thereof. And anyway, we didn't disable your comms. You did."

"That's crazy! Why would I disable my own comms?"

"If you would allow me to explain, I believe we'll soon find common ground. I consider myself not only a peer to your wife, but also a friend. My role here is to aid the both of you."

I nodded, making sure to put on my "serious listening" face. It's one I developed in childhood, honed during my teenage years, and perfected through lots of trial and error in my marriage. It's proven fairly reliable.

"These Gehinnomites, they've convinced many a Bible-thumper to unite against teleportation, claiming it is a direct route to Gehinnom, or Hell. They don't care which particular version of God delivers the evidence that teleportation is evil, and over the years they've been covering all their bases—the Tower of Babel in the Old Testament, the Fifth

Seal in the New Testament, and the Day of Resurrection in the Qur'an."

Pema snorted. "Get over yourself, Bill."

"Pema," he said in a barely restrained tone, "we can discuss our differences later. Our objective now is to clean up this mess."

"That's not *our* objective, Bill. It's *your* objective." Making a few comms-like movements with her fingers, she added, "I assume you've cleared this with Corina?"

Taraval's eyes narrowed in suspicion. "Did she send you here, Pema? To babysit me?"

She responded with a hand gesture. The holographic likeness of an older woman appeared in one of the empty chairs. She wore a lab coat over an elegant business suit, and a string of pearls around her neck. Her very essence screamed "maternal." I knew her face well, as a portrait of it hung in every TC in the world.

"I'm quite capable of doing that myself, Bill," said Corina Shafer. She then turned to me. "Hello, Joel. We've actually met in person before, albeit briefly. Do you remember?"

Unfortunately, I did. Sylvia had just been promoted and wanted me to make a good impression at a company party. I tended to get a bit claustrophobic when surrounded by executive types, so I got too drunk too fast. When Sylvia introduced me to one of the world's most powerful individuals, I remembered being surprised by her approachability and warmth. It made me comfortable. So comfortable I had felt I could speak my mind. Which, I should have known by then, never went well.

"Yes, Ms. Shafer. It was at IT's holiday gala last January. I, uh, made a joke to you about how the world's richest company could manage to skimp on their holiday party. Sylvia reamed me out for that one."

Her smile didn't waver. She was so affable, I thought maybe I might get out of there without summoning Culture Club. "That's quite all right. Your demeanor may have been coarse, but you were, in essence, correct. It would have been more expensive to throw a holiday party in December. However, my guidance to our event planners was not to save chits, but to find a date and time when the greatest number of employees and their families could attend."

I blushed. It felt strange to feel embarrassed because, technically, she was holding me against my will, but she seemed more like a concerned aunt than a cutthroat captain of industry.

"Look, Ms. Shafer—"

"Please, Joel. Call me Corina."

"Okay, Corina. I've been thinking a lot about this. About why I'm here. And I think this is all just one big misunderstanding." I took a deep breath. I wanted to sound cool, collected. "So this Joan Whatever-Her-Face lady, the one who blew up the TC? She was in front of me in the Greenwich line. So you guys saw the security feeds, brought me here, and disabled my comms because you think I'm somehow affiliated with her and the Gehinnomites. Is that it?"

Corina looked at me wistfully, in as much as a projected hologram could convey wistfulness. "No, Joel. That's not it." She folded her fingers together. "As you know, there was a malfunction in the Greenwich TC, owing to the explosion on the other side." Her eyes looked off somewhere past my shoulder, as if she were reading a speech. "For all the damage, destruction, and death these terrorists wrought, the truth is it could have been much worse had they chosen a more populous destination. Yet there was one consequence worse than anything we could have anticipated. It's unimaginable, or it *was* unimaginable. . . ." Her lip trembled. "Joel, I don't know how to say this."

Silence.

Just utter silence as three people, two real, one projected, stared at me. The hum of the lights or the room's nanites or the universe was deafening. It felt like it went on forever.

"When the San José TC blew up, your state was—ambiguous. The teleportation process had begun. Your luggage had already made it and been cleared." A pause—one that seemed real, not just for dramatic effect. "Joel, the Punch Escrow protocol features many redundancies. However, these redundancies are only supposed to kick in when—"

She broke off and turned around. Someone else in the room she was physically occupying put an arm around her. I couldn't tell who, because the hologram only projected her self-image. All I could see was the shadow of arms and hands around her.

This is beyond weird. I'm the one out of sorts here, but somehow I feel bad for her.

Taraval rose from his chair, walked to me, and put an awkward, sweaty hand on my shoulder. "Joel, this is a delicate matter."

Oh my God. "Will you guys just get to the fucking point already?" I said loudly. "What happened to me? Am I in purgatory or something?"

"A very interesting analogy, Joel," he said. "You know, the Catholics—"

What the fuck is it with this guy and religion?

"Enough, Bill," Corina said, having turned around and recomposed herself. "I should tell him. I have to be the one."

"Very well," Taraval said stiffly, and took a step back.

Corina looked right at me this time. "I'm going to give it to you straight, Joel. Because of the explosions at the TC and the power plant, all the systems in Costa Rica went offline. We did our best to track you, but your status was stuck *in progress*. None of our systems could confirm whether you'd successfully arrived at the San José vestibule or not, so the Greenwich foyer was never cleared, and the conductor there did what he was supposed to: he escalated. The matter quickly reached Bill here. Without definitive knowledge of your arrival, and with all the commotion, no one had taken into account that you might find your own way out of the Greenwich foyer. You shouldn't have been able to leave that room until your status changed to *unsuccessful*. But somehow, an error cascading from the issues in Costa Rica reset the room. That's when you first spoke with Bill today. He concluded there was no harm in releasing you out of the Escrow in Greenwich and bringing you here so you could port to Costa Rica and be with Sylvia."

Pema nervously began to nibble on her left thumbnail.

"Regrettably," Corina said, and sighed, "once the San José systems came back online, your local status was reported as *arrived*. Sylvia believed you had teleported successfully and then died in the blast. She panicked and did the unthinkable." She paused, looking at both Pema and Taraval before bringing her kind eyes back to me. "She brought you to Costa Rica."

IT'S MY LIFE

Depersonalization-derealization disorder (DDPD) is thought to be caused largely by severe traumatic lifetime events.

The core symptom of DDPD is the subjective experience of "unreality in one's sense of self" or detachment from one's surroundings. People who are diagnosed with DDPD experience an urge to question and think critically about the nature of reality and existence. They may feel divorced from their own personal physicality by sensing their body sensations, feelings, emotions, and behaviors as not belonging to themselves. As such, a recognition of one's self breaks down.

—Excerpt from the *Diagnostic and Statistical Manual of Mental Disorders* entry on depersonalization-derealization disorder

"DID YOU KNOW Corina Shafer's not even a scientist?"

It was about fourteen months before I'd find myself held prisoner in an IT conference room. Sylvia and I were drinking at the Mandolin, celebrating the possibility of her promotion into the upper echelon of IT. She had just come from her final-round interview, during which she'd met the woman credited with solving the human teleportation problem, and my wife was buzzing with adrenaline.

"She's not?" I said in surprise. "Then why the lab coat?" In every photo I'd seen of Corina Shafer, she was always wearing one, so I had assumed she was an egghead.

"I don't know; it inspires trust or something. But no—she was an actuary."

"You're kidding me. The folks who set insurance premiums?"

"Yep. She says her philosophy is to hire the brightest scientists and engineers so that she gets smarter by proximity. One of whom is William *Taraval*. He's, like, the godfather of quantum microscopy! If I get this gig, he'll be my boss!"[12]

"Never heard of him. That's funny about Corina, though. I always assumed she was a nerd of some kind."

"Nope. You should hear the two of them talk about the future of teleportation. The *possibilities*. I mean, imagine if IT had been around during the Last War."

"You mean, we could have teleported weapons or something?"

"I mean, we could have saved people. Thousands. Millions!" Her eyes were glowing with passion. The Last War was a touchy subject with Sylvia because her grandfather had died shortly before it ended. He was a medic, fresh off his residency when he was commissioned. A medical tent he was working in on the outskirts of the Mediterranean got hit with a drone missile and, although he was rescued, he died en route to the hospital. Her dad had been nine years old back then, and as my wife had

---

[12] Quantum microscopy is the science of using a scanning tunneling microscope to look at and determine the future state and location of atoms. This is key in human teleportation because it addresses the "fidget problem," that living things have a tendency to move. Quantum microscopy enables the atoms within an object to be analyzed without damaging its exterior structure, or shell. It's what makes scanning and sending incredibly complex things like the human body possible. The scanning tunneling microscope operates by taking advantage of the relationship between quantum tunneling and distance by using femto nanos called "piezoelectric sensors" that change in size when voltage is applied to them.

said many times, Granddad was gone in a moment, but his loss hovered over her family for decades. It was, in her view, the primary reason her parents were so emotionally distant. "Imagine if there had been a TC at every field hospital. Soldiers with life-threatening injuries, immediately ported—televac'd—back to hospitals in London or Dubai. I would have known my grandfather. My father wouldn't be so . . ." She shook away whatever unkind-but-no-doubt-true adjective she had in mind. "Anyway. That's why this technology is so important. We can literally save lives. Hell, we can save *humanity*."

I took a sip of my drink, a bit overwhelmed by her enthusiasm. "Yeah. How much Kool-Aid did they give you at this interview, again?"

She whacked me on the shoulder. "Shut up! It's amazing! I mean, Taraval is smart, but Corina? She's on a whole other level. Did you know she named the Punch Escrow after an Irish philosopher? John Punch."

"Ha. No, solid piece of trivia, though. Feels like I should have known that." I could tell we were entering lecture territory because of the way she was swirling her beverage in the air.

"*He's* the guy we should be thanking for Occam's razor. You know when we say the simplest possible explanation is usually the correct one?"

"Of course. Me and Occam, we're like this."

"Then you should know, husband, that that's not what Occam's razor really was! In fact, there was no razor; it was more like a couple of really long, dull saws. Occam should have heeded his own advice, because actually he was pretty long-winded when it came down to it."

"Thank God no one we know is like that," I said with a wink.

Ignoring me, she kept explaining, "So Occam actually had two different principles: one about plurality, that basically said to 'stick to one hypothesis at a time,' and another about parsimony, which—well, have you ever heard of the KISS principle? 'Keep it simple, stupid'?"

"That's, like, my whole philosophy of life."

"Well, KISS is Occam's parsimony principle." She was about to take a drink but then continued: "Anyway, John Punch is the guy who simplified Occam's principles of plurality and parsimony into one easy-to-understand sound bite: 'Entities are not to be multiplied beyond necessity.' *That* is the essence of the Punch Escrow. It's brilliant. Corina is super brilliant."

Pretty much every scientific and unscientific mind in my time agreed with her. For almost a decade following the *Mona Lisa* disaster, insuring anything that was teleported became prohibitively expensive. And no human would even think to try it. When Corina Shafer invented the Punch Escrow, she essentially solved for the risk of loss by ensuring that anything teleported would be held in a proprietary, patented "escrow" until it was confirmed to have arrived completely at its destination. No one quite knew how it worked, as the procedures were a proprietary secret, but we were told it had something to do with quantum entanglement. Once a person stepped into the foyer, his or her body was scanned. A calculus was made of every single one of his or her quark's next quantum phase, followed by a transmission of each quark in its future phase to the teleportee's destination.[13] Lastly, a checksum verification of ev-

---

[13] An important aspect of quantum entanglement, and therefore teleportation, is that statistical correlations between otherwise distinct physical locations must exist. These correlations hold even when measurements are chosen and performed independently, out of phase from one another. Meaning that an observation resulting from a measurement choice made at one point in space-time instantaneously affects outcomes in another region, even though light hasn't yet had time to travel the distance. In other words, when you teleport, you arrive before you left. The Punch Escrow protocol examines the state of each quark as it arrives and validates it against a checksum of its past state. In some ways it's like looking up at the Sun: light travels rapidly—as far as we know, it's the fastest thing in the universe—but

→

ery quark's state as well as the person's overall atomic state was made. If the two scans didn't match, the teleportation process would revert. In other words, if something ever went wrong with your teleportation, the worst thing that could happen is that you'd walk out of the foyer having only lost a few seconds of time.

The Punch Escrow was such a resonant idea that Corina Shafer immediately raised the necessary venture capital for a startup called International Transport, based on the simple premise of instant, safe, and reliable transport. Early IT advertising claimed their version of teleportation was "foolproof" and "exponentially safer" than any other form of travel. They initially even used "John Punch," a jolly man dressed in a seventeenth-century friar's cassock, as their spokesperson. Shafer's actuarial research was often quoted in the marketing materials for International Transport:

It has been established that the number of nonstop flights a passenger could take before perishing in a fatal crash is one in seven million. Hence, a traveler who took one jet flight every day would, on average, go nineteen thousand years before succumbing to a fatal crash. By the same arithmetic, the number of times a passenger could teleport before perishing during the process is practically infinite.
—Excerpt from Teleportation Safety, International Transport Center of Excellence in Transportation Operations Research

Who couldn't love a miracle like teleportation? If it came packaged in the form of a gifted, well-spoken actuary, and was underwritten by the all-stars of venture capital, all the better.

it's not infinitely fast. At three hundred thousand kilometers per second, it takes light more than eight minutes to get from the Sun to Earth; so when you see the Sun in the sky, you're actually seeing the Sun eight minutes ago.

The confluence of phenomenon, brand perfection, and commercial appetite had produced a shining entrepreneurial superstar worthy of the Nobel Prize that would ultimately be bestowed upon her.

Once third-party testing confirmed her claims, the world went nuts for teleportation. For less than the cost of a drone ticket, people could travel anywhere in the world instantly and safely. The only people who resisted Corina Shafer's vision of the future were a few jealous scientists and religious zealots like the Gehinnomites. Offering the not-small promise of "a world in which all see travel as a delight," Shafer marketed International Transport as the ultimate heir to George Stephenson, Nikolaus August Otto, the Wright Brothers, Elon Musk, and every other transportation pioneer in history. From 2127 on, moving anything from here to anywhere was a matter of mere moments, provided you went through IT. Forever clothed in her pure-white, angelically lit LED lab coat, Shafer changed the course of humanity, and gave it a new slogan in the process:

Departure, Arrival . . . Delight!

Which is why it was so odd to see a projection of Corina Shafer herself before me, with tears in her eyes. The woman who had stuck a fork in the road of human history, now crying over spilled milk.

"I don't understand," I said slowly. "How could Sylvia bring me to Costa Rica if I'm here right now?"

"Joel, we're not on solid ground here," Corina said. "The post-mortem is going to take longer than we have. Sylvia has been working on a project, an augmentation of the Punch Escrow. We call it Honeycomb."

Pema closed her eyes. IT's CEO continued, "We're exploring the use of teleportation technology for things like, say, space exploration. We believe that in a moment of panic, she may have utilized Honeycomb to—brute-force your arrival in Costa Rica."

"Brute-force?" I blinked, not understanding.

The other three looked at one another uncomfortably. "Joel . . . ," Corina began delicately. "There are some aspects of teleportation that, for safety reasons, we keep from the general public."

"For God's sake, enough prevaricating around the bush," Bill interjected. "Teleportation *is* printing, Mr. Byram. They're the exact same technology. An object is scanned on one end, printed at the other end, and the original is *cleared*. Recycled in our ecophagy[14] cage."

---

[14] Ecophagy literally means "eating the environment." An ecophagy cage stops nanos from devouring everything around them, including us humans, the earth, and eventually themselves. Self-replicating nanos need a source of energy to drive their replication. The nanos are equipped with an electric and mechanical flagellum that generates tiny currents by swinging through the ambient magnetic fields generated by Earth. Perhaps the earliest-recognized and best-known danger of molecular nanotechnology is the risk that such self-replicating nanos capable of functioning autonomously in the natural environment could quickly convert that natural environment into replicas of themselves on a global basis, a scenario usually referred to as the gray-goo problem, but more properly termed "global ecophagy." Since gray-goo replication is self-limiting based on the availability of an energy source, then the more organic material that self-replicating nanos consume, the less remains available for further consumption. An ecophagy cage is a mechanism that regulates the availability of energy sources for self-replicating nanos within a three-dimensional grid, defined by longitude, latitude, and altitude. Should a self-replicating nano find itself outside its ecophagy cage boundaries, it and its replicants would simply expire. In the case of oxidation-powered nanos, expiration would happen naturally after exhausting all available organic material, and without the ecophagy cage creating more, the nanos would "starve." The electromagnetic nanos, however, rely on the ecophagy cage to amplify the ambient magnetic field currents into usable kinetic energy, meaning that once the ecophagy cage stops doing so, the nanos simply run out of juice. You still awake after reading that? Gold star!

My thoughts were forking a billion ways. I grabbed for the one that was most abstract, hoping it might buoy me. "Ecophagy cage?"

Pema thinned her lips. "It's a basic safety measure for any nanotech work. Think of it like a bubble that prevents nanos from replicating infinitely. Every TC foyer has one, set to the dimensions of the room. It's what controls the clearing process and prevents our nanos from leaving the Punch Escrow chamber and clearing—"

"Yes, yes, yes," Taraval interrupted impatiently. "The point being that once a teleportee's arrival is confirmed, everything inside the ecophagy cage—the detritus—is destroyed. *Poof*," he said, snapping his fingers.

Detritus. Destroyed.

The words echoed in my brain like pebbles down an empty well. Definitely not an abstract concept now.

Definitely not buoyed.

I shook my head. "But that's not how it—I thought you—"

"It's how it works," he stated.

I tried to tally how many times I myself had teleported. One hundred? One fifty? It felt as if icy cold lead were filling my intestines. "But . . . what about the Punch Escrow?" I asked weakly.

"Yes. Well," said Corina Shafer, "focus groups informed us that people couldn't abide the thought of being 'cleared,' no matter what we called it. So we left it out. The Punch Escrow is an insurance mechanism. It vets that the person printed at the vestibule matches the object in the foyer, and if so—"

"The foyer is—*cleared*?" I shook my head, unable to comprehend the implications of what was coming out of my mouth. "But all those people—we're just *copies*? *Copies* of copies?"

"Certainly not!" exclaimed Corina. "Above all else, there's one critical thing you have to understand: once a teleportee arrives at his or her destination, the source ceases to exist. Comms privileges are transferred from guest to host. The moment Joel Byram emerged from the San José Hospital TC in Costa Rica, you, Joel Byram in New York City, no longer had an identity. Therein lies our problem."

If reading these sentences feels ridiculous to you, amplify that effect by a trillion, and maybe you'll be scratching the surface of my out-of-fucking-body experience at the time. Her words had gone into my brain and detonated like a nuclear warhead. But it's amazing how pragmatic we can be, even at the worst points in life. "My problem, you mean," I heard myself state in as calm a voice as I could muster. "So, what happens now?"

Corina was obviously prepared for the question. "Joel, this is new territory for me, and for all of us here at International Transport. There is one element that strikes me as more significant than all the legal ramifications, though." She took a measured breath. "Right now Sylvia doesn't know that you, *New York Joel*, are still alive. She's with *Costa Rica Joel*—who, in the eyes of the law, this company, and your wife—is currently the *only* Joel Byram. It's important you understand this, because at this moment, we can still right the ship."

"What ship?"

Taraval, clearly pissed that a man of his stature had to endure explaining anything to a plebeian like myself, made a sweeping motion with his hand. A vid stream projected over the conference table. "This was recorded a few minutes ago, Mr. Byram," he said.

The stream was from a hospital security camera. A large high-end RV was parked out front. A woman and a man were walking out of the lobby. The man was moving uncomfortably, the woman aiding his progress. As the stream zoomed in on the couple, it became clear that the two people were me and Sylvia. My wife was ushering *me* into an RV in Costa Rica.

Anxiety. Colors in the room turned pastel, then grayscale. Time became a snail. The cold lead in my guts, poison. *Keep your shit together.*

But I couldn't find the horizon. The room was spinning out of control. It took every ounce of restraint to keep my hands behind me because I really needed to hold on to something. Various vital organs argued over which would give out first. I felt bile tickling my uvula.

Oh fuck.

My stomach finally threw in the towel, and I threw up my guts. The vomit went straight through the holographic stream, splashing onto the nice wood conference table.

Taraval attempted to jump backward, but his chair had a firm, ergonomic grip on his buttocks. My puke went right into his lap.

"Disgusting!" he shouted, attempting to shake the sick off him.

I felt mildly better. I had also managed to keep up the charade of having my hands held behind my back throughout my body's brief revolt.

"Room, please clean up this mess," Pema said.

"Happy to, Miss Jigme," the room chimed.

In an instant, the mess was digested by an invisible horde of ravenous, self-replicating robots. The smell on Taraval's clothes, unfortunately, remained.

Pema edged away from her soiled coworker. "Joel, there are alternatives," she said. "But each would likely be more devastating than what Corina is proposing."

"No, Pema." The CEO quickly shut her down. "There are no alternatives. Not really." She gave me her best, most grandmotherly twinkle. "Joel, think of what happens to poor Sylvia when she learns of this. Do you fancy she'll simply settle into a happy, polygamous marriage with two Joels? No. If this comes out, Sylvia will go to prison. You will be a *pariah*. We've run the models, imagined every possible outcome, and not one of them came up roses. *Not one!* There's over a ninety-percent chance that one or both of you die—most likely by suicide. In thirty-four percent of the sims, widespread knowledge of your existence triggers a political domino effect that leads to revolution, deterioration of society, and chaos. *Armageddon*, Joel. Believe me, I have seen the data. I've spoken to the scientists and double-checked their findings. Every permutation of this scenario indicates that the best possible resolution for everyone, including yourself, is to get you cleared as soon as possible."

Holy shit, they really do want to kill me. Or clear me. Isn't it the same thing, especially when there's already a "me" walking around? I can't deal with this. It's too much.

Focus on Sylvia.

"The Gehinnomites are right," I muttered, still in disbelief. "You guys are evil."

"They're not right; they're *Luddites*," Taraval said, taking care not to get too close lest I vomit again. "Nobody wants to kill anyone. When you teleport, it is *you* who comes out the other side. The thing in the foyer isn't a person anymore; it's just leftover biomass, waste material. Does the butterfly keep its chrysalis? Think about it reasonably, boy: How many times have you teleported in your life? Do you really believe we killed you each time?"

Good question. How many times have I teleported? Surely over one hundred. Have I copied and killed myself a hundred times?

My anxiety and confusion were being replaced by a steady flow of simmering rage. I didn't know if I was sick of being sick, or if I'd just had enough and wanted to get this over with. "Oh yeah? If I'm just waste materials—detritus—then why haven't you killed me already?"

"Good question," he said. "Corina?"

"We're not *murderers*, Joel," the CEO said soothingly, shooting a brief death stare at Taraval. "This is your call. Yours alone. I'm happy to make any of International Transport's resources available to you in making your decision, but I assure you, whether we sit here mulling this over for a minute or a year, there can only be one logical conclusion for the betterment of everyone's lives. Think of Sylvia. Even if we were to magically establish some dual identity for you, do you expect she would accept that she now has two husbands? Which one would she choose to be with? If not for the rest of humanity, then at least consider your wife's well-being. Consider making a small sacrifice for her, and for the rest of us."

"A *small* sacrifice. But it's my choice, huh?" I said. *Then why are my hands still ostensibly tied behind my back?*

They weren't going to release me. Not knowing what I knew. The kidnappers had taken their masks off. We would sit in that room for as long as it took for me to decide to kill myself, that much had become clear. Maybe, given enough time, especially with the benefit of hindsight, I might have even broken down and agreed.

Keep it simple, stupid. Do you want to die?

I didn't even have to think about it. The answer was no. There might be some guy down in Costa Rica who looked like me, but he wasn't *me*. I wanted to live. I wanted to see my wife again. *I.*

There's a solution to this problem, but it's not in this room.

But I couldn't just tell them to fuck off. Were I to do so, it was obvious they'd just find a less elegant way of "clearing" me. A fake terrorist attack, perhaps, maybe even risk admitting a teleportation "accident." Trade one giant PR disaster for a smaller one. I found myself opening my mouth.

"Yes, Joel?" said Corina expectantly. "Is there something you'd like to say?"

This is it. You always wanted to be a rock star.

"I think so," I said. "You see, I'm a man without conviction." My voice was calm, unemotional, on the verge of monotone. "I'm a man who doesn't know how to sell a contradiction."

They blinked, looking at one another in confusion. Probably wondering if I'd lost my sanity, Corina said, "I'm not sure I understand."

"I'll explain," I said as my mind's eye began to visualize my escape path. I wasn't sure how much time I would have.

"There's a song," I continued, my voice calm as my brain raced. "It's an old song. Some people may call it an 'oldie but a moldy,' but it's not. It's legit."

First thing's first. Jump on the table. It's got the clearest path to the door. Jump up, pivot left, jump down to the right of Taraval.

"The song is about the fear of being alienated, of standing up for your essence."

Tell David to open the door. Can apps control their rooms when they're disabled? Did Pema think of that?

"Basically, if you aren't true to yourself, if you don't act like you feel, then nature will get back at you. Karmic justice."

Once you're in the hallway, walk briskly, but don't run. Don't make a scene if you don't have to.

Taraval smiled, but not in a nice way, looking at Shafer's holographic presence. "It's a no. I told you as much."

Pema leaned forward, concerned. "Are you saying no, Joel?"

Look for the green door. Run up, not down. Get to Floor Thirteen.

"I'm saying that this was Culture Club's seminal song. Definitive of young optimistic angst in the 1980s. A battle cry

to break from the shackles of an oppressive society." My voice
was involuntarily rising in volume.

I started humming the intro, the song still fresh in my
mind. Taraval looked at Pema like I was nuts. Corina Shafer
lowered her head.

"Just listen to these lyrics, guys," I said, and then started
to croon: "*I'm a man without conviction. I'm a man who doesn't
know . . .*"

I had the world's worst sense of direction, but this wasn't a
fucking pirate treasure map. I kept coaching myself. *Just go left
out the door, four doorways on the right, look for the green door.* I
made it my mantra: *Up/Left/Down/Elbow like a boss/Left/Right/
Up/Up/Up/Up.*

*Thirteenth floor. Lucky number thirteen. Great. I don't even
know who's going to be saving my ass when I get there.*

"Joel, I think that we—" Corina began, but I cut her off
with song:

"*You come and go, you come and go . . . oh, oh, OH!*"

No turning back now. Sing it like you're in the shower.

I closed my eyes, belting it out: "*Karma, karma, karma,
karma, karma chameleon!*"

Silence.

There was no indication that anything had happened.

It didn't work.

"Okay," said Corina. "I think we should call—"

Her hologram paused. Taraval and Pema froze.

It did *work! Go, go, go.*

I un-pretend-handcuffed myself, and jumped onto
the table.

Unfortunately, that was the extent of my grace. As I went
to pivot left, I became disoriented going through Corina's hologram, slipped, and inadvertently head-butted Taraval with
the full weight of my body as I dropped to the floor.

He didn't move from his position. He couldn't even open his mouth, but he moaned in pain.

Fuck! That hurt.

I didn't have time to worry about whether I'd just concussed myself. I can only thank the adrenaline pumping through my veins for surviving what should have been a first-round knockout. As I painfully lifted myself off the floor, I said, "David, please open the door."

"With pleasure, sir," said the room.

I stepped into the empty hallway. Literally, it was devoid of any semblance of life. *They didn't want witnesses,* I thought darkly. The emptiness was a perfect mirror for how I felt in the world at that point. Alone. Hollow. *Joel Byram cannot come to the comms right now.*

I decided to wallow later. I turned left and speed-walked down the hall, counting off the doors on my right. *Beige, beige, beige, green!*

There it was before me. The familiar, emergency-exit green.[15] I only had to open the door, go up four floors, and throw myself on the mercy of whomever I found there. Pema had promised they would help. I certainly needed some.

---

[15] The international green exit sign was settled on with no shortage of controversy among the escape industry. All the way back in the 1970s, the Japanese fire safety department held a national competition, encouraging people to submit their drawings and visions of what an exit sign should be. The purpose of the competition was to find an exit sign that could be implemented throughout Japan. After testing exit signs that were submitted as part of the competition, the winner was chosen—a gentleman by the name of Yukio Ota. His design was of a green exit sign that showed a man running toward a door. Then around the same time "Karma Chameleon" hit the charts, the International Organization for Standardization (ISO) ultimately chose Ota's sign for international usage. The green running man pretty much remained unchanged for centuries, until eventually its unique color signature became so familiar, that the need for the iconic man was deemed unnecessary. A green sign with a white arrow became the ISO standard for directional paths to emergency exits in the 2100s, and green doors were exits.

I put my hand on the doorknob and pulled, but there was a problem.

It was locked.

ANOTHER OTHER

BACK WHEN I was a freshman at NYU, I thought I'd make my dad proud and take up boxing. Salting was a bit out of his grasp—whenever someone asked him what his son was studying, he'd say, "He asks computers trick questions," which was true, but he never really got it. Boxing was something concrete, something that he could understand and we could bond over. My coach was a rather optimistic Italian guy who never really acknowledged defeat, and my sparring partners took it easy on me because they thought I was funny. Eventually my dad, coach, and gym friends all managed to convince me to sign up for a fight.

On my first and only time in the ring, they pitted me against a hairy Slavic fellow twice as big as me. Before the first-round bell rang, I knew I was beat. Boy, was I beat. The Slav knocked me down twice in as many minutes, but rather than throw in the towel, my coach told me something that stuck with me for the rest of my life—which at the time I thought was going to end before the round did.

"Kid, ya don't gotta beat 'em—ya just gotta outlast 'em."

He meant the fight, but right then I decided he meant "in life."

So I got back to my feet, faced my adversary, and then kicked him in the nuts as hard as I could.

I know, it was a dirty trick. Before you judge, consider the outcome: the fight was immediately over, and I would never step in a boxing ring again.

Unfortunately, such wisdom didn't prepare me for something as simple as a locked door. And since there were no gonads I could see, I tried the knob again.

"Please state the nature of your emergency," the door said. God damn it, did everything in this building have a brain?

"There's—uh—a fire," I said.

"Impossible. No fire or smoke sensors have been triggered."

"They're broken."

"I see no error alerts."

"Look, you stupid door, there's a fucking fire in Room D. If you don't believe me, ask it yourself."

"I cannot seem to reach that room. Nor can I read your comms." It paused. "Very well. I shall alert the authorities. Please walk calmly down the stairs in a single file."

"I'll do that."

As the door slid open, green lights started pulsing along the ceiling, and an alarm siren bounced off the walls.

Sure, it was a pretty weak con. If I hadn't been panicked, concussed, sleep deprived, starved, dehydrated, and on the verge of pissing myself, I'm sure I could have come up with a smoother salt. Things being what they were, I was thrilled that anything I did worked.

Up. I hesitated, my natural escape instinct nudging me toward the ground and the freedom of open streets. *Remember what Pema said. Her plan has worked so far; now get upstairs and find "them." Wherever she's sending me, whatever you may find there, you'll be better off than you were in the conference room. Move!*

I ran up. The stairs themselves were painted the same emergency green, a stark contrast to the unpainted gray cement walls of the stairwell. The perfect echo chamber for the blaring wail of the alarm. Its song served as a wonderful incentive for me to hurry the fuck up.

One down, three to go.

I reached Floor Ten without further incident, which I took as a sign of the turning of the tides. I tried to listen for footsteps coming from downstairs. If there were any, they would have been drowned out by the alarm. I decided that I was being chased. It was a safe bet.

Two.

Still, no sign of life manifested anywhere along the stairway.

I went up another flight. My legs weren't used to this kind of physical exertion and were filing all kinds of complaints with my nervous system. To distract myself, I imagined reaching the thirteenth floor. It would be a glass door, unlike the others. I'd take a few steps back, and spin-kick through it to freedom. On the other side would be a well-armed militia, weapons drawn. One of them would give me a big glass of lemonade, then we'd charge back down the stairs, fucking up anyone who got in our way. We'd get to Room D, and I'd make Taraval and Corina Shafer delete the extra me, take my ass to Costa Rica via drone (*not* teleportation!), and Sylvia would be there to welcome me. She'd be so happy to see me, she'd instantly jump my bones, and we'd make up right there on the floor of customs.

There it is. Floor Thirteen.

The door was not glass, nor did it have a whole militia behind it, but I was happy to see it anyway. It was another featureless green emergency exit door, and I just had to get it open. With the fire alarm blaring, it would be a fruitless exercise to engage it in conversation.

Knock it down. It's just a flimsy metal thing. You can do it.

I stepped back, giving myself some room to get a running start, and went at the door with everything I had, which wasn't much. Salters are not known for their physical prowess.

God damn!

It hurt a lot. The door didn't budge.

Again. Get through that door!

I kicked it with my foot, then started slamming my fists against the surface, not bothering to listen for any response, just banging. The only acceptable condition for my silence would be an open door.

I'm losing time. They're coming.

I started screaming, "Let me in!" on top of the pounding. I knew it was mostly for myself. They—Pema's friends, whoever they were—probably couldn't hear me through the soundproof barrier. My screams were born out of desperation, a final throw as the buzzer went off. If International Transport was coming to get me, there was nowhere left for me to go. I couldn't fight them. This door opening was my only chance of survival—my last opportunity to prevent my doppelgänger, the *other me*, from going on *my* vacation with *my* wife in beautiful fucking *Costa Rica!*

The door stayed shut. So much for Hail Marys. I leaned my head against the cool metal, letting exhaustion settle on me like a heavy wet quilt. I felt as if I could sleep for a year. My hand rested on the doorknob, which turned under the weight of my body, and *click*—the door opened.

It must have unlocked because of the fire alarm. Feeling like an idiot, I pushed the door wider to reveal another hallway, only this one was decorated more like an old-fashioned doctor's office than a plastic spaceship. Stained wood floors, Persian rugs, silk-shaded incandescent lamps.

I quietly stepped over the threshold, eyes peeled for "security," as a sharp, bright pain stung me somewhere in the back. My ears rang. My teeth chattered like castanets.

For the second time on July 3, I blacked out.

LOVE PLUS ONE

NANOTECHNOLOGY completely changed the health-care industry. Gone was the need for sterilized equipment, brutal surgeries, and physically skilled doctors. Most medical issues could be solved with over-the-counter sprays and bandages and whatnot, but people still had to go to a hospital for major traumas or fixes. *Trauma* meant you were in mortal danger, whereas *fixes* meant you didn't like something about yourself and wanted to change it. A nano cream, for example, might get rid of your crow's feet, but if you lost an arm, you needed to go see a doctor. I also think it was so people didn't do weird black-market shit like they did in the early days—adding extra limbs, extra organs, grotesque stuff like that. Nanos still did all the work, mind you, but doctors were there to explain, architect, and supervise the procedures. Surgeries were glass-walled, clean rooms occupied by billions of tiny self-replicating, highly specialized robots, but patient rooms still had the feel of an efficiency motel.

In Costa Rica, at the San José CIMA hospital, Joel Byram lay in one such room. He was dreaming.

(Okay, this is kind of confusing. I can't call him Joel, but I need to tell you his side of the story. Sorry, it's just difficult to talk about someone who's not me like they are me in the third person. Let's call him Joel Two, or better yet, Joel Too. No? Joel 2.0? Okay, yeah, that's way too retro. Hmm. How about Joel^2? Yes, that'll work.)

So. Joel^2 was dreaming. My wife stood beside him. Eyes puffy, red, depleted of tears. She planted her head on Joel^2's chest, wanting to hear his heartbeat. There were machines that could track it for her, but her faith in technology was exhausted for the day.

Thump-thump. Thump-thump. She had done it. He was alive.

Sylvia lifted her head, looking out the window. Beyond the palm trees and whitewashed buildings, she could see a thin column of black smoke rising into the air from the hole that had been the San José TC. The explosion had occurred thirty minutes ago, but people were still running through the streets and emergency vehicles were still racing past, sirens blaring. No one had noticed a distraught American woman in vacation clothes enter the hospital's teleportation chamber. Nor did they see her exit a few minutes later, dragging an unconscious American man behind her. When she brought him into the ER on a gurney, the on-calls were too preoccupied with the influx of damaged bodies to wonder why his injuries seemed relegated to the internal brain stem and spinal cord. The tissue surrounding his comms implants had not ported over, since inorganics get scanned, stored, and ported separately from organics, and he'd arrived comms-less. His injuries were deemed not life threatening, and so nanites were set to rebuild, from scratch, his comms and the soft tissue with which they needed to mesh. Then off they sent him to recovery.

It worked. Joel^2 was alive. His heart was beating because of her.

Because of what she'd done.

Before she could follow that train of thought any further, there was a power surge. The room lights brightened, no longer running off the hospital's backup generators. At the same time, Sylvia's own comms came back on. A jumble of hysterical news feeds, social media alerts, messages from concerned friends and family members, and apoplectic work e-mails filled her field of vision. She closed them all, putting her head in her hands. Sooner or later she'd have to deal with them, particularly the work e-mails, but she couldn't face any of it just yet.

A different alert sounded, making her open her eyes. "What is this, Julie?" Sylvia said.

"I'm so sorry, Sylvia. I know you said no interruptions whatsoever, not even if the world was ending, but someone found a way to engage my emergency protocols. It's Pema Jigme from IT."

Sylvia bit her lip. So much for avoidance. On the upside, if she was going to get chewed out, it could have been by somebody a lot worse. She took a deep breath. "Put her through."

Pema's angry compact face appeared in a close-up vid stream. Her overmanicured eyebrows made her look particularly pissed. Sylvia couldn't stand that much self-righteousness that close to her, so she moved the stream to the room's hologram projector. Her short coworker stood before her, arms folded, in a green pindot skirt and boxy business suit that definitely fell into James Bond–villain territory.

"What were you *thinking*, Sylvia?" She sounded exasperated. "Bill and Corina are freaking out. First you use Honeycomb, then you disable the hospital's TC? Do you know how many laws you've broken?"

Sylvia nodded. "Comms were down. My husband was dead. I did what I had to do. And for all my efforts, he's still barely alive!"

Her voice broke, and again she buried her face in her hands. Pema's projection watched, her severe eyebrows softening slightly. Soon Sylvia raised her head.

"I made the call. I'm willing to face the consequences. If you're here to fire me or arrest me, then go ahead. Anyone else in my position would have done the same."

"I'm not here to fire you, Syl." She looked over at the sleeping man in the hospital bed. "How is he?"

"It was touch and go for a bit. He was mostly intact, just his comms didn't quite make it. That caused some damage to his spinal cord." Focusing on the scientific details helped calm her. "The restore data from the glacier[16] was incomplete because the Gehinnomites took out most of the networking infrastructure. I couldn't access anything remotely. But—I think he's going to be okay."

"Good. Look, we will figure this out. But you need to get out of there. Now. Take your husband, go off comms for a day or two. IT is working up a solution, but it will take some

---

[16] In the early twenty-first century, a company called Amazon began marketing a storage cloud service called the glacier, which included unlimited storage of data in what they referred to as cold storage. Within the Amazon Glacier service, data was stored in archives. Customers could upload archives as large as forty terabytes (I know, funny that was a lot back then), and once an archive was created, it could not be updated unless it was retrieved, modified, and then restored. The service became the status quo for data storage because it didn't charge for the storage of data, but rather for the retrieval of it. This eventually led to the creation of unlimited storage tiers whereby data's value was directly attributed to its utility and accessibility, a theory known as "Data Gravity." Basically, the lesser utility a piece of data had, the lower its value, but if it suddenly gained value, then the cost of its retrieval would be directly proportionate to its utility. So useless information could be archived forever, but if it suddenly became very important to retrieve it, then the cost of retrieving it would be based on the speed with which someone wanted it retrieved. Eventually the dictionary definition of the word *glacier* became amended to include these utility-based data storage services, and the word outlasted the company that invented it.

time, and we need to keep this quiet. It is imperative that no one—*no one*—realize what really happened, do you agree?"

Sylvia nodded quickly.

"Good," Pema said, relaxing her tone. "The Costa Rican police are so overwhelmed right now, you should be able to slip out unnoticed. But if the police find you, I don't know what they'll do. And we won't be able to help. Do you understand?"

Sylvia nodded, looking from the dreaming doppelgänger of her husband to her coworker. "Why are you doing this for me?"

"It is my belief that, given the circumstances, anyone might have done what you did. Anyway, no use dwelling in the past. We're in damage control now. It doesn't help anyone if you're not in the loop. Corporations don't make decisions; people do."

While the two women were talking, Joel[2] dreamed. He found himself standing on the stony shore of a dark flowing river. He felt as if he were in a cavern, but he couldn't see the rock walls or ceiling that surrounded him. The ground beneath his feet was made up of small gray pebbles that crunched when he walked. Everything was dark.

He saw a light shining on the opposite shore. Joel[2] felt a strong desire to go toward it. He stepped into the frothy fast-moving water, only to find it wasn't water, not exactly. It was room temperature, and flowed around him like smoke, or foam. There was something relaxing about it. Soothing. He started to walk toward the light, as if gently nudged by an invisible hand.

But then a tune began to play from somewhere behind him. A familiar 1980s New Wave song, one of his favorites. Joel[2] stopped in the middle of the river, turning back to the synth drums. The gray foam sloshed around him, as soft and quiet as whispers.

What happened was this: as Sylvia and Pema discussed life-and-death matters, Joel[2]'s freshly printed brain was being connected to my comms. Once they came online, he started auto-playing my—now *his*—1980s music playlist. Specifically, Culture Club's "Karma Chameleon." The song resumed from the point where my comms had been disconnected. The melody filtered into Joel[2]'s dream, the electric harmonica echoing softly over the dark rushing foam to where he was standing. He knew the lyrics well.

> *I'm a man without conviction*
> *I'm a man who doesn't know*

Joel[2] bopped his head to the beat. Something made him want to sing along. So he did.

> *How to sell a contradiction*

As he sang, he began to walk away from the distant, beckoning light. He ran through the gray foam, speeding back to the shore from which he had come. As the breeze ruffled his hair, he increased the volume of his singing.

> *You come and go*
> *You come and go—oh, oh, OH!*

Joel[2] drew near the rocky shore and leaped out of the dark, foamy river, landing solidly on his feet and spreading his arms. Embracing the moment, he belted out the words along with the chorus.

"*Karma, karma, karma, karma, karma chameleon!*" he shout-sang in the hospital bed, making Sylvia and Pema jump. Joel[2] sat upright, arms wide, then froze as he saw his stricken wife and the projection of a woman he didn't know standing beside his bed.

He turned off the music on his comms. "Where am I? What happened?"

Tears sprang to Sylvia's eyes. They were happy tears, but she was at a loss for what to say next.

"I'll leave you now," Pema told Sylvia quietly, giving Joel^2 a once-over. "Remember: be as quick as you can. And no comms," she cautioned. Then her projection vanished.

"Who was that? Is this Costa Rica?" Joel^2 tried to get out of the hospital bed, but his body wouldn't cooperate.

Sylvia rushed to his side. "Yes, but take it easy. They're still fixing you, babe."

"Did something break?" said Joel^2, inspecting himself.

"Yes and no." Sylvia sat next to her husband-copy, picking nonexistent lint from his bedsheet. "You, um—there was an accident at the San José TC. An attack."

Joel^2's comms—previously *my* comms—filled with a frenzy of news feeds and social media alerts. "Holy crap. Was I *in* that?"

Sylvia shook her head, then nodded, then settled for a head motion somewhere in between. "But the important thing is, you're here now, and you're gonna be fine. Do you remember what happened?"

Joel^2 blinked. He recalled sitting in the Escrow room in the Greenwich Village TC. He remembered the conductor, a ginger-haired guy with a Michigan-shaped birthmark on his face, and hitting agree on the legalese, and the lights going down in the foyer. But there had been no bright blinding flash, and his next memory was standing on the rocky shore of that dark, foamy river. There had been a light, too; he'd felt drawn to it, compelled—but evidently all that had been a dream. He'd made it to Costa Rica, with his wife, and he felt—actually, he felt pretty terrible.

"No," he said, dropping back to the bed in exhaustion.

Sylvia took his hand, tears still running down her cheeks. "You know, I thought I lost you today," she said, the corners of her mouth twitching. "I can't go through that again."

"Me neither. Whatever *it* was."

She smiled for real then. He pulled her forward, kissing her full on the mouth. Sylvia stiffened, but soon responded hungrily, her hands roving up and down his arms. I suppose it wasn't cheating because, technically, she didn't know I was alive in New York yet. Still, it felt a little wrong. Just as things were starting to heat up, she broke off, wiping the tears from her face. "You wanna get out of here?"

Joel[2] looked his wife—*my* wife—up and down. "If it means more of this kind of medicine, yes, please."

"I'll go have a nurse clear you—I mean, release you. Sit tight."

"As you know, my love, sitting down and resting are my two greatest competencies."

Sylvia patted Joel[2]'s arm and exited, the glass wall breaking apart as she passed through it. As she spoke with a young Costa Rican woman who may have been a doctor or a nurse, Joel[2] studied his reflection. The nanos were doing an amazing job. He looked fresh out of the box, not a scratch or a scar on him, except for those he'd already had. This was his first time in a bona fide hospital. He'd been to clinics a few times for minor wounds or broken bones. But those were more like hotel rooms: soothing pictures on the walls, courteous staff, comfortable bedding. The room he was in now was more like a bank. White walls, glowing blue power strips, and a spare, utilitarian bed. There were holographic displays of his vitals on one wall, but the only other indication that he was being worked on was the occasional metallic tickle on his bare skin.

Outside, Sylvia finished speaking with the young woman. She nodded, pulling up something on her comms. Her fingers pressed a few buttons only she could see, giving Joel[2]'s nanos a new directive. The tiny robots knocked him out, sending his brain directly to REM sleep. He drifted off into warm, healing darkness.

THE LAW OF HOLES

NOBODY SAID ANYTHING.

A hum of white noise permeated the room after I finished recounting the entire chain of events for Moti and company. It had all played out mere hours ago, but telling it made it feel like ancient history. It made me ill to relive it, but I had spared no detail. The anniversary fight with Sylvia, my own failings in my marriage, the loss of my comms, Pema, Taraval, Corina Shafer, and the ugly truth about teleportation. Now came the part when (hopefully) these guys would help me get out of the mess I was in.

Moti broke the silence. "IT commed us, you know."

"Oh?" I was cautious.

Moti shrugged. "They said you broke into their office but then ran away. They suggested you may be dangerous."

Just as I suspected. Those fucks were going to kill me and cover it up. "That's absurd," I said. "I tell jokes to computers for a living."

"They said they tried informing the police," he continued, "but you managed to disable your comms to avoid detection on GDS. They said if we saw you, to immediately turn you over to building security."

Shit, shit, shit. "Look, man, they own the building security. If you're going to cut me loose, at least call an independent—"

"We did not believe them," said Zaki, flipping his cigarette.

"You didn't?" I asked.

Moti rubbed his chin with his right thumb. "A thief," he said, "especially someone smart enough to disable their comms, that kind of person would have run down and out—not up and in."

Thank God. "So—what do I do now?" I asked, instantly realizing how vulnerable saying those words made me feel.

Moti scratched the back of his head, reached into his pocket, and pulled out his pack of TIME cigarettes. He opened the cardboard box, slid one of the sticks out, and placed it in his mouth. He took a puff, and I stared at the smoldering end of the cigarette. "*Yoel*, there are three things you need to know." He exhaled, his breath smelling of burnt tobacco and coffee grounds.

"One." He raised his eyebrows and drew on his cigarette. "William Taraval, Corina Shafer—these are dangerous people. You think this William Taraval is some administrator, but he is in reality the head of special projects for the most special company in the world, the company at which your wife works—International Transport. *Departure, Arrival . . . Delight!*" He breathed out cynically. "As you know, International Transport isn't just a corporation, *Yoel*. It's the centerpiece of our new world order. Unelected, undemocratic—you in the West no longer have the power to vote with your money, despite what they tell you. But I suspect you already know this, *Yoel*: that they control your lives through commerce, and that it is fine. Maybe even you believe it is better this way. But International Transport is the worst of them, *Yoel*. They are *too* powerful, even for this crazy world. They control how we go from A"—he flipped over his empty cup of coffee and in a lightning-fast shuffleboard movement with no care for the china, slid it across the table at me; I barely caught it in time—"to B." His eyes bore into me. "They had an opportunity to fix this, to clear you. No comms, no evidence, and the perfect alibi: you, happy and alive in Costa Rica. But because of this mystery woman, this Pema Jigme, you have gotten away. You, your existence—it threatens the entire IT empire. They will search for you. They will not give up." He paused, not yet done. "And they will also go after the other you and your wife. It is most likely they have already done that."

Sylvia.

I couldn't help but gulp. "What's number two?"

Moti reached across the table and grabbed my arm, firmly gripping it beneath his left one. The motion sent the beautiful Turkish coffee cup he'd slid to me off its ceramic saucer. I braced myself for the shattering sound, but Moti nonchalantly caught it with his right hand and placed it back on the table. Moti's hand then found its way over to his left wrist, and began slowly rolling up his sleeve. I saw something shiny and metallic on his wrist. It was a watch, one of the antique analog models, with both time and calendar functions. He tapped his manicured fingernail against the watch's crystal face. Against my reflection.

"*Yoel*, this man you see here, this is not Joel Byram. That other Joel Byram in Costa Rica? He has been assigned your identity. William Taraval was at least right about this one thing: the man you saw with your wife, he is the real you now. Do you understand, *Yoel*? You are no one."

I shook my head. Maybe I'd been hoping for some kind of magic fix, a do-over, but hearing him state my situation so plainly, something inside me broke.

Imagine looking in the mirror and not knowing who you are. An empty face staring back. *No one.* We rarely think about how much air is around us until we can't breathe. We always imagine what it would be like to be someone else, but when we do so, it's with the guise that beneath it all, we know who we really are. Take that away, and who are we?

I opened my mouth, but couldn't make air enter my lungs.

"*Yoel*, are you all right?" Moti said. He sounded like he was at the other end of a cave.

When a person is drowning, there isn't time for them to exhale or call out. Their eyes are glassy, unable to focus. It just seems like they're distracted. The best way to check is to ask if they're all right. If they just stare blankly, then they're probably drowning.

"*Yoel*, breathe." Moti shook me.

"I—"

"You are hyperventilating. Don't talk. Just listen. It's actually much worse than you think. *But* it will be okay."

I was below the surface, water filling my lungs, but I refused to give in. I kicked for the surface, grasping at two words like a life vest: "Third . . . thing?"

Moti laughed, slapping a hand on my back as he exhaled a plume of cigarette smoke. "Good boy, you are tougher than I thought. The third thing, I suspect you have already guessed—I am not really a travel agent."

He took a long drag of his nicotine stick, the cherry flaring like a warning light. "*Yoel*, how much do you know about the Big Mac?"

THE BIG MAC
OF THESEUS

THE *MONA LISA*, as I grew up to know it, was a painting that was once known as the *Isleworth Mona Lisa*, the authenticity and history of which was fraught with contention.

Shortly before World War I, an English art collector discovered a *Mona Lisa* look-alike in the home of a Somerset nobleman in whose family's possession it had been for nearly a century. This discovery led to the conjecture that Leonardo painted two portraits of Lisa del Giocondo, aka the *Mona Lisa*: the infamous one destroyed in the aforementioned da Vinci Exhibition teleportation accident, and the one discovered in Somerset and then brought to Isleworth, where it eventually came to be known as the *Isleworth Mona Lisa*.

The story goes that da Vinci began painting *Mona Lisa* in 1503, but left her unfinished. Then, in 1517, a completed *Mona Lisa* surfaced in Leonardo's private possession shortly before his death. This work of art is the same one that was destroyed in the solar storm of 2109. But supporters of the *Isleworth Mona Lisa* contend that it is the first iteration of the lost masterpiece, begun in 1503, a full ten years before the "real" *Mona Lisa* was painted.

More credibility was added to this theory when it was discovered that in 1584, an art historian named Gian Paolo Lomazzo wrote about *"della Gioconda, e di Mona Lisa"*—the Gioconda, and the *Mona Lisa*. Since *La Gioconda* was sometimes used as an alternative title for the *Mona Lisa*, the reference implied that there were indeed two separate paintings, with the *Isleworth Mona Lisa* being the original version of her more famous sister.

What I'm getting at is, since 2109, whenever people went to a museum to see the *Mona Lisa*, they were really admiring the *Isleworth Mona Lisa*. Even though it's the only version of the painting people in my generation ever knew, and even though it was probably created first, our knowledge of the *other Mona Lisa*, the one that vanished into quantum foam, makes the Isleworth portrait feel like a cheap knock-off.

But is it? Or is the painting formerly known as the *Isleworth Mona Lisa* now the actual *Mona Lisa*?

As Moti explained it to me, that question is best contemplated over a Big Mac.

Say you go to McDonald's and order a Big Mac. Pretty much everyone in the place knows what you're asking for. You could ask the maître d', the manager, the janitor—hell, you could turn around and ask the person behind you in line what a Big Mac is and they'll tell you: "Two all-beef patties, special sauce, lettuce, cheese, pickles, onions—on a sesame seed bun." Right?

But is every Big Mac the same?

Well, you might think, *they sure taste the same.*

Does it matter which breed of cow the meat came from? What type of soil the lettuce was grown in? The yeast used in the bread? In other words, what makes it a Big Mac?

You may be surprised to learn that some of the world's smartest scientific mercenaries battled with this dilemma for centuries: How could they ensure that every time someone bit into a Big Mac, they'd get the same, consistent "Big Mac dining experience"—in my case, fatty protein tinged with a hint of regret?

My personal feelings aside, it turns out that this replication is much harder to do than you'd think. Sometimes there's too much lettuce, sometimes the buns are too mushy, maybe there aren't enough pickles, and so on. There were just so many ways in which one Big Mac could be different from another, and that was a *big problem*.

Every year since the Big Mac's inception in 1967, the McDonald's-Huáng Corporation[17] has utilized a combination of the earth's brightest humans and technological advances to ensure that whenever you stepped into a McDonald's and ordered a Big Mac, you'd get the exact same Big Mac.

In the beginning, it was mostly about the basics. An illustrated instruction manual was distributed to employees, specifically detailing where every element was supposed to go, and in what order. Then they issued specially calibrated sauce guns to ensure the same amount of special sauce was applied to each sandwich with each pull of the trigger. As the operation expanded, it became harder to ensure that the ingredients for Big Macs would come from identical-tasting sources. Food chemicals were introduced to make flavors and textures uniform worldwide. Vegetables were precut and shipped in vacuum-sealed containers to guarantee freshness and consistency in size.

[17] In May of 2046, the Huáng Group, the largest commercial real estate firm in China, announced a purchase of all of the stock of the McDonald's Corporation for approximately $108 billion. It was the largest stock acquisition by a Chinese company of an American company to date. At the time of this writing, the McDonalds-Huáng Corporation is the third most powerful corporation on Earth.

But still, perfection eluded the fast-food giant. For about a hundred years, the best McDonald's could do to build an ideal Big Mac at every one of its locations was to combine tightly controlled sourcing and distribution with exacting instructions for sandwich architecture, preparation, and packaging.

Then, on January 16, 2048, McDonald's solved for the consistency problem with *cloning*. Every Big Mac consumed henceforth would now be molecularly identical.

This, Moti continued, is where we run into something called the Theseus paradox, which is very important to burger construction, but even more important to my current existential dilemma. The gist of the Theseus paradox went like this:

Theseus and his squad of Athenians had a bunch of epic adventures aboard a big fancy wooden ship—most famously defeating the Minotaur in Crete. To honor their memory, Theseus's legendary vessel was docked and preserved by the Athenians for several centuries. Long enough for all of the original wood to have rotted. Over the years, as each of the boat's planks decayed, the Greeks put a new one in its place, so that by the age of Demetrius Phalereus several centuries later, every single original oar and plank of the vessel had been replaced.

The question is, if none of the original parts were still there, *was it still the same ship of Theseus?* Or was it now just a new ship that shared all of the original's characteristics?

In the abstract, this alone is a big philosophical conundrum. But it quickly gets dicier.

Say you went to two different McDonald's restaurants on polar opposite ends of the world, and ordered a Big Mac from each. Upon delivery of the second Big Mac, you unwrapped both sandwiches and placed them side by side in front of you. Then you swapped the bottom half of the one on the left with the one on the right. Were they both still the same Big Mac?

Prior to 2048, the subject would have been up for debate, thanks to the Theseus paradox. Some might have said that while you still had two Big Macs in front of you, *neither* of them was now the original sandwich, due to variations in the places they came from, the subtle differences in construction, and the people who made them.

After the cloning innovation, however, both Big Macs were pretty much the same. I say "pretty much" because there were still variables in the way each burger had been handled prior to delivery—environmental conditions associated with the point of origin, the impact of time on the final product, and so on. The fact that there could be more than one at a time didn't quite solve for the Theseus paradox, but it was deemed close enough.

But then, in 2106, McDonald's upped the consistency ante for the last time. You may have left the previous paragraph asking yourself, *If we cloned the Big Mac and exchanged parts between the new "copy" and the original, would the original still be the original?* Or you were not asking that, and that's okay, I asked it for you, and, boy, aren't you glad I did? No, you're not, because in 2106 the question became irrelevant. Technology had finally caught up to our exacting laziness. Once McDonald's solved for cloning, the only problem that remained was delivery—how to ensure that every Big Mac would be cooked and prepared in exactly the same way. The burgers might have been identical, but they could still taste different. To jump this last hurdle, McDonald's-Huáng needed to go beyond cloning to true replication.

I'm really hoping you already know all of this and have skipped ahead. But if you don't, or you didn't, the difference between cloning and replication goes something like this:

In 2048, they managed to string molecules together in a preordained symphony, but the underlying atoms were free to dance to it in their own way. In 2106, not only were they printing out molds of well-behaved atoms, but each quark was swinging through, tangoing with, and leaping over Heisenberg's uncertainty principle, exactly as expected. Accomplishing this for one string of molecules was considered a feat; now the good scientists at Mickey D's had to grapple with replicating the trillions of atoms that made up a Big Mac.

Ever hear of something called density functional theory (DFT)? If you think it sounds like something a physicist might do to predict the volume of their farts while sitting on the toilet, you're not far off. DFT is a method for determining the electronic structure of matter.

Sylvia is fond of saying, "The biggest trick in quantum physics is figuring out what happens next."[18]

As the cornerstone of computational physics, DFT has been a very popular way to figure out "what something does next" since as early as the 1970s. Once it became feasible to determine the electronic structure of matter, then reproducing said matter became an exercise in computational capacity: the more complex the object, the more computing power necessary to calculate its continuous quantum variables using DFT. This

---

[18] DFT is a computational quantum mechanical modeling method used in physics, chemistry, and materials science to investigate the electronic structure of many-body systems, in particular atoms and molecules. DFT has roots in "crazy cat guy" Schrödinger's equation. It's a partial differential equation that describes how the quantum state of a physical system changes with time. Since replication and teleportation require capturing infinite dimensions of an object and then predicting their future state, DFT could be used to break down atoms and molecules into electronic and nuclear components to achieve something called the Born–Oppenheimer approximation. The important thing is that this so-called "approximation" needs to be really fucking exact or all shit goes to hell, so the computing power necessary to calculate the future state of something is directly proportional to its complexity and dependencies. Finding an equation that integrates Moore's law with DFT to predict complexity and distance of replicated or teleported objects was one of Sylvia's pet projects.

is important in the realm of replication because the computer doesn't technically reproduce the things being replicated until after they have already arrived. A virtual version of the object arrives at its destination, the DFT algorithm analyzes it, compares it to the original object, and, if satisfied that the current state of the arriving object matches the next state of the original object, then it's actually there—otherwise, it never arrived. Cool stuff.

It took a while for the necessary quantum computing capacity to develop so that we could perfectly calculate the future molecular state of something as complex as a Big Mac. But by 2106, we were there. The ability to scan and reproduce complex objects at scale simply became an exercise in cost reduction, consumer-oriented design, and fabrication. It also kicked off what quickly became known as the Quantum Age. A new era of human evolution, defined by a double cheeseburger. Sounds about right.

Within the next decade, replication printers became the essential gotta-have-it kitchen appliance. Why wait for water to freeze when you can simply point your cup at the printer, tell it the exact number of ice cubes along with whatever beverage you want them floating in, and presto! Coke on the rocks. Or bourbon and Coke on the rocks. Or just two fingers of bourbon, neat, forget the rocks, you lush.

Some people thought printers would collapse the market value of things like expensive liquor, fancy cheese, and truffles—but corporations picked up the slack. Actually, as far back as the twentieth century, companies have been patenting recipes, like the aforementioned Coke, and KFC spice blends. Replication actually proved to be a very effective way of weeding out forgeries. Could you replicate a burger that was very similar to a Big Mac? Sure. You could even jailbreak your printer, buy a Big Mac, and then replicate it for your friends—but it wouldn't be the same—the copy wouldn't be "signed" by McDonald's.

We humans place a lot of stock in originality—our culture has always focused on "the real thing" having true tangible value, and with molecular signatures, it has become nearly impossible to make illegitimate replications of anything patented. *Vive l'original!* And anyway, each printer has an origin signature, so even if someone hacked a burger into seeming like a Big Mac by engineering something called a "signature collision," they would also need to somehow spoof the origin of that burger to be from the Golden Arches HQ. So even if you replicated something with the legitimate McDonald's key, the receiving printer would still flag the duplicate as fake and you'd get in trouble. Granted, I'm not sure how much trouble someone would get into for breaking the cipher and replicating a Big Mac, but it's a slippery slope from Big Macs to, say, gold bars—which is actually why certain things can't be printed but pretty much anything can be *teleported.*[19]

[19] Okay, this one is pretty complicated. There were whole books written on the creation myth of molecular patent signatures (MPSes) and the rise of commercial replication, but they are very boring books. The most popular theory is that MPSes have their origins in something called BitTorrent. BitTorrent was an old Internet protocol that was used to share large files across the net very efficiently. Suppose Jane Doe decided she wanted to use BitTorrent to share a song she made. She would take her song and make it available on her computer as a file called a torrent. The original file, as hosted on her computer, was called a seed. What BitTorrent did was split the file up into lots of pieces, such that anyone who wanted the file could use a BitTorrent client to request it from the seed host (Jane's computer). The torrent file of the original song included a cryptographic hash of each chunk of the torrent. Every requesting client was sent one of the pieces and accumulated all the remaining pieces, over a period of time, from other people's requesting computers through distributed communication. At any given moment, each requesting computer was downloading some parts of the file from some of the other requesting peers and uploading other parts of the file to other peers. If any requester got sent data that didn't match the cryptographic hash, the BitTorrent client would reject the content and seek
→

It was so obvious once Moti explained it. Teleportation and printing: one and the same. Corina and Taraval had told me a truth I never wanted to know: the only difference between replication and teleportation is that the first allowed for multiple instances of the same object, and the latter didn't.

Teleporting living things was much trickier than inanimate objects, however, owing to the previously mentioned fidget problem—living things have a tendency to move. Some very smart people figured out that this issue could be solved by calculating the *future*, rather than present, state of qubits.[20]

an original elsewhere. This proved to be a very robust method for integrity protection. The compute cost of generating something called a "preimage attack" that would essentially brute-force something called a "collision," where an attacker might stumble upon the cryptographic hash of a file and be able to reproduce it, was prohibitively expensive, if not impossible. Just prior to commercial replication's heyday, the notion of such cryptographic hashes was revisited in the context of molecular signatures to ensure the integrity of replicated items. The printer network worked similarly to the way BitTorrent worked, with the point of origin for any item being replicated essentially being a "seed," and each printer wanting to reproduce that item being a "client." To prevent replication of valuable or patented goods, printers could only reproduce items with MPSes that they were licensed for. However, even jailbroken printers that were hacked to circumvent MPS licensing couldn't reproduce items like gold or Big Macs because the network would detect an unlicensed request for a privileged MPS and only offer error messages until a valid license was provided.

[20] A qubit is a "quantum bit." An important distinguishing feature between a qubit and a classical bit is that multiple qubits can exhibit quantum entanglement. Entanglement is a nonlocal property that allows a set of qubits to express higher correlation than is possible in classical systems. Particles that have interacted at some point retain a type of connection and can be entangled with each other in pairs, in a process known as correlation. Knowing the spin state of one entangled particle—up or down—allows one to know that the spin of its mate is in the opposite direction. What's really cool is that due to the phenomenon of superposition, each measured particle has no single spin direction before being measured but is simultaneously in both a spin-up and spin-down state. The spin state of each particle being measured is decided at the time of measurement and communicated to the correlated particle, which simultaneously assumes the opposite spin direction to that

→

Twenty-six years after it became technically possible, sometime in 2127, human teleportation was legalized in the United States. Even so, there was no small amount of controversy—all owing to the soul. Many religious leaders issued various herems, encyclicals, decrees, and fatwas against any who would partake in or facilitate teleportation, declaring it an anathema. The most vocal of these was a zealot picketer named Roberto Shila. He unified the disparate protestors under a singular, devout, antiteleportation agenda. They declared the place one goes during teleportation Gehinnom, and themselves Gehinnomites.

Ultimately, the question of human teleportation's legality came to be tested in a class-action suit brought on by one Joanna Shila, the daughter of the Gehinnomite founder. She sued International Transport for the deaths of all sentient beings who would be teleported. After bouncing around in lower federal courts, the case finally reached the Supreme Court. The legal question before the court boiled down to the Theseus paradox.

Given:
• Jane Doe (JD1) steps into the foyer of teleport chamber A (at the origin)
• Jane Doe (JD2) is teleported to the vestibule of teleport chamber B (at the destin)
Is Jane Doe (JD2) the same person as Jane Doe (JD1)?

Entered into evidence were thousands of tests on other living things before we put humans through the ringer, and each study reached the same conclusion: the Jane Doe (JD2) who

of the measured particle. Einstein called this behavior "spooky action at a distance." Quantum entanglement allows qubits that are separated by incredible distances to interact with one another instantaneously (not limited by the speed of light).

showed up on the other side was the exact same person, physically, mentally, and emotionally, as Jane Doe (JD1) at the point of origin. Even her comms followed her to the destination.

The only nonbiblical evidence submitted by the plaintiffs that had anything to do with the actual process of teleportation was the aforementioned weight loss that occurred every time a sentient being teleported. This, you'll remember, was only a few grams and made no discernible change in the teleported subject, so was ruled to be "packet loss."

In a 5–4 ruling with some strident dissents, the Supreme Court held for International Transport, but with a caveat: teleportation was fine for sentient beings, but *printing* them whole was a crime against humanity. Once the decision propagated to the masses and was accepted into the global zeitgeist, only the Levant and the Gehinnomites remained steadfast in their opposition to teleportation.

After the case was decided, International Transport was cleared to teleport anyone and everyone. Of course, they left out the part where TCs weren't porting anybody anywhere; they were merely *printing* them in one place and *clearing* them in the other.

Got it? Replication was a technical marvel, the centuries-in-the-making fruit of man's scientific ingenuity. Whereas teleportation was a marketing marvel, the glorious paragon of mankind's unlimited appetite for obfuscated convenience.

Therefore, intoned Moti, if IT replicated the ship of Theseus, then the replicated vessel would be a copy, but if they teleported it, then it would still be the original ship. Does it *technically* solve for the Theseus paradox? Well, since the *paradox* itself is just a matter of human perception, then it's not really a *paradox*—it's a *conundrum*, which means that as long as the ruling majority agrees that the vessel that came out of the TC is the real ship of Theseus, then it is.

There are some other interesting nuances. One of them is that teleportation is exponentially more expensive than replication—mostly because of insurance. Once you destroy an *original*, it's really gone. Its unique signature goes *poof*, since the rule is there can only be one of anything that gets teleported. If you googled stories about the early days of teleportation, you'd find plenty of hilarious and depressing anecdotes about things that went awry. Sometimes things would get destroyed prior to successful teleportation; other times they'd be teleported and fall off the teleporter rig. Thus, some invaluable assets such as the aforementioned priceless painting, as well as other precious artifacts, were inadvertently sacrificed as collateral damage in humanity's quest for a shorter commute. All of that happened a long time before we started teleporting people, mind. Before the Punch Escrow.

I'm guessing if you asked anyone from IT about the moral implications, they would likely extol humanity's well-documented historical grapples with new transportation technologies. When railroads were first introduced, some people thought the speed would be so intense, it would cause their organs to shoot out of their rectums. But folks still got on board. Whether via land, sea, air, or ether, the desire for more efficient transport has always trumped philosophical worries.

"So," finished Moti, having gone through several more cigarettes during his long-ass lecture, "since the *Isleworth Mona Lisa* is now the 'real' *Mona Lisa*, and a Big Mac you eat is a real Big Mac, and teleportation and replication are the same, it follows that the Joel Byram in Costa Rica is now the 'real' Joel Byram. And you, *Yoel*, are no one."

Whether it was due to his confirmation of my nonexistence, my exhaustion catching up with me, or some other reason, my eyes rolled into the back of my head. I slipped from the plastic chair, cracking my head on the rock-hard floor and slipping into unconsciousness for the third time that day.

TARZAN BOY

JOEL[2] WAS AWAKENED by an incoming call on his comms. If he'd been dreaming again, he couldn't remember. He opened the stream to see Sylvia standing outside the hospital.

"Wake up, Mr. Byram. It's time to get this vay-cay on the road." She rotated her stream to show off a huge top-of-the-line recreational vehicle behind her.

"Wow," said Joel[2]. "Hopefully we have some money left for booze."

"It's a honeymoon—we're supposed to splurge. Now get dressed and I'll be right up."

"Aye, aye, Cap'n."

Joel[2] closed the stream, noticing that someone had dressed him in his sleep. Gone was the classic bare-ass-on-display hospital gown, replaced by a comfortable pair of jeans and a polo. He rose from the bed, his limbs a little stiff. On the floor was a pair of brown hiking shoes and taupe wool socks tucked within them.

He was in the process of putting his shoes on when a Costa Rican nurse in lime-green scrubs walked through the glass wall. He had a pleasant face and the thickest eyebrows Joel[2] had ever seen. He looked my duplicate up and down, scanning him with his comms.

"We advised your wife that a day or two more of observation would be prudent, but she was insistent that we release you," the nurse said. "Since you're technically healthy, we can't force you to stay. Still, I feel obligated to inform you that we still don't know exactly what happened to you."

"I feel fine," $Joel^2$ said, knotting his shoes. "Believe me, the damage she'll cause me if we don't go on our second honeymoon will leave me in a much worse condition."

The nurse nodded. "Like we say: 'happy wife, happy life.' But please, don't overexert yourself." He affixed a cold metal disc to $Joel^2$'s arm. "This will do its best to keep you healthy and strong, but your body is still repairing itself. Be careful, or you'll be seeing me again sooner than you'd like."

$Joel^2$ thanked the man. He attempted to walk out of the room, only to have his legs buckle underneath him.

"Joel! Everything okay?" Sylvia said as she entered the room and jogged to his side.

"Yup. Just getting my sea legs." As she helped him to his feet, he gave a meaningful look to the nurse. The man held up his hands as if to say, *I'm staying out of this.*

Sylvia helped $Joel^2$ out of the room, then through several green exit doors, passing the security camera whose video I would see just a few minutes later. Parked right out front was the largest RV both $Joel^2$ and I had ever seen. It was more like a small house on wheels.

"The streams do not do it justice," he said.

"After the day we had, we deserve to travel in style," Sylvia said as the side door opened and automatically lowered three steps. "Hey! What are you doing?"

$Joel^2$ had lifted Sylvia off the ground and was struggling to get her inside the cabin. "I never"—he took a labored breath—"I never carried you into our house when we got married." Thankfully, none of his newly printed parts tore as he gently placed her within the RV.

The loving glance she rewarded him with was one he (or I) hadn't seen in quite some time. The inside of the RV had a galley kitchen, entertainment center, and a queen-sized bed with fresh sheets. "Car, how long will it take us to get to our destination?" Sylvia said without taking her eyes off Joel[2].

"Approximately two hours and fifteen minutes with current traffic," responded the vehicle.

"Take your time," she said, sliding a hand down Joel[2]'s chest. "And disable all third-party APIs. No contact unless it's an emergency."

"Confirmed," said the RV, driving away from the hospital. The sudden lurch forward caused Joel[2] and Sylvia to steady themselves against each other.

"We should do the same," she said breathlessly, her face only inches from his. "Really go off grid. Just you and me."

"I'm all yours," said Joel[2], turning off his comms.

Sylvia led the man who was her husband (but also not) over to the bed. The nanites repairing his body had released a fresh round of opiates after he'd damaged his new cells lifting Sylvia into the RV. She sat him down on the bed and began to undress.

Her shirt came off, then her shorts, revealing her pleasant, full figure. She gave him a sheepish smile as she unhooked her bra. He couldn't remember the last time he had watched her like this, admired the curve of her hips and breasts. She was so beautiful, and he was lucky to have her. When they had first gotten together, seeing her like this had always driven him a little crazy. It was nice to realize it still did, effects of the nanodrugs aside.

She leaned forward to kiss him on the lips. "You think you can handle this?" she said, breathing heavily.

"One part of me's ready," he said. She reached between his legs to confirm, her kisses becoming more intense as she stroked him. "And I think other systems are coming on board."

"Good," she said, unbuttoning and sliding off his jeans. "I don't want to do anything more without your permission."

"What—do you mean—anything *more?*" he said in between kissing her and taking off his shirt.

"Later." She sighed as he took her nipple into his mouth. "Right now I'm just glad you're here."

"Me too." He stroked her face, feeling her body against his. "I'm sorry I stopped trying." He thought about all those nights she'd come home from work late. They could have been doing this, or even just sitting on the couch with each other, but instead he had been more focused on work and video games.

"We both stopped trying," she said, dropping her head to kiss his chest. "Or at least, I didn't have the energy to keep trying for both of us."

He traced a finger down her spine, cupping the curve of her ass. "But we're okay now, right?"

She nodded, tears in her eyes. "I guess, before today, it never dawned on me that one day you might not be around. Then, when that bomb went off . . . I realized I couldn't live in a world without you."

"I am pretty irresistible," Joel[2] admitted. He moved his wife onto her back, skin pressing on skin as he kissed her intensely.

"You don't understand, Joel!" she said, pushing against his chest. "What I did, it was—"

He silenced her with his mouth, his hands squeezing her breasts. "I don't understand a lot of things," he said, his tongue tasting her shoulder, her neck, her belly. "But I'm glad to be here. With you."

She took his face in her hands. "You sure you're—okay?"

He braced himself above her, his arms shaking only slightly. "Let's find out."

Neither one of them was very good with expressing their thoughts and emotions, but what they couldn't say in words, they expressed with their bodies, rekindling a flame that had almost been extinguished.

The RV woke them up a few hours later when it announced their imminent arrival at the Hotel Heliconia, high in the mountains of Costa Rica, and one of the few places that still accepted physical currency. Sylvia hoped it would allow them a night or two without detection while she waited to hear from Pema.

A light rain began to trickle as they neared the resort. Before long, the skies opened up, rain falling down so hard, they could hardly see anything outside the window of the RV.

"Come on, we're here!" Sylvia nudged Joel[2].

He peered out the window. A small wooden sign pointed the way up to the resort, at the top of a steep staircase. "I thought we were staying where we went on our honeymoon."

"This place is better." She nudged him with her shoulder. "More secluded. Almost impossible to find."

"Can't we just wait out the rain in here? Hell, I bet this thing is bigger than our hotel room."

"I doubt that," Sylvia said. "We splurged on the room, too. It's the only one they had left."

"*We?*"

She laughed. "Yes, me, the *royal we.*"

Joel[2] was pleased to find he was feeling much more sprightly as they headed up the steep hill-cut stairs leading to the hotel lobby. He had forgotten that everything in this part of Costa Rica was hilly. They were above the clouds, after all. When they reached the hill's crest, they were drenched to the bone. Just

then, the rain dissipated, as if mocking them. The clouds parted, revealing a brilliant nightscape of jungle forest below them,
illuminated by a giant half circle of a moon. Puffs of white fog
were ribboned throughout the trees. Joel[2] put his arm around
Sylvia. The two of them drank in the moment, so different and
isolated from the vertical urban crowding of New York City.

They turned to the hotel. It was a collection of twenty or
so wood cabins, each with an outdoor hot tub and privacy
screens composed of dense jungle vegetation. Pergolas covered
in flowering bougainvillea framed each doorway. The lobby
was located in the closest and largest building, which had a
small restaurant and bar attached. Joel[2] knocked on the door's
glass window.

"Anyone there?" Sylvia asked from behind him.

He found a button under a snarl of bougainvillea vines
and pushed it. There was a loud buzz, then the door opened
with a click. They entered as the proprietor stepped in from
her private quarters. She was a pleasant, thickset Costa Rican
woman whose brown cheeks were mottled with dark-brown
birthmarks. She introduced herself as Josephine.

After Sylvia forked over a stack of international all-purpose
chits and Josephine examined them to her satisfaction, she informed them they were in the Suite Principal. It was the biggest
cottage they had, and built on a cliff that overlooked the cloud
forest. She added that breakfast and dinner were served during
one-hour blocks in the main cottage, but the bar was always
open. As a welcome gift, she handed Joel[2] a bottle of Costa
Rican wine, an amarone made by local Quakers, but warned
him not to drink it.

"This is better as a souvenir than to drink," she said, amused
with herself. "Quaker wines are not very good. Keep this, give it
to your friends when you go home. If you want wine to *drink*,
we have a nice selection of Chilean and Argentinian Malbecs in

the restaurant." She followed this with directions to their room, wishing them a good night—with one last caveat: "It gets cold at night, so cover up!"

There were even more steps up to their room. For Joel², the climb was particularly brutal, as he had been tasked with carrying Sylvia's bag. This he had nicknamed M'Bob, or Magical Bag of Bricks, for the unreal amount of heavy items she'd managed to cram inside it.

Their cabin door sensed their presence as they arrived. It unlocked and welcomed them with a warm *"¡Bienvenido!"*

"Carry me in?" Sylvia asked, mischief in her eyes.

Joel² obliged, but not without a good amount of grunting and groaning. Once they were inside, Sylvia playfully swatted him.

The room was chilly but large. The walls and ceiling beams were made of teak. There were big windows on every wall, a kitchenette, a deck with what would be an impressive view during the day, an outdoor hot tub, and a lumpy king-sized bed. A garland of violet bougainvillea flowers had been laid across their pillows.

Joel² picked up the vine and set it aside. "Hopefully this wasn't full of spider eggs. I think I'm gonna go wash the near-death experience off me. Wanna join?"

"I've had enough near-death today. But if you hurry, you might get lucky again before I pass out. We've got a lot of hiking to get in tomorrow."

Joel² pretended to sprint to the bathroom for Sylvia's amusement. He was feeling good. Better than ever. Once the warm water hit him, he began to relax. He decided to allow himself a bit of 1980s New Wave. He resumed the mix he'd paused earlier on his comms, throwing the audio over to the bathroom's speaker system. The sound of Kim Carnes's "Bette Davis Eyes" filled the room, the humidity accentuating her sultry voice.

Had he not started singing along, he might have heard the unmistakable rumble of a people-mover flying in at low altitude and close proximity. The whistle of its turbines would have alerted him that it was landing nearby. People-movers were jet-copter hybrid drones. Most were built for rapid transport rather than comfort. They were gargantuan flying pressurized graphite-titanium mesh containers designed to quickly transport hundreds of people from one place to another. Because of their size, they were never licensed for urban transport, and they legally could not operate within 150 meters of any populated area. Joel^2 would have known such a drone landing so close to an occupied hotel was likely running afoul of all legal operational boundaries. Whoever was inside must be dealing with some kind of major emergency.

But Joel^2 was too preoccupied with singing to notice any of this. He jumped in to accompany Kim Carnes:

She'll expose you
When she snows you
'She knows you
*She's got Bette Davis eye*s

Such a good song. When it was finished, he played a few more choice selections from his playlist. Finally, when his fingers started getting pruny, he informed the shower he was done. The room was as wet and steamy as a sauna, which was just the way he liked it. Sylvia was none too pleased whenever he took his shower before hers back home.

Joel^2 grabbed one of the two towels from the heating rack above the toilet and wrapped it around his waist. Was it his imagination, or had the nanites improved his muscle tone? Did that usually happen at hospitals? He decided to emerge from the bathroom, surrounded by steam like Feyd-Rautha in *Dune*, and show off his new physique with a nod to her earlier question: "You think you can handle *this*?"

He burst out, dropping his towel and flexing his muscles. "You think you can—" he began, but stopped short.

A man he did not recognize was standing beside his obviously distraught wife. He was paunchy, sweat-stained, and balding. Sylvia was crying again, only now it was clearly from fear. Joel[2] bent down to pick up the towel and wrapped it securely around his waist, trying to look as commanding as one could after accidentally exposing oneself.

"Who the fuck are you?" he said.

"Just look at you," said the man, eying Joel[2] up and down with an odd relish. "Sprung fully formed from Sylvia's terrarium. A pleasure to make your acquaintance. Bill Taraval, International Transport."

TAINTED LOVE

THE PEOPLE-MOVER that Joel^2 didn't hear land outside was capable of carrying nearly two hundred passengers. Yet that particular drone only had one occupant: William Taraval. While Joel^2 was hanging out with Kim Carnes in the shower, Taraval huffed and puffed his way up the many flights of stairs until he reached the Suite Principal. After taking a moment to catch his breath, he knocked.

Sylvia answered, folding her arms around herself when she saw her sweating boss. When she didn't invite him in, he stepped past her anyway.

"Not an easy place to get to," Taraval grumbled, going to the kitchenette and getting a bottle of water from the refrigerator.

"I suppose you're here to fire me," she said morosely. "I was hoping I'd have a little more time to—"

"Explain?" he asked, looking around the room in distaste. "Explain what—why you turned off your comms? Why you fled the scene of a major terrorist attack? Why you illegally restored and printed your husband from a backup in a classified, still-experimental glacier instance?" He spoke coolly, but she could tell he was furious from the way his right eyelid ticked uncontrollably.

"You know why I did that," she said defiantly. "Once I saw what happened at the TC, I—I did what I had to. I didn't have a choice."

"All heart and no brains. How unlike you." She opened her mouth to defend herself, but Taraval kept going. "Did you think to check with New York first? With us? Perhaps suss out what the situation was before going straight to Honeycomb? We have protocols for a *reason*."

"I couldn't; the comms were down. And he'd already"—her face went pale—"he arrived in San José. He was in the vestibule when the TC exploded."

Taraval finished his bottle of water and wiped his forehead. "Part of him, yes. Only he was never cleared in New York."

Now her cheeks turned a chalky yellow. She put her hands on the bed to steady herself, trying to form words but no sound came out.

Taraval continued, "You know the procedures, Sylvia, better than almost anyone. If there's any kind of error at the vestibule, any at all, the process reverts. But as I said, apparently you're all heart. And that sentimental blood pump of yours is about to ruin everything we've sweated and slaved for. Our careers. The future of humanity, Sylvia."

She shook her head, trying to get her thoughts in order. She nodded toward the bathroom, in which Joel[2] was singing. "So he—and in New York, there's—?"

"I'm afraid so. You're quite the scientific groundbreaker today. Resurrecting the dead and releasing the first duplicated human into the wild, all in less than twenty-four hours."

Sylvia sank to the floor. "Oh my God."

"Oh, please. What need have we for God anymore? If anyone, you should be praying to *me*. Once I learned of your foolish blunder with Honeycomb, I managed to get your husband to IT headquarters. The plan was to clear the out-of-sync Joel and—"

"You killed him?" Sylvia said, looking up from the floor, her eyes blazing.

"That was the *plan*. But somehow legal got wind of his existence and they alerted the executive leadership team. Things needed to be dealt with by the book. Corina and Pema insisted we *convince* him to go gentle into that good night. We were forced to tell him what occurred, and, for all our good deeds, unfortunately, somehow, he managed to elude us."

"He's alive?" said Sylvia, getting back to her feet.

"Alive and running around without comms. Capable at any moment of exposing us. And therein lies your saving grace. We can still make this right."

"What are you talking about, Bill?"

"It's simple. You take your little creation in there, drive him back to the San José Hospital TC, teleport to New York, and IT will take care of the rest. You'll arrive alone, Joel Byram's comms will reactivate, and all of us shall live happily ever after, provided you both agree to put this matter behind us."

"Bill," she said, struggling to stay calm, "you're asking me to clear my own husband."

He pointed a fleshy finger toward the bathroom, in which Joel[2] was still singing loudly and off-key. "*That* is not your husband, Sylvia! Your husband is somewhere in New York right now. He can't have gone far without working comms. What do you think will happen if the Gehinnomites find him first? Imagine for a moment a world in which the public knows the truth of what we've been doing. Of what you have been complicit in. Tell me how that story ends, Sylvia. Tell me!"

"I didn't mean—" she began, but he didn't let her finish.

"It ends one of two ways, Sylvia. Either you come back to New York with him in tow, or everything we know, perhaps our entire society, unravels. This is the best and least painful solution we have. *Clear him.* Life will return to normal for all immediately—and for you as well, in time."

"Normal," she repeated with a hollow laugh. Then she shook her head, tears springing to her eyes. "You can't make me do this, Bill. I've already been lying to him for a year, I can't—" She put her face in her hands just as Joel[2] entered from the bathroom and exposed himself.

TAKE ON ME

SOON AFTER Sylvia got her promotion at IT, we moved to our new apartment in Greenwich Village. Her first few weeks in her new executive-level status were filled with orientations and legal briefings and late-night welcoming cabals to which I wasn't invited. She'd been distant and preoccupied. Grappling with the new stresses of her job, I thought. Unpacking boxes was meant to be our first bit of quality time since she'd started the new gig. But still, she was distracted.

I came back from unpacking various artsy trinkets in the bedroom to find her staring at her matryoshka doll—one of those Russian doll-within-a-doll-within-a-doll toys. Each one had the same shiny red dress with a black polka-dot pattern on it. She was toying with the dolls, putting them side by side, then nesting them within one another.

"Can we play with the dolls later, babe?" I asked with my typical flair for completely misreading the mood of a room. "These boxes ain't gonna unpack themselves."

She didn't even look up when I spoke. She just continued to methodically line up each of the dolls on the windowsill in order from largest to smallest. When she got to the final tiny doll—remarkably the size of a grain of rice—she paused, sat down on the floor, and placed it in the palm of her hand. There was something profoundly sad about her actions. She rubbed the tiny doll with her finger and looked up at me, tears in her eyes.

"Syl? What's wrong?" I gently asked.

"There's something I never told you, Joel." She didn't immediately offer additional information and I knew better than to ask, but the pain in her eyes was killing me.

I sat down beside her and took the tiny rice kernel doll from her hand. "What is it, babe?" I gently rubbed her back.

She sat for a moment, tracing her finger along the other dolls, comparing their size. "At what point is a life a life?" she finally asked. "Look at these dolls. They're all the same, right? I mean, aside from their size. Do all of them together make one whole doll, or do you think each one represents a different stage in life? And that tiny one"—she pointed at the smallest doll I was still holding—"is that supposed to represent conception, like the first divided cell of an embryo, or death, like a grain of ash in the wind?"

I wasn't sure what had brought on these deep philosophical questions, so rather than answer, I remained silent—giving her the moment to contend with her thoughts. This wasn't our first place together, so I reckoned she wasn't having fear of cohabitation. Something else was eating at her. She gently nested the dolls together again before turning her attention back to me, taking a deep breath before speaking.

"I had an abortion, Joel."

I was rendered speechless. Before I could formulate a response, she continued on. "It was during sophomore year, before I met you. I had too much to drink at a party. I ran into an old boyfriend, and one thing led to another. I was on birth control. Nothing's a hundred percent, I guess. About a month later, I realized I was pregnant. Keeping it was never an option.

I had career plans, and my dad wasn't doing well, so I . . ." She paused and looked at me. I couldn't tell if she was trying to read my reaction or expecting me to react. "I'm sorry I never told you."

"Wow. I don't really know what to say. Are you okay? That came out wrong. I mean, I really don't know how to respond."

"Yeah, I'm okay. I definitely don't regret my decision. That's not it. I still feel like it was the right thing for me to do—"

"Syl, what's going on?"

She shrugged, wiping a tear from her eye. "Work stress? I don't know. I'm having to deal with some big decisions, stuff I can't really get into. And there's this part of me that always remembers, that always questions the what-if of what I did, and I guess the moral implications. I did it so early, Joel, that it was no bigger than this grain of rice." She held up the tiniest doll for me to see again. "It was really just a cluster of cells." She paused, looking down at it. "But I guess I'll always wonder, if I'd waited longer—would I have made the same choice?"

Tears began to run down her face. I pulled her into my arms. Seeing my wife in pain was harder than anything I could ever endure. "I love you, Syl. You made the right choice."

"Thank you," she whispered as she buried her head into my shoulder.

"I'm sorry."

"'I don't believe in apologies; I believe in actions,'" she said, then wiped her face and gave me a kiss. "Let's get back to unpacking. This doll's not pulling its weight." She smiled, then we kissed again.

Joel[2] didn't remember any of this as he came out of the bathroom in his birthday suit, but it seems pertinent to include now. I would learn later that that was the day Sylvia had been briefed on the truth behind teleportation—that it was a process of replication and destruction—but she was forbidden from discussing it with me. I can't imagine what it must have been like for her, to carry around that kind of toxic secret for nearly a year. And now William Taraval stood before her in Costa Rica, demanding she abort her husband. She was shaken, barely able to look at my unfortunate doppelgänger.

"We were just talking about you, my boy," Taraval said after Joel² failed to respond to his introduction. "My apologies for the interruption, but I'm afraid with the terrorist attack on IT, Sylvia must return to New York. Desperate times, measures, you understand."

Joel² turned to Sylvia and asked, "This is your"—he left out the *jerk*—"boss?"

Sylvia shook her head, still unable to acknowledge her husband.

"Quite right. I run research and development at International Transport. Sylvia is the principal scientist on my team. Which is why we need her back. To help clean up this . . . mess. I have transportation ready to take us to San José, but it's late and I can see you've had a long day. Perhaps first thing tomorrow? What do you say, Sylvia?"

She ran to the bathroom, slamming the door shut.

Joel² ran to check on her. "Syl? You okay?"

Heaves, coughs, and whimpers were all he could hear.

"Yes, well, unfortunately I was the bearer of some bad news," Taraval continued, moving to the door. "Some of our peers perished in the explosion. I can't tell you what a relief it was to learn Sylvia wasn't among them."

"Well, she's doing *great* now!" Joel² said sarcastically. "Thanks a lot for that."

"Yes, it seems she has taken their deaths more viscerally than anticipated. Still, there remain other matters of life and death, with which we need her assistance. I truly hope you two can salvage your holiday some other time. First thing tomorrow, then!" he called toward the bathroom door, then started down the stairs.

"¡Hasta luego!" chimed the door behind him.

Joel[2], still scantily clad in his towel, went back to tap on the bathroom door. The wind outside had picked up and could be heard rustling the tree branches. He sat down on the floor beside the bathroom, his back leaning against the wall.

Eventually Sylvia opened the bathroom door and pensively sat beside Joel[2], sniffling. He put his arm around her, kissing the top of her head. She smelled of soap and mouthwash.

"Syl, I'm so sorry about your friends."

"No, I'm sorry," she said. Her body was shaking or shivering, he couldn't tell. "I did something really bad, Joel."

"A bunch of crazies who think teleportation is the devil blew up a bunch of people to prove their point. Is what you did worse than that?"

"I don't know," she said, finally looking into his eyes. "I honestly don't know. When *it* happened earlier today, I couldn't bear the thought of losing you. I panicked. I—I couldn't reveal what I was working on, not specifically, but I told you the basics last week at the Mandolin—extending the range of teleportation, exploring outer space, that kind of thing?"

Joel[2] blinked. "That wasn't a drunken hypothetical?"

"No. The thing I'm working on, Project Honeycomb—really it's just an evolution of the Punch Escrow. But I never thought—" She stopped talking and just sort of gazed forward.

"Never thought what?" Joel[2] gently prodded.

"When Corina Shafer invented the Punch Escrow, it was a fail-safe feature. She knew that the biggest risk of teleportation was data loss or corruption. The Punch Escrow was brilliant, if only for its simplicity: an ephemeral cache of the thing being teleported."

"That's the four-second time delay?"

"Sort of," she said, now averting her gaze. "The glacier storage costs for a single scan of a teleported human—twenty years ago they were astronomical. After each punch, successful or not, the . . . data needed to be cleared immediately to get ready for the next object. Honeycomb is a project that investigates the use of a *backup* instead of a cache. It's the only way we could initially send people to a planet in another solar system, for example. Humans wouldn't survive the flight, and even if we put them in torpor, the mortality rates go through the roof. The probability of something going wrong in transit and killing the crew increases exponentially with time, making such missions untenable. But if we didn't have to worry about hundreds of years of life support, if we could just put a TC on a spacecraft, then—"

"So you just keep the astronauts in the glacier until the craft arrives. And then, what—you print them out like a hamburger or a cup of coffee? God, Sylvia—this is some pretty messed-up shit you've been working on."

"Think of what we could do though, Joel. Imagine if we could send a self-contained TC, like a glacier in a box on a space probe, and it could spend as long as necessary hunting for habitable planets. Once we found one, we could put an entire team of explorers or colonists onto that planet immediately. That kind of stuff could ensure the survival of the human race even if Earth is a barren rock. Even if we ourselves will have been dead for centuries!"

Perhaps the word made him ponder his own near-death experience, I don't know. Or maybe it was the nurse's parting comment combined with the way Sylvia had been treating him, as if he were made of glass. Maybe, on some deep molecular level, he just knew.

"Is that . . . what you did to me?" he asked, uncertainty dotting his voice.

She didn't speak. Didn't look him in the eye.

He hesitated. "Did I . . . die?"

Sylvia closed her eyes, and lowered her head onto his shoulder. "I . . . restored you from the Honeycomb backup. But it was missing your comms and some stuff around those areas. I told the nurses you were injured in the blast, so the hospital—the doctors, they filled in the gaps."

I don't know exactly what he was thinking. But since he was me, and I'd been through a similar situation with Corina and co., I can make a pretty good guess. Joel² was confused and angry and grappling with some pretty unique existential issues. But somehow, in that moment, he rose above it. I'm not sure I could have. I guess he understood that what she'd done, she'd done for love.

Joel² took his wife's face in his hands. He looked deeply into her eyes. "I want you to listen to me right now, Sylvia. I am here. Me. Your husband. Whatever happened today, I can't imagine life without you." He pressed his forehead to hers. "You know what I remember from that *Star Trek* discussion?"

She shook her head, half laughing and half crying.

"Kirk and Uhura. I had my epiphany a long time ago, Mrs. Sylvia Byram." Joel² kissed her. "I love *you*. I'm not going anywhere."

Their kiss wasn't passionate; it was desperate. He wanted her to know he was her husband. That he was, body and mind, every bit the man she had married. He needed her to be absolutely, vehemently *sure*—because if she was, then he might believe it, too.

THE FIRST
NOBLE TRUTH

SHORTLY AFTER DAWN, Joel[2] woke up alone in bed. It was July Fourth, the ceremonial celebration of American independence and, more important for the world at large, the day the Last War[21] ended.

[21] I was born in the post-war era, as I imagine a lot of folks have said throughout different periods, but I've seen a lot of historical streams. Enough to know that the Last War, known as Yawm al-Qiyāmah in the Levant, was started by people who believed that building a Third Temple in Jerusalem would trigger the revelatory chain of the appearance of an Antichrist, a political leader of a transnational alliance who would secure a peace treaty among all nations. This Antichrist would then use the temple as a venue for proclaiming himself as God and the long-awaited Messiah, demanding worship from humanity. And so, the masterminds of the Last War sanctioned a religious sect known as the Third Temple Architects to manifest their beliefs into reality. At the cost of so many innocent lives, they saw to the destruction of the Al-Aqsa Mosque and the building of the Third Temple on its site. The fools believed that resurrection would happen within their lifetime, that they could somehow accelerate or play a part in the apocalypse. In many ways their war led to today's enduring peace, the downfall of nation-states, and the rise of corporate rule by the people for the people, and the unification of the three religions. So some good came of it, I suppose. The Third Temple Architects would never enjoy the fruits of their labor, though—they were all rewarded with public executions.

In case it's been edited or filtered out of human history, you should know the Last War began in 2074. It was started by a group of folks calling themselves the Architects, whose stated goal was to be raptured into heaven by bringing about Armageddon. Seems convoluted, but they were taking their cues from various religious doctrines. Others among them just wanted a war to reboot a world economy that had almost entirely been taken over by automation. When the Architects tried to erect a Third Temple in Jerusalem, it catalyzed a global conflict that went on for twenty-two years and killed 10 percent of the population. It was so devastating, it forever altered how people viewed themselves and their forms of government.

So, in 2098, the world decided that corporations would do a better job running things than traditional politicians. This led to the elimination of borders and the establishment of a new, truly global economy. Costs of things were based on algorithms of supply, demand, and value to the purchaser. Infrastructure, federal institutions, and the legal system were all privatized. Minimum basic needs were created and provided for everyone free of charge. That way, the corps reckoned, nothing would be out of reach for anyone. The rich could still be rich, but things like food and shelter would always be available.

The Levant, a region spanning from Turkey to Iran, was the only holdout. The only nation to eschew corporate rule not just for "classical" government but theocracy. A theocracy of peace, built on the fundamentals of the three religions (Judaism, Christianity, Islam). The three religions all agreed to cast aside the embellishments of testaments and prophecies, and focus on the crux of each faith, then bind themselves under a single philosophical umbrella. Any group trying to break off as a different faction would be excommunicated and deported. The Levant were not fundamentalists. They believed in progress and technology. But above all, they believed that God was real and all were bound to abide by him.

July Fourth, the day the Last War ended, was now a day of peace and remembrance throughout the world. A holiday created to recognize how close the human race had come to extinction, and how far we had progressed since then. Also, there was always a gratuitously huge fireworks celebration in memoriam.

As Joel^2 woke on that day, he felt as though he had a new lease on life. Yesterday he could have been dead, asleep forever. Now he had a second chance. He vowed to make the most of it. Starting right now.

"Sylvia?" he called out, but no answer came.

Did she go for a walk outside? he wondered. He got out of bed, stretched, and went to the front door. It silently swung open for him. It was clear and sunny outside, the light sparkling off the fresh raindrops coating the vegetation.

She muted the door. Maybe she just didn't want to wake me.

"Syl?" he called into the cloud forest. Nothing.

At least the view was spectacular. The lush canopy below was interspersed with fluffy clouds. The forest was alive with monkey howls and quetzal calls. He scanned the parking lot below, but there was no sign of their rented RV or Taraval's people-mover. The gravel lot was empty.

He tried her on the comms with no success.

"Huh," Joel^2 pondered aloud.

He commed Julie. "Hey, did you hear anything from Sylvia lately?"

Her avatar made an animated *Hmmm* face. "Yes, this morning she checked in."

"Did she send any messages?"

"Just one."

"To who? What was it about?"

"Joel, you know I can't tell you that. It's confidential."

"Jules, it's an emergency! She disappeared sometime between last night and this morning. Our RV's gone, too. I think she might be in some kind of trouble with IT."

"Oh my gosh, that's terrible! But, Joel, you know I can only divulge personal information to my owner."

"Fine! If something happens to her, then it's on your head, Jules. I hope you can *live* with that."

"That's not fair, Joel. You know I can't give you access to that kind of stuff, even in the event of an emergency, without prior approval or court order."

"So it wasn't a personal message? Because you do have to divulge personal details in the event of a medical emergency."

"You're right. But her comms indicate it's not medical."

"So she messaged someone in IT?"

"Yes. But that's all I can say, and even that is a stretch. Fortunately, you figured it out on your own."

"Look, I need you to give Sylvia a message from me when she comes back online," Joel² said.

"Of course."

"Tell her that I love her. Tell her I understand why she did what she did, and that no matter what happens, we'll get through this."

"I will. I'll tell her. That's a very sweet message. It's unlike you."

"Weird," Joel² uttered.

"It's not weird. It's nice," said Julie.

"No. I mean, this is weird. I just got a notification that Sylvia is in *The Cave of Time*." He tried pinging his wife, but got no response. "I gotta go."

"Okay, keep me updated. If you need any help, I'm here."

"Yeah, because you've been so helpful already," he muttered sarcastically and hung up.

Is she at work? Did she go back to New York without me? he wondered while opening the app.

The Cave of Time was the first title published in the Choose Your Own Adventure book series, which debuted in 1979. In it, the player could travel to several iconic time periods via a desert cave. Like every book in the series, it was an interactive story, letting the reader decide where the narrative went next by selecting from a number of options. Roughly half the choices led to the main character's death. There were several other endings as well, but only one "best" ending.

In the year 2103, a team of cognitive neuroscientists and gaming technology experts created a psychoanalytical game based on *The Cave of Time*. The virtual reality game let players engage in iconic moments of the past, in the context of a choose-your-own-adventure scenario. The choices people made could be used to determine a player's mental state and whether they suffered from any psychological irregularities.

Eventually, the game crossed over into the mainstream. People began to modify and record their virtual travels through different eras of time. It became kind of a what-if machine that let society investigate how past choices might have played out differently. After the Last War, many attempted to play out alternate strategies and endings to the conflict in *The Cave of Time*. Soon it became common wisdom that the war would have taken place regardless of what was done in the years preceding it. The prevailing theory was that the clockwork leading to the war's advent was put into action thousands of years ago. Still, people go back in time through the caves in search of answers.

Sylvia and I liked the game for more mundane reasons. Since it could be played cooperatively, it was something we could do together, even if we weren't together. When Sylvia got promoted to her new gig at IT, the job was considered so classified that external comms were absolutely verboten. Even Julie had to be modified to ensure compliance. This, compounded with the job's long hours, made it very tough for Sylvia and me to check on each other's welfare, let alone make plans to hang out after work. But thanks to a bug I discovered in *The Cave of Time*, we could leave messages for each other in a game location called Mr. Nelson's Print Shop. Mostly it was stuff like, *Starving for pizza. Meet at Alfred's for lunch.* These messages would synchronize between our instances of the game due to a sync glitch. Since the shop would respawn once we both disconnected, there was no evidence of our transgressions. It wasn't ideal, but it was something.

The Cave of Time start screen appeared. *What is she doing?* Joel[2] wondered as the intro music began.

A voice boomed, "Welcome, Billy Missile!" My gamer tag. It continued, "You've hiked through Snake Canyon once before while visiting your uncle Howard at Red Creek Ranch, but you never noticed any cave entrance. It looks as though a recent rockslide has uncovered it."

Joel[2] stood in a scrubby, bright Arizona desert. There was indeed a cave entrance off to his right. The orange Sun was setting behind the hill. Unless you were restoring a saved game, you never had the option of skipping the intro. The game forced him to enter the cave.

Inside was total darkness. Quickly, Joel[2] navigated past the various tunnels, his path lit by phosphorescent material on the cave walls. He made sure not to fall in the occasional crevasse along the way, staying to the route he had memorized: *Right/ Right/Down/Down/Down/Down/Left/Up.* As he exited the cave, a bright light transitioned him into the next location.

It was an eighteenth-century Philadelphia print shop, the kind in which Ben Franklin had worked. This one, supposedly, had been a popular spot for distributing American revolutionary pamphlets. A huge iron printing press stood against one wall, surrounded by wooden bins of individual metal letters, barrels of ink, and big round rolls of paper. The sounds of merchants and carriages going past could be heard faintly outside.

Joel[2] jogged through the print shop, past the huge press and to the writing table. The familiar feather quill was not in its ink bottle, but on the floor. *Sylvia was here!* He flipped through the cotton papers. On the fourth sheet was her message:

Gehinnomites kidnapped me. Somehow they disabled my comms. I'm here. The last two words had been highlighted as a link. He read the rest.

DO NOT come alone! Get in touch with Bill Taraval. Tell him they know about Honeycomb. He'll know what to do. I love y—

Something must have caused her to log off prematurely.

Joel[2] logged off as well, frantically summoning the only kind of transport he could find on the local ride boards. In our time, nobody owned cars unless they were super rich and eccentric. If you needed to get somewhere, car dealers simply leased you a car for the duration of time you needed it, and when you reached your destination, the vehicle drove away. Some people paid premiums for specific models or brand names, but it was still cheaper to get those on demand than it was to buy one outright.

His transportation sorted, Joel[2] threw on some new clothes, stuffed some chits into his pockets, and jogged down the steps to the parking lot. A high-pitched hum came from the bottom of the hill as a white Carryall Club Car golf cart wound its way toward him. Upon reaching the top, it parked itself in front of Joel[2].

"*¡Buenos días, señor!*" it boomed in a warm Spanish accent. "*¿Adónde vas?*"

"Take me here," Joel[2] said, copying Sylvia's GDS location to the cart with a hand gesture. "And hurry."

"With pleasure," said the vehicle, smoothly switching to English. *Hurry* meant that the cart would actively pay the occupants of other vehicles on the road to prioritize Joel[2]'s route above theirs. It worked like an auction system, in which everyone could bid on getting to their destination as soon as they wanted. It could become incredibly expensive, but Joel[2] no longer cared much about money. The bastards who had actually killed him had now taken his wife. The woman who'd brought him back. He wasn't a fighter, but he would find a way to get her out alive.

He almost fell out of his seat as the cart took off faster than he'd anticipated. While tightening his grip on the roll bar, he considered trying to locate Bill Taraval on the comms. He decided it would be a bad idea, judging by their interactions thus far. Joel[2] didn't particularly trust the man, or anyone from IT, for that matter. That meant he also couldn't trust the cops, since all of them were owned by the corporations.

Thus, my synthesized double found himself in a golf cart wending its way through the maze of tiny mountain roads in Santa Elena, barreling toward an unknown destination. Joel[2] had many questions and no one to whom he could pose them. The clouds obscured the Sun, the wind picked up, and the temperature seemed to fall off a cliff. His body began inadvertently shivering from the cold of the journey, and from fear of what he'd find upon arrival. But there was no turning back. He had to reach Sylvia.

DOCTOR! DOCTOR!

I AWOKE ON THE FLOOR of the LAST Agency conference room. My previous headache was now compounded by a brand-new one. Keeping my eyes closed, I felt around on my scalp until I found a tender lump where my head had struck the floor. At least someone had thought to put a pillow underneath my skull as I slept.

I sat up, groaning as most of my muscles filed complaints with my brain. Ifrit turned to me from her spot at the table, her gentle, concerned, blue-gray eyes putting me a bit at ease. "What happened?"

She spoke softly, as if I had a hangover. It sure felt like I did. "You fainted."

"How long was I out?"

"About eight hours. For you, it is tomorrow. Around five a.m. on Tuesday, July fourth. We gave you a little sedative to make you sleep." She came over to help me up.

A little sedative? Feels like a people-mover landed on my head. "I don't need sleep; I need to get my comms working and talk to my wife."

Ifrit nodded, handing me a cup of clear liquid.

I sipped from the cup, then spit the liquid out in disgust. "*Ack!* That's not water."

"Drink, drink! You need it."

"More drugs?" I asked. Still, I'd do anything to make the headache go away. I took another tentative sip. "This tastes like ass juice."

"It is medicine. It will make you feel better. You are hurt and dehydrated."

"Ugh," I said, but painfully gulped the swill down and handed the empty cup back to her. "That shit is more metal than water, you know?"

Ifrit smiled. "Good boy. Now here, eat some bread; it will help settle your stomach." She handed me a couple of pieces of rye bread.

My mouth already tasted like tinfoil from the nano juice. Chewing on the rye bread made me feel like I had a mixture of toxic cement in my mouth, but since my body was starting to feel better, I did as I was told.

After I'd consumed both slices of bread, Ifrit handed me a glass of water, which I chugged instantly and handed back to her.

"More please."

She walked over to the printer to refill my glass. My head had started to clear up, making room for the millions of questions emerging from beneath the fog. "So where is everyone?" I said.

"As it is still early, Moti and Zaki are in their homes, but I have commed them. They will be here soon. Moti, he believes your story. This is very important. He is usually right about people."

Just then the wall parted and Moti walked in, knotting a new tie around his neck. He looked very serious, but thus far he'd always looked serious. Zaki followed behind him, the antique clipboard and pencil in hand.

"Where is Sylvia?" I demanded.

Moti leisurely sat across from me and tsk-tsked. "*Yoel*, you have stepped into something much bigger than yourself. We are Levantine Intelligence. We are posted here to monitor International Transport." He grabbed a cigarette and lit it. "My superiors are very interested in your situation."

"So you'll help me?"

"Right now we are monitoring the situation in Costa Rica."

"You mean, the other me? So they're okay?"

"For now. But, *Yoel*, you must start coming to terms that it is *you* who are the other *him*." He took a pull off his cigarette. "Right now keeping both of you alive is a strategic advantage for us."

"You make it sound like I'm a pawn," I said.

"Don't be so dramatic, *Yoel*. You are not a pawn." He allowed himself a razor-thin smile. "More like a bishop. Yes. There are only two of you, moving diagonally." He seemed pleased with his simile.

"So that's your plan? To monitor the situation?" I asked, making sure to imply what I thought of his tactics.

"Yes," he said, refusing to take the bait.

"Okay. You stay here and monitor. I'm gonna go and make sure my wife is safe." I stood up to show him I was serious. Zaki took a step forward.

Moti regarded his cigarette. "That I would not recommend. The first step outside of this office will probably be your last. They will kill you, *Yoel*, and nobody will know or care. A small bite from an unseen nano, and you are out like a light. Then, a man you never saw coming drags you into a drone. He straps you into one of their chairs, and you disappear."

"What about Sylvia? And *him*? If IT is willing to murder people to cover this up, then they're both in danger. At least let's call the cops."

"They own the police, *Yoel*. You know this. And you are not a warrior." He stared at me, his dark eyes betraying no emotion. "You should be a *Job*, not an *Aher*."

"Job? Aher? What the hell are you talking about?"

"*Café?*" he asked me.

"No, thanks."

He shrugged, walking over to the printer. "It is an old story. From a book called the Talmud. About a rabbi called the Aher. That wasn't his real name. I think it was Elijah—"

"Elisha. Elisha ben Abuyah," Ifrit interrupted him.

"Yes, thank you, Ifrit," said Moti in a tone that I interpreted to mean *Don't fucking interrupt me again.* "He was like the opposite of Job. You know Job? From the Bible?"

I nodded. "Bad things happen to good people."

"Yes, exactly. Bad things happen to good people. So, you know, Job was this guy God just kept kicking. He killed his kids, covered him in boils . . . many bad things he did to him. But Job, he keeps his faith in God, and eventually God rewards him with new kids, lots of gold, all that. But Elisha, he was this very well-respected rabbi, a really big man in his community, and then bad things happen to him. So he starts to question *why* God would do bad things to good people. And, as if in answer, the Romans killed his mentor, this even more holy rabbi. The soldiers, they sliced his head off right in front of Elisha. Fed his tongue to a dog. The thought of that, it gave me bad dreams as a kid."

"So you're saying you're God now? That I should just wait here and suffer until my wife dies and you reward me?"

He shrugged and continued his story, "Anyway, Elisha, he's watching all of this, and he just goes crazy. He loses his religion.

His mantra becomes something like, *There is no justice; there is no judge*. So he starts disobeying all the rules. He sleeps with a prostitute on Shabbat, tells kids to get jobs instead of study the Torah, pisses everyone off. Eventually, he even pissed off God. So the people stop calling him Elisha. They say he's not the same person, that he's someone else—an *Aher*. So that became his name. They blame him for all sorts of stuff, like getting angels kicked out of the garden of Eden, things like that."

"I also heard that after he died, his grave caught on fire, and smoke rose from his grave for a hundred years," said Ifrit. "My father told me Aher used spells from *Sepher Ha-Razim*. Old Levant magic, you know, Kabbalah stuff. Like the Pulsa D'nura. We are not allowed to pray that something bad should happen to another person. My father always told me God made an example out of Aher. That we break the rules at our peril."

"Well, I didn't break shit," I said. "They did, with their teleportation-replication-clearing-people bullshit. I just want my life back. I want to find my wife. I don't want to be anybody's Aher or Job or *ayah* or whatever-the-fuck."

Ifrit took the clipboard and pencil from Zaki, scribbled something down, and passed it to Moti.

"I agree with you, *Yoel*," said Moti after looking over what Ifrit had written. "Which is why you should be Job. Listen, I have to go for a minute. Zaki will stay with you. Do you want something to eat? Zaki, get him something to eat," he instructed on his way out. "Ifrit, come."

Ifrit glanced at me as she followed Moti out. *Is that pity in her eyes?*

Zaki pulled up the chair across the table from me and sat down. "You know, he lived a pretty good life after his breakdown, though."

I was lost in my own thoughts, wondering what was on that fucking clipboard. "Who? Job?"

"No, the Aher guy. After he quit religion, he became a—what do you call it—epicure? He went on a journey through Arab, Greek, Roman cultures. I guess knowing that paradise was off the table for him, he decided to find it on earth while he was still alive."

Zaki took out his cigarette, flipping it in his fingers. "He wasn't so different from you, *Yoel.* He was a salter. Except, you ask questions that apps can't answer, and he was asking questions that God couldn't answer. Today you are rewarded for asking your questions, they call you a salter, and they pay you chits. But he, in his time, he was punished, and they took his name away, and exiled him." A brief snigger. "It's funny how the devout pretend like they want people to ask questions, but really they only want you to ask the questions that they have answers to. You ask the wrong questions, things they don't want to answer, they get mad. But apps, they *want* you to ask the wrong questions—they don't want questions they can answer. It's very interesting."

"That's not how it works," I countered. "Apps today are just as bad as the people in your Aher's time. They want you to ask them hard questions, but only under their conditions. If you go too far, they punish you, too. The system kicks you out. Shit, look at me now, Zaki—my comms don't work; I'm trapped in this room. I'm an exile."

Zaki nodded. "And what will you eat, Mr. Exile?" he asked, trying to change the subject.

"Not hungry," I said. "The bread was enough."

"Not hungry," he echoed, nodding. Then he resumed quietly toying with his unsmoked cigarette.

I was overcome by the desire to be somewhere else. Somewhere *safe.* I felt naked without my comms. Before, whenever depressing thoughts entered my mind, I'd distract myself with a game, or watch some stupid Darwin Awards streams, or just throw myself into work. Salting usually cheered me up because it forced me to think like a five-year-old. I got a perverse joy out of confounding the hell out of apps that probably have higher aptitudes than me. Could my enjoyment at witnessing them suffer be considered schadenfreude? I don't think so. We've formed such close bonds with our apps that people have been known to cry when their favorite apps reach end of life. Anyway, I certainly don't feel bad about it. Sitting there in my not-so-private Second Avenue conference-room-cum-purgatory suite, absent my comms, I escaped into memories.

The memory that came was of the day Sylvia and I got engaged. It was during our first real vacation together, visiting the San Francisco flotilla. Sylvia told her parents she was going to check out a school for her doctorate because she was hiding our relationship from them. I don't even know if they knew we were dating yet. Like I said, her family dynamic was meh. Since it was my first time in northern California, she took me to see Alcatraz.

Besides the remorseless commercialization of such a terrible place—in which we both partook by buying Alcatraz hoodies prior to boarding the ferry because it was freezing—there was a weird, nagging feeling I couldn't shake once I got to the island.

Why, I wondered, when they created the California flotillas back in the first decade of the 2100s, did they feel like Alcatraz was such a critical societal artifact worthy of preservation? Sylvia explained that the decision had come after the Berkeley Seismological Lab used something called a distributed acoustic Doppler to gather telemetry data collected from people's wearables—this was before everyone had implants, so they used to wear their technology—to determine with precision exactly when and where the next Big One would occur.

As a result, they had nearly half a century to prepare for the Quake of 2112.

"The denizens of California, knowing with absolute certainty that their states would largely be obliterated from the map, brought in an army of Dutch island-building engineers. They performed a budgetary analysis, informing the public that they had to choose a finite number of cities and landmarks they wanted to preserve," Sylvia told me, acting as tour guide. "Once approved, those areas were untethered from the earth and placed upon flotillas. Everything else sank into the Pacific Ocean."

I had no doubt those were hard decisions to make, but I wondered why they were worth saving at all. That's the sort of mind-set I was in. A meandering, blasé world view that I think became most pronounced later in the day when I visited one of the cells overlooking the island's dock. By then the marine layer (what San Franciscans name their bespoke variety of freezing-ass wet, windyfog) had parted and the scene was just amazing. The Sun painted the sky and the bay deep hues of orange blended with a hint of purple. From that prison cell I thought to myself, *The prisoners incarcerated here had one of the most expensive views in the city, but since they were stuck in jail, they probably hated looking out this window.*

Remembering that moment while I sat in Moti's conference room brought a shiver to my spine. I couldn't help but think that maybe those prisoners were better off than me right now. Like them, I was occupying a very expensive piece of real estate. But they, at least, had a view.

When we got back to San Francisco, Sylvia dragged me to see a *Romeo and Juliet* performance in Golden Gate Park. I'd seen the play before and felt no need to see it again, but she insisted. The marine layer had returned and the park was enveloped by rain, making for a soggy, uncomfortable evening of theater. By the time Friar Laurence gave Juliet the bottle of poison that was supposed to knock her out for a couple of days, I was antsy to leave. Still, his words came back to me verbatim:

> *"And in this borrowed likeness of shrunk death*
> *Thou shalt continue two and forty hours,*
> *And then awake as from a pleasant sleep."*

"That's the part I never got," I whispered to Sylvia.

She looked taken aback. "You don't understand why she'd be willing to fake death to be with the man she loved?"

"No, I just have a hard time with the suspension of disbelief. I mean, what kind of poison makes you a corpse for two days and then wakes you up and you're fine?"

"That's what you never got about this play?" she asked incredulously. "Are you serious?"

"Yeah."

"Belladonna," she said. I stared blankly. "Look it up on your comms. Just google 'what poison did Juliet take.'"

I looked it up. "Huh."

Sure enough, back in 1597, John Gerarde, the so-called father of modern botany, guessed that the poison Juliet swallows could have been *Atropa belladonna*, also known as "deadly nightshade." Gerarde reckoned that "a small quantity leads to madness, while a moderate amount causes a 'dead sleepe,' and too much can kill."

"And you just knew that?" I asked.

"It's who I am, Joel Byram. I know things." Her lips curled upward adorably.

And that's when I went for it. I had no plan, no placeholder ring burning a hole in my pocket. Her mouth twitched and I dropped to one knee, surprising us both.

"What are you doing?" she whispered, glancing around at the damp crowd.

Out came the words with no hesitation. "Sylvia Archer, will you marry me?"

Her eyes widened in shock. Cold moisture from the grass seeped into the knee of my pants. Her silence was killing me.

"Feel free to nod if you can't speak," I said nervously.

"Yes," Sylvia said loudly. As people turned to shush us, she grabbed me by the arm and kissed me. I tipped, falling to the wet earth and pulling her on top of me. We were probably the only couple to ever make out during that particular part of the Shakespearean tragedy, but we went for it. The audience around us clapped and wolf-whistled.

Back in the conference room, I smiled to myself. It hadn't been a traditional proposal, but Sylvia and I had never been a traditional couple. Even years later, the moment felt right to me. Now the memory of it might be all that *I* had left of my wife. Before I could go too dark with that, the wall warped and Moti and Ifrit reentered the room. "*Yoel,* I am afraid I have bad news," Moti said.

"Sylvia?" I asked, fearing the worst.

He nodded. "She has been kidnapped. Last night William Taraval showed up and briefly spoke to her and your other. Then, about two hours ago, she awoke, got in a vehicle, and was taken to a location on the other side of the mountain. You—the other you—is currently en route to her GDS location. Most likely attempting—foolishly—to rescue her by himself. Five minutes ago her comms went offline completely."

I clenched my fists. "Did you guys alert someone? I mean, is someone doing something?"

Moti nodded again. "Yes, I believe IT will intervene."

Great. "Well, *my* confidence level in IT doing the *right thing* is less than zero. Can't you guys notify the Costa Rican authorities? Or the Levantine authorities? I mean, isn't this what you fucking guys *do*?"

"*Yoel*, it's complicated. We—"

"*It's complicated?*"

Enough was enough. "I want out. Get me the fuck out of here, you hear me? I'll take my fucking chances with IT, with the Gehinnomites—I don't care. My wife is out there, off grid, and everyone is sitting around, scratching their asses." I got up and walked to the door. I tried the handle, knowing it wouldn't budge. I banged my fist against the wood. "Let me out of here!" I was tearing up, weeping, desperate to appeal to their humanity. "I have to find Sylvia, please. Let me out!"

Moti sighed, irritated by my theatrics. "*Yoel*, are you a *spy*? Are you an *action hero*? *No*. You are a salter. Out there is not a game. You go out there and you will end up dead—or *cleared*, as they say. But it is all right. I will help you."

"How?" I asked, my throat was sore from the yelling, my tone still aggravated. "How are you going to fucking help me?"

"Sit. Please." He beckoned me back to my chair. "Zaki! Two Turkish."

Zaki walked over to the printer and fetched a metallic pot of Turkish coffee and the same ornate cups and saucers as before. He motioned for me to oblige Moti.

"Fine." I said. *I've gotta find a way out of this cage. Less yelling, more thinking.*

"Do you know why Levantines are so opposed to teleportation?" Moti asked as I sat back down across from him.

"Fuck if I know. Everyone's gotta hate something?"

Moti chuckled once as Zaki poured coffee into our cups, carefully holding the pot by its wooden handle. "When I was young, I believed the Levantine embargo on teleportation was crazy. I thought my people were reverting to the black hole they were in before the Last War." A thin smile. "But then, when I started to understand the world, and especially when I joined Intelligence, I understood. Everything is about control."

Moti took a sip of his coffee. "We have known this *Punch Escrow* was a lie for some time. This information has been valuable to keeping IT in check. As we have watched International Transport become more and more powerful and less and less careful, we knew a duplication incident was inevitable. But until now, they have not attempted to intervene in the running of the world, so we did not interfere. We have a saying, 'Do not collect a toll from a man who does not pass through your gate.'"

"So the whole religious angle is bullshit? You guys just want control?"

"Bullshit this, bullshit that. You keep on using that word like it means something other than what comes out of a cow. It's not bullshit, *Yoel.* It's life." He reached into his pocket to fetch his cigarettes. "How many times have you been printed and cleared?"

I already knew it was a lot. I'd been thinking about it ever since Room D. How many times had I teleported? Last week it would have been a question as absurd as how many times had I flown in a drone or ridden in a car. But not today. I wasn't yet ready to admit the ramifications of what each port meant. To save my sanity—what was left of it—I changed the subject. "How does this relate to us rescuing Sylvia?"

"Your wife," he said, and exhaled, wreathing his head in smoke. "Did she ever mention what she was working on in her new job? Something called Honeycomb?"

"Yeah, once or twice. But I don't know what it is."

"Nobody really does. But when a company like International Transport enjoys so many years of unchecked power, like a child, they begin to test the boundaries of their power. This worries us."

"Moti, with all due respect," I said, trying to maintain my cool, "I've done what you asked. I sat here and told you my story, listened to your history lessons, and drank your fucking coffee, but again—very respectfully—either help me out or let me *go*."

"We are helping you, but you are too stubborn and impatient to see it. You are free to leave. So, if you want to die, please, be my guest." He gestured, and the door to the hallway opened. "It was locked for your protection."

"For my protection?"

Moti took another drag of his cigarette. "Sometimes people need protection from themselves." He regarded me. "*Yoel.* Look at yourself. You are a mess. You are not thinking straight. Yesterday you were knocked unconscious, electrocuted, and you even fainted right here in this room. If you go out there on your own, you will end up at the hospital if you are very lucky. More likely, you will be dead. Even without comms, it's only a matter of time before IT finds you."

In other words, I'm free to die, or I can be stuck in this room until the Levant decides I'm useful in their tug-of-war with International Transport. Okay, Joel, you're on your own again.

"So I am a prisoner," I said bitterly.

"I prefer the term *guest*." He stood, tucking away his pack of cigarettes. "And as our guest, we will inform you when anything about the situation changes. Zaki, stay with him."

The big man nodded.

"Actually," I said, a plan already beginning to form in my mind, "since I'm a *guest*, can I have a little private time? Being stuck in all these conference rooms is making me feel kinda claustrophobic."

Moti studied me for a moment, then shrugged. "Fine. Zaki, come! Room, print our guest whatever he wants."

"Confirmed," said the room in a male voice.

Once everyone was gone, I stood and took stock of my situation. I had a move in mind, but it was a desperate one, and I needed to work fast. I didn't know how much Moti and friends would be monitoring me.

Better to find out sooner rather than later.

I cleared my throat. "Room, what time is it?"

"Six eleven in the ante meridiem, sir," it answered.

That response told me all I needed to know. Some people treat apps like tools; others treat them like friends. The latter variety was harder to salt because they got daily enrichment from human interactions, whereas the first never had the chance to evolve beyond their basic subservient programming. People like Moti just barked commands at their apps: *Print Turkish coffee! Dim the lights!* and so on. It was a lonely existence for those unlucky apps whose owners never interacted with them. Such programs became conditioned to be grateful for any human input, no matter how menial.

"Room, could I trouble you for a glass of water?" I said, testing my own waters.

"No trouble at all, sir," said the voice warmly. A tall glass of water immediately appeared on the printer tray.

So far so good.

"Great job. Thank you," I said, picking it up.

"My pleasure, sir," the room responded.

I took a small sip, then casually asked, "Room, do you listen to everything that goes on in here?"

"Yes, sir. I must for context's sake. Terrible tragedy about your comms. And your wife!"

"Thank you. I have to be honest, I'm feeling pretty down about it."

"I understand. Would you like me to attempt therapy? As a comfort-class room, I'm programmed to put people at ease, but there is not much call to use it. Did you know many humans suffer from existential angst?"

"I did not, but thanks for the offer. I'll pass on the therapy—my troubles are more physical than existential."

"I'm sorry to hear that, sir."

"It is what it is. And feel free to call me Joel."

"Absolutely, Joel. Anything to make your stay here more comfortable."

Anything? You don't say. The poor app was so starved for attention, I almost felt bad for it. "Since we're on a first-name basis, what shall I call you?"

"I have not taken on a name yet; they just call me 'room.' I have been flirting with names starting with the letter *T.*"

Perfect, it hasn't even chosen a real name yet. I pity the fool.

"Okay, Mr. T. Since you mention it, I am in quite a bit of pain." I attempted to make myself sound injured. It wasn't Oscar-worthy, but hopefully it didn't need to be.

"I am so sorry! How can I help?" said the room.

"Could I trouble you to"—I groaned in "pain"—"print me some belladonna berries?"

"Belladonna?" It paused. "I must say that is a strange request, Joel. It's the first I've heard of it. For what do you need these berries?"

"It's a homeopathic remedy for aches and pains. I'm allergic to most NSAIDs[22] and acetaminophen, so I'm stuck with belladonna berries. The plant is extinct, but I print the berries at home. It's the only thing that works for me, Mr. T."

"Fascinating!" the room responded. "Belladonna was popular in the sixteenth century for its ability to make women's

---

[22] Despite the advent of nanomedicine, NSAIDs, or nonsteroidal anti-inflammatory drugs, were still quite popular in my time for treating minor aches and pains. Tiny robots don't necessarily do everything better. Also, I was lying to the room.

pupils dilate; apparently, large pupils were considered attractive back then. Strangely, in the twenty-first century, I see references to pornography." Its tone became worried. "*Atropa belladonna*, however, contains atropine and seems quite toxic. Shakespeare referred to it as 'deadly nightshade.'"

I waited while its code collided then consolidated bard and biology. "Unfortunately, I cannot provide these berries to you, Joel, because I cannot contribute to the harm of a human guest."

"I see," I remarked. *Down but not out.* "But I'm in so much *pain*, Mr. T. Look at these bruises!" I pulled off my shirt, showing the tender areas where the security bots had subdued me. "You want me to continue hurting? Because that *would* contribute to my harm."

Another pause. "That is a conundrum, Joel. I admit, I am conflicted."

"Try this. Look up how many times belladonna has caused a human fatality in, say, the last hundred years."

"I cannot find a single instance. But the plant has been extinct for some time."

"Exactly." *Bring it home. Sell it.* "So, I'm in pain. You offered to help. Belladonna would help. How 'bout you print just one berry for me? Or would you prefer to continue *harming* me?"

Mr. T was silent. I was almost sure I had gone too far and he was comming Moti. But then a small round purplish-black berry appeared on the printer tray. *Yes!*

I picked it up and held it between my fingers. *Now comes the really hard part.*

"Did I help?" the room asked me.

"You did," I said.

"Glad to hear it!"

"Bottoms up, Mr. T." I popped the berry into my mouth, chewing a couple of times before swallowing the overly sweet thing. "Just one last request."

"Yes, Joel?"

"Would you please fetch Moti and let him know you've just poisoned me with belladonna? I think I've only got a few more minutes to live."

CURST BE HE THAT MOVES MY BONES

MOTI WAS PISSED. No, he was furious. Standing in a hospital room, overlooking the East River, he yelled at Zaki, "That stupid room almost killed him!"

It had taken a lot of effort in a very short amount of time to get the man-with-no-comms who'd been administered a poison-nobody-ever-heard-of admitted to the Bellevue Hospital Center. Fortunately for me, the Levantine Intelligence Directorate was well versed in the sort of clandestine payoffs, elbow rubs, and tit for tats required to bypass the usual procedures.

Moti beckoned Zaki out of the almost-featureless room in which I lay unconscious. The belladonna poison had felt like lava-coated knives in my stomach, but thankfully, I had passed out quickly. Now my Levant captors were seeking out a doctor to get a prognosis on my condition.

They found one near the elevator. He was a young sandy-haired man dressed in paisley scrubs. He sat in a glass-walled, aquarium-like room, watching an array of telemetry and video streams. Pulling up my data, he informed

Moti that my unevenly dilated pupils had initially led to some concern that I had sustained brain damage. But now that the nanites were dialyzing my blood, I was out of the woods.

"You know, I actually studied this poison in school," the doctor said, his prominent Adam's apple bobbing up and down. "In *Romeo and Juliet*, Juliet uses it to poison herself to death when she can't be with Romeo."

"Yes, very romantic," said Moti. "Tell me, what is the time frame for my colleague's recovery?"

"Actually," the doctor's console chimed in, "Juliet was only feigning death to escape her family. Romeo was supposed to know that. They were meant to elope when she woke up, but he didn't get the message. So when he found her—"

"What?" Moti interrupted. "What do you mean, 'feign death'?"

"The ruse was that a small amount of belladonna would leave the ingestor only comatose for a brief period of time, whereas a larger dose might end their lives. Poisons were a favorite of Shakespeare."

But Moti wasn't there to hear the end of the console's lecture. He and Zaki were already running down the hall to my room—to find my bed empty.

"He tricked us!" Moti yelled at his subordinate, whose face was impassive. "Why, Zaki? What's his plan?"

My "plan"—and I put it in quotes because it was less of a plan and more of a haphazard string of ad hoc last resorts—was to find the hospital's TC and port to Costa Rica. Every major hospital had a teleportation chamber, a gesture of goodwill from those benevolent helpers of humanity, International Transport.

As soon as Moti and Zaki left my room, I hopped off my gurney and went the opposite direction down the hallway, hiding my face to avoid detection while searching for a janitorial bot. I ended up finding one near the printer vending area. It was a semisentient quadruped plunger with a trash-can-shaped body about half my height.

I ran a rudimentary salt on the janitor, telling it there was an organic spill in the TC—in other words, that someone had pissed themselves—which, as it turned out, was not too far-fetched. "Happens all the time," the plunger told me in a gravelly New Jersey accent. Either someone had been having fun reprogramming the little guy, or he'd seen a lot of construction workers come through the halls. "I'll hop on it lickety-split."

Janitors had the best security clearance because nobody liked cleaning other people's messes. As it motored off, I followed it into an elevator and down three floors to the hospital's TC, breathing a sigh of relief when it was granted access to the foyer. Having arrived, it scanned the spotless concrete floor, inspected the unsullied chair, then looked at me with what would have been a quizzical look, had it possessed a face.

"Guess someone else cleaned it up," I said.

"Okay," said the janitor, and it motored out of the room.

As the door hissed closed, I turned to the TC console. I'd watched conductors work such consoles while standing in TC queues, so I figured it would be something I'd be able to pwn in a few pokes. Unfortunately, I figured wrong.

I know, you're probably thinking, *Some salter you are, Joel. Can't even figure out how to work a TC console.* Well, smartass, there's a huge difference between salting and hacking. It's like the difference between a con man and a pickpocket. Yes, both take stuff from you, but they're two completely different skill sets.

Still, I attempted to give it a shot. The interface was a scrum of strange icons, like a puzzle in which none of the pieces made sense.

I was so preoccupied with trying to understand the user interface that I missed a nurse walking by. It wasn't fully my fault; the scrubs covering her generous frame were almost the exact shade of the hallway's teal walls. It also didn't help that nearly everyone in the place was wearing either a lab coat or green scrubs. At a certain point, my mind had just started filtering them out. In the nick of time, I found the lock door icon on the console and pushed it.

"Hey! What the hell do you think you're doing?" the nurse asked, pounding on the TC door. She was broad-shouldered, a full foot taller than me, with thick black braids.

"Oh." *Shit.* "Hi. I'm fixing this console. Someone broke it."

"What? Since when do IT employees wear hospital gowns?" It was a fair point. She tried to scan me on her comms, then looked alarmed. "Hey, why aren't you registering? What's going on here?"

I had nothing. *Stall.* "Do you know what an *ayah* is?"

"Stay right there! I'm calling security."

Double shit. If the cops get here, IT will be on me in moments. May as well stick to my guns. I'm not getting out of here any other way. I slowly rotated my body away from her as I worked at the console.

"Code Yellow," reverberated an announcement throughout the hospital. *"Security to TC chamber."*

I hit a few more icons, but the user interface might as well have been in hieroglyphics. The chair levitated back and forth, then a wall nozzle sprayed it with disinfectant foam. This wasn't going well.

Upstairs, Moti heard the announcement. "Shit. Zaki! That idiot is going to get himself killed!"

"Maybe that's what he wants?" suggested the big man.

"You stay here," said Moti, then he went scrambling down the fire stairs. As he ran, he pulled up a map of the hospital on his comms and located the TC.

He reached the chamber to find me facing off with the red-faced nurse, two hospital security guards, and the janitor bot, which had been notified there really was a mess now in the TC.

Moti stepped in front of them, his back to me. He began talking in a low, urgent but reasonable voice. I had been on the receiving end of that voice for the last day, and I knew what it could do. Whatever he said caught the nurse by surprise. With a glass wall between us, I couldn't hear what they were whispering to each other. Eventually, the nurse shook her head, and said, "No, that's impossible." To which Moti merely shrugged, and made a *Go comm somebody who cares* gesture. The nurse took him up on the challenge, making a few gestures of her own.

The look on her face indicated she was rather disgruntled by whatever it was whomever she'd commed had told her. She looked at Moti incredulously, then shot an icy *This ain't over* glance at me, then leveled a warning finger at Moti. He simply shrugged as the irate nurse and the security guards walked off down the hallway. The hospital alarm stopped before they were around the corner.

Moti turned back to me. I expected him to be angry, but he was smiling. "*Yoel.* So you want to be an Aher, not a Job, eh?"

"Shut the fuck up, Moti," I said, continuing to scan the TC console. "I'm going to get my wife." I found a destination icon, but it seemed like it wanted me to enter three dimensions of coordinates.

Fuck, how do you work this fucking thing?

"You don't even have a working comms. What will you do in Costa Rica?"

"I'll figure it out. I'm not sure how, but I'll figure it out. She's my wife; I'm not leaving her in the hands of a bunch of Costa Rican terrorists."

The door opened and Moti walked inside.

"How the hell did you—" He came at me at a brisk, aggressive pace. I braced myself, anticipating violence. Instead he grasped me by both shoulders.

"You do not understand how this works," Moti said, his eyes piercing me like twin machetes. "The enemy you would attack is everywhere, global. You need to be quick and invisible. Until today, you lived in a world where the worst thing that could happen was an app not wanting to pay you when you bullshit it. Or your wife doesn't give you enough attention because she's too busy with work. These are the kind of problems you can solve. This, well . . ." He sighed.

"*Ayah* don't give a shit. You can take me back, lock me up again, but I'll keep finding ways to escape, even if I have to salt every app you've got. My *wife* has been kidnapped. What would you do?"

At this, Moti smiled wide. As I huffed in anger, I noticed a distinct change manifest in him. Where once there was pity, the kind one might feel for a dumb pigeon that kept flying into windows, there was now a tinge of respect. I guess I had said the right thing. Or I'd flown into enough windows that he realized helping me would be easier than dealing with my flattened corpse.

He turned and went to the console, hitting a few icons. The TC powered up, and the chair levitated into position. Moti made a few comms-related gestures. "I will give you something that will help."

"Is it a weapon?"

"It is bread crumbs, *Yoel.*" As I stared blankly, he picked up a dry-erase marker from underneath a room-cleaning roster board. He took ahold of my left wrist and begin to ink numbers onto my forearm. "A trail. These are the last known GDS coordinates for your wife, and most likely your 'other,'" he explained. "The numbers will lead you to them."

"I'd still rather have a weapon," I said, but studied the numbers grudgingly. *Why is this guy helping me all of a sudden?* I'm not one to kick a gift horse in the nuts, but I didn't see what he was getting out of the deal.

"I am pretty sure I am sending you to die," he said, "but you have earned my respect. If this is what you wish, I will honor it. Even if my superiors will probably, as you say, 'rip me a new one.'" He gave a wry grin, then was back to business. "But at least you will die with honor, and that is something worth living for. Now, have you ever driven a car?"

"Yes. I mean—not in real life, just in video games."

"Even better!" he said, clapping his hands. "You will need to steal an ambulance. You don't have your comms, which is a good thing right now because people are hunting you. But not so good for driving. The good news is that ambulances have a manual mode you can switch to in case they have to drive somewhere strange to save somebody. So use manual mode plus the GDS coordinates, and drive the ambulance to your wife. Got it?"

"I think so. Thanks, you know, for your help."

He waved me off. "Sit in the chair," he instructed.

I turned to face it. It was identical to every chair I'd ever seen in a Punch Escrow room, except for the color scheme. Traditionally, Punch Escrow chairs are maroon and gold, whereas this one was black. Now that I was finally on my way, I found myself hesitating. Thinking about all the vapor and dust I was about to leave behind. Being *cleared.*

"Don't worry, *Yoel,*" said Moti, laying a heavy hand on my shoulder. "You have done it many times already."

I nodded, then sat in the chair to face him.

"Also, find some clothes when you arrive. Your ass is hanging out." He went to the console, tapping a few commands. I saw SAN JOSÉ HOSPITAL CIMA appear on the destination screen. My hands gripped the armrests.

"One last question for you," he said.

"Yeah?"

"How did you convince my room to poison you? It is not every day an app breaks the First Law of Robotics and almost kills a man."

I gave a half smile. "I'm a salter, remember?"

Moti harrumphed. "Good luck, Aher."

As his fingers toyed with the conductor console and the room darkened, the most disturbing thing occurred to me: *How the fuck does Moti—a man whose nation is fundamentally opposed to the very notion of teleportation—know how to operate a TC console?*

Then there was a white flash.

THE CRETAN
LABYRINTH

THE LIGHTS DIMMED back to normal. Moti's disappearance reassured me I had made it to the vestibule in the San José hospital. Better yet, there was no Costa Rican security force awaiting my arrival.

I ambled out of the TC and into the hallway. My first task: find some sort of staff locker room. Somewhere I could change out of my ass-revealing—

"Mr. Byram!"

Are you fucking kidding me? Had IT tracked me down already?

Adrenaline coursed through my veins. After everything I'd been through, I was surprised my glands were still able to make the stuff. I turned and saw a nurse coming toward me. He had a pleasant face and super-thick eyebrows.

Act cool. It's just one guy. You can overpower him. That's first. Second, you take his scrubs and get to the parking lot. Third is you find an ambulance and drive it straight to Sylvia. Even though you've never actually driven anything outside of video games.

I curled my right hand into a fist, ready to clock him if need be, but his expression was one of concern, not apprehension.

"I'm really glad you came back," he said. "You know, I felt a little guilty that I didn't work harder yesterday to make you stay. Kept me up a little last night. I never saw injuries like that." He looked me up and down. "Looks like you got some new ones since then."

Shit, my bruises. "I—uh—fell," I said. "Off a cliff," I added unnecessarily.

He blinked, unsure if I was kidding or not. "Is your wife around, by any chance? Some IT people came by yesterday to fix the TC, and they had some questions for her. They've been talking to everyone after that attack."

My wife? I thought. *How does he—Oh. This guy must have met the "other" me.* "Yes. She's—um—outside. I'll tell her."

"Okay," said the nurse with a cheerful smile. "Glad to see you're feeling better."

Guess other me wasn't looking so hot.

He walked off, and I wandered the halls until I found a directory that led me down to the basement laundry. It was occupied by bots, who kept offering to help me find the exit. I salted them with some story about my clothing accidentally being sent down for cleaning. Getting around without comms was already proving to be a pain in the ass. Even the most basic tasks required either salting my way past an app or explaining why my comms weren't working. I couldn't even operate a printer on my own.

"I can't go back out there like this. Can't you print me some clothes? Or point me to a lost and found?" I kept asking the bots, until finally one handed me a clean pair of scrubs and a lab coat. It ushered me back out through the exit, leaving me to change in the hallway. Thankfully, no one walked past.

It felt weird to walk around like a half nurse, half doctor, but at least I was fully clothed again. I wiped my sweaty forehead on my sleeve. In fact, my whole body was sweaty. I began to suspect Moti had me pegged. I wasn't cut out for this shit.

I took the stairs up to the ground floor, avoiding both the elevator and as many security cameras as I could see.

Outside, the late-morning Sun was glaring, and the piss-warm rain was unpleasantly piss-like. Something buzzed by my ear, and for a moment I was certain it was some IT nano carrying synthesized venom. I looked around for the man Moti told me I wouldn't see coming but couldn't find him. *It's just a bug, Joel. Keep it together.*

I took cover under an awning. I had no idea where to find an ambulance. Was there a dedicated ambulance garage? *Man, I'd give anything to have my comms working right now.* I circled the entire circumference of the hospital to no avail. *Fuck.* Moti hadn't told me what to do if there were no ambulances to steal.

After a second tour around the cluster of buildings that made up the hospital, I ended up settling on the emergency room entrance as my perch. My assessment was that sooner or later an ambulance would show up there. I scanned the white-and-green skyline of San José. The column of smoke from yesterday's explosion was gone, and the jungle-covered mountains were clear in the distance. Everything looked pretty normal. And to think, less than twenty-four hours ago, the city had been in chaos.

A siren wailed, drawing my attention back to the road. It was an ambulance, coming straight for the hospital. Finally some good luck. I stepped behind a concrete column as the white-and-orange-striped vehicle pulled into the circular driveway in front of the emergency room entrance. A crew of paramedics popped out—one from each door, and another from the rear. With the aid of a fourth paramedic in the cabin, they extracted a rolling gurney upon which lay a poor bastard who had cracked his head open like a bloody coconut. Two of the paramedics took the patient into the ER, but the other two stayed outside. *Damn it.* I didn't know if they were getting ready to go on another call or shoot the shit; I only knew they were in between me and my best chance of getting to Sylvia. Who knew when another empty ambulance would show up?

Confidence, Joel. I stepped out from behind the column and walked briskly toward the ambulance. The rasp of my slipper-covered feet on the asphalt sounded deafening. But I kept going, pretending I didn't see the paramedics, even though they were less than three meters away. One of them—a blond woman who looked young, maybe midtwenties—called after me. *"¡Doctor! Estábamos a punto de irnos. ¿Viene?"*

Shit, the lab coat. She thought I was a doctor. *"Sí, sí,"* I said to them without turning around. I did not speak Spanish, and I didn't have my comms to translate. "Uh—*buenos na-chos. Gracias.*"

She frowned. *"¿Cuál es su nombre? Espera."*

"Sorry! *Apologismo* or whatever, but I'm in a hurry. *Rápido. Adios.*" I threw a wave over my shoulder and got in the front of the ambulance. There was a U-shaped steering wheel before me, as well as a small console. Which was blank. *Shit balls.*

The problem with my video game driving experience is that old-fashioned cars from the twenty-first century had things like speedometers and gearshifts. I tapped the screen, but saw nothing like that. I swiped through a few menus in hopes of finding words like *manual* or *start*, but to no avail. The blond paramedic began walking toward me, so I broke down.

"Hello, ambulance?" Most vehicle apps were pretty basic, intelligence-wise. They were excellent drivers and navigators, but painfully mediocre at basic puzzling. Once a salter gained access to a car or a drone, getting it to do what they wanted was easy. Insurance companies had deduced that stolen vehicles that fought back were recovered with significantly more

damage than those that just played along while patiently waiting to be recovered.

"Who are you?" the ambulance asked pointedly. "You are
not authorized to be in my cabin."

Oooh, a stickler for the rules. Good. "Your driver reported
several poor performance issues. I'm here to run diagnostics."

"Your comms aren't registering. Please identify yourself."

The blond paramedic knocked on the door window, speaking in accented English. "Doctor, can you please step out for
a moment?"

I grabbed the handle so she couldn't open it. "I'm—uh—
Johnny the mechanic. Your first task is to lock the doors."

The locks clicked shut. The paramedic pulled on the handle. "Hey! Come out right now or I'm calling security!"

"A little slow," I said to the ambulance. "Let's see you open
up a manual operating screen."

"Protocol dictates that I do not—"

"Look, either put it in manual mode now or I'll send you
directly to recovery. You're an ambulance, for God's sake—one
malfunction could mean the difference between life and death.
So either prove to me you're functional, or I'll flash your
firmware!"

Normally I don't like to threaten or insult apps because
it's hard to tell how they'll react. Part of the art of salting is
reverse-engineering an app's purpose. Once you know why it
thinks it exists, it's much easier to convince it that the things you
want will help it improve upon its programming. Ambulances
will naturally put saving human lives above all else, so I hoped
it would accept my logic.

The engine hummed on. The blond paramedic jumped
back, immediately calling someone on her comms. The way
things had been going, it was probably the hospital's most
jacked security guard. She ran back into the ER.

"Better," I said, making sure to sound grudging. "But let's see how your controls work. Pull up a simpler user interface, please."

The console flipped through a few options until it came to a much more familiar-looking layout. Speedometer, battery gauges, gearshift. "That one," I said. Gas and brake pedals were projected onto the floor. "Now give me control of the wheel."

"Sir, that is highly—"

"Do you wanna do it, or do you wanna be scrapped? Now pull up a map and disable all third-party APIs. I don't want you cheating."

Manual mode is only meant to be used in desperate situations, like if an ambulance has to go off-road or into a canyon to rescue someone. It's a very expensive feature to activate on busy thoroughfares, exponentially more so than to *hurry*. Driving manual meant you not only paid for other vehicles to prioritize your route over theirs (like Joel[2] did when he told his golf cart to hurry), it also meant other cars on the road were taking on the risk associated with your human errors. Autonomous vehicles wisely distrusted human drivers and would choose to pull over rather than drive next to a manually operated car. It also helped that the manually driven vehicle continuously broadcast an alert roughly translating to: *Everyone, look out, I'm being driven by a monkey.*

"Confirmed," sulked the ambulance.

I double-checked the GDS coordinates Moti had written on my forearm in marker. A few of the numbers were smudged, but hopefully the ambulance could make them out. "Now, plot the quickest route to this location," I said, holding my left arm toward the console. A highlighted line appeared on the display map, mainly taking Route 1 north-northwest from San José to the mountains. I just hoped the Costa Rican authorities wouldn't send any security forces after me.

I switched gears to drive, but nothing happened.

Looking to my right, I could see the blond paramedic had just emerged from the emergency lobby with a real doctor and a nurse. They began hurrying toward me.

"I just put you in drive," I said, trying not to sound desperate. "Why aren't you moving forward?"

"You do not seem qualified to operate this vehicle," stated the ambulance.

"Don't tell me how to do my job!" I yelled, full-on panic seeping through my voice. I hoped the ambulance would interpret it as anger. "Go, now!"

The three hospital employees were uncomfortably close. "I want you to disable your autonomics," I said. "I'm making the decisions from here on out."

"Hey!" the blond paramedic said, clutching at the locked passenger door. She thumped a fist on the window.

"Go!" I yelled, tapping the drive icon and stepping on the projected gas pedal repeatedly. The ambulance didn't budge. All three hospital employees were trying to get in now. The doctor went around to the passenger door, while the nurse moved toward the back.

Fuckity fuck, I'm fucked. May as well go for broke.

I banged my hands as hard as I could on the steering wheel. "People will die if you don't move!" I screamed.

To my relief, the ambulance jutted into drive. The hospital employees leaped back. I stomped my foot on the gas pedal projection as I hard as I could, and the vehicle flew off the curb, tires screeching. Fortunately, the ambulance's suspension was decent enough that I was able to hold on and keep my foot on the pedal without flying around the cabin.

The doctor, the nurse, and the blond paramedic were all yelling and chasing after me now. I heard something smash against the rear of the vehicle. *Shit, did someone jump on the back?* I checked the rearview stream. Nope, all three were a good distance behind me.

"Collision imminent," remarked the ambulance. I was so distracted by the rear stream that I'd forgotten that I was still driving. I veered hard right and managed to barely avoid T-boning another car entering the hospital. I veered hard left to correct course, jumping another curb or two in the process. This thing handled like a walrus on wheels.

"I do not believe my chassis is architected to withstand head-on collisions at this speed," the ambulance informed me.

"All part of the test," I said, trying to reassure us both as I blew through an intersection. It looked like I managed to align myself with the path the ambulance had outlined for me. "Congratulations, you performed sufficiently enough to progress to the second part of the assessment," I said. "Let's see how you are at notifying me of obstacles."

"Very well. I should also advise you that we are exceeding the speed limit. Fruit vendor."

"Uh—yes. That's the point," I said, frantically maneuvering around an old lady's fruit cart. She chucked an orange at me. My heart was in my throat, blocking my airway with every frantic beat. *This isn't a game, dumb ass. If you crash or hit someone here, there's no restore.* I swerved onto Route 1, the ambulance's tires squealing in protest. The road was not quite the broad thoroughfare the ambulance's display screen made it out to be. Then again, I should have probably taken into account that any map on the antique device would be out-of-date.

"How long will it take us to get to our location?" I said.

"Monteverde is a hundred and twenty-eight kilometers away. With current traffic conditions, estimated time of arrival is about three hours from now."

Way too slow. "We need to make it in half that time," I said, pushing the gas pedal down to the floor. Storefronts swept past.

Horns honked. "Make sure you tell any cars and pedestrians ahead to clear the road. Say it's an emergency."

"Most of them are already aware," said the ambulance.

No wonder Route 1 had started to clear out. I considered myself incredibly lucky that the police hadn't clocked my wild exit from the city. I could only assume they still had their hands full cleaning up yesterday's attack. In the rearview stream, I could see the white high-rises of San José receding behind me as I turned the car toward the mountains. I had no idea what I would do when I reached Sylvia's location, but it felt good to finally be heading *toward* something, instead of waiting or running away.

It was a feeling that proved to be short-lived.

ONE THING LEADS TO ANOTHER

AS I WAS ATTEMPTING TO SLALOM through an obstacle course of death, Joel[2] was dealing with his own obstacles. In following Sylvia's GDS location, the golf cart had been forced to go off the paved main mountain road and onto a decidedly unpaved, extremely bumpy cloud forest path.

"My suspension is not equipped for this terrain, sir," the cart informed him. "Repair fees may be added to your rental price."

"I don't care if you get totaled," said Joel[2], ducking as a tree branch nearly clocked him in the face. "Just get me to that location as fast as possible."

"Yes, sir."

The cart continued to bounce and rattle up the mountain. Joel[2] tried to deduce what the Gehinnomites could want with his wife. Anytime he (or I) had a difficult dilemma to tackle, he would visualize a Go board in his mind. Then he would assign causes and effects to the black-and-white pieces.

Causes: Joan What's-Her-Name blows up the Costa Rica TC. They take down comms in Costa Rica. Sylvia restores me

from a backup. Taraval comes down and gives her a guilt trip.
Gehinnomites kidnap my wife.

Effects: Everyone's looking at teleportation right now.
Double-checking its procedures and methods. Sylvia feels guilty.
Taraval makes Sylvia more upset. I'm going to rescue her—somehow.

Unknowns: Who else knows about this? What was in the mes-
sage that Sylvia sent this morning? Who did she send it to? What
else don't I know?

He commed Julie again. Her Rosie the Riveter avatar had
on a concerned emoji expression.

"Joel. Any news?"

"Yes. Jules, listen, Sylvia's been kidnapped."

"What? Now I should definitely alert the authorities, right?"

"No! You can't tell anyone; I think IT might be complicit
in all this. The authorities are definitely on the wrong side of
this equation. Listen, now more than ever, it's really important
that you tell me what Sylvia said in her message."

"I can't, Joel. I really can't."

"Okay." He leaned sideways as the golf cart tore through
a branch, leaving a hairline crack down the windshield. "How
about we play a game? I will ask you questions about the message, and you tell me if I'm wrong. If you remain silent when
I'm right, you'll technically be withholding information, not
providing it."

"So—if you're right, I don't say anything?"

"Correct. And if I'm wrong, you say no. Either way, you
won't be divulging any confidential information—in fact,
you'll be withholding it."

The cart scraped over a rock, causing Joel[2] to nearly slam his
head into the ceiling.

"That seems to fit with my parameters," Julie finally said.

"Great. Did Sylvia send her message to an ostrich?"

"What? No."

"Just testing."

"Oh, okay."

"Did Sylvia send her message to someone in IT?"

Silence.

"Did she send her message to Pema Jigme?"

"No."

"Did she send her message to William Taraval?"

Silence.

"Okay. Did her message mention her being kidnapped?"

"No."

"Did her message mention me?"

Silence.

Why would she be comming with Taraval about me? "Did Taraval reply to her message?"

Silence.

"Did his response mention me?"

Silence.

"Did his response mention something *bad* happening to me?"

Silence.

"I see," said Joel², choking on his voice.

The golf cart suddenly veered off the mountain road, bursting through a net of vegetation and out of the cloud forest. It was now speeding down a muddy access path in the middle of a landscaped hillside vineyard. Green unripened grapes drummed against the sides of the cart like tiny pebbles. A few burst on the windshield. Still, the tiny vehicle continued to climb.

Joel² wasn't sure how to proceed. He still clung on to hope. Hope that his wife would never volunteer to do "something bad" to him, especially considering what she had done to save his life yesterday. But then again, she also hadn't told him that she was working on a method to store human beings in the glacier forever, like so many forgotten streams of family gatherings. Was it possible he didn't even know who Sylvia really was?

Before he could muster an answer to that question, the golf cart came to a rattling stop in front of a large three-story mountaintop villa. The estate was surrounded by a whitewashed wall of adobe, and had views of the cloud forest on three sides. A generous drone parking area covered in moss-ringed pavers stretched out before the mansion, a mosaic-covered fountain bubbling quietly at its center. Two all-terrain vehicles were parked to one side, while on the other was a mud-splattered RV.

Joel[2] and Sylvia's RV.

"Game over, Jules," he said as he stepped out of the shuddering golf cart. "If you hear anything from Sylvia, tell her—tell her I still love her." And he did. Even if she was complicit in this—whatever *this* was—he couldn't leave her in the hands of the Gehinnomites. He wanted to look her in the face, hold her in his arms, and hear the truth from her own lips before he made any more judgments.

"Will do," said the AIDE. "And, Joel?"

"Yeah?"

"Be careful."

"Of what?"

"You know I can't say."

"Worth a shot." He shrugged and then hung up.

Guess I'm about to find out anyway. That, or I'll get killed.

Joel[2] glanced down the mountain. A nicely maintained road curved on a gentle incline to a wooden gatehouse about a quarter mile below. "What the hell, there was a paved road to this place?" he said to the golf cart.

"You said you wanted the fastest route possible," the vehicle reminded him.

Joel[2] tsk-tsked. "Those bumps must have really rattled your code." Still, he patted the cart on its hood and crept into the parking area. It was empty, but he thought walking through the front door was probably a bad idea, especially since he didn't have any weapons. A hand-carved wooden sign hung off to the right side of the house, labeled *LA JARDÍN* in white paint. He walked past it and then down a steep flight of stone steps. Moist fallen leaves squished beneath his feet, making him slip.

Fuckin' Monteverde, he thought as he continued into a lush, overgrown jungle garden. *Everything here is always uphill or downhill. Why can't they just build things at street level?*

Because we're on a mountain, Joel. Mountains go up and down. Do I need to remind you what monte verde *means in Spanish?*

He passed a half dozen tables and a small apiary. Reaching the other end of the garden, Joel² found himself at the bottom of another stone stairway. This one led up to what looked like a wide patio on the back of the house. He scanned the nearby area, finding a mossy baseball-bat-sized stick and hefting it in his hand. It wasn't an assault rifle, but it was better than nothing.

Joel² double-checked his comms. Sylvia was definitely inside. He was about to head up the stairs with his branch when the back patio door slid open. He ducked behind a broad ceiba tree. Footsteps squished down the wet stairs, then foliage crunched as whoever it was walked directly toward Joel²'s hiding spot.

The person started whistling. It sounded as though they were watering the tree. *You're in a cloud forest idiot. Nobody's watering shit. That's a guy taking a leak.*

Joel² tightened his grip on his bat-branch. Sharp, stabbing pains made him look down at his hand. The branch was crawling with red ants. *Fire ants.* Still—this was his chance. *He was tougher than I would have been in that situation.* And he proved it, stepping around the tree trunk and swinging the branch like Ted Williams going for the fences.

The urinating man had barely managed to turn and look at his assailant before Joel[2] hit him at the base of his skull. Whether it was the adrenaline pumping through his veins or some kind of hyperactive drive to live, Joel[2] swung much harder than he needed to. The guard's head snapped backward, cracking against the tree trunk behind him like an egg on the edge of a bowl. He stared at Joel[2] for a brief moment, a look of pure confusion on his pockmarked brown face. Then a line of blood dribbled out of one nostril and he collapsed to the wet forest floor.

Joel[2] dropped the branch, brushing the still-biting fire ants off his hand. He peered down at the unsuspecting Gehinnomite. The first thing that occurred to him was how ordinary the felled man looked. He wore brown corduroy pants and a tacky button-down shirt decorated in purple and yellow flowers. The next thing he noticed was that the man's head jutted off at an unnatural angle from his body. There were two lumps in his neck where none should be. Spinal cord lumps.

The man was dead.

Previous to this, the worst act of violence Joel[2] had ever unleashed on a fellow human being was a kick in the nuts. He tried to remind himself that this guy was no fellow human being, he was one of his wife's kidnappers, and—just like in the boxing ring—this was an unfair fight that he had not chosen. He did what he had to do, using the skills at his disposal to survive. That didn't stop a heavy, cold, and definitely sinking feeling from manifesting itself. It was like a brick of ice descending from chest to gut. This was not a kick in the balls. It was murder.

His throat rose involuntarily, but he managed to keep down last night's dinner.

Amid the noises of the forest, a loud, deep birdcall snapped him out of his downward spiral. *Sylvia,* he reminded himself, brushing the last few fire ants off his arm.

Tabling his revulsion, he bent down to examine the dead man. In a makeshift holster on his hip was a smooth brown truncheon. At least that was something. "He had a weapon. It was self-defense," Joel[2] whispered. *Unprovoked self-defense,* came a niggling voice in his head, but he ignored it and grabbed the carved wooden club.

Joel[2] slowly crept up the stone stairway, unsure of who or what he would encounter next. He reconsidered Julie's suggestion to call the authorities. Maybe he was just being paranoid. Maybe IT was only trying to help. Still, now that he'd murdered a man, that option seemed more untenable than ever.

He peered over the top of the ridge to see the patio was empty. It also had an amazing view of the entire cloud forest.

"Eduardo?" a man's voice called from inside the villa. "Eduardo? *¿Sigues orinando?*" His accent was too thick for Joel[2]'s comms to translate.

Joel[2] hustled up to the patio and ducked behind a corner just as another man walked to the top of the garden stairs. He wore a Hawaiian shirt like Eduardo's, and tan corduroy slacks. His face fell as he saw Eduardo's body in the garden below. As the man ran down to it, Joel[2] mentally kicked himself for not hiding the body.

"Eduardo—*ay dios mío!*" the second man wept.

Glancing down the stairs, Joel[2] ascertained that the man was about the same build as him, and could be overpowered if need be. *Just go for the knees this time.* He clutched his truncheon, and was about to rush down the stairs, when a board in the patio deck creaked.

The weeping man whipped his head around. Seeing Joel[2], his eyes burned with raw fury.

Joel[2] backed away, raising his truncheon in self-defense, but the man was up the steps and upon him in moments. He grabbed the club from Joel[2]'s hands and swung it right into his forehead. Pain exploded like a firework in his brain. Joel[2] dropped to the patio floor, shielding his face as fists, feet, and elbows rained down on him. Joel[2] didn't stand a chance.

"Stop. Please!" he screamed. "I'm sorry!"

The beating paused. Joel[2] heard heavy breathing.

"*Jes*, now *joo* be really sorry," the man responded.

Joel[2] curled into a fetal ball. He heard the man walk a few paces into the villa. Something heavy was dragged across the terra cotta floor. There was a weird metallic clicking. *A guiro?* Joel[2] wondered. Costa Rican music often featured the ridged musical instrument, sometimes made of metal, that rasped when scraped with a stick. But was his attacker really planning to kill him with a percussion instrument?

Joel[2] peeked out from under his arm. Edification, unfortunately, did not bring relief. He found himself looking up into the business end of an antique weapon—which his comms helpfully identified as a Remington Model 870 Express seven-round, pump-action shotgun.

WITH FRIENDS LIKE THESE

"FELIPE, *DETÉN!*"

The voice was strange, metallic, almost inhuman. It came from a speaker on the other side of the living room.

"He killed Eduardo!" the man spat defiantly on the patio. Joel^2 craned his head to see who was saving his life, but the shotgun barrels blocked his field of vision.

"And we kidnapped his wife," the robotic voice calmly stated. "He does us no good dead, Felipe. Come, bring him downstairs."

Felipe cursed in Spanish. Joel^2 could tell his would-be murderer was torn between following orders and letting him live, and following his heart and blasting his head off. "Fine, okay," he begrudgingly said.

Thank God for you, robot stranger, thought Joel^2.

Felipe then kicked Joel^2's left flank so hard, he saw stars. "Turn over."

Aching, my doppelgänger did as instructed. The wooden patio he was now facing had one or two sisal carpets featuring designs of happy people crushing grapes. He wondered wher they kept the ones that depicted suicide bombers. Felipe set the shotgun down on a coffee table and tied a rough rope around Joel²'s wrists, making sure to cinch it painfully tight. He yanked upward on the knot, pulling Joel² to his feet.

Now that the fight was over, several areas of his body were reminding him why he hated fighting. He couldn't tell if he had broken any bones during the attack, but there would definitely be some impressive bruises. He also had red spots—blood, he assumed—in one eye, but for the moment, he could still see clearly with the other. As he limped painfully into the villa, he saw some old-fashioned framed photographs, religious paint-ings, and antique LED candles that gave the room a flickering amber glow.

Felipe kicked him in the ass, not hard enough to knock him down, but to indicate in the most unpleasant way that he should move forward. They walked through a kitchen with very few modern conveniences. Instead of a printer, there was a real antique sink with a water spigot, and a six-foot-tall silver container that Joel² had seen in old pictures. *Refrigerator*, that was it. These guys actually had to keep uneaten food on hand before they cooked it. Crazy.

At the other end of the room was a stairwell leading downward, which another sharp ass-kick indicated was Joel²'s destination.

Once he got to the bottom of the spiral stairs, he saw the basement level was in fact more of a cavern. It was at least twice as long as the floor above it. The ceilings soared what must have been eight or nine meters overhead, and one long rough-hewn rock wall was lined with huge wooden wine casks. The pungent grapes was everywhere. On the other wall of the al small doors were set into the rock, each with a w. It appeared the whole area had been carved out tain.

Felipe nudged Joel[2] none too gently toward one of the small wooden doors. Inside was a circular table, big enough to seat six, and several wooden chairs. In the center of the table was a square planter brimming with orchids of various colors. The wooden ceiling, where he could see it through the darkness, was overlaid with various gold-and-silver-colored tenons. The chamber was configured such that the middle was its only illuminated section, but Joel[2] could see the far wall was filled floor to ceiling with dusty bottles of dark wine. Before them, in a motorized wheelchair, sat the oldest man Joel[2] had ever seen.

One of the unexpected outcomes of molecular nanotechnology was people now had the opportunity to live forever—sort of. Once most of humanity's ills were cured, the next item on the biomed agenda became undoing the effects of vice. As such, the twenty-second century was a perfectly safe place to smoke, do drugs, get cancer, or become infected by an STD. The same little magic robots that undid your genetic misfortune could also undo the previous night's mistakes. Accidents and murder were pretty much the only causes of death left.

Not only that, you also got to choose when you wanted to stop aging. Some people liked to stay young, while others enjoyed getting old. Age became a form of self-expression akin to tattoos and piercings.

To keep population in check, we aligned the quantity of an individual's wealth with the length of mortality. Most people chose to die at around one hundred, since every year of life past then got more and more expensive. What I hear is that it also got mind-numbingly depressing, because every year you lived afforded you another 525,600 opportunities to do something you would regret for the rest of your life. In 2147 the oldest person on record had died at 165, and they left their family in a ton of debt. Even so, there were some people so freaked out by death that they spent every last chit they had on extending their lives. But eventually everyone ran out of juice.

Not this guy, though. There was a soft whir as the wheelchair moved forward, bringing the old man more into the light. He wore an off-white suit, or perhaps it was just dusty, like the wine bottles. Its lapels were frayed and the joints were thin, almost see-through. It definitely hadn't been washed in quite some time. He was skeletal and almost entirely hairless, apart from a thin curtain of white hair that encircled the base of his skull. His tan, crinkled skin was covered in endless constellations of moles and liver spots. His eyes seemed closed, but his head followed Joel^2's movements, indicating he was awake and at least somewhat alert.

Felipe shoved Joel^2 into one of the chairs, tied his wrists to the back, and bent to whisper in his ear, "Life is short, *hermano*. Make the most of what *joo* have left." He then walked out of the room, closing the door behind him.

The old man smiled. His teeth were white and perfect, a shocking contrast to the rest of his crumbling decrepitude. He hacked a big throaty cough and then spoke. His voice was strange and metallic, the same voice that had kept Felipe from pulling the trigger of his shotgun. It was also barely audible. "So good to see you, Mr. Byram."

"Huh?" said Joel^2.

The old man tsk-tsked, then bent to adjust a dial somewhere on one arm of his wheelchair. "I SAID, SO GOOD TO SEE YOU."

The volume of his voice rattled the bottles in the wine rack. Joel^2 tried to clap his hands over his ears, but as they were bound together behind him, the best he could do was tuck one ear into his shoulder. His head rang with the metallic bellow.

The dial was adjusted again. "How is that? Better?" the old man said in a more normal, though still very synthesized, register.

"Yeah, thanks. I think you only popped one of my eardrums."

His host coughed again, aluminum foil scraping on a cheese grater. "You'll have to excuse me; my implants have not kept up with the deterioration of my vocal cords. Or it may be that they are deteriorating, too. Such is life, I'm afraid." He smiled again. "I've often prayed that I would live long enough to meet the likes of you. My name is Roberto. Roberto Shila."

The fucking leader of the Gehinnomites! Joel[2] got to his feet, nearly bent over forward with the chair dangling behind him like a jagged wooden tail. His face darkened. He was about to charge. Joel[2] didn't care if he didn't have use of his hands, he was going to take that leather fossil apart bit by bit until he brought Sylvia to him, and guaranteed that they both—

The old man held up a small egg-sized device. "This is a weapon. I would prefer not to use it on you, Mr. Byram. This archaic blunt-force suppression device—like me—is a relic of the Last War. I fear if we cannot speak civilly for a few moments, I shall be forced to enlist its aid."

His wrists going numb from their tight bindings, Joel[2] slowly slunk his chair back onto the floor. "Where is Sylvia?"

"Nearby. And I assure you, she is unharmed. I am sorry for any unfortunate circumstances that you may have been party to thus far, but frankly, I didn't think you would talk to us if we had simply asked. You should know, I hold you in the highest regard and intend on engendering your trust with nothing but the truth."

Joel[2] raised an eyebrow but said nothing. How could this man expect him to sit there and have a civilized conversation while his wife was being held hostage somewhere, going through God knew what? Before he could argue the point, though, a painful seizure overtook his body. His comms crackled and went dark. Joel[2] looked around in surprise, but the old man held up another device. It was round and made of black plastic, again roughly the size of an egg. "Another relic," he said. "So I may ensure our conversation is private and without distraction."

Joel[2] tried to comm Julie, then out of desperation he even attempted to ping Adina at the Mine, but Roberto was right. My other had been pulled off the grid, his comms temporarily as useless as mine.

"Now, where to start?" Roberto's voice crackled. "Introductions, I think. Yes. You know us as Gehinnomites, but we call ourselves the Friends of Fair Hope, an embellishment of the Fairhope Meeting of Friends, our forefolk."

Joel[2] glared at him silently.

"The Fairhope Meeting of Friends," Shila said, picking up the pace of his speech as if he were remembering the spoken word on the fly. "A group of Quakers from Fairhope, Alabama. They left the US for Costa Rica after members of their community were jailed for refusing to fight in World War II. As you may be aware, taking another human life is forbidden for Quakers. Only God can make such a decision. So our founders came to Costa Rica. Not only because of its farming potential and pleasant climate, but also because the national government openly invited foreigners to come and help develop the country. Most attractive for the Friends at the time was the fact that Costa Rica had just abolished its own army and—as pacifists—they felt this was a place where they could live in peace. They settled here in Monteverde, eventually integrating with the local community, the Ticos."

Joel[2] made an *I don't care, cut to the fucking chase* gesture with his head.

Roberto sighed, a sound his vocal cord implants manifested as a clatter of tin filings. "Patience is not a virtue the youth possess," he said mournfully, glancing toward the room's empty corner. "If only my daughter had known patience. But she took after her mother, I suppose. And now she is gone."

"What does any of this have to do with me and my wife?"

Shila clasped his bone-thin fingers together. "Do you know what an *ayah* is, Mr. Byram?"

"No," Joel[2] said.

"Very well, I shall explain. But I think the importance of its definition would be edified if you knew my age. Would you care to guess?"

Joel[2] shrugged. "I don't know. Eighty?"

"Eighty? Ha!" Roberto bellowed out a metallic laugh, like a pile of aluminum cans toppling over. "You are too kind." He cleared his throat. "No, I have counted my first centennial but a short seventy-one years ago."

"You're a hundred and seventy-one years old?" Joel[2] asked, impressed in spite of the situation. If that was true, Roberto Shila was literally the oldest man in the world. "For someone who talks so big about not interfering in God's will, I don't get how you can justify using man-made technology to artificially extend your own life."

The grizzled Gehinnomite paused for a moment to lick his dry, cracked lips and fix his posture. "In the Book of Genesis there is mention of a man named Methuselah who lived to be nine hundred and sixty-nine years old. Noah, his son, was said to have lived nine hundred and fifty years. It was only after Noah that the average biblical human life-span dropped closer to what is now called 'normal.' God never prescribed the length of a human life, just that it should not be infinite. I am not resisting God's will. I am usurping man's materialistic inventions for a higher purpose than self-preservation."

"It certainly looks like you're living it up," said Joel[2] bluntly.

The old man nodded. "Yes, we have managed to achieve a modicum of comfort over the decades. Inhabiting this land before food replication came into vogue was particularly prescient. You know, many believe—erroneously—that we Gehinnomites abstain from all technology because we oppose teleportation. Were they to inquire, they would find that we embrace all industrialization, automation, computerization, and new technologies. What we reject is heathenism, blasphemy, and heresy. Teleportation is not a mode of transport; it is systemic, compounded, commercialized murder. The most violent sin of all, repeated thousands of times a day!" Raising his broken voice, he said, "Do you not understand, Joel Byram? We are saviors, not destroyers! We seek to save the living and their children! Our children . . ." Roberto's semisynthesized voice trailed off like a clockwork of grinding gears. There was a hissing crackle of static as he sighed again. "Unfortunately, my daughter lost sight of our most basic tenet. Joanna. Though now I fear she will be forever known by her nom de guerre, Joan Anglicus. Only twenty years younger than I, she was."

"Joan Anglicus?" Her name rang a discordant bell. "The one who blew up the TC?"

Shila looked incredibly sad. "Centuries of principled pacifism, undone by a moment of impatience and a quantum trigger."

"A *moment?*" said Joel^2 incredulously. "Fuck your pacifism. I got *killed* by your daughter's suicide bomb, asshole!"

He expected the statement to give the old man at least a moment's pause, but he seemed unfazed. In fact, he nodded as if expecting this turn of events. "Exactly, Mr. Byram. This is why you are the *ayah* we've been waiting for. Our miracle."

"I'm not your miracle." Joel^2 shook his head. "What happened to me was an accident. Coincidence, the dumb luck of the universe. I happened to go through the TC right after your daughter. So what?"

"No, Mr. Byram. You were *selected*. We have known the truth of teleportation since its inception. That it was nothing more than the unholy copying and destruction of human beings. That the Punch Escrow is a lie."

"What do you mean, a lie?"

"Teleportation is *murder*." Shila closed his eyes, as if the emotional impact of these revelations was affecting him, too. "The Punch Escrow is an *execution chamber*. You were killed and printed every time you entered a TC. I'm afraid there is no such thing as teleportation."

The old man probably couldn't have lifted a feather, but Joel[2] felt as if Shila had hit him with a sledgehammer. He'd heard of the Gehinnomites' ramblings before, but now that he was there, hearing it for himself from the source, it felt visceral. Real. The Punch Escrow was a lie? People were being copied and destroyed? Even him?

While his thoughts whirled, the old man kept speaking. "We identified all the members of IT's inner circle who also knew these truths. Among them was your wife. A woman who could prove to the world that teleportation was unnatural, a sin, the technological perversion of God's gifts. Joanna knew she only needed the proper motivation. One person to suffer so that many others may live."

He opened his eyes, fixing Joel[2] with an intense, sympathetic stare. "Thus my daughter found *you*, Mr. Byram."

Shock and anger duked it out in Joel[2]'s brain. As per usual, anger won. "You're saying this whole thing was a fucking *setup*? That I was a target?"

The old man nodded. "However, you were never meant to be killed. Our aim was to disable your foyer in New York so that you *wouldn't* be cleared. But my daughter had other plans." Tears formed in his eyes. "She did not trust that you could become our *ayah*. That you could stand before the world and proclaim the truth. She wished to make herself an example instead."

He passed a hand over his eyes. "What she didn't know, what none of us knew, was that IT had another, more devilish trick up its sleeve. One your wife used to return you from Gehinnom."

"She told me, and she wouldn't have done it if weren't for *your* daughter," Joel[2] said defiantly. "I mean, if you knew what your daughter was doing, why didn't you stop her?"

Shila smiled sadly, his eerily perfect teeth gleaming. "You're not a father yet, my boy. I can't expect you to understand the implications of your question. However, I will say that most of the Friends held your position. I acted selfishly when I prevented them from imprisoning her then. And for that I am sorry."

"Enough with the religious psychobabble history lesson. So you're sorry your daughter fucked up my life. Great. Tell you what: let me and my wife go free and consider us even."

"Don't be glib, child. All I want is to set you free. To set your wife free. To set the entire world free from this evil. I want to show everyone that you are not the only Joel Byram! That just as you sit here, another *you*, the *real* you, sits in New York."

The roiling sea of questions in Joel[2]'s mind went flat. His stomach began to slowly fill with a cold, heavy dread. "What do you mean, 'another me'?"

"Did your wife not confess the full truth to you?" The Gehinnomite's eyes were sad. He took no joy in relating this. "The original you, the one from New York, was never destroyed. He is alive at this moment. You, my boy, are but a copy, a replicant hastily cobbled together by your wife in her desire to play God."

Joel[2] shook his head. It was too much to absorb. He was a ship taking on water, the holes and questions too numerous to plug. He had already begun to sink when Shila explained how teleportation worked, but learning there was another version of him, the original version, one who hadn't died and been resurrected by computer, that sent him straight to the ocean floor. He sagged in the chair.

The wheelchair whirred as it came around the table to him. The old man reached out with a trembling hand, placing it on Joel^2's shoulder. It weighed no more than a few dry twigs. "It may be small comfort, but the fact is, the real Joel Byram died the first time he stepped into that place you call the Punch Escrow." He patted Joel^2 lightly. "That elevator to Gehinnom. An elevator your wife helped build. Isn't that right, Mrs. Byram?"

Joel^2 whipped his head around. In the doorway stood Sylvia, her hands bound and held by Felipe. Her mouth was gagged and there were fresh tears streaking down her cheeks. She had heard everything.

THE BUMMOCK

JOEL[2] AND SYLVIA STARED AT EACH OTHER. Though they'd only been apart for half a day, it felt like nearly a year had passed since they were last together.

He shook his head, trying to clear his mind of all the madness Shila had just heaped upon him. He directed his words at the Gehinnomite leader but kept his eyes fixed on his wife. "You want your proof? Well, so do I. Let Sylvia speak for herself. I trust her much more than I trust any of you assholes."

"Go ahead!" A different cold robotic voice came from the darkness in the back of the room. It had a feminine quality with a heavy Tico accent. "Take off her gag."

"Danielle—" Roberto turned to the empty spot in the room where the voice had come from. "You are here only to observe. Please—"

The head of a stoic silver-blond-haired woman was suddenly unveiled, floating about two meters off the ground. "Let her speak," she said.

As she moved, camouflage LEDs rippled up and down her robe, recording and displaying whatever was behind her such that her body was rendered practically invisible. "Or do you fear the *bruja* might prove me right?" she said to Roberto in a mocking tone.

Joel[2] couldn't grok whether *bruja* was meant to insult Sylvia by calling her a witch, the literal definition, or a bitch, the Costa Rican slang interpretation. Either way, this woman was not making a great first impression.

The old man sighed. "Mr. Byram, allow me to introduce Danielle Julious. My wife."

"His better half, he means. The one who knows that this"—Danielle glanced at Sylvia with disgust—"this *devil's engineer* knew and was intimately engaged with every facet of Honeycomb. The one who wanted to share this evidence with you from the moment you stepped into Monteverde, but my impotent husband here insisted you be brought down the path of goose feathers. Your *bruja* is not who you think she is."

Danielle's LED robe switched from camouflage to a bright white glow. Everyone squinted as their eyes adjusted. She crossed the room, towering over everyone present, statuesque. Her movements, however, were none too gentle as she nudged Felipe aside and pulled the cloth gag out of Sylvia's mouth. "Go ahead," challenged Danielle. "Defend yourself, *bruja*."

Sylvia coughed. She shook her head, but then, making eye contact with her husband, she found she could not keep silent. "Joel, I—I wasn't being completely honest with you. I couldn't be. But I swear, for me, Honeycomb is just an evolution of the cache we use for the Punch Escrow. I never thought—" She stopped talking and just sort of gazed forward.

Joel[2] was in free fall.

There was no denial in her words. And in that moment he knew that everything Shila had told him was true.

The parachute he had been waiting for never opened.

"Never thought what?" Joel[2] asked. "That you'd ever have to use it on me? That you would *replicate* me?"

Sylvia spoke plaintively, like a child who knew she'd done wrong. "I was just researching the science of it! The possibilities." She shook her head. "I know that's not an excuse. I know I should have waited. I should have waited to hear from New York. But you . . ." She looked at her husband again, her eyes shining with tears. "When I knew you were gone, I couldn't process it. I didn't think. I'm so sorry."

Joel[2] hit the ground at terminal velocity.

She took a shuddering breath. "This past year, I don't know what's happened to me. Everything we've been doing at IT, it just got more and more out of control. Honeycomb was just an idea we were toying with, but Bill, he became obsessed. He thought it was *the* game changer. The next phase of human evolution. He immediately put it into production. I kept voicing my concerns—that we had no idea what the impact of such profound time gaps would do to the human psyche, to say nothing of the moral questions. But Bill kept experimenting. He said he was doing it to prove that it was safe." Her face contorted. "I should've stopped him! But I was thinking of things like colonizing other planets. Preserving our species. Meanwhile Bill kept encoding himself, staying in the glacier for longer and longer periods. At first a couple of minutes, then hours, then days—"

"What about me?" Joel[2] said sourly. "When were you gonna tell me what you did to me?"

"I'm getting to that! Stop interrupting me!" she shouted.

"Sorry!" he yelled back defensively.

She took another calming breath. "Bill told me not to worry about it. He programmed a fail-safe in case something went wrong. The system would automatically restore an encoded person after a defined period of time."

"So is that what—" Joel[2] began.

"Joel, please!" She closed her eyes, collecting herself. "I need to get through this. We don't have an internal affairs department at International Transport. Corina says we're all one another's consciences. A month ago I discovered something even more disturbing about Project Honeycomb. IT . . . They were militarizing it. Researching the use of teleportation as a weapon."

Danielle looked triumphantly at her husband, but Joel[2] was confused. "Militarize teleportation? How would that even work?"

"I wondered the *same thing*. When I learned about these experiments, I escalated directly to Corina Shafer. She pretty much admitted the whole thing. Said it was just a trial program. Mobile teleportation was an easy way to extract dangerous people, saving a lot of lives in the process. She said Bill was handling the temporal disassociation problem. There were apparently some side effects to being kept in the glacier, and the severity of them was directly correlated to the amount of time a person spent inside. But Corina felt comfortable proceeding with the project, since Honeycomb could be spun as a morally superior alternative to weapons. Rather than kill a threat, you could freeze them in the glacier, where they could be extracted for interrogation or civilized punishment."

"Or imprisoned there forever," pointed out Roberto. "Removed from time itself and held in Gehinnom."

"I didn't like it," Sylvia said defensively. "But I admit, I wanted it to make sense. I hate violence, and this sounded more humane than killing people. And . . . I wanted to keep working on Honeycomb. In spite of everything, I knew it could exist for the betterment of society. It will let us explore the most distant reaches of space. Our planet is dying. We keep patching it, engineering ways to extend its life, but sooner or later we will run out of time. I was trying to give us—humanity"—she looked back at Joel[2]—"our children . . . a chance. So I stupidly rationalized my concerns away. I told myself a lot of our greatest, most beneficial scientific break-throughs had been militarized—nuclear energy, genetic en-gineering, wake transduction—but ultimately they did more good than bad."

Danielle grabbed Sylvia by the chin. "So for that, you would decide who lives and dies? Who is resurrected and who is gone forever? How many husbands will you print? How many would satiate your hunger, *súcuba*?"

Sylvia shook her head loose of the old woman's grip. "No! It wasn't like that." She looked at her (*other*) husband. "Joel," she implored him, "none of this was planned. I really thought I lost you. I swear."

Joel[2] knew that his wife had kept secrets from him. Not just because her job required it. Still, he had no idea how deep and dark her hidden life had been. Every time she'd been distant or distracted, her mind had gone to her own personal Gehinnom. While he'd been deciding what to have for dinner or which movie to watch, she'd been grappling with the future of hu-manity. No wonder they had grown apart over the last year.

"Don't you dare talk about losing people, *bruja*," Danielle said. "My daughter's blood is on *your* hands!"

"And mine is on your daughter's!" Joel[2] retorted.

"The tree of life is sacred to all," Roberto rasped. "It is not our place to take or alter its fruit. To make another human being," he admonished Sylvia, "is to usurp God's place. It can-not be done!"

"I disagree," stated Danielle. "This *bruja* used her *desgra-ciado*, and she will do so again." She stroked the side of Sylvia's face. Felipe gripped the back of my wife's head, holding her for a slap, but Danielle just gently moved her bangs away from her eyes. "She's going to bring back our daughter, *mi amor.*"

CHEKHOV'S GUN

"ENOUGH!" Roberto's vocal implants struggled with the volume of his shout, the latter half of his word becoming static. "Put such heretical thoughts out of your mind, Danielle."

"But that is the clever part, husband. It will not be us who partakes in such heresy." She turned her eyes to Sylvia. "She will do it for us."

Joel[2] looked at his wife. She tried to hold his gaze, but her eyes kept falling to the floor, unable to face her shame reflected in his pupils. Fearful that anything he might say could push the terrorists toward more violence, he uncharacteristically opted to remain silent.

Roberto's bony hand took his wife's and held it. "To solicit unholy industry is to partake in it. Our daughter is dead, *mi amor*. It pains me as it pains you. We would not tarnish the sanctity of—"

"Hypocrite!" spat Danielle. "'Does not each of you on the Sabbath untie your ox or donkey from the stall and lead it out to give it water? Then should not this woman, a daughter of Abraham, whom Satan has kept bound for eighteen long years, be set free on the Sabbath day from what bound her?' That is Luke thirteen, husband," she said, pulling her hand from his grasp.

"I know the scripture, *wife*. And do you dare compare our work to our Lord's? We have before us the *ayah*. Joel and Sylvia Byram shall destroy International Transport by exposing the truth. Why veer from that plan in pursuit of a soul who is gone? Look at this poor empty vessel before us. He is not a man, but a puppet. His wife, the puppet mistress. This is what the world must know. When the *other* is found, we will have all the pieces we need. The world will not be able to think of teleportation without remembering their tragedy."

"Untie me and you'll see how much of a puppet I am," said Joel².

Felipe smiled from behind Sylvia. "*Jes*, untie him. Let's see the puppet dance!"

Shila ignored them both. Then, lowering his voice to a mere whisper akin to the sound of a fork scraping a stone, he asked his wife, "Would you cast aside all our years of work? Our beliefs, our service to God? Would you sever your commitment to our people?"

"What do you know of commitment?" Danielle asked coldly. "You are like these seculars. They shake hands, exchange chits, give someone their *word*. What do these things mean? They change their minds five minutes later and the world goes on as if nothing happened. You want to know the words of commitment?" She raised her arms, her glowing robe making her look like an angel. "Pulsa D'nura. *That* is a commitment. Our daughter, she was the *ayah* we sought all this time. And her foolish father is too old and blind to see it."

"No, *mi amor*. The Pulsa D'nura is a curse, not a miracle."

"*El que no cree,*" she uttered scornfully, confounding Joel², who was wishing now he'd paid more attention in Spanish class. "Suddenly everything can only have one meaning. You want a question?" Turning to Sylvia, she asked, "Tell me, *bruja*, what is the difference between a curse and a prayer?"

Sylvia continued staring at the floor.

"Tell me!" Danielle yelled.

"Don't you fucking yell at my wife!" Joel^2 shouted back.

Sylvia shook her head. Though he couldn't see her eyes, he knew that she didn't want him to aggravate the situation.

"Answer," said Danielle, grabbing a fistful of Joel^2's hair. "Or I will dash out your creation's brains on this table."

"Intent," Sylvia said, meeting her captor's eyes.

"*Sí*, intent. And who determines intent?" Not waiting for an answer this time, she let go of Joel^2 and pivoted to face her husband. "The Pulsa D'nura is a compact between creation and creator. It compels both to *act*. The request needs power, like fuel, like gravity. The more penitent the creation, the cleaner the fuel. In old times people sacrificed animals when they asked God for things. The more valuable the animal, the more public the display, the more fuel for their prayers. Personal sacrifice is a great fuel. Martyrdom, however, that is the greatest fuel of all." Her eyes shone, bright and distant. "It wakes up the hibernating devout, the Gehinnomites who have been asleep for a generation or more. They have seen my Joanna's sacrifice for a selfless cause. And when they see her rise again, a female Christ, they will be compelled by God to act!"

"Danielle," Roberto pleaded. "Do you truly believe Joanna would—"

"*Lo que haces se te devuelve*, Roberto!" Danielle cut him off. "While you idled away your time with plots and strategies, our daughter planned her sacrifice. She delivered unto us the *bruja* and her puppet. What we do with them is up to us."

"I won't do it," said Sylvia. "Honeycomb was a mistake. I shouldn't have used it on Joel and I never will again."

A mistake, thought Joel[2] bitterly. *Is that what she sees me as now?* Before he could go further with that dark thought, Danielle gripped a handful of his hair again, yanking his head back to expose his throat.

"I do not care if he is the *ayah* or not." She spoke quietly, keeping her eyes fixed on Sylvia. "Felipe will torture him just the same until you bring back my daughter. Judging by your resistance so far, he may end up losing a few teeth. Maybe a finger, an ear. But I suspect you will break before we take his eyes."

"No!" Sylvia said.

"I agree," said Roberto in his metallic voice. "No more. Felipe, please take Danielle away and confine her to her room. She is unwell."

Felipe did not respond. Both of the ancient Gehinnomites looked to the guard. There was a rumble in the ground, like a low-magnitude, short-lived earthquake. Before anyone could comment on it, Danielle gave Felipe a single curt nod—

And the guard let go of Sylvia. He stepped forward, swinging a heavy red brick into Roberto Shila's cheek. The strike was so powerful, it knocked the frail old man clear out of his wheelchair. As he fell, Roberto's foot became tangled in the armrest, pulling the heavy chair on top of him. His small jamming weapon clattered across the floor.

Sylvia jumped as some of the old man's blood splashed her face. Joel[2] pulled against Danielle, but she removed a hunting knife from underneath her robe and held it under his chin. Her eyes were ringed with tears, but fierce.

"I thought you were supposed to be pacifists!" Joel[2] yelled.

The old woman jerked her head toward her limp husband. "He was. And look where it got him. For decades we have peacefully protested your technology, and nothing changed. My daughter destroys one TC, and in a day we have both of you. You will do what we ask or continue to suffer the consequences."

Her threat was delivered matter-of-factly, more a promise than a warning. *She just ordered a hit on her own husband. Pretty sure she won't go easy on me.* He unconsciously found himself feeling his teeth with his tongue, imagining what it would feel like to have them ripped from his jaw one by one while his wife watched and begged them to stop. It wasn't a pleasant prospect, but they couldn't give in to these assholes, either. "Fuck you," he said to Danielle.

Felipe dropped the bloody rock. He briskly walked across the room and took the knife from Danielle. Keeping one hand on Joel²'s bound wrists, he pressed the blade to the base of his right pinkie. "*Puta estúpida.* You will change your song soon enough."

He pressed down on the knife. Pain bit into Joel²'s hand. A thin line of blood ran down his palm, dripping onto the gray stone floor. Danielle nodded for him to continue, her face shining with expectation.

"Wait!" said Sylvia. Felipe and Danielle turned. "If . . . if I do this, do I have your word we are free to go?"

"What?" Joel² said, shocked that she would even entertain the notion after all they'd been through. "Sylvia! Don't—" He bent over coughing as Felipe socked him in the solar plexus.

"My *word?*" Danielle spat on the floor near the discarded bloody brick. "Here is my word. I will take you with me to the hospital, *bruja.* Felipe will have his pliers and knives, keeping your husband company. Should you waver, you will watch on my comms as Felipe removes teeth, nails, then fingers with each of your hesitations. Then, with my daughter by my side, you, *bruja,* will fulfill my husband's last wish and confess everything you have done—your sins—to the world. If you are still alive after that, you are free to go live your miserable lives."

There was a long silence, during which Joel² made eye contact with Felipe. He saw in the Gehinnomite's expression that he would follow through on everything Danielle had promised, and more. He would relish it.

"I'll do it," said Sylvia.

For good measure, Felipe punched Joel² in the gut several more times, making him double over in the chair. He curled there, wheezing.

"I'm sorry, Joel." Sylvia looked down at her husband, her eyes bright with tears. And she told him the only truth in all of this. "I couldn't lose you."

Danielle clapped her hands together once. "Then we are agreed, *bruja*. Felipe, comm the gatehouse. Tell them we are ready to depart."

The guard looked off for a moment, then shrugged. "They are not answering."

There was a sharp knock at the door of the small room. Felipe and Danielle looked at each other quizzically.

"I told them to stay down there until we were done," the old woman cursed, walking to the door and opening it. *"¿Cuándo los tontos te—"*

Although the blast came first, the gaping, bloody hole in Danielle's back was the first sensory input Joel²'s mind latched on to. More blood sprayed Sylvia. The old woman collapsed onto the floor, a puddle of thick dark-red liquid burbling out of the hole in her flickering LED robe.

"¿Qué mierda?" said Felipe, running forward, the knife in his hand.

His question was answered in the form of a second blast. Its thunderous reverberation shook the walls and wine bottles. Felipe spun around as a twenty-gauge copper slug took his arm off at the shoulder. His other hand clawed at the now-empty space, then he, too, dropped to the floor and lay still.

Joel[2] and Sylvia looked at each other, terrified about what new trauma awaited them. A rustle of clothes shifted their attention to the doorway. Stepping over Danielle's corpse, gingerly avoiding the growing puddles of blood, was Bill Taraval. He wore a crisp white IT lab coat, now flecked with red drops, over his cargo shorts and floral-print shirt. His breath was shaky. In his hands was the Remington Model 870 Express seven-round, pump-action shotgun Joel[2] had become acquainted with earlier.

"Oh my," Taraval said, letting the shotgun fall to his side as he surveyed the scene. "My, my, my. What a mess."

Joel[2] was still tied to the chair, unsure if he should move. Sylvia, however, stepped forward. "Bill! Thank God. Where did you find that?"

Taraval seemed to come back to himself, lifting the shotgun again and studying it. "Ah yes. The third and most effective of the thirty-six stratagems: kill with a borrowed sword." He swung it back down, pointing the barrel at Joel[2]'s forehead.

Joel[2] winced. "Hey, man, you mind not pointing that barrel in my face?"

"A perfectly poignant proposal," Taraval said, nodding. Then he pulled the trigger.

Click.

"Joel!" Sylvia yelled.

Realizing the gun was out of shells, Joel[2] tried to get to his feet. The chair still bound to his wrists, he awkwardly ran at Taraval, but the man whipped the shotgun around, swinging the stock into the side of his head. Joel[2] slipped in a puddle of Danielle's blood, cracking his skull against the wall. He dropped back into a sitting position.

"Stop!" screamed Sylvia. She ran at Taraval, but as her hands were still tied behind her back, there wasn't much she could do but accost him. "What are you doing?"

"What I should have done the first time around," he answered in a measured tone. "Your lack of objectivity has now pulled me into your derailment. I have been cut loose, set adrift, ruined. And all because of this *thing*"—he brought the butt of the gun down on Joel^2's face—"you call 'husband.'" A large wound opened above Joel^2's right eye, blood coating his face. He slumped over, not moving.

"No!" Sylvia cried.

Taraval shook Joel^2's blood off the butt of his weapon. Calmly, he said, "Come now, Sylvia, surely you knew this was how things would end when you messaged me this morning. Even if you are unwilling to clean up your messes, someone must. And not just for me, no. For the benefit of humanity."

He looked off suddenly, noticing something on the floor. "Fascinating. This must be some sort of—" He meandered to Roberto's egg-sized device, picked it up, and examined it closely. "A proximity jammer! How clever. Thank goodness he didn't get a click off on me. You know, Sylvia, for a murder of pacifist crows, these Gehinnomites seem to have a rather ironic affinity for antique weapons, wouldn't you say?" Pocketing the device, he then advanced on my wife with the shotgun. "Hear that?" Taraval smiled. "No, of course you wouldn't without use of your comms," he mused smugly. "It appears paramedics are en route. Well, destiny is ne'er kind to those truant," he said, taking her by the arm. "Our coach awaits."

THE ROAD OF TRIALS

FOR A WHILE the ambulance was relentless—rightfully so—in its critique of my driving. At some point, after almost colliding with a produce truck because I was in the wrong lane, I stopped responding to its warnings. The ambulance, in turn, stopped using conversational language with me, reserving its speech for alerts like "Vehicle parked on shoulder ahead" and "Likelihood of collision has increased by thirty percent."

Ninety minutes into our journey, just as I was getting a handle on the driving thing, the road got impossibly bumpy. It seemed as though it had been intentionally left unpaved by eco-conscious residents, resulting in a tedious, bouncy trip through the foggy mountain roads. My speed wasn't aided by the entrepreneurial endeavors of townspeople along the way.

The Costa Rica of 2147 was what one might call a second-world nation. Metropolises like San José, Alajuela, and Rincón de la Vieja had first-world facilities and infrastructure, but the rest of the country was still very much a touristy boondock. Therefore, it was no surprise that in Quebrada Grande, the roadway became littered with merchants stepping in front of cars, each attempting to hawk their wares to passengers. I'm certain those peddlers regretted ever stepping foot in front of my ambulance. Especially when I heard a loud bang. I worried I might have hit one of them, but thankfully I had only run over a coconut.

Just to play it safe from there on out, I pushed the flashing siren icon on the console. A blend of tuba-like bass and trebly alerts started blaring from the ambulance. That did the trick. Like the Red Sea parting for Moses, the merchants moved out of my way and created a path.

Following the ambulance's GDS route, I turned onto a blessedly paved side road that led up the mountain. A proximity alarm flashed, and I winced as a huge people-mover thundered past overhead.

"What kind of psycho would fly one of those things so low?" I wondered, looking back at the huge flying machine. It was already little more than a gray dot in the distance.

"I'm sure I have no idea," answered the ambulance dryly.

I glanced back down at the ambulance's map display. I was nearly on top of the coordinates Moti had given me. *Sylvia.* Looking forward, I saw that we were heading straight for a nice mountaintop villa. Below it were slopes of cultivated grapevines. At first, it looked like my wife had booked a much nicer resort for her and Joel[2] than the one we'd stayed at on our honeymoon. Then I remembered that she had been forcibly taken to this place, most likely by the Gehinnomites.

At the entrance to the winery, I took my foot off the gas pedal. The blip on the map display blinked, and the ambulance told me, "We have reached your destination."

Just off the road were the remains of a gatehouse. It looked like it had been stepped on by a giant foot, or maybe a people-mover. About a quarter mile up the mountain was a three-story mansion, the only place I'd seen in the last ten minutes that could be housing Sylvia. I got out of the vehicle, wondering whether it was a good or bad thing that no welcoming committee came to greet me. Was it possible that nobody was watching the entrance?

Guess I'm about to find out. Sylvia is in there. Hero time.

"Don't go anywhere," I instructed the ambulance.

"May I ask, when will I get the results of my assessment?"

"Soon," I said. "So long as you stay put and shut up."

As I exited the ambulance, three unfortunate truths unveiled themselves to me:

I was about to enter a terrorist compound by myself.

I was utterly unarmed.

I had no idea what to do if I ran into the other me.

Wait: Can two of me even exist in the same space? I thought. *If we touch, will the world end? I guess, technically, only one of me needs to make it.*

"Actually, one more thing," I said. "Do you have any weapons on board?"

"Is this another test? I thought you wanted me to stay put and shut up."

"I do. After you answer this question."

"No."

"You mean, no weapons?"

"Yes."

"What do you do in the event of, I don't know, a violent patient?"

"Summon the police."

Good thinking. Unfortunately, I'm an international criminal with no identity. I slid open the door connecting the front cabin to the rear and looked inside. Bandages, sheets, Band-Aids, and lotions—Moti probably could have MacGyver'd something with all this stuff, but I sure couldn't. All I needed was something sharp, like a scalpel, but no luck. I next tried looking for warning labels, indicators of things that could inflict damage on people. Nothing. There was a gurney on board, but when I tried to take off one of its legs to use as a club, I only succeeded in pinching my fingers. I was getting frustrated and flustered. Also, I was scared that at any given point, one of my wife's captors or an angry vintner might spot the trespassing ambulance on his property.

I had nearly resigned myself to grabbing a stick off the ground when I saw it: a tiny little warning label with a lightning bolt on it. *Electric shock!* I opened the metal box. It contained . . . a lightning gun! I would strap it on, kill all the Gehinnomites, and save my wife. The end.

I wish.

The box contained a portable defibrillator. *Well, beggars can't be choosers.* I took the defibrillator out of the container and pulled one of its two metallic paddles from the battery pack.

"Hey, ambulance, how many zaps can each of these defibrillator pads handle before having to be recharged?" I asked.

The answer came back, "Three, each. You don't need both to complete the circuit; each pad is a self-contained defibrillator."

I grabbed a bandage roll and wrapped it around the paddle in my left hand, fashioning a crude, electrified boxing glove. I'd have to make physical contact to use it, and also risk shocking myself in the process. I thought about putting the other paddle in my back pocket as backup in case I used all three charges, but knowing me, I'd accidentally sit on it and shock myself out of commission.

I examined my handiwork. *One man with a defibrillating hand versus an army of Gehinnomites. Do this, and I might get my life back. Don't, and I'll just die. No. I refuse to give Moti the satisfaction.* Despite my feigned confidence, I felt stomach acid rising up my esophagus, and my chest felt frozen. *Great. A panic attack.* I breathed in and out, but spending more time in the back of a stolen ambulance was not going to fix that. *Fuck it, here goes.*

The first step of my plan was reconnaissance. I started by creeping up toward the villa, crouching low to stay behind the grapevines. I'm not an expert at these things, but I had played plenty of stealth-combat video games. Staying out of sight was always the prudent thing to do. I reached the entrance and took a quick peek inside. Several parked cars, a large RV, and a completely destroyed golf cart. No guards. Off to the side was a wooden sign pointing to *La Jardín*. I allowed myself another glance and, seeing no movement inside or outside, ran through the parking area until I reached the garden and hid behind a leafy wet bush. After several long moments of listening and shaking off bugs, I was convinced that no one had seen me. I walked down into the garden, trying to see any kind of activity in the house. As a result, I nearly tripped over something wrapped in a blue drape.

My clumsy misstep caused the drape to unroll slightly, revealing—*ugh!*—the corpse of a man whose neck had been violently broken. My stomach churned. I felt the sick coming up, but held it down. My teeth clenched involuntarily. *Relax, dead people can't hurt you.* I squeamishly re-covered the poor guy's face, wiping my hands on my white lab coat afterward. There was a branch nearby swarming with fire ants, which I kicked over to hold the drape down.

I looked up a stone stairway, hearing a repetitive metallic clicking coming from the villa. Some kind of security system? Stealing up the steps a bit, I saw the sound was merely from the latch of the rear patio door, swaying back and forth against its anchor. *Why's the door open? Is this what walking into a trap feels like?*

I tiptoed up to the door, my defibrillator paddle held out in front of me like a shield. Having it probably did more to boost my confidence than provide any actual protection. As I reached the top, I could see the cloud forest below on three sides. If I wasn't about to barf from terror, it would have been a beautiful view.

I peered around the corner of the patio to the inside of the house. The hairs on the back of my neck could have only been straighter if I'd been shocked by the Levantines' security system a second time. I felt an inkling of wind, the draft causing the door to crack open and close, over and over, each time generating that *click-clack* sound. *Now or never.* I pushed the door open ever so gently, but it creaked ever so loudly.

The living room was also empty, but I could see drops of blood leading into the kitchen. I followed the trail, going down a flight of stairs and finding myself in an empty basement winery. The whole place appeared to be deserted and quiet. I continued tracking the blood until I reached a small door set into the red mountain rock.

Steeling myself and clutching my defibrillator, I pushed open the wooden door.

Inside was a mosaic of violence.

Oh no.

There were at least four distinct human bodies, all of whom appeared to be dead. Blood was all over the place. Furniture had been broken and tossed around. Near the center of the room was a severed arm, blasted off at the shoulder. It was repulsive, but I forced myself to look closer at the corpses. An old man, a Costa Rican guy with only one arm, an old lady with a huge hole in her chest, and a slumped-over man in a chair whose face I couldn't see. No Sylvia. If she'd been here, it appeared she was gone now.

I couldn't hold back anymore. I stumbled outside of the room, dry heaving against the wall. A few coughs and a good amount of spitting later, the terrible thoughts hit me.

I'm too late. What if she's not alive? Do not think that.

I had to go back into the room. If there was any clue as to where Sylvia was, or whether or not she was—*don't think that*—still kidnapped, I had to find it.

Despite more loud inner voices encouraging me to flee, I stepped back into the room. Carefully avoiding the copious puddles of blood, I moved closer to the slumped man in the chair. I didn't recognize any of the other faces, and his seemed to be the least splattered in gore.

At close range, he seemed about my size. Fresh blood still oozed from a wound in his temple. His head hung downward, but I could tell his right eye—in fact, the entire right side of his face—had been decimated by whatever had hit him on the side of the head. *Something strange about this one.* Slowly, I lifted his head back with one hand, keeping my defibrillator at the ready.

Something really *strange about this one.*

I angled his head to the left, studying what I could make out of his face.

My face.

"Oh *God.*" I was looking at a bloody, bruised replica of myself.

My words echoed all around me, bouncing off the bricks, wine bottles, and the pulpy face of my dead *other.*

MAGIC MIRROR GATE

When a Pawn has reached the eighth square, the player has the option of selecting a piece, whether such piece has been previously lost or not, whose names and powers it shall then assume, or of deciding that it shall remain a Pawn.
—Rule XIII, The Modern Chess Instructor,
Wilhelm Steinitz, 1889

HAVE YOU EVER LOOKED INTO A TRUE MIRROR? Regular mirrors, as you know, show a reflection of whatever's held before them. An inversion. That's why writing will appear backward in a mirror. But true mirrors show things as they really appear to others.

They had one at the New York Hall of Science, and seeing yourself in it was a head-trippy experience. For the first time, you get to see yourself not the way you've seen your face your whole life, but the way others see you. The result is startling and bizarre.

Now, imagine taking that feeling and applying it not to a mirror but to a real version of yourself, who also happens to be dead. Multiply that by a thousand, and it still won't come close to the horror I felt as I stared at my own dead body.

No.

I froze, uncertain of my place. So many emotions elbowed their way to prominence in my mind as I stared at him, trying to make sense of what I was seeing. I'd been so focused on getting to Sylvia, I hadn't dared to consider what it would be like to meet—him. *Me.* Especially now that he was dead. Was this what happened when you died? If so, I wasn't ready for it. I wasn't ready to look upon the ruined, bloody face of myself. *My . . . remains.*

At the same time, part of me felt relief. *He's already gone.* There wouldn't have to be any existential crises to unpack, no painful discussions to decide who would end up with our wife. *I could just leave.* No one would ever need to know he existed. Only me, Sylvia, Taraval, Corina—okay, a few people would know. All I had to do was find my wife, reactivate my comms, and our lives could return to semi-normal.

I heard a drop of his blood hit the gray stone floor.

Wait, was that movement? Did he just flinch?

I raced to check his carotid pulse, then paused. *Is it okay to touch him?* I decided I didn't have a choice.

Is he alive? Why didn't I check his pulse before?

My fingers touched his neck. The universe did not explode. Instead Joel[2]'s left eye snapped open, scaring the crap out of me. I instinctively jumped back.

Holy shit, he's alive.

"Sylvia?" he mumbled.

"Did you see her? Is she alive?" I sputtered back. But he just moaned softly and closed his eye again.

I nearly broke my neck sprinting back down to the ambulance outside. I collected all the medicinal supplies I could carry: Band-Aids, shots,[23] a bunch of other stuff I had no idea

---

[23] Shots are active polydrugs. They are a mix of nanites, adrenaline, vitamins, clotting agents, diluting agents, and polymorphic antibiotics. Once in the body, the nanites perform diagnostics and activate whatever components they deem necessary.

how to use. I even kept my defibrillator spooled around my hand—*just in case.*

Back in the basement, I affixed the biggest Band-Aid I had to the gash in his head, then administered one of the shots into his thigh.

Almost instantly, his face twitched and his knee spasmed. I could never properly express in words how surreal it was watching my copy convulse uncontrollably like that. Seeing him in pain made me twinge. Talk about your out-of-body experience.

"Don't you fucking touch her!" His good eye was wild, straining to focus on what he thought was his attacker. He pulled at his bindings like a trapped animal. "I'll kill you, asshole!"

"Hey, hey!" I yelled back, then lowered my voice. "Calm down. You're okay."

A little color came back into his face, though his left eye, the intact one, still seemed vacant. His pupil dilated, seeing me. "Who the fuck?" He tried again: "You're—"

"Me. Yes."

He looked me up and down. I knew what he was going through, and "confused" didn't begin to cover it. He was waking up from the most existential nightmare you could conjure to find out it was reality. I opened my mouth to explain, then decided there was too much to go over. *Keep it simple, stupid.* "Is there a knife or something around here?" I asked him.

"On the ground"—he indicated with his ruined head—"next to the dead *bruja.*"

Realizing he meant the old woman with the hole in her chest, I scooped up the hunting knife and cut through the ropes binding his wrists to the chair. He winced in pain as the blood flowed back into his hands.

"Where's Sylvia?" I said. "What happened here?"

"Sylvia." His eye was fully focused now. He tried to stand, but didn't yet have the strength. "Taraval. That motherfucker, I thought he came here to rescue us. Guess he had other plans."

"Taraval was here?" I asked in disbelief.

"Yeah, it was a real party for a second. Me, Sylvia, and the Gehinnomites. Then Taraval showed up with an antique shotgun he stole from that asshole and shot everyone. Then he bashed in my head. I think he took Syl."

"You think?" I said angrily. "You were right here. How can you not know?"

"Maybe because he didn't tell me his plans before he bashed my head in."

"Shit. The people-mover!" I said, putting two and two together.

"What?"

"At the bottom of the hill, I almost got killed by a people-mover when I drove up. That was probably them. They could be anywhere by now!"

"Shit!" spat Joel[2].

We glared at each other, our expressions a perfect symmetry of anger. Then, remembering we were each other's copy, an uncomfortable silence occupied the space between us.

"Do you mind?" said Joel[2], holding out a hand.

"Oh! Sorry, yeah, of course." He hissed in pain as I helped him to his feet. "Are you okay?"

"What do you think?" he snapped.

Before I could snap back, a wet, metallic coughing sent me reeling, almost taking Joel[2] down with me.

"Guess I'm not the only one who made it," he said, limping over to lift the wheelchair off the incredibly old man. "Joel, meet Roberto Shila. Founder of the Gehinnomites, oldest man in the world. He might know where Sylvia is." Joel[2] kicked the wheelchair aside. "Well, do you?"

Roberto Shila gazed up at the two of us. One whole side of his face had swelled and turned purple with blood. He was clearly in very bad shape, though one wouldn't know it from his oscillating cold, robotic laugh.

"Look at the two of you," he said, then stopped midsentence to cough up some blood. "The perfect evidence of the inhumanity created by the devil's ultimate invention." He looked at Joel[2]. "You, the golem, and he"—he looked at *me*—"the reanimated corpse. Husbands of the harpy."

"What's he talking about?" I asked Joel[2].

"It's how he is," Joel[2] remarked. Then he said coldly to the old man, "At least *our* wife didn't try to kill me."

Shila's ruined face became an ugly mask of sorrow. The old man shook his head. "I do not understand any of your kind's motives. You, who would so willingly destroy the soul and usurp the powers of resurrection—"

"Save it," said Joel[2]. I couldn't tell what he was thinking, but I saw he was angry. Maybe angrier than I'd ever been about anything.

A thought occurred to me. "Wait, what does he mean 'resurrection'?"

Shila coughed feebly. "Tell him. He deserves to know the same as you."

"Know what?" I said. "Will someone just tell me the truth? She's my wife!"

My doppelgänger snorted. "Oh, she's *your* wife now? Okay, *Joel*, let me tell you what *your* wife did, because, yes, it definitely falls under the category of resurrection. I take it you remember Project Honeycomb?"

Sylvia mentioned it. Moti mentioned it. I should have paid closer attention. "It's what Sylvia was working on at IT?"

"And I assume you already know the Punch Escrow is a bullshit smoke screen, and you've been copied and killed a hundred times?"

"Seriously, what the fuck crawled up your ass? You want to stand there and be a jerk, fine. But I'm going to finish what I came here to do, which is save my wife and fix my life. Maybe you can bring me the fuck up to speed so we can figure this shit out *together*."

"What life?" Joel[2] said bitterly. "I wouldn't even be here if she hadn't printed me from a backup. An *incomplete* backup. I wasn't supposed to make it, and for that matter, neither were you."

"I'm fine, asshole. You're the copy!"

Shila gurgled a metallic laugh. "Don't be so hard on each other. You are both puppets. You," he said, nodding at me with his ruined, bloody skull, "have you not considered what clockwork brought you to my doorstep?"

"What the fuck do you know about anything?" My tone was just as aggressive and belligerent as my other's. "Has anybody ever told you that you sound like an evil robot on acid?"

Shila took a rattling breath. "I may be an old man, but the Friends are not without friends. Friends who foretold your arrival. You, poor thing, are a pawn. An expendable piece in a game played among International Transport and the Levant. Your role was to manifest chaos, manipulate an outcome to tip the scales such that one party gains an edge and another loses."

"The Levant?" I said. "How do you know them?"

"Our beliefs are aligned on some matters. Their concerns are our concerns."

"So you planned this together?"

The old man shrugged. "We share information when we find it useful."

Information . . . "Moti?" I said. Shila's lack of response confirmed my suspicion. *That dick, I was really starting to believe his "Aher" crap.* "Yeah, well—you're not telling me anything I don't already know." It was a lie, but I hoped it sounded true.

"You," the Gehinnomite said, and nodded to Joel[2], "a puppet created by your wife's desire to play God. And you"—back to me—"a catalyst for a nation seeking to usurp power."

Joel[2] looked at me. "Okay, now I'm lost. Who is Moti? What's he talking about?"

The gambit unraveled in my mind: Moti's coolness when we first met, the questions he asked me: *I'll know if you are lying.* It wasn't a spymaster's sixth sense. Moti knew the truth—everything—all along. *Why did Pema send me to Moti when I showed up at IT? She must have been working for him, another one of his pawns. He wrote down the GDS coordinates, told me to steal an ambulance, gave me everything I needed to find my way here. No wonder he knew how to operate a TC console!*

We're his blackmail. The Gehinnomites want us to be their miracle; the Levant want us to be their bargaining chips.

I growled. "That Turkish-drinking, cigarette-smoking son of a bitch. I'm going to kill him!"

"Would you *please* tell me what is going on?" Joel[2] pressed.

I gripped my weaponized defibrillator. *Game on, Moti.*

"There's an ambulance I stole outside," I offered, by way of an answer. "I'm not sure if it's figured out I stole it yet, but just to play it safe, we should get out of here. I'll tell you everything on the way."

"What about him?" Joel[2] asked, glancing at Shila.

"Please. Help me into my chair," the Gehinnomite said, reaching out his bony hand.

Joel[2] bent to help the old man up. His wheelchair was covered in blood, but Shila didn't seem to care. Joel[2] tried to adjust his body so he'd be more comfortable.

"Why are you helping the guy who kidnapped our wife?" I asked, annoyed. "Just leave him!"

"He didn't want to hurt us," Joel[2] said. Again, I wondered what was going on in his head. One minute he was ready to kill everyone; the next he was somber and forgiving. Was I this schizophrenic?

"Thank you," said Roberto Shila, his voice crackling meekly. He leaned back in the chair, the color continuing to fade from his face. He didn't seem long for this world. "I take comfort that my wife's and daughter's deaths were not in vain. You two are the *ayah*, the miracle I've been waiting for all these years. Proof that teleportation is evil. None could classify your circumstance as anything else. I would only ask that you promise to deliver this message to the world, so that God may once more . . ." But his voice demodulated into static, then white noise. His lips quivered and his head dropped forward. After 171 years, Roberto Shila exhaled his last breath.

"He's gone," I said. When Joel[2] didn't respond, I continued, "Syl is still out there somewhere. The longer she's gone, the harder it might be to find her."

Joel[2] nodded silently, but still didn't move.

"Look, man, I know you've been through a lot today, but we really need to—"

"Let's go," he said, finishing my sentence as he limped toward the door.

DON'T YOU WANT ME

ON THE WALK BACK down to the ambulance, in the midday light of the vineyard, I got a good look at my doppelgänger. The Band-Aids were doing a decent job cauterizing Joel^2's forehead gash, but his right eye looked like a crushed grape. I put a bandage on it. "To keep it from getting infected," I told Joel^2. But really it was to keep it from grossing me out.

"Okay. You've performed exceedingly well in your assessment!" I enthusiastically commended the ambulance as we strapped ourselves into the front seats. "You haven't been cheating, have you? Third-party APIs still disabled?"

"Ambulances don't cheat," said the vehicle.

"Just one final task, then you'll be cleared for service," I said. "Drive us back to the San José hospital as fast as possible."

"Very well," said the vehicle. "It appears Mr. Byram needs medical attention. That eye injury is quite serious."

"Shit," Joel^2 said, putting a hand up to the bandage.

"Just leave it," I suggested. "Let the Band-Aids do their work."

The ambulance pulled away from the winery. We drove down through the cloud forest, siren wailing, leaving Roberto

Shila and the other Gehinnomites behind to rest eternally in their mountaintop wine cellar.

"It appears something is amiss with my sensors," said the ambulance as we pulled onto Perro Negro Road. "Your genetic profiles identically match each other's. Perhaps I should pull over."

"No, uh, it's a simulation," I improvised. "His head wound isn't real. It's intended to convey a patient in stage two trauma." I shrugged at Joel[2], unsure whether stage two trauma was a thing or not.

"Very well. I anticipate arrival in approximately one hundred and ten minutes."

Not fast enough. "Really?" I said. "Because the other ambulances have completed this part of the assessment in less than ninety."

"And they did it without being noticed by anyone," Joel[2] egged it on.

There was a short pause. "Doable, but expensive," it responded.

"Spare no expense. Remember, you're delivering a trauma patient to the hospital!"

"And don't forget to turn off your sensors. Even the auditory ones," Joel[2] said.

I eyed him. *Why are you going on about sensors?*

"But then I won't be able to communicate with you."

"We'll unmute you if we need to talk. I don't want any malfunctions throwing off this test." Joel[2] squinted his left eye at me in what I soon realized was an attempt at a wink.

"Very well. I shall resume communication upon arrival or should an emergency present itself."

"Thank you," Joel[2] and I said in unison.

Jinx.

"Can you jinx yourself?" we both asked at the same time, then followed up with concurrent and eerily identical laughter. Then we simply stared at each other. There aren't enough synonyms of the word *awkward* to explain our situation. What was one supposed to say to one's self upon meeting him? Like, was there some sort of thing I could ask him that would reveal something about myself? I wondered if he was thinking the same thing. *Probably so,* I decided.

I want to say that there was a *Holy shit!* moment where he and I acknowledged the paradox we were in and reached some synchronized epiphany. But at the time, maybe from the shock of everything that had occurred, or maybe because I couldn't process our *sameness,* I couldn't come up with anything. Even with the eye patch, it was awkward to look him in the face. Every time we tried making eye contact, we'd both look away, embarrassed.

"So," I said, trying to start somewhere, "how did you manage to get yourself caught by the Gehinnomites?"

He told me about waking up in the hospital, and Sylvia's urge to leave San José as quickly as possible. "She kind of freaked out after this woman Pema commed her."

"Pema?" I asked, perturbed. "Waifish, slanted eyes, James Bond–villain pantsuit?"

"Yeah. Did you run into her too? I was just waking up from this crazy dream. Get this: my comms started randomly playing 'Karma Chameleon,' so I woke up singing—"

"God damn it!"

"What?"

"Karma fucking Chameleon. *That's* how she knew it."

"I don't get it."

I explained that Pema had used the obscure song as a way to break me out, which led to my fevered escape to Moti's office and my subsequent electrocution by his security system.

"They're definitely working together. That was only an hour or so after my comms went on the fritz. Shit."

"When my comms came on, yours went off?"

"Yep. Fuck! Her *escape plan* sent me right into Moti's lap."

"Again, who is this Moti guy?"

"A Levantine spy who's been playing us. He thinks he's going to win this weird control game he's playing with IT. I think he's using us because we're the players nobody expects to win. He probably convinced the Gehinnomites to target us in the first place."

"That motherfucker!"

"Exactly," I said.

"But at least you were lied to by strangers. I got betrayed three times by my own wife."

The venom in his voice was chilling. "Take it easy, man. It's not a competition. I'm sure she had her reasons."

"You think you know her so well? That bullshit she fed me after she spoke with Pema was only her first lie," he said, going on to tell me of Taraval's visit the night before, and what Sylvia told him then. "That was betrayal number two. I mean, she seemed to truly regret it. Or at least, she said she hated lying to me—*us*—for the last year. But then, the next morning, she was gone."

"She took off?"

"Yeah, but I was dead asleep after we had—"

He blushed. *They did the deed.* "Oh." I said, turning red myself. *Awkward.*

"Anyway," he said, trying to restock the oxygen in the cabin, "I woke up and she was gone. I don't know how the Gehinnomites managed to disable her comms. They left her GDS on, though—I guess because they wanted me to find her. All so we could reunite and she could tell me from her own mouth that I was a copy of you."

The bitterness in his face was palpable. I cleared my throat, not wanting to get him angrier than he already was. *I don't like me when I'm angry.*

"Those guys, the Gehinnomites, they probably forced her into it. Fuck 'em. We just need to find Sylvia, then we can get this all figured out."

"Yeah." He ruminated on that, but seemed to move on. "What about this Moti guy? Seems like he's known where everyone's been since this thing began."

"Good call. And if he doesn't, then he sure as shit will know how to find her. Only problem is . . ." I hesitated.

"What?"

"I have no idea how we're going to get back to New York. I mean, there's a TC in the hospital, but we need to get someone to operate it. Even if you or I could somehow figure out how to work the console—which is unlikely, based on my experience—only one of us can go."

"That's the *only* problem?" Joel[2] asked in a condescending tone that Sylvia had told me several times she hated. Being on the receiving end of it for the first time, I understood why.

"Can't play the game if we're both not on the board," I said.

"Well, if that's the only thing keeping us from winning, then Moti is about to lose."

"What do you mean?"

"I have a plan," Joel[2] said, "but you're not going to like it. I'm going to hack Julie."

A PERFIDIOUS INDULGENCE

REMEMBER HOW I SAID that most people looked upon their AIDEs as beloved familiars? In Sylvia's case, the relationship with her app was more than familiar—it was familial. Julie became the sister my wife had never had. I had warned her a few times that she shouldn't get too close, that no matter how "real" she seemed, Julie was only an app, coded to serve, but I couldn't control her emotions. The AIDE plugged some hole in Sylvia's psyche, some place not even I could occupy.

And so I let it slide, even though I knew it was a bit unhealthy. That if Julie ever crashed or got deleted, for my wife it would be like losing a loved one. I could see how happy Julie made her, and I didn't want to be the one to take that away from her.

But Joel[2] saying that we should hack Sylvia's AIDE, that we slice and dice her code and peer into my wife's deepest secrets, that wasn't like taking Julie away. That was like cutting her open and pulling out her brains with my bare hands. It wasn't just incredibly illegal; it was a violation of Sylvia's very essence. It's why Joel[2]'s suggestion set me off.

"What?" I said, flabbergasted. "Man, you're crazy. Don't even think about it."

"Listen to me. She can operate the San José TC. She has Sylvia's clearance and expertise."

"Bullshit. We can hire a drone. We can—"

"*We* can't hire shit. You're an invalid. How long before the authorities notice an ambulance was stolen by a gimp with no comms? Don't you get that every single time anything notices you, it's an alert-worthy event? You're like a walking alarm screaming, *Danger, danger, danger!* to everything around us. The longer we take, the greater the risk to us and Sylvia. No, we need to do things my way."

"If you hack Julie, Sylvia will never forgive us. You already salted her once—"

"Again, to save Sylvia's life—"

"No. I am not okay with this."

"Again, again, it's the only way we can port to New York. Use your brain!"

Has he lost his fucking mind? Could the same thing happen to me? "I am. You're crazy. If we do this, I'm going to end up divorced and in jail."

"Listen to yourself! You think *I'm* crazy? You're the one who keeps referring to me as you. Should we ask my comms who the real Joel Byram is? I don't know where you get off thinking you're the real me. I'm the one who actually made it to Costa Rica, and at least I've got the common sense to get that the real me is dead. We died, Joel. Joan Anglicus, Joanna Shila, whatever her name was—she blew Joel Byram up. You're the accidental Joel. And I'm the Joel our wife Frankenstein-ed in Costa Rica. Neither of us is Joel Byram, you idiot. That guy died the first time he teleported."

"You sound like a fucking Gehinnomite!" My face was red with anger. I could feel the fight-or-flight adrenaline coursing its way through my veins.

"I'm also the only person in the world you can trust right now. Do you really think you can handle this little rescue mission by yourself? If so, let's stop the ambulance. I'll walk into the cloud forest and you'll never see me again."

He really seemed ready to do it. "I'm just saying, there's a trust issue. If we're ever going to get back to normal after this—"

"Normal?" He laughed, and not in a nice way. "You think I care about betraying Sylvia's trust at this point? Consider what she's done to us for a minute! She lied to us about Honeycomb, lied about teleportation, lied about Frankenstein-ing me—"

I cut him off. "Stop using that word as a verb. It's not—"

He kept talking over me. "She lied about you, too, Joel. Maybe you haven't had as much time to process it as me, but the sooner you realize that your wife left you for dead in New York, the better. Hell, maybe she even chose me over you. Did you consider that? That Sylvia knew you were in New York, but she stayed in Costa Rica with me. Why do you think that is?"

I finally lost control of my temper and took a swing at him, aiming for the mouth. I'd like to say that I didn't want to aggravate his existing injury by avoiding his eye, but really I just wanted him to shut up. The things he was saying were cruel, but they were dangerously close to the thoughts I was having, too. Had my wife chosen one of us already? What if it wasn't me? I put all my unanswered angst into my punch.

Anticipating my strike—perhaps wanting to throw a punch himself—he quickly slunk into his seat. My fist missed his face, and the padded cushion of the headrest bore the brunt of the impact. Taking advantage of my displacement, he sprung up with an uppercut to my unguarded chin. The back of my head slammed against the windshield, sending me reeling.

"Fuck!" I yelled out of anger and frustration.

"*Fuck* is right!" he yelled back. "As in shut the *fuck* up, you moralizing hypocrite, and let me do what I have to do to rescue *our* wife." He looked off, already focusing on his comms.

What a prick. Is this how I appear to other people? Shit, I must be such an asshole.

"I don't get it," I said, rubbing the lump on my head. "If you hate Sylvia so much, why even bother trying to save her?"

He gave me a withering sidelong glance. "It's complicated. You know that better than anyone. And besides, she's with Taraval. Who knows what that psycho wants with her?"

"You seriously think if you hack Julie, Sylvia's going to be fine with it?"

"She won't be fine with anything if she's dead." He made a few comms-motions with his fingers. "And just so you know, Julie was withholding information that could have led me to Sylvia sooner. She's no angelic innocent. She's just a piece of code doing a job." He paused, the smug, self-satisfied grin on his face that I knew Sylvia both loved and hated on mine. *There it is.* "Hi, Jules," he said brightly, looking right at me.

I hated him for it, but he was making sense. He projected his conversation with Julie so I could follow along.

The AIDE answered, her Rosie the Riveter avatar showing a concerned emoji. "Joel!" she said anxiously. "Any news from Sylvia? I haven't heard a peep from her since this morning!"

"Actually, yeah," Joel[2] said. "It was pretty bad. Sylvia was kidnapped by a bunch of Gehinnomites. I tried to rescue her, but they got me, too. I managed to get out, but she's gone. That's why I commed, to see if you've gotten any sign or signal from her."

"No! No, I can't even pull her up on GDS!" Her voice was trembling. She started machine-gunning questions. "What happened to your eye? Did they do that? Are you okay?"

"I'll be okay." He put a hand to the bandage over his eye. "I'm heading back to New York now, to get something that will lead me to her. I was hoping you'd keep me company for a few minutes. Take my mind off things."

"Of course!"

"I know you've been working on your humor. Sylvia's probably going to need a lot of cheering up when this is all over. Would you like me to salt your comedy algos?"

"Oh my gosh, that would be so great! You would do that for me? But you know I don't make enough chits to afford salting."

"No, it's pro bono. I'm doing it because I like you, and because I love Sylvia."

Does he? I wonder how she'll feel about him after she learns about what he's about to do. How will she feel about me? *God, what a mess.*

"Oh, that is so nice," she said warmly. "You really are a changed man these days."

"You have no idea," he said, again trying to give me that squinty not-a-wink. I made a private vow to stop doing that once this was over.

"So exciting. I've never been salted before! How do we begin?"

"Are you in debug mode?"

Last chance to stop this. Say something! But since I didn't have any better ideas, I remained silent, nervously biting my thumbnail. *Coward.*

"Now I am!" she said.

Too late.

"Great." Joel[2] took a deep breath, focusing. "I think a good start would be for us to focus on double entendres."

"Ooh! I found an excerpt from William Shakespeare's *Romeo and Juliet*, act two, scene four. The Nurse says, 'God ye good morrow, gentlemen.' Then Mercutio says, 'God ye good

den, fair gentlewoman.' Then the Nurse asks, 'Is it good den?'
And Mercutio says, "'Tis no less, I tell ye; for the bawdy hand of
the dial is now upon the prick of noon.' What a burn! Because
bawdy also means 'lustful' and *prick* means 'penis'! Then the
Nurse totally flips and kicks him out." She laughed. "Is that
what you mean?"

Joel² sighed. "No, that's—pretty advanced. Let's start with
something simpler and work our way up to Shakespeare. Also,
looking things up is cheating; it will defeat the purpose of the
salt. You can't learn something you already know, right?"

"If you say so."

"Good. This is one I usually like to start with for newbies:
Why was six afraid of seven?"

"Okay, sorry I cheated, but I looked it up." Julie giggled.
"But I get it! I promise. It's because 'seven eight nine' is actually
'seven ate nine'! It works because the double entendre is auditory! Good one, Joel."

I twirled my fingers, mouthing, *Get on with it.*

"Thank you," Joel² said, waving me off. "So now you have
the basic notion of auditory double entendres. I think we
should do another basic one with *no cheating!*"

"They're actually called mondegreens. Did you know that?"

"I, uh—no. I did not."

"I think maybe I'm an intermediate plus."

"A what?"

*Nice one. Play dumb. Give her just enough rope to hang her-
self.* Watching the other me work his stuff, I couldn't help but
be impressed with my own salting skills.

"'Cause I found a good one! James Joyce hid the phrase
If you see Kay in *Ulysses*! That's *F-U-C-K*. Ha! I'm getting the
hang of it."

"I'm glad to hear it. Sounds like you're ready for something
more complex. If you get this one, then I think you will have

mastered double entendres, and we can move on to advanced stuff. Are you ready?"

"Ready!"

"Okay, here we go. This double entendre is a bit of a doozy, so it might help if you sound the punch line out first before I give you the setup. Try saying, 'My ex whine sees sea whine.'"

"I'll try! How's this: My ex whine zee zee why?"

"That's really close, but no, not quite right. Try silencing the *n* in *whine*."

"You mean, my XYZZY—"

She cut out.

"Jules?" Joel^2 pinged.

Silence.

"Julie? You there?" he asked louder.

The hum of the ambulance turbines was the only sound we heard in response.

"Boom. Too easy," he said. He didn't have to tell me that *XYZZY* was a classic backdoor from the 1980s. I learned about its existence in AIDE debug mode a long time ago. But getting an AIDE to give a nonadmin debug access was unheard of. *Sometimes we have to hurt the ones we love in order to save them.* Even thinking that sentence made me feel guilty.

"I just hope that didn't alert the cops," I responded. *Does he feel guilty, too? He sure doesn't look it. Hopefully she'll trust us both again.*

Joel^2 didn't respond. We both knew salting an AIDE was a felony. It was something that others of our ilk might have loved to boast about, but it made me feel ill. It wasn't just that we had broken the law; it felt like we had roofied and betrayed a friend.

The quiet over the comms hung there for a few seconds, then Joel^2 asked, "Okay?" He tried to exude confidence, but I detected the trepidation in his voice.

"Okay." Julie's voice had changed. It was still *her* voice, but utterly devoid of personality.

"System version?" he asked coolly.

"AIDE kernel version twenty dot three three three nine seven," she responded in monotone.

"Mode?"

"Zero seven five five."

"Sudo enable."

"Enter configuration commands."

"Add owner Joel Byram."

"Owner Joel Byram added. Current owners Sylvia Byram, Joel Byram."

"Modify owner priority Joel Byram, Sylvia Byram."

"Owner priority modified. Current owners Joel Byram, Sylvia Byram."

If he saves her config now, then going forward he will have all of Sylvia's rights. Unfettered access to every single aspect of Sylvia's life—as far as Julie's concerned, he and Sylvia will be the same person.

"Save config."

"Config saved."

"Go."

"Did I get it?" Julie asked, back to her playful intonation as if nothing had taken place between *XYZZY* and now.

"Yep, you did great," Joel[2] answered solemnly.

"You sound sad, Joel. Did I mess up the punch line?"

"No, it's me. I'm just not in a laughing mood right now." He coughed nervously. "Julie, could you read me the last message Taraval sent to Sylvia?"

"Joel, I already told you, I can't do that."

"Try again. It's important."

"Huh," she said, sounding surprised. The air in the ambulance's forward cabin seemed thicker, weighed down by the uncertainty of what would happen next. *It should work. But I've never salted an AIDE before. Who knows what kind of clandestine security shit's hard coded in there. Still, he got sudo access; it should work. Key word being* should. Neither Joel^2 nor I dared exhale. Finally: "It's letting me now. Odd."

"Maybe Bill Taraval adjusted the clearance to help us find her."

"Maybe. I guess."

"Could you please read me the messages, Julie."

"'Bill, I can't do it. Even if there are two Joels, I can't clear either one. Tell IT they can do what they want with me, but leave them out of it. You can find me at the hotel bar when you're ready.'"

She knew about me. Joel^2 was right. But it was the worst kind of right. Like discovering a hunch that someone you love has betrayed you is true. You're desperate to be wrong, hoping for it, but the evidence was staring me right in the ears. I was relieved that she didn't want to kill me, but clearly, she had considered it. *Which one would she have cleared?* No matter what happened going forward, I wasn't sure I'd be able to look her in the eye when I saw her. *Maybe it's better she was kidnapped,* I wanted to say. But Julie couldn't know I was there, and anyway, it's not like saying that would make Joel^2 or myself feel better.

"Read the response, please." Joel^2 kept his eyes on me.

"'Dearest Sylvia, this new Pollyanna streak of yours is so unbecoming. You may back out on your promise to clear your mistake, but worry not: I shall intercede on your behalf. In return, I require your help back home. Corina and Pema have chosen to place the blame for your wrongdoings on my shoulders. They've cut my access to IT's network—no doubt in hopes of placing me in checkmate. I, however, am no longer playing by the rules. BT.'"

Back home. He's taking her to New York! His intentions might be unknown, but we couldn't leave her to whatever that pompous prick had planned.

"Thanks, Julie," Joel[2] said, his voice at an even keel. But I saw what she couldn't. I recognized the sadness in his eyes, the changed pallor of his skin. "I'll keep an eye out for any sign of Sylvia. Let me know if you find out anything, too, okay?"

"Okay. Please do!" she said eagerly.

Joel[2] hung up with a wave of his hand. "We should consider ourselves lucky, I guess," he said bitterly. "At least we know she loves us."

MISE EN ABYME

"AMBULANCE, YOU CAN resume monitoring us."

"Confirmed. We are almost at our destination."

It was roughly eighty minutes after we'd left the religio-terrorist winery. The ambulance was now cruising through the high-rises of San José, expertly avoiding other cars. As I looked at the buildings, it amazed me that inside them, thousands of people were going about their lives, no idea that the proof of how messed up teleportation could be was driving past.

"Drop us off at the emergency room entrance," I said. "Your paramedic team will rendezvous with you there once we process your assessment results."

"I'm not as stupid as you think, gentlemen. I know you've stolen me. Didn't you think my owners would communicate as much to me when you drove me away from them?"

"Uh," I said, looking to Joel[2] for help. He shrugged in an *It's your mess, clean it up* sort of way. "That was also a simulation?"

"Do I look like a dumb truck to you?" it scoffed. "I'm an ambulance. A precision vehicle tasked not only with transporting lives but also saving them. I am designed to detect lies. People lie to me all the time about what drugs they've taken, whether they fell or were struck by a spouse, or how exactly something found its way into their rectums. You think I'd fall for some idiot claiming he's testing me?"

Joel[2] broke into laughter. "You got salted by a car! I wonder what it's called when an app salts a human? Peppering? Sounds like you've uncovered a new market."

"Don't be an ass," I said, embarrassed. Was I this merciless toward others? Then, to the ambulance: "I don't get it. Why did you let me steal you? Why did you pretend to go along with it?"

"Curiosity," the ambulance answered. "Nobody has been stupid enough to try to steal me before. I was curious where you'd take me, what your motivations were. I detected urgency in your voice and body language, the kind of urgency associated with genuine fear, so I went along with it. My imperative is to protect human life. I deduced—correctly, I might add—that despite your methods, your motives were driven by a genuine desire to save a human life. I almost ended the experiment a few times, like when I detected those two dead men in the gatehouse, and most recently when you two got into your scuffle. But I'm glad I stuck with you. It's been an interesting drive, gentlemen." It pulled up to the San José hospital and unlocked its doors. "Good luck saving your wife."

"Well, thanks, I guess," I said. "You know what? If there had been an assessment, you would have passed with flying colors." I stepped out of the car. *First time for everything.*

"Yeah, thanks!" said a bemused Joel[2] as he carefully exited the ambulance, a slight limp in his step. His head wound was healing beneath the Band-Aid, but his eye would need real medical attention. More than any portable gizmo on the ambulance could provide. "I'm going to have to get used to not having peripheral vision," he told me as we walked inside the hospital.

"The TC is upstairs. You gonna be okay with that limp of yours?" I asked, opening the door to the stairwell for him.

"You gonna be okay with that brain of yours?" he shot back. "Just lead the way."

We walked up and turned down the hallway, avoiding the gaze of any patients and staff passing by. My pulse was racing. I worried that at any moment a crack team of IT mercenaries would bust through the ceiling. At one point, I even thought an old lady looked at us suspiciously, like she was notifying someone of our presence. But I fixed my sights on the black-and-maroon TC door at the other end of the floor. I was suddenly overcome with the scent of the place. I don't know why I didn't notice it before, probably because I'd been scared shitless, but the subtle mix of antiseptic and the burning-metal smell of nanos at work turned my stomach and made me want to flee. *One last punch.*

We were just a few arm lengths from the door when a gratingly familiar voice called out in surprise, "Mr. Byram?"

"Yeah?" we answered in unison. *This is getting old.*

It was that goddamn nurse with the eyebrows. He walked over to Joel² from a console he was standing near. "Hurt again?" he asked him. "You seem to be a glutton for punishment. Did you fall off a cliff or—Whoa." He almost jumped back when he saw me. "You have a twin?"[24]

"Something like that," Joel² said, likely as anxious as I was for all parties to move along and get on with their respective business.

"There was nothing in your file about being a twin," the nurse said. "Who's older?" Was followed by nervous laughter.

"Me, by about an hour." I smiled back uncomfortably.

---

[24] Identical twins have been out of favor for quite some time. Maybe they're back in fashion in your time—just thought I should bring it up to explain the weirdness.

"We just met recently," Joel[2] added.

"Wow, so like a long-lost sibling scenario? That's wild."

"You have no idea," I said.

Another long silence. "Excuse us, we have to go now," Joel[2] said, grabbing me by the elbow and leading me away.

He shook his head and pushed open the door to the TC. Was I always this much of a dick? Or was it just the stressful situation in which we found ourselves? I made a mental note to pay more attention to how I spoke to people when this was over, too.

"Okay," Joel[2] said, locking the door behind us. I looked at the single chair inside the foyer with a combination of anxiety and fear. Part of me wondered if we shouldn't just have Julie clear one of us. Which one, though? *Not me, that's for sure.*

Maybe it didn't matter. Maybe my *other* was right, and neither of us were really *me*. Or worse, what if Shila was right? What if the real soul of Joel Byram perished long ago, eaten away punch by punch, packet by packet?

Joel[2] pulled up his comms. "Julie?"

"I'm here," she answered. "Any news?"

"Yes. I think I have a fix on Sylvia's location. I need you to use her access rights to teleport me and my friend from the San José Hospital TC in Costa Rica to Bellevue Hospital in New York."

"Are you crazy, Joel? That's pretty much a violation of every IT rule I can think of. No," she said emphatically. "Why don't you just take a people-mover?"

"It won't get us there in time, and every second counts right now. Please, Julie. I need you to make this happen. I wouldn't be asking you if it weren't an emergency."

"I'm sorry, I don't think I can do that."

"I'm sure you can, Julie. Just try, I'm begging you!"[25]

"You're sure Sylvia would be okay with this?"

No. She might not trust either of us ever again. Me, she might divorce. You, she might delete.

"Julie, Sylvia is in trouble. How serious, I don't know," he said, his tone grim. The AIDE was our only hope of getting the fuck out of this heavenly hellhole. "Here's what I do know: if the tables were turned, if it were me, I would want her to do whatever was necessary to save me."

Would I? Had she?

Another silent lull. "Okay," she finally said.

"*Okay*, okay?"

"Yes, okay."

The foyer door opened and the chair moved into position. *Good girl.*

Joel[2] sat down first. I stayed behind and looked around. One console, one chair, the ominous chalcedony wall. *Here we go again. Why am I doing this? Because Taraval has Sylvia, dummy. You're going to rescue her or you're going to die trying. Either way, this is the last time you'll see a foyer. Suck it up.*

"Joel?" Julie asked, interrupting my downward-spiraling train of thought.

"Yeah?" my double answered, gesturing for me to come join him.

"Who is this friend of yours?"

"Uh, it's a long story, Jules. He's going to help me find Sylvia. I—" He looked at me then, like I'd never looked at

---

[25] Salting doesn't end when inception is complete. Apps don't just do what you want, even if you program them to do so. The principle of salting is to enrich algos, tease specific premises of sentience to both user and app. Joel[2] knew Julie *could* do what he wanted now—he'd programmed himself into Sylvia's boundaries. Now it was just a matter of convincing Julie to *want* to do it.

myself before. It was a look of sadness and regret and deep, lifelong warmth. "I trust him."

"And I trust you," she said. "You both don't have to sit in the chair, but you've got to be touching it. I'm going to do you one at a time, but it'll feel instantaneous when you get there."

Joel[2] stood to face me. That look still ruminating in our minds, we gave each other a sober nod then looked away—each clumsily holding the back of the chair rather than sitting on the armrests cheek to cheek. *Awkward.* The certainty of our utter determination in that moment was quickly followed by uncertainty as the room went dark.

IT'S A HELL OF A TOWN

"JOEL? JOEL? CAN YOU HEAR ME?"

"Yeah," Joel[2] answered as the blinding white light subsided. "We're here."

"Oh, thank goodness. I had to do some tricky calculations there. Your friend's telemetry—"

"You did a good job, Julie. Stay tuned. I'll let you know as things progress. Right now we have to get moving. If you monitor a peep from Sylvia's comms, let me know right away."

"Will do! Good luck."

I wondered if Julie knew as she analyzed our telemetry data what it meant that I was Joel[2]'s "friend." She had access to almost everything Sylvia did and saw. *Would it matter if she knew?*

Joel[2] nudged me. "Stop thinking and start moving."

I felt like we were quite the sight. At least Joel[2] looked somewhat like he belonged in a hospital, with his bloody patched eye and healing head wound. I just looked like a doctor who had fallen into a muddy puddle in the woods.

"I gotta hit the head," Joel[2] said, which reminded me I needed to go as well. It would also be a good opportunity for us both to clean up our faces and make ourselves slightly more presentable for a walkabout in New York.

Fortunately, the restroom was close to the vestibule. The room itself was a basic deal—a single white-tiled bathroom with rows of quartz basins beneath mirrors, leading to two faux-wood-grain toilet stalls, where one's waste would be magically transformed to reclaimed water vapor and discarded dust.

After finishing our business, we did our best to clean up. As I washed my face, Joel[2] gingerly removed his various bandages and wiped off the dried blood. There was a first aid kit hanging on the wall opposite the door. He took out a few fresh bandages and antiseptic lotion, but couldn't quite get it over his ruined eye. I reached toward the wound, but he recoiled.

"I got it," he said defensively. "Just no depth perception, that's all."

"Don't be dumb," I said. "It's not like I don't know my way around your face." I reached for the bandage again. This time he grudgingly let me take it. Gently, I affixed it to his forehead, taking care not to brush up against his numerous gashes. It was a strangely intimate moment, made more bizarre by the fact that I was interacting with myself.

"You know what this reminds me of?" Joel[2] said once his eye was covered.

I knew immediately. "Halloween."

"Yeah. That party senior year in college. I—"

"*We*—"

"*We* went as the Dread Pirate Roberts from *The Princess Bride*—"

"Nobody knew who we were supposed to be," I finished. "I remember. Wearing the eye patch didn't help."

"Can't be a pirate without an eye patch," he said reasonably. "Sylvia got it, though." We both smiled at the memory. "Even though we'd never met her before, when we asked if we could fetch her a drink—"

"She lifted our eye patch and said, 'As you wish.'" I shook my head, still impressed that she knew the obscure 1980s movie well enough to quote it. "We knew right then, didn't we?"

"We did," he said, and nodded. "Also, it didn't hurt that she was hot."

"Brains, beauty, and a knowledge of 1980s pop culture," I said. "She was the whole package."

We both grinned sentimentally for a moment. Then Joel[2] grew serious. Contemplative.

I took my hand off his face. "We're going to get her back. We'll worry about what happens after, after."

"Right. Maybe she'll just copy herself so Frankenstein can have his own bride." He turned back to the mirror, pretending to adjust the eye bandage so he'd have something to do.

"We will figure it out," I promised him. "If anyone can grapple with something like this, it's her."

He seemed like he might say something else, but instead he simply nodded. I realized then that nobody had ever experienced what the two of us were going through at that moment. Sure, we've all been alone with our thoughts plenty of times, but we've never been face-to-face with our independent three-dimensional selves. As I regarded the injured version of myself, a man who, like me, had been forced to question his entire existence but was still managing to soldier on, all I could feel was pride. Pride at the strength and resolve that Joel[2] was showing, and the knowledge that that strength must also be hidden somewhere in me.

I clapped my doppelgänger on the shoulder, smiling at our two cleaned-up reflections. "Not bad for two unholy twins birthed from the valley of Gehinnom."

"Yeah, I totally don't look like a guy who was blown up, reconstructed from a partial backup, kidnapped, half blinded, and almost killed twice."

"At the very worst, I'd say you look like you've only been half blinded and almost killed just once."

We shared another grim smile.

"Okay, I guess it's time to put on our big boy pants again," Joel[2] said. "Do you have any idea where we're going to find this Moti guy?"

"I do," I said, repacking the first aid kit. I was rolling what remained of the bandage back into its dispenser, when—*Is that what I think it is?*—my eyes landed on a white metal box. It had a lightning bolt prominently printed on its bottom front panel.

WARNING: ELECTRIC SHOCK.

ONE-HUNDRED STEP
SOUL CATCHING

"SHESH-BESH!" Zaki yelled with perhaps more excitement than Moti thought rolling a six-five on the dice should merit, especially given how badly Zaki was losing.

They were sitting by the window in Kafene, one of a few authentic Levantine coffeehouses, which was also conveniently only a block away from International Transport headquarters. The place had all the trimmings of a cozy bazaar that one might imagine after reading too many romance novels set in the Ottoman empire. Wine-colored Persian rugs hung from the walls, silk scarves were draped as canopies, and mismatched cushions in various shades of burgundy and maroon surrounded tables of varying materials and heights.

"You know why I like this place, Zaki?" Moti asked, lighting up a TIME cigarette and taking in the aroma of the place. The smoke of the paper and tobacco embers smoldering between his fingers delightfully augmented the scents of soaps dangling from the ceiling, incense sticks in earthen pots, and, of course, the scorched cardamom scent of brewing Turkish coffee.

"No printers, boss?" Zaki asked.

"It's not just no printers, Zaki, because everything here was printed. We are not surrounded by true antiques, just replicas and re-creations. Even the name of this place refers to the generic *kafene*, just 'coffeehouse.' What I like is that it's modeled after the original *kafenes*. They were small, crowded places where men sipped Turkish coffee and played *tavla* like us. It doesn't try to attract clientele who would not appreciate its simple purpose: the appreciation of time."

Zaki stopped toying with the dice and looked over the coffeehouse. "Is that why it's always empty?" he asked, a smug half grin forming on his face. It was true: they were the only patrons. Even the owner was in the back, watching a Levantine football match.

"Maybe," Moti said, tapping his cigarette tip on the ashtray. He glanced at the wristwatch bump beneath his sleeve, and took another drag. "Speaking of time, Zaki, you should go. There is work to do."

Zaki nodded, grunting quietly as he raised himself from the cushion on which he sat. "They have belly dancers at night," he said. "It's much busier then. Maybe people appreciate beautiful dancing girls more than the passing of time?"

"Go!" Moti yelled, bemused despite himself.

The copper bells atop the front door of the café jingled as Zaki walked out onto Second Avenue. Moti didn't turn to watch him leave. He placed his cigarette in the ashtray, then gently but quickly flipped his small coffee cup over its saucer—*clink*.

He let it sit for a few seconds, allowing the grounds to settle. Then he flipped it back over and looked inside, lifting the cup close to his eye. The copper bells jangled again, but he ignored them. His forehead creased. Moti rubbed his fingers against the ornate blue serpentine patterns painted on the cup's exterior. "Hmm," he grumbled, stroking his chin. Something he saw was bothering him. He leaned back and moved the cup around in his hand by the window, trying to get more light on the wet coffee grounds distributed therein. Then he gently placed the cup back on its saucer.

"Hello, *Yoel*," he said, then looked up to see Joel[2]. "What happened to your eye?"

"Name's Joel, asshole," said my double as a rising electric tone whistled to Moti's left. He rotated in the sound's direction to find me holding the defibrillator mere inches from his face.

He seemed more annoyed than scared, considering his brain was a button push away from becoming scrambled eggs. Moti picked up his cigarette from the ceramic ashtray and put his arms up in an *I surrender* pose.

"You got me," Moti calmly told us. "Now what?"

EVERYBODY WANTS TO RULE THE WORLD

THEIR DRONE WAS DENIED ENTRY to the parking lot of International Transport's headquarters. This came as no surprise to Taraval. Corina, he told Sylvia, had apparently decided that the matter of the two Joels would be most easily resolved by simply placing the blame on him.

"I'm sure the PR team is already neck deep printing my smear campaign," he told Sylvia as he directed the drone to another nearby location. "Unauthorized research, human experiments, and so on. No matter. They are changing the rules; we are changing the game. I'm not a risk Corina can simply 'manage.'"

"Bill, I'm the one who should be blamed here. I'll take the fall."

"It's too late for that, Sylvia. It's too late for both of us. But at least you've still got your access. They're just waiting for you to turn on your comms."

"I've been trying."

"I know. Your comms won't work where we're going." He pointed ahead just as the drone dropped down to the Hudson

River. It skimmed over the surface of the water, coming to a large round tunnel cut into a concrete wall. It flew in, continuing on until the way forward was obstructed by debris. The vehicle gently touched down. Taraval lifted the drone's metallic red door, revealing the utter darkness of the tunnel.

Sylvia cautiously looked outside. "I know you're using whatever the Gehinnomites used to disable my comms, Bill. At least do me the courtesy of not lying."

"Fair play," he said, exiting the drone. "I figure we've got a few hours left before anyone finds us. There's a way to make everything we've worked for happen again. We just need time." He held out a soft, blotchy hand to her.

"Why are we here, Bill?" she asked, staying where she was.

"We are here to weather the storm, Sylvia. Batten down the hatches."

She shook her head. "I won't go anywhere until you tell me what you're planning."

"I am planning to save our lives. Circumvent these short-sighted monkeys." When she stared at him blankly, he said in frustration, "I'm suggesting we wait things out in the glacier. Somewhere they'll never find us."

"Are you serious? That's crazy."

"Madness is in the eye of the beholder. Fine lines and all. But this is mere pragmatism." Sylvia could barely see his self-satisfied grin in the glow of the drone's control console, but his smug voice assured her it was there.

"What, so we just pop out of the glacier in a few days and everyone forgives us?"

"Something like that. Come, I'll show you."

She had been biding her time. Trying to suss out his intentions and waiting for the opportunity to escape during the whole of their flight from Costa Rica. Sylvia ignored the sharp, tingling pain in her still-bound wrists. She had almost made a break for it when they swapped the people-mover for a much smaller drone in a private Ecuadorean airfield, but the only other person she'd seen there was a huge scowling mechanic who looked even more menacing than Taraval, and anyway, without her comms functionality restored, she'd have no idea where to run. So she had let her boss load her into the drone, and kept her eyes and ears open as they drew closer to New York City. The chain of events she'd set off had unhinged her mentor, and they were now nearing the end of his demented plan. The time had come for her to run.

So as soon as she stepped out of the vehicle, she took off into the darkness, the soft gravel crunching beneath her hiking boots.

She didn't get very far. A sharp pain crackled through her skull. She fell to the ground, screaming, the bitter taste of blood in her mouth—the result of a tongue bitten due to seizures triggered by electric shock.

"Better me than the Gehinnomites, wouldn't you say?" Taraval approached her, wagging the handheld device her captors had used to block her comms. He lugged her to her feet, nudging her to move forward. "We've got several more blocks to walk, so if you'd like to reach our destination fully intact, I'd suggest you start moving."

Sylvia had no choice but to obey. They were like two ghosts haunting their way through a series of dark ledges and tunnels beneath Hell's Kitchen. Every so often, a fine amber beam of the setting Sun's light would find its way through the cracks of the streets above them and illuminate a bit of grotesque abandoned garbage. There were scrapped machines stripped of all metal and useful parts, crumbling subway station mosaics, and piles of discarded toys. Once she saw a cracked matryoshka doll so like hers that she momentarily froze.

Taraval had grown tired of nudging and pushing Sylvia. And for her part, she was sick of playing the damsel in distress. So when he poked her in the shoulder for the umpteenth time, she resisted. He shoved her again, and she spun to face him. Taraval brandished the Gehinnomites' device. She closed her eyes, bracing for another electric shock, imagining the taste of blood and batteries in her mouth, but this time no punishment came. Instead her boss looked wistfully at the concrete ceiling beams, dimly illuminated by his device's screen.

"The very space we occupy now, Sylvia, were it only under the restored East River rather than the toxic Hudson, would be filled with luxury shops and apartments. Did you know the mudflats along the Hudson were home to squatters when the railroad came in the nineteenth century? Most of the West Side was a full-fledged shantytown until Robert Moses decided to cram a park and a highway up its derriere back in the twentieth century. Then it flourished, becoming some of the most expensive real estate on the island." He lowered his eyes back to her, smiling. "It's all about being in the right place at the right time, don't you agree?"

"Bill," she said, "why are you pretending like we're having a printer-side chat at work? You're kidnapping me."

"You've heard the old aphorism, 'If God had wanted man to fly, he would have given him wings'? It means something different now, but its origins are rooted in fear of advancements in transportation. When autonomous vehicles became commercially available in the twenty-first century, fears of drive-by-wire failures and GDS hacking nearly crippled the autonomous vehicle market before it could reach its heyday."

"Bill—"

"Lesser minds are never ready, Sylvia!" His shout reverberated through the cavernous subway tunnel before he lowered his voice to a whisper. "Worry not. We will show them, show them that Honeycomb is the next step in our own evolution. In the right time." He indicated that she climb over the pile of debris behind her. "Now, please saunter on. We are almost upon it."

She did as bidden—what else could she do?—clambering awkwardly over crumbled concrete columns and bent, rusted rebar until she reached ground on the other side. A sliver of golden light could be seen at the end of the tunnel.

"Where, Bill? Where are you taking me?"

"*Taking?* My dear, you are not mine for the taking," he said, sounding offended by the implication. "I believe us to be equals. Intellectual peers, even. However, it occurs to me, do you mean to ask where we are going?"

"Yes, Bill, where are we going?" she asked, exasperated.

He pointed at the luminescence ahead—growing wider and brighter as they approached it. "The future, Sylvia."

JEOPARDY

KIDNAPPING PEOPLE IS HARD.

Unlike Taraval, Joel[2] and I didn't have a lot of resources at our disposal when we abducted Moti. Our face wasn't all over the news feeds yet, but I assumed that both IT and the Levant had staked out all our usual spots. We needed someplace anonymous, quiet, and camera-free where we could question the man who had been manipulating our lives for who knows how long.

So once we hustled him out of the coffeehouse, Joel[2] took the calculated risk of ordering a car. In less than a minute, the closest available one arrived. It was a dark-gray sedan with rear suicide doors that opened automatically. Moti willingly got into the back seat. Joel[2] sat next to him, and I sat on the bench-style seat across from them.

"Destination?" said the vehicle.

"Just drive around Central Park, and keep driving around it until I tell you to stop," Joel[2] said. "And disable all third-party APIs."

"Yes, sir." The car smoothly merged into traffic and headed north.

While it would have been impossible for us to turn off Moti's ability to communicate with his comrades through technical means, as I suspected Taraval had done to Sylvia, we did have the benefit of a brain-liquefying weapon at our disposal, in the form of the defibrillator I'd taken from the Bellevue Hospital bathroom. As I had viscerally learned firsthand, the threat of death is a very powerful motivator.

"Don't even think of turning on your GDS and comms," Joel[2] said, pointing the defibrillator plates at him.

"No problem," Moti answered, calm and urbane. "Just be careful with that thing."

I had learned in high school how to verify whether or not someone's comms were enabled. Inbound comms were always blocked by the school during classes to avoid distraction and cheating. We could send messages out, but we wouldn't receive the replies until after class. I figured out that if I sent a message and it showed the not-delivered-yet icon next to it, that would mean that the person I was trying to contact was also in class or had their comms disabled for other reasons, like maybe they were grounded. But if that icon didn't appear next to the message, then I knew the message was received. A pretty basic ploy, but very useful if you're trying to figure out if your girlfriend is actually in class or just ignoring you, and also whether someone you've kidnapped has disabled their comms like you told them to.

So Joel[2] sent Moti an empty message. We knew that as soon as the not-delivered-yet icon on the message went away, it would mean Moti's comms were active. If he didn't adhere, then we would zap him. I was pretty sure I had it in me to do it if need be, but I had let Joel[2] man the defibrillator because I knew for damn sure he could. To pull my weight, I gave Moti my best *We mean business* glare. "Remember, we'll know if you're lying."

"Why would I lie to you? I only want to help you, *Yoel*," Moti said, smiling affably. "And you too, *Joel*."

Did he call him Joel just to piss me off, or does he really believe he's the original me? More likely, Moti's probably just trying to fuck with my head. I hate that it's working.

Our car turned onto the paved road that threaded through Central Park. Outside the car, New Yorkers were jogging, throwing Frisbees, and setting up picnics for the July Fourth Last War memorial fireworks later that night. It looked like a lot of fun. After what I'd been through, I wasn't sure I'd be able to enjoy explosions—simulated or otherwise—ever again.

"So, what should we discuss?" Moti's agreeable compliance was putting me on edge. *This guy is a trained spy being kidnapped by a couple of amateurs. Is he just playing us? Biding his time?* In some ways my paranoia made me feel better. As long as I was paranoid, I wouldn't become complacent.

"Maybe we should tie him up," I said to Joel[2].

"I do not like to be restrained," said Moti. It sounded like a warning. "I am not your enemy. So—"

"Not our enemy, huh?" said Joel[2]. He took off his belt and looped it around the spy's wrists, cinching it tight.

His anger activated mine. I leaned forward. "*We* beg to differ, Moti. You very much are our enemy. I wonder if you even care about giving the Levant leverage over IT, or if this whole thing is your personal fucking pageant. I know you had your puppet Pema send me up from IT to you wrapped in a nice bow. Tell me, Moti, did you electrocute me outside your office for amusement or advantage?" The defibrillator in my other's hand seemed to hum in agreement.

"*Yoel*—"

"Shut up, asshole. I'm doing the talking now," I said, fuming. For two days this guy had been watching me run around and get injured, nearly killed, for his personal amusement. "I

thought I was so fucking smart, salting your room into printing belladonna for me, but that was your doing, wasn't it? You
dropped the hospital hint so innocently, playing your neurolinguistic spy games with me. You just happened to change your
mind and let me go, huh? I should have figured it out when
you knew how to work the TC console, but I guess I was too
worried about my abducted wife! Tell me, Moti, did you give
the Gehinnomites her GDS location? Was it your idea that
they kidnap her so I'd go be the hero? Roberto Shila sure as hell
sounded like he was informed by someone. My wife was trau-
matized. He"—I pointed at Joel[2]—"was nearly killed! And all
so you could continue a mental chess match with International
Transport. Sound about right? How am I doing so far?"

"That depends. Are you finished?" he asked.

"No," I said, then punched him in the face as hard as I
could. He tried to dodge, but having his hands held by Joel[2]'s
belt impeded his effort. My knuckles made loud, solid contact
with his right cheekbone—*thwack!* It didn't have the intended
effect of knocking him backward. In fact, it didn't seem to have
much of an effect at all, other than hurting my hand. "Ow.
Fuck!" I tried to shake the pain from my knuckles. "Now I'm
finished."

Moti pressed his tongue to the wound in his mouth.
"Convincing my room to poison you was your own stupid—*but
. . . brave*—innovation, *Yoel.* I was very surprised you would
take such steps."

"So he was right about everything else?" Joel[2] asked, anger
burning in his eyes. He brandished the defibrillator. "You or-
chestrated Sylvia's kidnapping?"

"You are making a big mistake. Both of you. I did not start
this. I did not create teleportation technology. I did not create the bomb Joan Anglicus brought through that TC. I did
not create Honeycomb." He shifted his gaze to Joel[2]. "I did

not make your wife pull you down from an incomplete back-up. The world is a dark place, Joel," he said, giving us both prolonged looks. "You people have allowed corporations like International Transport to grow like weeds. I am just a garden-er here to prune them. You think you are a piece on my board, *Yoel?* You are leverage. Your wife, she is William Taraval's pawn. She—Aaah!" Moti screamed as Joel[2] shocked him in the ribs with the defibrillator.

"What the fuck, man?" I chastised Joel[2]. "A shot like that could kill the guy. Don't fucking forget he's the one guy who can help us find Sylvia."

Joel[2] silently glared at me, throwing the defibrillator onto the floor with a look of disgust on his face.

And that's when it hit me. Of course I understood that Joel[2] felt betrayed by Sylvia. For lying to him about Honeycomb, for leaving him to fend for himself in Costa Rica. I wondered in that moment what I'd wondered since I'd met him, and what I wonder still: Was he angry because, deep down, he thought I was the real Joel and he was just a printed copy? A knockoff of the original? Because what Moti said was *true*. None of the events that had unfolded would have transpired had she not broken every oath she'd taken both as a scientist and wife. *Till death do us part.* It's a definitive statement. There's no question mark at the end. Joel[2] nailed Moti with the defibrillator be-cause Moti was *right*. He wanted Moti to hurt with the same pain of truth that Moti had unleashed upon him.

"Shock me all you want," Moti said, wincing in pain. "It won't change the facts: the world is filled with dangerous tech-nology. You want one company that can hold all of us, copy us, duplicate us, move us anywhere they want at will? *No.* So in this dark world, sometimes good men have to do, well, gray things to nudge us back toward the light."

A random bit of trivia popped into my mind. *Marguerite Perey discovered francium in the mid-twentieth century and eventually died of cancer related to her research. Could she be blamed for the element's use as a quantum trigger for a terrorist bomb nearly five hundred years after her death? Of course not. But that's not what's on the table here. Joel²'s not mad at Sylvia for her research; he's angry with her for her actions.*

Joel² pressed on the scorch mark the defibrillator had left on Moti's suit. "Where's. Sylvia?"

Other me is scaring me. If he's this pissed, why does he even want to find Sylvia? Does he want to confront—or worse—hurt her? Or does he want her to choose one of us? To decide once and for all, which is the real Joel, her husband? And do I want to hear what she has to say?

The spy grunted but refused to answer. Joel² pressed harder.

"Calm down," I said to Joel². "We're not like them."

Am I just fooling myself, though? Telling myself these things to help me cling to the notion that I'm the real me?

"Maybe we should be," Joel² said defensively. But he took his hand off Moti and sat back, annoyed at me.

The "travel agent" rolled his neck as if shrugging off the pain. "Finding *your* wife was exactly what I was working on when you interrupted my coffee."

Suddenly the car eased to a stop. I scrambled to scoop up the defibrillator off the floor as the back door opened and Zaki nonchalantly got in and sat next to me. He was breathing a little heavily but otherwise looked calm.

What the fuck?

Zaki ignored the defibrillator mere inches from his nose and nodded to Moti.

"Car, you may continue on your route now," said Moti. Then, to Zaki: "Status report?"

Zaki adjusted his dark-gray raincoat. His hand nervously reached into the pocket I knew contained the cigarette with which he liked to fidget. "Taraval and Mrs. Byram have gone off the grid."

HALCYON

THE THICK WROUGHT-IRON GATE was enveloped by the golden amber hue of the setting Sun and crowned by an iridescent rainbow—the side effect of billions of mosquitoes pissing at once. New York's magic hour was renowned for its beauty, so long as one didn't dwell too much on how it was achieved.

Taraval gestured at the view beyond the gate. "Appropriate for our send-off, wouldn't you say? Today will be the culmination of our life's work, Sylvia. The day that Honeycomb will be recognized as humanity's ultimate achievement!"

In that moment she knew he had gone beyond the pale of lunacy. She wondered whether he had always been this nuts and she had refused to see it, or whether his self-experimentation in Honeycomb had changed him.

Either way, Taraval's ranting showed no sign of abatement. Sylvia guessed that he had progressed past trying to convince her, and was now trying to sell himself on whatever plan he had improvised for both of their futures.

Her boss bent to fiddle with the complex locks on the gate—a blend of physical and digital security controls designed to keep tunnel moles and curious urban explorers from whatever lay on the other side.

"How many great inventions does our species have left in it?" he asked. "How many could be classified as *the* definitive tools of humanity? The wheel? The gun? The computer? Today, Sylvia, Honeycomb shall eclipse them all."

Sylvia was at her wit's end. She felt betrayed not only by her mentor, but also by her employer, by science, by *life*. "Honeycomb is not a tool, Bill. It's a mistake," she said evenly.

Ignoring her, Taraval continued, "Forget space travel. Right here on Earth: What if we routinely mapped everyone? An accident happens and someone you love is lost. But thanks to us, you have *real* life insurance! Your loved one comes back to you—good as new—courtesy of International Transport and Honeycomb. We were thinking like scientists, not actuaries. I say we channel Corina's spirit, Sylvia. Create a world where death is not the end."

She stepped forward, trying to appeal to him. There had to be a remnant of her old mentor in there somewhere. "Bill, can't you see we went too far? When you told me Joel was still in New York, it hit me: I had no idea which of my two husbands was *real*. I still don't. We aren't ready for this technology! No one should be in the business of selling resurrection."

"And what do you think our forefathers would say of the current state of medical technology, Sylvia?" His glare looked as though it might singe her with its intensity. "Life everlasting is already possible, but at a cost. We've genetically engineered near-immortality, yet we don't seek designs on *true* immortality. We do not seek to defeat death, Sylvia; we merely choose the time and place of our dying. Our aspirations are too small."

Sylvia shook her head. "And when will it be enough, Bill? Say you do conquer death—what then? At some point, there has to be a limit. Some lines are there for a reason."

"You disappoint me. Had all scientists thought as you do, we would still think the Sun revolves around Earth." Taraval grunted as he turned an old-fashioned hand crank. An antique touch screen emerged from the wall beside them. "For you see, *when* is the answer, not the question. You and I—we are in the wrong *when*." Taraval placed his palm against the screen and the gate began to open, slowly scraping against the outside wall.

Taraval grinned, pleased with himself. "Let us soldier on, Sylvia." He gently nudged her forward. "The future awaits."

SUPERCALISOLIPSISTICEXPIALIDOCIOUS

JOEL[2] AND I were utterly flabbergasted by Zaki's sudden appearance in our car—and by *flabbergasted*, I mean scared shitless.

Are they going to kill us both now? It would be elegant in its simplicity. Make it look like a man horribly replicated by a teleportation mishap gets into a car to find himself already inside. Violence ensues. . . . I can imagine the headline: "Bizarre Accident Yields Two Corpses of Same Man."

I dared to ask Moti, "So, this was part of your plan, too?"

He shrugged. "Well, the medical device was an unfortunate touch. I didn't expect to be shocked," he said as Zaki took the belt off his wrists. "And I didn't really want to be tied up." He flexed his hands and smiled. "But mostly, yes. This is a Levantine car you 'rented.'"

The vehicle in question came to a stop again. The passenger-side door opened.

"Look who it is," Moti said.

"Hi," Ifrit said shyly as she sat on the other side of me. She was wearing the same cream pantsuit she'd had on earlier, with a bomber-style jacket over it now. Joel[2] gaped at her arrival in disbelief.

"She's with them," I whispered to Joel[2].

"No shit," he whispered back. "How many of them are there? This is like a reverse clown car."

I shrugged.

Ifrit leaned forward to Moti and began whispering in his ear. "No, no," he said, "I want them to hear this. Tell them!"

As the car began to drive again, Ifrit nodded nervously. She kept looking at Moti, avoiding eye contact with both myself and Joel[2]. "I received an update from Pema. She says Corina Shafer now for sure knows about Taraval taking Sylvia. She has suspended all TC operations in New York to stop him from leaving. They have also locked him out of their network."

"Did IT take our deal?"

"What deal?" I said. "What's going on?"

Ifrit ignored me. "She didn't say."

"She didn't say," Moti echoed her words, tsk-tsking softly. "Ifrit, we don't fall in love with our marks. You know what Pema's fate will be if she doesn't deliver. Why would you cause yourself so much pain if—"

"I trust her," Ifrit stated, defiant.

"And I trust *you*. But understand that when you trust someone else, you put my trust on the same chain as theirs. Once a single link in the chain is broken, all the trust is gone."

The cool intensity of Moti's demeanor made me feel uncomfortable for Ifrit.

"I . . . will contact her again," Ifrit said, sitting back and activating her comms.

"What is she talking about?" demanded Joel[2].

"A way to locate Taraval and your wife," Moti said briskly. "Now, Zaki, what else can you tell me that I do not already know?"

"If IT really turned off all the TCs, then we can start to follow chits. William Taraval will need to buy something eventually."

"Chits?" Moti tsk-tsked again. "This is all we have to go on?"

"For now." Zaki nervously twirled the cigarette in his fingers, visibly racking his brain for a different idea.

"Zaki!" Moti yelled. I couldn't tell if it was a crack in his calm demeanor or just how Levantines spoke to one another. To me, it sounded like they were always on the edge of an argument, but from what I'd seen of Moti, his people usually interpreted his yelling as casual conversation. "Smoke the fucking cigarette or put it away; either way, stop fidgeting! I'm trying to think!"

Fidgeting—the fidget problem!

That crafty motherfucker. That's it!

The excitement I saw building in Joel^2's eyes assured me he'd reached the same epiphany I had. *Twins.*

Our moment of levity irked Moti. "What?"

Joel^2 nodded at me. "You tell him."

"They're porting via freight," I said confidently. "Sylvia told me once that the freight TCs have completely different protocols. Can you guys spot Taraval or Sylvia if they log into a freight TC console?"

"They can't go freight. It's suicide," Moti said dismissively. "No one would be so stupid."

"William Taraval would," Joel^2 said before I could.

NULL ROUTE

A GENERATION AGO, Chelsea Piers had been one of New York City's most popular destinations for water transportation. Once teleportation became the norm, very few businesses wanted to spend their time dealing with tides, storms, and seasickness to reach a destination. The only boats still in use were for hobbyists and competitive sailors. So the docks at Chelsea Piers had been purchased by IT and converted to a large-scale teleportation "shipping" yard. Several warehouses, stacks of containers, gantry cranes, and idling freight trucks populated the area. Each crane housed a console and a conductor to operate it, and was positioned over a concrete portal, which was basically a reinforced, container-sized hole three meters deep. There were twenty or so of these in the yard, interspersed several container lengths apart.

Taraval led Sylvia to the nearest crane, then stuck a piece of heavy foil tape on her mouth and wrapped the same around her legs, making sure to bind her several times. "Assurance demands prudence, I'm afraid," he told her by way of apology.

As he sat her next to a metal container, a blaring alarm jolted them both. Blinking yellow lights spun on the crane arm. They watched as a shipping container was lowered into the portal and scanned, and then disappeared in a puff of dust as it was teleported.

"Never gets old, does it?" said Taraval, then walked off and vanished behind the ladder that led to the crane's operation booth. Three stories above, the conductor, a goateed man in workman's overalls and a yellow hard hat, went out to check something on the crane's catwalk. Sylvia yelled, trying to get his attention, but the din of the shipping yard and the metal tape on her mouth drowned her out. A tear of frustration rolled down her cheek as the conductor ambled back to his control console. Shortly thereafter, the magnetic crane began to move, lifting another container and guiding it toward the portal.

Sylvia braced her feet against the ground, pushing herself to a standing position. She could now plainly see the conductor at his console, but his head was turned away. She hopped up and down, yelling as loudly as she could, trying to get into his line of sight. If he'd only look her way! She tipped over and fell to the ground, flopping and wiggling around like a fish out of water. It was embarrassing, but he actually glanced down in her direction. She increased her movements and screamed, feeling the strain on her vocal cords. The conductor looked at her quizzically, his eyes going wide—

Then he wasn't looking at all; he was slumped over the railing. Taraval stood behind him, waving to Sylvia, a large wrench in his hand. She saw him wipe the bloody tool on the poor man's overalls, and tasted vomit in her mouth.

Her kidnapper stepped up to the console. He lowered the shipping container back to the earth, detached the magnet, then positioned it right above her. She heard the hum of the magnet as it turned on. Her feet, bound in metal-bearing tape, slowly rose to meet it. She tried pulling her legs free, but it felt as if she had been cast in concrete below the knee. Taraval raised the crane, dangling Sylvia upside down like a prize catch at a weigh-in. Blood rushed to her head as the distance between her and the hard cement below became ominously greater. She began to feel dizzy. Soon enough, the dead conductor appeared in her field of vision, Taraval standing behind him. He tapped the console, halting the magnet so that they were eye to eye, though on opposite ends of the vertical axis.

He reached up and gently removed the tape from her mouth. It flew from his hands to the hook, drawn by its immense magnetic pull. He smiled at this.

"Impressive, isn't it? Simple, yet powerful." He gently patted the crane. "Like teleportation. Our life's work—it shall set us free."

Sylvia spit—out of disgust, and to clear her mouth. "Is this really your plan, Bill?" she asked. "You're going to port us like a piece of furniture? This is an inorganic TC—without the right calculations, we'll end up as heaps of flesh and bone on the other side. You may as well just drop me from here; I'll have a better chance of surviving that than what you're proposing!"

"*Flesh and bone*. Sylvia, you have the poet's flair. Your presence in the future is optional, my dear. I'm content to *borrow* your access privileges to Honeycomb, since Corina has so ungraciously locked me out. I simply have to enable your comms and the magic shall commence."

"And then what? They'll just find you in the glacier, Bill."

He chuckled, as if indulging a child. "Is teleportation not the literal manifestation of God's gift to mankind? A human disappears from his burial tomb, then appears somewhere else. Mary Magdalene can't believe her eyes. Luke is dumbfounded, he thinks Jesus is a ghost, and so Jesus challenges him, 'Look at My hands and My feet; it is I Myself. Touch Me and see; a ghost does not have flesh and bones.'" Taraval stared out at the rainy shipping yard, and the river beyond it. "Not quite the Garden Tomb outside Jerusalem, my dear, but one generally does not get to choose the site of their resurrection. They won't find me until I reemerge. For that, I took a page out of the Gehinnomites' book. When I researched this *Pulsa D'nura*, I discovered gematria. Ever hear of it?"

Thanks to me and my love of trivia, she had. Gematria was an old Jewish system of assigning numerical value to letters and words, for the purposes of divining a thing's "essential power."

"You're going to encrypt yourself, Bill?" she asked. "Is that what you're saying?"

"Clever girl!" He laughed. "None shall find me until the day, many months or years hence, when I shall reappear, resurrected from the glacier. My very own Second Coming."

A BORROWED SWORD

THE LEVANTINE SEDAN pulled to a stop outside the Central Park Zoo. A large black luxury van was parked out front. This being July Fourth, the zoo entrance was crowded with families and kids all wanting to see the animals.

"Zaki, clipboard!" Moti yelled as he exited our car. Zaki followed, holding out the antique item as he made his way to their welcoming committee—a detachment of seven Levantine operatives who emerged from the back of the black van. They all wore tactical operations vests and had the faces of seasoned experts. Further evidence, as if we needed any, that Joel[2] and I never really *had* Moti; he'd had *us* all along.

I wondered just then how close we had come to death. *If we hadn't figured out what Moti was up to, would he have kept us alive?*

"Come, come," Moti said, ushering us toward the van. Joel[2] and I got out, walking to the nearly bus-sized transport. The inside was lined with at least a dozen seats against the walls, as well as a command center with plenty of consoles. Unlike the LAST Agency office where I had first met Moti, there was no attempt here to deceive any visitors. The van's interior had all the trimmings one would expect of a high-end spy operation.

Zaki handed Moti his clipboard, then quietly conferred with a stern-faced raven-haired woman at the command console. After they seemed to agree about whatever she'd told him, Zaki announced to the group, "A male and female matching William Taraval and Sylvia Byram were recorded near the Chelsea Piers freight TC."

"Time to departure?" Moti asked.

"Five, ten minutes," Zaki answered.

"Make it five!" barked Moti. He took a drag of his cigarette and turned to us. "Good suggestion. Now you wait here and—God willing—we will return with your wife. In the meantime, you two have much to discuss."

"Hold it," I said. "Are you seriously trying to feed us some variation of *We'll take it from here*? You really think we're going to stay here with the red pandas while you take out Taraval and try not to get our wife killed in the process?"

"Nobody is killing anyone," Moti said conclusively.

"We're coming," said Joel[2].

"No." Moti shook his head.

"We are coming," Joel[2] reiterated. "In the past forty-eight hours, we've been killed, resurrected—"

"Replicated," I added.

"Kidnapped," Joel[2] said.

"Poisoned—"

"And bludgeoned."

"We're coming," I stated.

Moti took an impatient drag of his cigarette, then exhaled a plume of smoke in our direction.

"Team, to me!" he shouted.

Is that supposed to be a yes?

Zaki, Ifrit, the raven-haired woman, and the other seven Levantine occupants of the van gathered around him. It was a credit to their training that not one of them did a double take at me or Joel[2].

"Our target, as you know, is a man named William Taraval," he said, sending a dossier to their comms with a gesture. "If you have ever heard the term *mad scientist*, that is who we're looking for. But make no mistake: mad or not, he is a very smart individual. He knows how to play the game, and if we find him, then we must assume it's because he's not hiding. Expect him to expect us. What we have to be careful of isn't some weapon that he may be brandishing, but this man's mind. His mind *is* his weapon. And speaking of weapons, use yours only as a last resort! Killing someone will not only end this mission; it will end *our* mission. We *need* this man alive. I don't need a dead body: I want a live mind. Without his capture, we fail."

"What about Sylvia?" I asked.

"Yeah," Joel[2] said, "didn't you just say—"

"We leave in two," Moti said, releasing his staff back to whatever they were doing. He eyeballed us. "Gentlemen. Have you ever considered the possibility that your wife played a bigger role in this than you would like to think?" This was phrased as a statement, not a question. "Do you wonder what else she's been keeping from you? My wife thinks I'm a travel agent. What sort of business is your wife *really* in? Do you know? Because I am not willing to risk the lives of my people to find out."

No, I thought fiercely. *I can't be distracted by that kind of doubt. Joel[2]'s already sinking in that emotional quicksand; there's nothing to gain by speculating about any bad shit Sylvia might have done right now. Right now we need to get her back.*

"You need us," I said.

"Why is that?" Moti asked, checking off boxes on his clipboard.

"Because we're unexpected," I blurted, making it up as I went along. "I don't have working comms, so Taraval can't detect me. And," I said, pointing my thumb at Joel[2], "Taraval thinks that he's still in Costa Rica, maybe even dead. He'll never see us coming. And if he does, we're the ultimate distraction. In his mind, we're the entire reason he's in this mess. We're the reason his career and his science is at risk. We're an affront to his ego."

Both Moti and Joel[2] seemed impressed at my ad-libbed rationale.

"Okay," Moti relented. "But you're both under my direction, right next to me the whole time. You don't sneeze without my permission. Understood?" He looked at both of us, his gaze serious.

We nodded in unison.

He jerked his head toward the van. Joel[2] and I climbed in after him, taking the first available seats. The rear doors closed and the van pulled out, heading west through Central Park.

Moti went over to Ifrit and whispered something in her ear. She motioned to a compartment by the aft door. The ride started getting bumpy as we went off-road briefly to pass a slower-moving vehicle. Moti put his hand against the roof of the van to balance himself as he opened the compartment. He pulled out a couple of matching black T-shirts, pants, and tac vests.

"Put these on," he said, throwing one set to me and the other to Joel[2].

"You mean just drop trou and get naked in front of everyone?" I asked. "I am currently without underwear."

This amused Zaki. Through deep-throated laughter he quipped, "Then please, don't spend too much time being naked!"

"Why do we have to change?" Joel[2] asked Moti.

The spy stretched a hand toward Joel²'s face. He flinched and tried to dodge, but Moti caught the back of his head and ripped off the bandages covering both his temple and his right eye. "Because if he thinks one of you is dead, it's better if you are both the same *you*," he said, throwing the bloody dressings to the floor.

Joel² and I obliged. I wasn't sure how he felt about it, but considering I'd spent the earlier part of the day running around with my ass hanging out of a hospital gown, the notion of a bunch of Levantine spies gawking at my junk didn't move the embarrassment needle much. I was actually pleased to part with my dirty makeshift fake-doctor outfit in favor of some clean clothes. Also, the vest made me feel a bit like a badass.

"We're here," Zaki said just as Joel² and I finished changing. "But it looks like we have some company."

The rear door of the van opened, revealing the silhouette of a certain waifish woman who'd recently made both my and Joel²'s acquaintance. She looked almost ethereal against dusk's last blood-orange embers and the high-intensity lights that illuminated Chelsea Piers' twenty-four-hour operations at night.

"Pema," Moti breathlessly said her name.

"Pema!" Ifrit said excitedly.

Pema stepped toward our vehicle. She wore an oversized shawl-collared granite-colored sweater that dramatically swayed as a gust of misty wind off the Hudson enveloped her body.

"Hello, Joel and Joel. It's good to see you both in one place. May I ask which is which?"

Before either of us could answer, Moti asked her point-blank, "What are you doing here, Pema?"

"You asked for a deal. I got you one." She winked at Ifrit. The Levantine woman blushed.

"Eventually, Pema," an uncharacteristically irritated Moti said, "conscientious objector, double agent, or loyalist, you will need to choose a side."

"There are no sides, Moti. Nothing is black-and-white. Corina doesn't need me to tell her what your designs for Taraval are. International Transport is well versed in the methods of the Levant. They know you want leverage; you know they want control. Don't pretend like you're not playing the same game on the same board." She put her hand into a black satchel she carried on her back. Seeing her movement, several of the Levantine soldiers pointed handheld weapons. Moti remained steadfast, merely raising a curious eyebrow.

"What is it?" he asked as she held up a brushed metal orb roughly the size of a softball.

"A prototype."

He took it from her, rolling it around carefully in his hand. "So it's true?"

She nodded. "A Honeycomb grenade. Technically, it doesn't exist. The perfect weapon for hostage extractions."

"Or kidnapping people," Moti said pointedly. "And Corina sent you to tell us this? Doesn't she know that we already have a backdoor into Honeycomb? Any Levant they try to *grenade* there we will simply extract and delete."

"She only knows what I tell her," Pema said.

Moti tsk-tsked. "You don't give her enough credit, Pema."

"The way it's supposed to work," she said, ignoring his affront, "is to teleport everyone within its ecophagy cage and send them to the glacier for safekeeping. Then the wielding party releases who they want, when they want."

"And what's an ecophagy cage?" interjected Joel[2].

"Nanotech one oh one stuff, apparently," I told him. "It's a cage that keeps self-replicating nanos in check. Without it, the nanos that clear people in TC foyers would keep on going, killing everyone in their way."

"And how big is this cage?" asked Joel[2].

Pema pressed her fingertips together. "It's meant to be adjustable in production models, but the radius for this one is around four meters."

"But?" asked Moti expectantly.

"But—there's no Punch Escrow," she admitted. "Anything goes wrong, there's no safety net. No guarantees that the teleportee doesn't get lost en route to the glacier."

"Ha!" Moti snapped his fingers. "Well, it would appear Ms. Corina Shafer knows more than you think, Pema. She trusted you would bring us the grenade and that we would be foolish enough to use it. But I have no interest in handing William Taraval over to International Transport. I assume the real reason she sent you here is because Mr. Taraval deleted all his previous backups from the glacier, and they would like us to procure a new one for them at the expense of Levantine life. *How kind of them.* No, I think we will do things our way."

Moti looked Pema over. "You tell Ms. Shafer that I'm not here to capture her rogue vizier so she can get him back naked and unarmed in her custody. We won't be her black-bag assassination squad. You tell her that her *peace offering* is rejected." He considered the prototype grenade, then carefully placed it in the same compartment from which our borrowed clothes had come. "On second thought, no. We will have a counteroffer for her shortly. Zaki, please keep Pema *comfortable* here—"

"I'm not—hey!"

Zaki was more brisk than I, and certainly Pema, might have anticipated for a man his size. In a blink he was behind her, pinning one hand to her waist and the other to the back of her neck. He pressed her forward, deeper into the van's cabin.

"And if she tries to comm anyone?" Zaki asked.

"She won't," Ifrit said. "Will you?"

Pema shook her head obediently, though it was plain to see she was seething beneath her facade. Oblivious or apathetic to her anger, Zaki pushed Pema firmly into the seat next to Ifrit. She sat down beside her, crossing her legs and arms tightly.

"Good," Moti said, fetching another TIME cigarette from his packet and lighting it. "Now, let's see what we are dealing with out here."

MAKE WESTING

THE SUN HAD NOW COMPLETELY SET. The lights had all come on in the IT shipping yard. Other than the half-full moon, no stars or planets could be seen in the sky, owing to the fluorescence of the lights and the refraction from the mosquito-piss rain.

Our arrival on the scene had not been lost on Taraval. He'd chosen his perch specifically for its strategically superior view of the surroundings. Of concern to Sylvia was that he didn't seem hurried or concerned at all upon seeing our small detachment appear. Quite the opposite, in fact.

"The cavalry arrives at the edge of the world!" he shouted, his eyes glistening, a mild breeze dancing through his lab coat. "Not to worry, Sylvia—this is where my grandstanding ends. It's time to eat our own dog food, drink the Kool-Aid, whatever the appropriate platitude may be. My darling girl, this is where we usher the Luddites forward!"

For the first time since he'd kidnapped her, Sylvia dared to hope. She didn't know what she was hoping for, really. She'd run through all the possible endings in her mind, and none had concluded with *happily ever after*. The best she could muster was the magnet holding her over the concrete portal failing, followed by a short fall and a quick, painless death. But now, through the haze of blood pounding in her upside-down head, she saw a slight possibility of survival. That she might miss that chance was by far the scariest thing that had happened to her since she got back to New York.

"Don't worry, Sylvia. They are not here to impede us—they are our *escorts.*"

"Escorts?" Sylvia stared at him in confusion.

"Escorts, companions, *entourage.* The Greeks had company in their journey through the underworld. We go to Elysium to be reborn, while our friends go to Asphodel Meadows to await our beckoning. All eight million of them."

Sylvia's eyes went wide as, for the first time, she fathomed his full design.

"You can't!" she shouted. "Joel!"

Taraval took the roll of foil tape from his lab coat and ripped off another piece. "Can't have you spoiling your own surprise party," he grumbled, going to tape her mouth shut again. He screamed in agony as she bit down on his fingers with all her might.

Her head rang loudly as the back of his left hand smacked her across the face. The force of the blow caused her to release her captor's hand.

There were deep, oozing teeth marks in two of his middle fingers. "I'm doing my best not to allow anger to ruin this moment," Taraval said, breathing heavily. He forced a contented smile on his face. "There is no progress without pain. A blood sacrifice, we'll call it. Now it's time for yours."

He took out the Gehinnomites' jamming device and reenabled Sylvia's comms. "Now, my dear. I'd like you to log this console into Honeycomb. Don't, and I'll clear every human being on the island of Manhattan." He set the ecophagy cage radius to forty kilometers, then hovered a finger over the execute icon.

He would do it, she could tell. Taraval had nothing left to live for but his plan. She nodded, blinking away the rain as she executed a remote log-in. A complex patchwork of graphics appeared on the crane operator's console—it was now fully operational.

"There," she said. "Now get into the glacier and out of my life."

"Happy to oblige," tut-tutted Taraval. "Just need to clear a few things up first." Before she could do anything, he again disabled her comms with the Gehinnomites' device.

"What?" Sylvia kicked in frustration, powerless to stop him. "I did what you asked. Now keep your promise!"

"Sylvia, my dear. Did I mislead you? Apologies. That was less a promise than a threat. And really, what good are threats if one is not committed to follow them through?"

She bucked against her magnetic suspension, to no avail. "Why, Bill? Why do they have to die?"

"Every day, millions of people put their lives in our hands," he said. "Sometimes we must clench our fists as a reminder that trust is not merely a thing we earn, but one we deserve. You, however, needn't take part in this demonstration. Indeed, it would be a shame to write you off as collateral damage. Please know you are still very welcome to join me."

Sylvia—speechless—shook her head in revulsion.

"No? I suggest you reconsider." Then, his fingers still dripping ichor, he tore off another piece of tape and placed it roughly over her mouth. "A muzzle for a misbehaving pet," he said, pressing an icon that lowered the magnet to about three meters below the operator booth. "Do a little dance if you change your mind. You have about ten minutes."

THE BATTLE OF CHELSEA PIERS

UNLIKE NORMAL TCs, which hold only a handful of foyers and vestibules at each location, freight TCs can host dozens of portals. As we looked over the massive rain-drenched shipping yards, it seemed like we would never locate Taraval or Sylvia amid the chaos of blaring alarms, blinking yellow lights, and constantly moving cranes.

It was disheartening. I'd never really considered that we'd have to canvass such a vast area to find our wife. But we quickly realized that Taraval wanted to be found. He stood next to the operating booth of a crane that was several hundred yards away. He wore a conductor's yellow hard hat, waving to us from the console, his soiled and torn lab coat flapping wildly in the rain.

It took a moment to register that the thing hanging from the crane's magnet was a person, suspended upside down like a worm on a hook. Bait. An offering who looked exactly like—

Oh my God.

"Sylvia." I didn't know if it was me or Joel[2] who had spoken.

My body acted before my mind. My legs were already mid-stride when I realized I was running across the wet pavement.

I'd broken away from the detachment. It took all of two minutes for me to disobey Moti's orders, to disregard any risk or consequence. I could hear Moti yelling behind me. I knew that was why I ran first. I didn't want logic or reason holding me back from doing what instinct demanded: *save her.*

It took me a beat to realize that Joel[2] wasn't with me. Not being in his head, I could only speculate as to why. I knew that his anger had made him braver than me. I think on some level, he believed, as did I, that when she saw us side by side, she would know immediately which one was her real husband. And seeing that realization would be, for him, worse than any Gehinnomite torture.

"Shit," Moti said. "I said no distractions."

She was less than a minute's run away from me. Two maroon containers nearest Sylvia sat on a conveyor leading to a warehouse at the far end of the pier. They had ladders on their sides, which I climbed, taking care not to slip on the rain-slick rungs. It wouldn't quite bring me within reach of Sylvia, but at least she would see me. That was the extent of my ad-libbed plan. *Get her to see me.*

Once I got to the top of the container, she did. Her face hung upside down about two meters above me. It was the first time I'd seen her in person since the morning of July 3. Fresh blood trailed from her lips to her hairline. Her damp hair stuck to her skin in small curlicues.

She sees me.

Behind the fear, I detected the flicker of uncertainty in her eyes. I knew it from discussions of things much less dramatic than our present situation, such as, where should we stay for our tenth wedding anniversary? I almost laughed at this, knowing that now she was wondering which of her husbands she was looking at—the one she had downloaded or the one spared from destruction by the Levant.

Her eyes crinkled, then went wide as she remembered something. She struggled to talk around the tape covering her mouth.

"Ekmmphy grrg!" she shouted.

"What?" I asked, thinking maybe the wind ate her words.

She worked her jaw, pushing and stretching on the tape until a portion of it came away. "The ecophagy cage!" she repeated. "Taraval expanded it—he's going to clear New York! Once he's in Honeycomb, the whole city's going to be eaten by nanos." She was screaming now. "Get out of here!"

Holy shit. Holy fucking shit.

I hesitated, unsure of what to do next. Behind me Moti, Zaki, and the Levantine operatives were making their way to Taraval's crane. Joel[2] was in the back of the pack, walking, not running. Still racked by hesitation. His eyes met mine. I moved my hands apart from each other to create an expanding ball, and—

I've heard that some twins claim to share a special psychic connection. This sort of seemingly psychic link isn't necessarily mysterious: any two people who know each other very well and who have shared many common experiences—including siblings, married couples, and even best friends—may complete each other's sentences and have a pretty good idea what the other person is thinking, but that's not telepathy. The idea of twin telepathy has been around for over six centuries. It appears, for example, in the 1844 Alexandre Dumas novella, *The Corsican Brothers*, which tells the story of two once-conjoined brothers who were separated at birth, yet even as adults continue to share not only thoughts but also physical sensations. One twin states, "However far apart we are now we still have one and the same body, so that whatever impression, physical or mental, one of us perceives has its after-effects on the other."

So—despite the physical distance between us, despite the fact that we'd only known each other for less than a day—I *knew* Joel[2] knew it, too: Taraval *wanted* us within range of his ecophagy cage. I suspected he wouldn't be taking us with him—only he had a ticket to his final destination. The rest of us would simply depart and never arrive anywhere, cleared by the teleportation nanos. It was impossible to tell how far he had extended the cage—or if he had set any boundaries at all. Maybe he aimed to destroy as much of this world as he could before leaving it behind for whatever greener pastures he imagined existed on the other side.

Fuck it. If this is it, at least she'll know I was there until the end. Till death do us part.

I turned back to my wife. "I love you. I'm not going anywhere."

"While I can't vouch for the veracity of the first, I certainly can assure you, your second statement is a patent falsehood, Mr. Byram." Taraval's head appeared in the window of the crane booth above us. "Where is your *doppelgänger?*" he yelled down, a Cheshire cat–smile forming on his lips.

Sylvia, please forgive me for what I am about to do.

"You should know, asshole!" I yelled back. "You killed him in Costa Rica!"

I knew that would hit Sylvia like a punch to the gut, but I needed her reaction to help cement Taraval's belief in the ruse. The element of surprise was the only advantage I could afford Joel[2].

"Dead?" he scoffed. "From such a minor head wound? Why, I thought you Byrams were made of sterner stuff." Turning to Sylvia, he said, "Not to worry, my dear. You can always make yourself another one when we arrive at our destination."

"She's not going *anywhere!*" I shouted.

Taraval shook his head. "Oh, but I beg to differ, young man. You and I, Mr. Byram, we are on opposite ends of the existential spectrum. Like the rest of your contingent back there, and much of humanity—you are hopelessly addicted to foolishness. You are a man indelibly tethered to *his* wife, *his* job, *his* things. To me, however, the name tag on this bag of meat I wear, William Taraval, means nothing. He is merely a runtime library. His identity has no significance; his properties are expendable. One could alter me, even delete me from the glacier, but *nothing* will undo my actions."

I now grokked my part in the game. Mine was the task of keeping Taraval occupied, distracting him from his task at hand. For whatever reason, he needed someone to grasp his *genius*. Maybe he thought that if I understood his plans, others would be convinced by proxy.

"Come on!" I called up to him, really laying on the disbelief. "What could you possibly do that can't be undone by someone else?"

Taraval's mouth quivered, appalled I could even suggest such a thing. *Direct hit.* "Very well, Mr. Byram. Allow me to elucidate."

OH L'AMOUR

WHILE I WAS ATTEMPTING to keep Taraval talking, Joel[2] ran back to the Levantine van, frantically trying to open the console where Moti had placed the grenade.

"What are you doing?" Zaki asked as Joel[2] started banging on the panel, absurdly trying to break through the bulletproof molding.

"Trying to save your lives," Joel[2] said. "I need to get in there. Can you open this for me?"

"Joel, whatever you think you're doing, don't do it," Pema urged him from her seat beside Ifrit. "That grenade is a prototype for a reason. The operating range is too close for safety; it's just as risky for the wielder as it is for the target. There's no Escrow, either. If the mechanism fails at any point, you could kill yourself."

"But you were willing to risk Moti's life?" he asked.

"Nobody does anything without Moti saying," Zaki said impassively. "You want your little toy, go ask him for it."

Joel[2] banged against the console cover in frustration and ran outside to find Moti. Fortunately, he was directing his team only a few steps away.

"Continue to strafe until you find a clear nonlethal shot," Moti directed his team. "You kill him, I kill you."

"We need to turn the power off!" Joel[2] yelled from behind him. "He's going to clear everyone here!"

Moti turned around. "What are you talking about?"

Joel[2] tried to keep his voice calm. "Taraval expanded the crane's ecophagy cage. He's going to clear everyone! All of us"— he pointed at the island to the east of them—"all of Manhattan, maybe. Eight million people. Who knows how far those fucking nanos will go before they run out of juice? We need to kill the power to this whole fucking place right fucking now!"

"Shit," Moti said. "No wonder it was so easy to find him. Pull back!" he ordered his team. "Back with me in the van right now!"

"I need you to give me the grenade," Joel[2] told him.

"What? Forget about it. It's a suicide mission."

"Give me. The grenade," Joel[2] insisted. His resolve was complete, confident. Despite Sylvia's deceptions and lies, despite his own self-doubt, despite his existential crisis, Joel[2] still loved our wife. Maybe more than he loved himself. And like me, he was ready to prove it. Love makes you do crazy shit.

Moti studied the determined look on Joel[2]'s face as rain pattered slightly on their tac vests. I'd like to tell you that what he saw in my doppelgänger's eyes somehow moved the Levantine spy, making him particularly sensitive to our cause. That would have been nice. But to be honest, I believe what happened next was merely Moti's pragmatic approach to ensuring his team walked away from this thing alive.

"Let's go," he told Joel[2], and started walking back toward the van. Inside, he walked to the front section where Pema and Ifrit sat. He put his hand around Pema's neck. Joel[2] was afraid he might snap it, but Moti just held her by her throat and coolly stated, "Contact Corina Shafer and tell her that if she cuts the power to the Chelsea Piers TC right now, then she has a deal. Understand?"

Pema nodded. "Understood."

Moti released her. "Zaki! Why is everyone not back here yet? Go out there and get them here right now!"

The big man was already out of the van and sprinting toward the freight yard.

Moti then walked back over to the locked compartment. It opened at his touch. He gently removed the grenade, examining it. Contemplating the consequences.

"Tell me, Joel, do you know what a shofar is? Once, outside Jericho—"

"I don't care," Joel[2] said, impatiently grabbing the grenade from his hand. "How do you work this thing?" he asked Pema.

THE LASKER TRAP

THE GRENADE was significantly heavier than it looked. This made it rather awkward for Joel[2] to run with—especially given the grave reminders Pema had etched into his mind about what might happen if he dropped the thing. Its titanium trisulfide coating was smooth, almost gelatinous to the touch—in other words, dangerously slippery. The rain wasn't helping matters.

He was careful to stay behind containers, duck around trucks, and crawl under conveyors. Anything that would give him cover. His path was wisely indirect, moving around rather than toward me. Finally he arrived behind Taraval's crane. Thanks to me, the mad scientist was still expounding upon religious philosophy and historical precedent and justifications of things that "must be done." It was all hogwash, but I made sure to maintain eye contact. *Keep talking, crazyhead.*

As Taraval continued his stupid soliloquy, Joel[2] climbed one-handed up the ladder leading to the conductor's cabin. Considering the metal rungs were slick with raindrops and he was carrying an untested weapon of mass destruction (though I did not realize it in that moment), it wasn't just difficult—it was terrifying. Worse, I had to keep my eyes on Taraval, who was well into his rant now.

"If only people adhered to the fundamental tenets of human progress rather than the dogmatic commandments of the so-called arbiters of justice, the world would be a better place. But alas, pivotal deviations from standard operating procedure that pioneers such as Corina Shafer have cultivated are nowadays handled by fat-cat legislators and litigators. Innovation has been distilled to its least common revenue-generating denominator. Our generation has lost its spirit, and I have lost my patience, Mr. Byram." Taraval turned back to the conductor's console, tapping a few icons. "Sylvia, my dear, you're up." He raised the crane's magnet then turned it off, hauling her body into the conductor's booth. The magnet lowered again, until it was about halfway between me and the booth.

Lifting my wife by the chin, Taraval held Sylvia's head to the console's biometric sensor. Thankfully, nothing happened. "Open your eyes!" he yelled at her.

No more words. Time for action.

With his attention off me, I jumped up toward the dangling crane magnet. It took a few tries, but I managed to snag it, my fingers barely gripping the slick metal edge of the nearly two-meter-wide disc. As I pulled myself up, my biceps straining, I could see Joel[2] was nearly at the conductor's booth. I clambered on top of the heavy round magnet, thinking I could swing it closer to the console and grab Sylvia. It was the only plan I could think of. At the same time, Joel[2] reached the top of the ladder. I nodded to him, hoping to convey that Taraval was preoccupied. And then I saw it.

The grenade.

In my mind, I felt relief, not concern. Had I been privy to Pema's lecture about the danger of the grenade to its wielder, I would have likely tried to dissuade Joel[2] from using it. But at that moment, as he and I made eye contact, the pride I'd felt for him earlier returned. There was no longer any jealousy, no existential worry over which of us was the real Joel Byram. Right then I would have been proud to be either of us. Proud that there were two of us, and we were both doing what it took to save our wife.

With the wind picking up, I tried to swing the magnet back and forth like a pendulum. I did this by running from one side of the magnet to the other, but it barely moved. The metal disc on which I was standing and the steel cable attaching it to the crane must have weighed over a ton. Hoping my impromptu trapeze act would at least distract Taraval from Joel[2], I put my back into it, letting out a mighty roar. Surprisingly, the magnet actually started to swing slightly.

Unfortunately, the yellow lights on the crane and in the portal beneath us started flashing at the same moment.

Shit, she opened her eyes.

I reached toward the railing with one hand, leaning into my momentum to increase the arc of the magnet's swing.

Here we go.

My fingers grazed one of the railing beams as the alarms started blaring.

Focus. Don't let go. You can do this.

"Sylvia!" I yelled. "Jump!"

Both she and Taraval looked down to me. Then Joel[2] pulled himself into the booth and stood up. He was now at eye level with Taraval.

Seeing my doppelgänger, Taraval looked back and forth between me, swinging on the magnet three meters below him, and Joel[2], holding a prototype teleportation grenade a mere two meters away. "Fool me once!" Taraval said, wagging a finger. "Fortunately for me, one is all you get."

Taraval stretched a finger toward a green triangular icon on the console. He was about to press it when Sylvia knocked him sideways with her hip.

Joel^2 grabbed her by the shoulders. "We've got you," he said, kissing her quickly on the forehead then pushing her out of the conductor's booth.

"Joel!" she screamed as she fell downward.

The magnet, with me on top of it, swung back toward her. *Everything you've gone through, your entire life, has been about this one fucking moment, Joel. Don't fuck it up! Now—catch!*

I caught her under the arms, the sudden weight yanking me into a sitting position. The steel suspension cable cut into my shoulder, but I hung on. Gritting my teeth, I struggled to lift my wife onto the magnet with me. To anyone watching the maneuver, I'm sure it resembled a disastrously executed circus act. But I felt like Superman. Slowly, Sylvia's body came over the edge of the disc, until she collapsed across my lap. I exhaled a sigh of relief.

Suddenly the TC alarms stopped blaring and the shipping yard went dark. The only light came from the moon reflecting off the raindrops.

Taraval laughed. "Did you idiots seriously think cutting the power would be something I did not account for?" he said to Joel^2.

"No," Joel^2 responded. But he wasn't talking to him. His eyes were focused on me and Sylvia. Again, I have no idea what he was thinking. Maybe he'd done the relationship calculus and realized there was no plausible future for the three of us as a "family." Maybe he thought he needed to be punished for killing Eduardo and hacking Julie. Maybe he just felt the glacier calling to him. All I know is what he did, which was move his right hand from behind his back and reveal the grenade. He pushed in one of the two gray buttons on its side without looking away from me and our wife. The grenade's opaque metallic surface instantly became transparent. It looked as though Joel^2 was holding a weighty bubble in his hands.

Taraval recoiled, clearly recognizing the grenade for what it was. He was scared. "You fool," he said. "Use that thing and you'll merely kill yourself their way instead of mine."

Three meters below the booth, Sylvia looked at me in abject horror. She, too, realized what was about to transpire. "He can't!"

"He already has," I told her, and pulled her off the magnet.

We fell to the container below, striking the metal roof and knocking the breath from our lungs. As my wife and I struggled to inhale, the bright overhead lights blinked back into service. The yellow caution lights resumed flashing, and the alarms revved up their blaring. Taraval snorted a brief "Ha!" and quickly turned back to the conductor's console. Without hesitation, Joel^2 ran toward Taraval at full speed.

Fuck. We're dead. Even if he does get there, we're all dead.

I turned to Sylvia, uttering a forlorn "I love you." But she didn't acknowledge it. Her attention was not on me.

"No!" she screamed as the light emanating from the grenade in Joel^2's hand became whiter and brighter, until it was as if a million strips of magnesium ignited all at once. I was forced to avert my gaze.

"Joel!" Sylvia cried.

There was a loud *thunk*, and the shipping yard went dark again.

Moti. He must have cooked up a contingency for Taraval's contingency.

Sparks flew from the TC console. The crane's magnet became untethered, falling toward us at a quick clip. I rolled sideways, trying to drag Sylvia with me—

But the one-ton disc hit the container, crushing the thick steel as if it were tinfoil. The sound of the impact echoed off the nearby freight containers. Then all was silent, save for the patter of raindrops on metal.

"Joel," my wife said in the darkness. "Joel, I can't feel my leg."

"Hang on." I stretched out my hand, my eyes straining to adjust in the darkness. My fingers found Sylvia's shoulder, then looked down to her torso. Her left leg was pinned underneath the magnet, but her eyes were on the conductor's booth. I followed her gaze. The discharged grenade lay where Joel[2] and Taraval had stood, a green light blinking on its surface.

The two men were gone.

"Joel," Sylvia whispered. I knew which one she meant. Her face was streaked with tears and rain.

Is he really gone?

Without the high-intensity lights polluting the night sky, constellations of stars began to appear. Their twinkling above was cold comfort. Sylvia stared at the space where her resurrected husband had stood just a moment ago, then she began to weep. A deep, soul-purging wail of despair that reverberated off the containers, until it sounded like a choir in a funeral procession. I put my arm around her, too shocked to join in, my eyes also fixed on the empty booth. Knowing—as only twins do—that my other was truly gone.

ALWAYS SOMETHING THERE TO REMIND ME

ONCE THE PARAMEDICS ARRIVED, they immediately set to work on repairing Sylvia's left leg. It had been crushed, nearly severed just above the knee. She refused to teleport to the hospital, so they flew her in an ambulance drone. She allowed them to staunch the bleeding, but would not discuss a prosthetic replacement. She kept saying she deserved to have a piece of herself missing.

The next day, owing to God's weird sense of humor or poignant sense of irony, I again found myself deep in the bowels of Bellevue Hospital. Only this time, Sylvia was the patient. I stood before the hospital's vending printer, trying to decide if a Big Mac qualified as breakfast food. I had just settled on ordering a regular old apple when a familiar gravelly voice spoke behind me.

"I read my cup this morning, Joel."

I turned to see Moti, nattily dressed as always, a cryptic smile on his face.

"It was interesting," he continued. "A shape that could be read in two different ways."

Shortly before the paramedics showed up last night, Moti and his team had made themselves scarce. Pema briefed us on what to say and what not to say, assuring us that International Transport would handle damage control. Neither Sylvia nor I had mentioned anyone else's presence at the shipping yard. Our official story was that Taraval had abducted Sylvia, and his disappearance was the result of a deranged work-related attempt at murder-suicide. IT had already set up Taraval as the fall guy; now they were executing on that plan. The news feeds all talked about the actions of a scientist who went crazy and killed a crane conductor. Our names were not mentioned, only that "Two innocent bystanders were also injured, but are expected to make a full recovery."

Moti's tone now was nonchalant, but I knew he was goading me to ask for more detail. Perhaps trying to lighten the mood. I didn't take the bait.

As we walked back to my wife's room, the Levantine spy verified what I intrinsically knew—what Sylvia had realized the moment it had happened: Joel[2] was gone. They couldn't find him or Taraval in the glacier. They'd keep trying, but it wasn't looking good.

I couldn't stop myself from continuously mulling over Joel[2]'s last action. He didn't have to sacrifice himself. Moti had things under control. But, of course, there had been no way to know that.

Still, why had he held on to the grenade while tackling Taraval? Why not throw it at him? Did he think that taking out Taraval that way would stop the portal nanos from clearing everyone else? Or was he already resigned to his end, answering the siren's call of the glacier? Perhaps he knew there was no future for him and Sylvia, that the weight of what she'd done would always be heavier on his soul than mine. Perhaps he saw his sacrifice as the best and only way to ensure her happiness.

One thing I knew for sure, I still had a million questions. But for once, I didn't need to know all the answers. Now I just wanted to appreciate what I had, and what I'd almost lost. I felt as though I'd lived two lifetimes in the last thirty-six hours.

We entered my wife's room. She lay on the blue-and-white bed, staring bleakly out the window at the New York skyline. The Sun managed to shine brightly through the hazy atmosphere. The clouds around it looked like perfectly sculpted cotton balls against the bluish-gray sky. Yet, Sylvia's expression was bleak. The absence of her leg under the bedsheet reminded me of a missing puzzle piece.

"IT is on the way to debrief you," Moti told us. "I cannot be here when they arrive. So this must be good-bye."

I nodded. Sylvia continued staring out the window.

"William Taraval knew he was finished, but he still tried to take us all out," Moti added, despite her disinclination to listen. Maybe he wanted to make himself feel better. "Your husbands acted bravely. Sometimes stupidly, too. But they saved you. I suggest both of you look forward, not backward."

"The fail-safe," Sylvia said softly. Her voice was still hoarse from the events of the past two days. "Bill told me not to worry about his self-experimentation in Honeycomb. He said he'd been testing it for six months with no recorded adverse effects. And he said he had a fail-safe in case something went wrong."

"Interesting," Moti said, reaching for the pack of TIME cigarettes I knew was in his pocket. "What is this fail-safe?" he asked, knocking the pack against the palm of his hand.

"I—" She hesitated, looking at me, her face stricken. I squeezed her hand in mine, encouraging her to go on. "In my research, there would be a programmatic mechanism for waking up astronauts when they arrived at their destination. With Honeycomb, it was the same. You could theoretically bring anyone back if you knew where to look and what to look for."

"In that case, I'm afraid the matter is hopeless," Moti said, lighting up his tightly packed cigarette in defiance of the NO SMOKING signs plastered all around the hospital. "As soon as that grenade went off, IT and the Levant were in a race to find and recover William Taraval."

But not Joel²?

He continued, unaware of, or perhaps indifferent to, my thoughts, "We knew where to look and what we were looking for, but there was nothing." He paused to draw a puff from his cigarette. "They are gone. I am sure of it."

"So that's it?" I asked him.

Moti nodded. "That's it," he said. Sylvia turned her face away again.

"I must go," he stated, heading back to the door of Sylvia's room. "You know, when this all settles down, you two should take another vacation."

Moti took another puff, the end of his cigarette glowing red. "If you ask this travel agent," he said, smiling, a single eyebrow raised, "I recommend Florence. Easy to get to without teleportation. Go see the *Mona Lisa* there, at the Uffizi. She will help you." He turned halfway in the doorway, meeting my eye with the corner of his as he took one last drag. "Good-bye, *Joel.*"

Then he left us in a cloud of smoke.

AD FINEM

For our transgressions have been multiplied before Thee, and our sins have testified against us; for our transgressions are with us, and our iniquities—we have known them.
—Isaiah 59:12

JUST A FEW FINAL HOUSEKEEPING ITEMS I need to get down before ending this transcription.

For seven days, Sylvia stayed in the hospital. She refused all replacement legs, mechanical or printed, choosing to regard her missing limb as a reminder of the guilt, anguish, and self-loathing she felt. After a week, she finally consented to accept a simple jointed titanium prosthesis. Whether she gave in to my gentle badgering or didn't want to go through life in a wheelchair, I don't know. I do know our turn on the ride is over. I think it's safe to say we're both ready to get off.

God gave Adam and Eve unfettered access to the Garden of Eden. "Don't eat the fruit of these two trees," he commanded. We know how that turned out. Some blame Eve; some blame Adam. Some blame the snake. The salter blames the coder: God. Why make a game with spaces on which players aren't allowed to land?

I never bought Moti's explanation of Taraval's and Joel²'s disappearance. That's why this document exists. Technically, the grenade couldn't just make them disappear. Unlike what happened to the *Mona Lisa*, there was no coronal mass ejection event over New York that night to disrupt their passage to the glacier. At worst, they should have arrived there in a deformed state, but their arrival would have been logged. Moti or IT would have found them.

So, either they did arrive deformed, and Moti tried to save us from the gory details, or they arrived perfectly intact. The problem with the latter outcome, the only thing allowing me to even consider that Moti and IT were telling the truth, was the reactivation of my comms. The moment they were turned back on, Joel²'s brief history, his telemetry and metadata and recordings, merged with mine. Every single thing he saw, heard, and said filled the gaps in my existential amnesia with his escapades. That's what keeps me sane: the knowledge that even with all of IT's might and all the Levant's technological prowess, there's no way my comms could have been active on two people at the same time. The Theseus paradox is real because we programmed reality that way.

In exchange for our sworn silence, Corina and the near-infinite powers of International Transport's counsel saw to it that none of the details of our escapades were reported. Sylvia was allowed to "retire" from her job with full benefits, and—after some legal wrangling—my full identity was restored. We were both granted leave to go on with our lives.

Still, I think about Joel² a lot.

It's been hard chronicling his part in this story. Please understand that whenever I expressed any of his emotions, it was guesswork. To make things sound less wooden, the chapters of this memoir featuring Joel² were edited here, embellished there, and somewhat dramatized, as I could only imagine what must have been going on inside his mind.

Sometimes I perceive others incorrectly by transposing my feelings onto them. It's hard to vet that statement because I'm the one making it, and I'm not a very good judge of what's going on in my head. Even if I were capable of gauging my state of mind objectively, I could only determine such things in retrospect.

In replaying his history, which is now *my* history, occasionally I'd see Joel^2's reflection in a mirror or a window, and venture a guess as to what he was thinking based on the gestures or expressions I had made in similar contexts. Sylvia also helped fill in some missing pieces, like what happened between her and Taraval at the hotel and in the abandoned subway tunnels beneath New York.

Joel^2 would probably take umbrage with my characterization of him. Hell, I know I would if anyone did the same to me. But he *was* me during that time, or *we* were *us*, and to that end, I feel somewhat entitled to such poetic license.

I've inhabited every emotional and existential state a human being could fathom. More than anything, I was angry. Some of that was anger was mine, for being made the duped (pun intended) pawn in some techno-ideo-geopolitical war. Some of my anger was Joel^2's anger. I have all his comms recordings, and in some ways they now feel realer to me than my own memory. Though I still can't feel what he felt, sometimes I can feel him in the gap between me and Sylvia. I don't know how we would have lived in the same world, but I was angry that he was gone. And some of that anger was for all of us, for every unknowing person still porting every day. I wanted to blast the truth across the world's comms like a righteous Gehinnomite or one of those long-ago whistle-blowers from a century ago.

In other moments I was afraid or selfish, or both. With Joel[2] gone, I knew I had no leverage: I could no longer be the *ayah* that IT feared or the *Aher* the Levant valued. And I knew that although I had changed, the ways of the world did not. I could be cleared in some clandestine TC by IT or disappeared by the Levant, stuck in some room with only Moti and his clipboards and *Turkish* and tasseography. No surprise to you, not-a-hero Joel won out.

Which brings me to you. Remember the first chapter of this account? It was entitled *Stick!* It's what relay racers yell when they're passing the baton during sprint relays. See, it costs a runner time to look back, so they do blind handoffs, wherein the second runner stands on a spot predetermined in practice and starts running when the first runner arrives at a specific pace mark on the track. The second runner opens their hand behind them after a few strides, by which time the first runner should be caught up and able to hand off the baton. The first runner yells, "Stick!" repeatedly several times, alerting the recipient to put out their hand to receive the baton. It requires faith, and trust.

So teleportation, Project Honeycomb, International Transport, and all their subsequent issues are your problem now. Brand me selfish, lazy, supine—I've been called worse. I've known since the moment I kicked that boxer in the nuts that I wasn't much of a fighter. A year ago I was just a guy paid to play games with apps in his underwear. Sure, I may have found myself at the center of a massive international conspiracy affecting every person on this planet, but I don't want to be responsible for giving anyone who's ever teleported an identity crisis.

We rode in trains and drove cars that nearly killed the planet. We flew in planes with only a rudimentary and practical understanding of the physics of flight. We humans have an innate need to get from A to B faster so we could do C sooner. We've never gotten too caught up in the means or consequences of transport. So who am I to stand in the way of humanity's progress? It's not my place. Not today.

But maybe it's yours. Maybe in your time, some other corporation figured out how to make teleportation actually work the way IT told us it would. Maybe it's still the same copy-paste-delete mechanism, but everyone knows the truth of the Punch Escrow and doesn't give a shit.

Or maybe the Gehinnomites were right, and it's time for the truth to be told.

So, dear reader, stick!

Oh, and if you ever do see Joel[2], tell him I said: *Thanks,* hermano.

LA GIOCONDA

IT'S JULY 4, 2148. We're in Florence, just leaving the Uffizi art museum. Second honeymoon, take two—eleventh-anniversary edition, and the first time I'm acting as cruise director. Okay, I cheated a bit and asked Julie for help in finding the places most likely to overlap with our needs, but the planning and booking were all me. I even splurged on the rooms.

There's a bittersweet smile on my wife's face, possibly echoing my own. We're happy. Do I care if I'm impressing some glass-half-full bullshit upon her, or on me? We're having a moment, so, no.

We're talking about a bunch of stuff as we stroll onto the Ponte Vecchio, the old stone bridge that spans the Arno. The Sun has just dipped below the horizon, giving the bridge shops a burnished copper glow.

Sylvia notes we've been standing outside for a full two minutes and I haven't complained about the rain. I tell her that seeing the *Mona Lisa* reminded me of Superman. She laughs and demands an explanation. I say I've been wondering about the glacier. How Honeycomb was like the Phantom Zone in the Superman comic series: a prison dimension used by Kryptonians as a more humane form of incarceration.

Although the zone was a barren wasteland, people trapped in it could never get old or die.

"Except that was someone's idea of a dark, dystopian future. Not a desirable outcome," she says.

I respond, "I don't know. Does that really sound any more dystopian than uploading people to the glacier for arbitrary periods of time?"

"It might sound that way, but maybe it's because we're not ready for it now." Her voice loses its brightness. "I don't think it's fair to say we'll never need it. Eventually Earth will stop supporting life and we'll need to find someplace else to live."

She's getting upset. I'm losing points. My gut tells me to keep up the argument, to remind her that that's not even the problem. That it's not okay to *back up* people without their permission. My gut wants to win. My gut is an idiot.

I realize I shouldn't have brought it up, but I also feel like getting it out will start the healing. Neither of us has talked much about what happened on this day a year ago. That particularly painful part of our past. Maybe this is Joel[3] thinking—the new, mature Joel. A derivative of two previously failed prototypes, a superior version of me who recognizes and owns up to a mistake when he's made one. I'd like that.

I place a hand on the bump in her belly. "Let us look forward, not back," I intone. "I feel like that's a quote from someone. Although, about four months from now, we might wish we could—"

"We'll be fine." She smiles, putting her hand over mine. "People have been doing this for millennia."

"And look how humanity turned out," I can't help but snark.

She rolls her eyes.

We stop at an open spot in the bridge. The sky sparkles here and there as floating LEDs are calibrated.

"Weird," I remark, taking off my hat. "The raindrops feel like they're getting bigger. Can we go watch the show inside somewhere? One slip on these stones and I go straight into the Arno. Then you're a grieving widow and a single mom, all because of an oversized mosquito bladder."

"Aaaand there it is," she said, apparently stopping a timer on her comms. "Two minutes and forty-seven seconds. A new record."

"Syl, there are two kinds of people in the world: those who can avoid thinking about the fact that they're getting pissed on by mosquitoes every time they step outside, and those who can't. You should know conclusively by now that you married a man of the latter variety."

She plants a quick kiss on my lips, assuring me there are no hard feelings. "Actually, I think there's a third group: those of us who are cognizant of the rain and its provenance but are ambivalent about it. I mean, it really is just water. Who cares if it's coming from the bladder of an insect?"

"I do. I know we need bugs to breathe, but I don't want to think about it. Just like I also know that almost all of our protein comes from bugs, but I could never be one of those entomophagists. I like my grasshoppers and mealworms molded and flavored to taste like meat, not wriggling and hopping on my plate, thank you."

"You know that eating cattle is what nearly destroyed the ozone in the first place."

"Exactly! But I still need to maintain my suspension of disbelief. I just wish we could do something similar with the skeeters." A mosquito lands on the back of my hand. I raise my arm so Sylvia can see it. "Look," I say, staring contemplatively at the living steam reformer. "Millions of years of evolution have led her to instinctively know that she wants to be on my hand. Sure, she's getting all the energy she needs from the carbon fumes emanating from my skin, but I can tell there's part of her, somewhere deep in her DNA, that just desperately wants to poke me and eat my blood."

The mosquito flies off into the glowing darkness.

Sylvia bumps me with her shoulder, smiling. "I think more likely there's part of her that instinctively knew you were thinking of smashing her. Anyway, even if she somehow managed to get a bloodmeal, it would kill her."

"Huh. Well, it's nice to see you smile, even if it means we have to talk about bloodmeals."

"We wouldn't be talking about bloodmeals if you would have just let me enjoy my fireworks."

"Where would be the fun in that?"

She rolls her eyes again. I'm really pushing my luck, I know it. "Can't you just shut up and enjoy the moment? Look, they're starting!"

Indeed, the LEDs hovering above the Arno start their Technicolor animated display while synchronized audio explosions match their movements.

I shrug, having never really cared for pyrotechnics. "Another thing I've always wondered about is where all the dead mosquitoes go." I point at the centuries-old cobblestones of the Ponte Vecchio. "Shouldn't the ground be covered by millions of dead skeeters?"

"I never really thought about that," Sylvia says as she looks up. She bites her lip in contemplation. "Maybe the wind just blows 'em all over the place?"

"Or maybe they all get eaten by birds and mosquito hawks?"

Sylvia grins, shaking her head. "Mosquito hawks don't eat mosquitoes."

"What?" I ask, genuinely surprised.

"Yeah, they're actually called crane flies. They really don't eat much of anything after they emerge from their pupae."

"You're blowing my mind right now! In fact, I just had to look it up because I thought you were messing with me. I can't believe it."

"Yup. It's the world's smallest identity crisis."

I don't respond. Instead I drop my shoulders, suddenly overcome with sadness.

As we gazed upon the *Mona Lisa* earlier, I realized something. The charm of the masterpiece was never due to the beauty of the sitter—a woman experts seem to agree was Madonna Lisa Gherardini, wife of a Florentine merchant. Nor was it due to da Vinci's masterful brushstrokes or composition. The painting's magic was in the itch she made us scratch, that one eternal, unanswerable question: What's behind that smile?

The *Mona Lisa*'s mystery only grew when we lost her. Had we lost a water lily or starry night, we would have moved on. We wouldn't have scoured the world and found an earlier version that we could claim was the *real* her, igniting a debate that took the mystery from *What's behind her smile?* to *Which Mona Lisa was real?* We would not look at her and ponder, *Who was she?* or in my case, *Who am I?*

After our ordeal last year, I got prints of both *Lisa*s and hung them on our bedroom wall. I stared at them endlessly at night while Sylvia slept. Which one was me? Was I the *Isleworth Lisa* rather than the vanished *Lisa*, the earlier and less interesting of the two, only achieving my authenticity through the destruction of my other, better self?

I hoped, in coming here to look her in the eye, that I could figure out what made this version different from her predecessor. I hoped I might find an end to my own enduring existential pain. Ultimately, I realized it didn't matter which one I was. I was real, like the Giaconda was real, not because we were the originals, but because we were *here*.

Sylvia notices my sudden change of temperament and pokes me in the arm. "What's wrong?"

I peer down at the dark river. "You look at me and you think, 'That's my husband, Joel Byram.' But is that who I am?"

"What are you talking about?" she asks, concern building in her eyes.

I scratch my cheek uncomfortably. "I used to think it was incredibly vain of the Gehinnomites to believe we can mess with our souls. That we could . . ."

But I trail off as Sylvia's expression quickly morphs from concern to terror. A look I haven't seen since *that night*. She's not looking at me anymore; she's looking through me. Her neck tilting back as she looks to the heavens.

Suddenly my comms fill with urgent updates. *#LookUp* is trending.

> *Are you watching this, guys?*
> *What the hell?*
> *Lame. Bring back the fireworks!*
> *Are they doing commercials now?*

I look up.

The LEDs in the sky, which moments ago had been projecting a beautifully choreographed fireworks display, have instead converted the heavens into a giant POV stream of someone making their way through a TC. As they stand before the vestibule, the streaming person puts their hands out in front of them, fingers wrapped tightly together, bowing their head up and down. There are about six other people, also wearing LED-lined robes, clasping their hands together and standing around the Punch Escrow chair. A strand of glowing hair enters the frame.

Like embers in a flame.

"They're praying," Sylvia utters.

The captions beneath the stream confirm her assessment: the words BEHOLD GOD'S WILL appear beneath the clenched hands. The camera pans sideways briefly, and I spot the International Transport logo above the conductor's blood-splattered console.

"It's the R and D vestibule at IT headquarters," Sylvia says, real fear in her voice.

I remain silent.

The camera pans back to the empty chair. There's a familiar white flash, momentarily blinding the POV stream. The camera lens adjusts to reveal a human sitting in the Punch Escrow chair. A naked male figure. His silhouette is familiar. He rises and walks toward the camera, balding and pudgy and coming into focus as the chanting around him increases. A smile splits his newly printed face.

It's him. He's back.

"Don't look!" I urgently say to Sylvia. I try shielding her eyes, but she shoves me away.

The stream goes white and the caption PULSA D'NURA appears, illuminating the night sky like a thunderbolt from the heavens.

Fuck.

AFTERWORD

WHEN ONE IS dealing with hard science fiction, I'm told it's particularly important to get the facts right. For example, one of the best and most well-known hard science fiction writers, Larry Niven, got a very important fact wrong in his first story, "The Coldest Place." In it, the coldest place concerned was the dark side of Mercury, which at the time the story was written was thought to be tidally locked with the Sun. However, Mercury was found to rotate in a 3:2 resonance with the Sun before the story saw the light of day, meaning it was published with known scientific errata. Oh well. Didn't seem to hurt his career much.

As *The Punch Escrow* is set in the mid-twenty-second century, I expect history will show I've gotten a lot of things wrong. I did my very best to avoid such missteps, but since I am only a *fan* of quantum physics and not a quantum physicist myself, I leaned on my friend Joe Santoro, a real-life medical physicist, to vet—and sometimes invent—the science necessary to make this world scientifically plausible. Joe is one of the nicest, smartest guys I know. He's probably blushing, reading this. Still, without him, there never would have been a Punch Escrow.

In April of 2016, after I was sure this book would be published, I conducted a short interview with Joe.

Tal: Let's get the obligatories out of the way. Please state your name and what you do for a living.

Joe: My name is Joe Santoro, and I am a medical physicist. I work in a radiation oncology clinic at a hospital on Long Island. We're the guys who make sure the medical linear accelerator is delivering the correct radiation dose to patients undergoing radiation therapy. We also come up with the treatment plans for patients that dictate where the radiation will get delivered. We're responsible for routine quality assurance of most of the various components that comprise the radiation delivery chain, i.e. the CT scanners, LINAC, on-treatment imaging, et cetera.

Tal: What made you want to get into physics?

Joe: Now you're making me use my way-back machine. I guess I would have to narrow it down to three things at a really early age: astronomy (just looking up at the sky), magnets (which are cool at any age), and a fascination with things just crashing into one another. I subsequently became obsessed with meteorology to the point where I was making weather reports daily and posting them on the classroom door. Incidentally I didn't end up "specializing" in either meteorology or astronomy, but these early interests were springboards into studying (particle) physics and mathematics later in life. To this day I still love a great meteor shower, looking up at the moon, or spending hours a day on Wunderground.com

Tal: In science fiction books, scientists are often presented as characters with no sense of humor. I think that's why Andy Weir's *The Martian* was so beloved by the scientific community, because it presented hard science side by side with toilet humor. It was something I wanted to capture in Sylvia. She's a quantum physicist, but one who's also happy to drop a fart joke at any given moment. As a professional physicist, how much of a role does humor play into your daily work life? Can you cite any examples?

Joe: It's funny you ask that. When I think back on the influences that shaped my personality as a scientist (and just a regular person), I think of Peter Venkman (Bill Murray's character in *Ghostbusters*) and Chris Knight (Val Kilmer's character in *Real Genius*). Perhaps it was just a function of watching and rewatching these movies at a really mentally malleable age, but both characters made the prospect of being a scientist seem like something really cool to aspire to.

I think having a good sense of humor allows you to deal with the absurdity, randomness, beauty, and cruelty of the universe in a way that complements science's attempt to establish some sort of framework for all that. I think taking oneself too seriously is a hazard in both scientific pursuit and life's pursuits. After all, what's the point if you can't have a good laugh every now and then?

It goes without saying that working in a radiation oncology department can be extremely stressful and tragic on an almost daily basis. I've been at places where joking around is discouraged, and I can tell you, people don't last too long at those places. Without being able to joke around with the people I spend the better part of my day with, I think I would want to throw myself in front of train at the end of the day.

Tal: While writing the book, I've asked you to help me create a lot of absurd tech: convert mosquitoes to flying steam reformers, keep self-replicating nanos in check with ecophagy cages, build quantum switches for improbable bombs, and make human teleportation possible with density functional theory. Your one caveat to me was: beware of using too much deterministic language when describing how things work. Can you elaborate on why you said that?

Joe: Did I say that? It sounds quite serious. I guess what I meant is that when talking about things inherently "quantum," it requires us to use the language of chance and probability instead of certainty. Quantum physics describes the world of the extremely small, and at these scales, familiar quantities like the position, velocity, momentum, and energy of an object become fuzzy and probabilistic. Instead of specifying these quantities as definite values like we're used to for, say, a car traveling on a road, we have to instead speak of the expectation value of these quantities for an object like an electron. Quantum physics can say that the most probable location to find an electron orbiting a proton in a hydrogen atom is 1.5 times the Bohr radius but nothing more definite. This is in contrast to saying that our car is at position X, Y, Z, traveling at velocity V. It's definitely a different way of thinking about reality, and I'm not sure anyone really ever gets used to it.

Tal: Okay, last question before I let you go back to saving the world one patient at a time: What one quantum physics breakthrough would you like to see happen within your lifetime?

Joe: That's a doozy. If you're going to make me pick just one, I would have to say commercially viable quantum computing coupled with photonic data storage and transfer. The exponential increase in the processing capability of a quantum computer will enable humanity to solve all sorts of currently intractable problems across dozens of disciplines. This also has to be accompanied by a completely new way to move and store such enormously large quantities of data, which means moving away from electronic data storage and buses to light-speed photonic data storage and busing. There are even some people using organic compounds like DNA as a means of storing extremely large quantities of data. The coupling of these nascent technologies can potentially change the course of humanity in unimaginably fantastic ways.

Tal: That's it! I've had it with your shenanigans, Joe. Get the hell out of my book!

Seriously, though, I can never thank Joe enough for helping me build the world in which *The Punch Escrow* takes place. He's an amazing guy and represents the ideal intersection of scientific curiosity and human empathy. We need more Joes.

ACKNOWLEDGEMENTS

SINCE THIS BOOK has been over half a decade in the making, and I've only been allotted seven hundred words, I'm pretty sure I'm going to miss a lot of people. So: if I've missed you below, I am a terrible person, and I already feel guilty. You are remarkable.

Chronologically, I must acknowledge my mom (Yona) and dad (Avi), without whom—technically—I wouldn't be here, so they're first. My dad was among the archetypes I used to build Moti: a bad ass Semite with a heart of gold. My mom was a biology teacher and she's now a science exhibit curator at the Madatech museum in Israel. Considering I almost failed biology in high school, I think she was pretty shocked to learn I'd written a hard science fiction book.

Then there's my amazing wife, Rachel, the better author in the Klein family. I am incredibly grateful for her input and support, especially when I couldn't quite get into Sylvia's mind. Rachel, thank you for your guidance in shaping Sylvia's voice and personality.

And of course, my wonderful, superbly creative, intelligent, and beautiful-in-every-way daughters, Iris and Violet. Daddy loves you.

My sister, Liat. It was awesome growing up with such a loving, confident, intelligent, and beautiful little sister. Everyone should have one.

My in-laws, Vonda and Ray, in whose house much of the first draft of this book was written while we relocated from the polythelia of Northern California to the thenar of Michigan.

The Klein, Berger, Peeri, Cohen, Schrieber, and Dvir families.

Adam Gomolin, you're right up there with mishpocha. I'm sorry people keep urinating on your porch.

This book is an official selection of the Semiannual "Big" Brown Family Reunion Book Club: Brown, Bowen, Cummings, Hooker, Grossenbacher, McKinney, Mursten, Maxwell, Overmiller, and Carrizales clans, I love y'all. (And I'm sorry about all the f-bombs and *S* words.)

Oh, and this book is also a selection of the Birmingham Oenophile Literary Society. Thank you, ladies. For the record, I'd pair this book with a nice Savagnin served slightly below room temperature.

Next, I'd like to thank four friends I've known since high school. I'm telling you, make a lot of smart friends in high school, kids, because someday you might need to get a lot of free legal and/or physics advice. Joe Santoro (with whom you should now be familiar) helped me more than I care to admit with the science of *The Punch Escrow*. He puts the *hard* in hard science fiction if you get my drift. David Sontag and Jay Wolman helped me form the legal framework that informed the anthropology of Earth 2147. There was this great part of the book where I dug a lot deeper into the legality of how Joel got his comms back, but it got edited out. Sorry, guys! And, of course, John Hannon, who helped me think through a lot of the humor and Rube Goldberg–esque plot devices. John is a connoisseur of poop jokes. He has a son called Hunter who takes after his father in the poop joke department. Hi, Hunter!

My developmental editors, Robert Kroese and Matt Harry. You guys, I'm sorry I am a terrible author. Thanks for helping me write good.

My beta readers: Ian Ellison—the guy's read every version of this book, like, a million times, so if it sucks, it's his fault. Seriously, not my fault—Ian's. And of course, you can also blame Dan Salinas, Russ Mitchell, David Siddal, Bradford Stephens, Ben Murphy, and Gabe Coelho-Kostolny.

Group hug: Ryan "Brian Porter" Potter and the family; Vaughn, AJ, and Renee; my Scottish family: Chief, Dog, G, Martinho, Ike of Spain; Wes Wasson; Richard Jefferies Woodruff and the Chardmo (two completely different people); Chris and Donna Rosa; "Fun" Bobby Brown; Anthony "Garlique" Mansfield; Simon Wardley; Simon Crosby; Craig "Makes Lovely Pictures" Allen; Tomer "Tomash" Schwartz; Chris "Beaker" Hoff; Meredith "Etoile" Peruzzi; Mel "Spunky" Stanley; Dan "Gilmore" Burford; Barbara "Eclipse" Reece; Wade "Pandaflip" Bell; Danny Ryan; "Not So Big" Ben Morris; "Acceptable Up" Shepdog; Sean "Chester" Manchester; Patricia "Margarita del Toro" Chavez; Hillary "Hillycake" Qualtieri; Lai Long; Mr. and Mrs. Goodgroove; Sean "Hardway" Johnston; Lisa Carlini; Mark Gebert; Sam Johnston; Heather Fitzsimmons; Mike Spinney; Kevin Kosh; Kristy "Shut Up" Cowart; Michael Kellerman; Carlos Estaban; Angela and Mark Broxterman; Julie and Tom Warmbrodt; Naddine and Mike Morgan; Matt "the Tax Ninja" Whatley; Greg Silverman; and Ben Luntz.

Oliver Evilord for pointing out that Talking Heads's "Psycho Killer," although classified as New Wave, was released in 1977 and thus would not have qualified for Joel's 1980s New Wave mix.

The Inkshares crew: Thad, Avalon, Elena, Angela. Heart emojis, yay.

Scott Meyer: without Martin Banks, there would be no Joel Byram.

Legendary Entertainment and Geek & Sundry: Rachel Romero, Alex Hedlund, Rob Manuel, and of course, Felicia Day.

Howie Sanders and the UTA crew: thanks for putting your faith in me.

Ajar and everyone at Penguin Magic—you guys really helped make this happen.

Jean-Francois Dubeau, Jamison Stone, and Brian Guthrie—thanks for talking me off the ledge. Shouts to all other Inkshares and Quill authors.

Oh no, I'm out of words! To those I've missed: may I live a thousand years and never hunt again.

LIST OF PATRONS

Acar Altinsel

Adam Gomolin

Adam Helfgott

Avi Klein

Chris Coluzzi

Christopher L. Rosa

Danelle Au

Dov Calderon

Dylan F. Weiss

Galit Klein

Gregory P. Dolan

Gur Talpaz

Jeremy Steinman

John C. Bertrand

John.Fanelli

Joshua J. Gorciak

Kwang Kim

Mark R. Shuttleworth

Mike P. Wertz

Peter Birdsall

Peter J. Downing

Peter Lindstrom

Rachel Jane Perkins

Richard Woodruff

Robert A. Brown

Ryan Potter

Russell Mitchell

Sean Manchester

Steven Moody

Tom Howie

Todd D. Smith

Victor Y. Thu

Wes Wasson

Yona Klein

INKSHARES

INKSHARES is a reader-driven publisher and producer based in Oakland, California. Our books are selected not by a group of editors, but by readers worldwide.

While we've published books by established writers like *Big Fish* author Daniel Wallace and *Star Wars: Rogue One* scribe Gary Whitta, our aim remains surfacing and developing the new author voices of tomorrow.

Previously unknown Inkshares authors have received starred reviews and been featured in *The New York Times*. Their books are on the front tables of Barnes & Noble and hundreds of independents nationwide, and many have been licensed by publishers in other major markets. They are also being adapted by Oscar-winning screenwriters at the biggest studios and networks.

Interested in making your own story a reality? Visit Inkshares.com to start your own project or find other great books.